The Holts: An American Dynasty

HOMECOMING

AN AMERICAN DREAM OF CONQUEST TURNS
INTO A TROPICAL NIGHTMARE, A FAMILY
TORN BY BITTER CONFLICT FACES THE
THREAT OF TRAGEDY, TECHNOLOGY POINTS
THE WAY TO THE FUTURE IN THE SOUTH-
WESTERN DESERT . . . AND A YOUNG NA-
TION DISCOVERS RENEWED HOPE,
UNLIMITED POSSIBILITY, AND UNEXPECTED
DANGER AS IT CROSSES INTO A NEW FRON-
TIER: THE TWENTIETH CENTURY.

Frank Blake—After years of drifting, the adventurer
has finally returned to his family home in Washington,
D.C. Yet although his family connections promise him
a lucrative government career, he is once again seized
with wanderlust. And, in a moment of unanticipated
passion, he follows his destiny to a distant desert.

Henry Blake—A high-ranking officer in the U.S. intelligence service, he has grown increasingly disen-
chanted with his mission in Manila. Now an urgent
message from his family demands that he make a decision that could ultimately destroy his career and force
him to leave behind the beautiful woman who loves
him.

Cindy Blake—Her separation from her husband has been a long and bitter one. Now it seems that fate has conspired to throw them together for an unexpected reconciliation . . . or a final renunciation. If they fail to reach out across the chasm of time, anger, and hatred, they could end up destroying each other—and their family.

Midge Blake—At fifteen, she cannot accept the possibility that her mother and father may never be together again. And now she suffers even more, infected by an insidious disease. For the moment, her condition is the glue holding the family together; but each day, each hour, the stresses increase, threatening to tear the Blakes apart.

Dr. Janessa Lawrence—While working in a Cuban hospital, she once left her children in the care of Cindy Blake. Now she has a chance to return the favor . . . by coming home to the States and trying to save the life of Cindy's daughter, Midge.

Estrella Rodriguez—A young and beautiful Filipino mistress, she offers Henry Blake a refuge from loneliness, promising to love him, care for him, satisfy his every urge. She asks only one thing in return: that if he abandons her country, he not abandon her as well.

India Blackstone—Talented and rebellious, this promising young painter is determined to make her mark in an art establishment dominated by men. Her quest will take her to Taos, New Mexico, where she will explore new landscapes both artistic and sexual.

Michael Holt—A man with a vision of the future, he has come to Taos in the belief that the invention of the moving-picture machine offers the last chance to capture the essence of the frontier. But while he may hold the future in his hands with his Biograph camera, he will soon discover that the American West has lost nothing of its violent and dangerous past.

THE HOLTS: AN AMERICAN DYNASTY
VOLUME NINE

HOMECOMING

DANA FULLER ROSS

 BCI Producers of **The First Americans,**
White Indian, and The Robber Barons.

Book Creations Inc., Canaan, NY • Lyle Kenyon Engel, Founder

BANTAM BOOKS
NEW YORK • TORONTO • LONDON • SYDNEY • AUCKLAND

HOMECOMING

*A Bantam Domain Book / published by arrangement with
Book Creations Inc.*

Bantam edition / October 1994

*Produced by Book Creations Inc.
Lyle Kenyon Engel, Founder*

*DOMAIN and the portrayal of a boxed "d" are trademarks of
Bantam Books, a division of Bantam Doubleday Dell
Publishing Group, Inc.*

ISBN 0-553-56150-2

Published simultaneously in the United States and Canada

*Bantam Books are published by Bantam Books, a division of Bantam
Doubleday Dell Publishing Group, Inc. Its trademark, consisting of
the words "Bantam Books" and the potrayal of a rooster, is
Registered in U.S. Patent and Trademark Office and in other
countries. Marca Registrada. Bantam Books, 1540 Broadway, New
York, New York 10036.*

PRINTED IN THE UNITED STATES OF AMERICA

OPM   0 9 8 7 6 5 4 3 2 1

HOMECOMING

THE HOLTS *An American Dynasty*

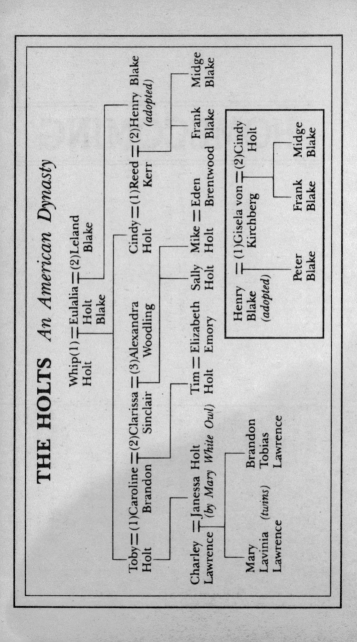

Whip(1) = Eulalia = (2)Leland
Holt   Holt   Blake
        Blake

Cindy = (1)Reed = (2)Henry Blake
Holt   Kerr   *(adopted)*

Midge
Blake

Toby = (1)Caroline = (2)Clarissa = (3)Alexandra
Holt   Brandon   Sinclair   Woodling

Frank
Brentwood Blake

Charley = Janessa Holt
Lawrence   *(by Mary White Owl)*

Tim = Elizabeth   Sally   Mike = Eden
Holt   Emory   Holt   Holt   Brentwood Blake

Mary   Brandon
Lavinia   Tobias
Lawrence   Lawrence
(twins)

Henry = (1)Gisela von = (2)Cindy
Blake   Kirchberg   Holt
(adopted)

Peter   Frank   Midge
Blake   Blake   Blake

THE BLAKES, THE BLACKSTONES, AND THE BRENTWOODS

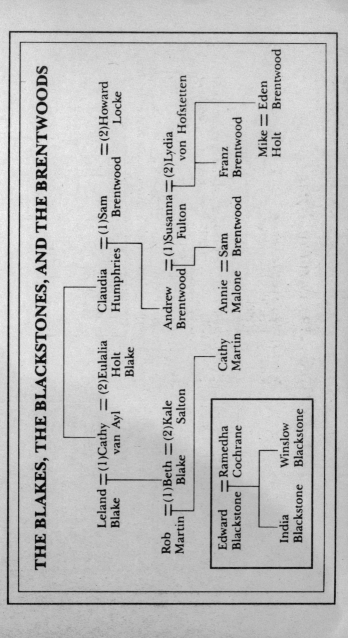

I

Washington, D.C., March 1899

"Hey!"

Frank Blake turned. A railroad bull was standing on the steps of the caboose, four cars down the line. Frank thought he resembled a packing crate in a navy blue overcoat. The man's black felt hat was powdered with a late March snow; his fingers were closed around the dark grip of a revolver.

"Good afternoon, Officer." Frank moved gracefully away from the doors of the boxcar and tipped his fedora, displaying his immaculate haircut and carefully trimmed nails.

The bull narrowed his eyes.

"I assure you I'm not a bum seeking transportation," Frank said. "I was just out for a stroll and thought perhaps I could take a shortcut through these yards."

"Well, you can't," the bull said. Railroad police were inclined toward suspicion, and this one was not quite mollified.

Frank smiled. "Yes, I'm afraid I found that out. I suppose I'll have to retrace my steps." He came close enough for the bull to note that his overcoat was new and

1

his shoes bore the polish of prosperity. No bindle on his back.

The bull holstered his gun. "You go on, sir, before you get hurt. This yard ain't a safe place. Trains moving through it all the time, and the 'boes'll roll you for your wallet if you ain't sharp." He turned to the boxcar doors. "Thieving bastards ain't going to ride *my* train."

Frank felt rather than heard the movement inside the car. A year ago he would have been the one huddled around his bindle in the darkest corner or stretched on the rods below, with rain and cinders in his eyes.

"You know, I'm not at all sure how I got here," he said quickly. "It's fearfully confusing. I'm afraid you're going to have to show me out if you want me out."

"That way." The bull pointed, exasperated. "Right past the flatcars."

"Well, I was just over there, and I still couldn't see the road. Then it started to snow. It's extraordinary how different it makes everything look."

Frank gazed up at the flakes falling from a sky made of gray powder. They clung briefly to the cars, limning the low ridges of the roofs. Frank had ridden the top deck, too, joyfully astride a boxcar in the summer sun, while the train's dragon curves whipped ahead of him and the whistle blew, lonely and mysterious, across the valley. It was easy now to forget he had been hungry then, too, and infested with lice. Maybe that was why he had come here this afternoon, to watch the hoboes hunkered down in the ditch along the tracks, waiting for a train, and remember what it had been like to be one. Maybe that would scratch the itch in his wandering foot. Frank was only twenty, and the itch was strong.

The bull was beginning to lose his temper. "You go right past that string of flatcars and bear left. You'll see a bunch of *N* and *W* boxcars. Go on around them and then just keep crossing the tracks till you get to the road that runs the far side of the yard. And for God's sake watch what you're about. They're making up trains." The low grumble of a switch engine was audible. "Damn fool idea to come down in here, anyway."

"Certainly, Officer." Frank gave up. The hobo in the boxcar was on his own; this bull wasn't going to be distracted. He had his job, and that was rousting 'boes so no one got a free ride off the railroad. Which made about as much sense as trying to keep birds from sitting on the cars, Frank thought. None of the wanderers, the down-and-outers, the jobless moving from town to town just trying to get work, had the money to pay for a ticket if they wanted to.

Frank dodged between the trains. He didn't need the bull's warning to look sharp; he had learned to read a railyard—the signal lights and the markings on the cars—three years before on his first voyage from home, a grandiose move in the old parent-child game of *I'll show you*. He eyed the puff of steam from the little switch engine cautiously and took care not to go between coupled cars. Over the couplings was nothing but a narrow plank (hoboes called them "death woods"). One good bang as the engine coupled on another car down the line, and you were in the works—or parts of you were. It was a rare railyard worker, coupling cars with the infamous link-and-pin assembly, who didn't display at least a missing finger, and the Railway Union magazine was full of advertisements for the newest prosthetic arms.

Frank was two tracks away when he heard a gunshot. He froze. Around him he heard clanging noises and the dull boom of cars being shunted into line. Maybe he had mistaken the sound. Maybe he should just go home like the good citizen he was.

Instead, he turned and retraced his steps, disinclined

toward citizenship. He moved at a swift dogtrot, ignoring the snow, which was falling heavily now and clinging to the dark ground. A yard worker with a signal lantern looked at him, and Frank nodded briskly, hoping his own overcoat—the same shade as the bull's—and his purposeful expression would make it appear he had business there.

Frank soon saw where the shot had come from. The railroad bull was having a good time. The boxcar door stood half open, and the hapless occupant was sprawled on the cinders below it. The bull had shaken out the old man's bindle and was putting a hole through anything of use it contained—probably because he couldn't get away with shooting the old man himself here in the switchyard. A kettle lay between the wheels, driven under the car by the bullet that had ruined it. Frank watched indignantly as the bull found a flour sack and upended it, spilling the contents into wet slush. He kicked a coffeepot into the middle of the filthy flour and took aim with the pistol again.

"Aw, boss, not my coffeepot!" the hobo pleaded.

"Show your face in my yard again, I'll put a hole in *you*," the bull said. He pulled the trigger, and the coffeepot jumped and rolled against the rails with a clang.

Frank gritted his teeth. That was too damned much. The old man's sole possessions were wrapped in that bindle. The hobo spotted him and crouched to flee, thinking now there were two of them, and they would surely beat him. Frank shook his head and put his finger to his lips. The other man froze, puzzled, and the railroad bull snapped his head around.

"I thought I told you to get out of here."

"Give him back his bindle," Frank said.

"And who the hell are you to tell me what to do?"

"A public-spirited citizen. Haven't you anything better to do on the railroad's pay than bully old men?"

The railroad bull holstered his revolver. He was about twice Frank's size. "I told you to get out of this yard. Now I'm gonna make you wish you had. This is railroad property."

Frank waited for him, balanced on the balls of his feet. The hobo stared. When the bull didn't turn back to him, the hobo started packing what was left of his belongings into his bindle with quick, squirrellike movements.

Before the railroad bull was quite close enough to swing his melon-shaped fists at Frank, Frank jumped him. The bull grunted and staggered, and then they were wrestling, sliding in the snow, each trying to get a punch in. The bull was nearly three hundred pounds of solid flesh, but not as much of it was muscle as might first be thought. Under Frank's coat, however, were the muscles of a former school boxing champion who had then lived off the proceeds of his own labor for three years, including a year digging through permafrost in the Yukon, mining gold. He slugged the bull in the stomach and felt the man's breath explode. The bull might have wished he had kept a grip on his revolver. Frank wasn't going to give him the chance to draw it again.

They grappled with each other, punching and clawing, slithering on the cold, slippery ground. Frank wasn't sure what he thought he was going to achieve, but his blood was up. Besides, the bull would pound him to jelly if he didn't get his own licks in first.

A heavy fist collided with Frank's jaw, and he staggered back, shaking his head. The bull reached for his gun; Frank lowered his head and charged that too-soft stomach. The bull let out a *woof* like a startled mastiff and stepped backward, his arms flapping for balance. He slowly toppled, his boots churning up wet snow. Frank, snowflakes clinging to his lashes, thought it was like watching a building slowly topple over from a wrecker's ball. He prepared to jump the man and make sure he didn't get up again, but it wasn't necessary.

The bull came down with a thud, his head smack against the steel rail. He didn't move.

Frank eased forward to peer at him. Still no movement. "Oh, hell," he muttered. He knelt, afraid that he had killed the man, and stuck his hand under the navy coat. The bull's shirtfront rose and fell rhythmically; the thump of his heartbeat could be felt beneath it. But he was out cold.

Frank felt a warm breath, laden with coffee and onions, floating past his ear. The hobo, bent over his shoulder, looked worried, his gray mustache twitching with unease. "Colder'n a cuckoo. You kill him?"

"No," Frank said, relieved. "But we better get out of here."

The hobo nodded, clutching his bindle. "I need a drink," he said hopefully.

"Nothing on me, friend. Sorry."

"Oh, well." The man apparently felt it had been a shot in the dark anyway. He beckoned Frank to follow him, and they slipped through the thickening snow away from the prostrate railroad bull. If nobody found him, he would be cold when he woke up but probably not suffer anything more than a headache. Not nearly as much injury as he'd been trying to inflict on the old man, leaving him with nothing and a snowstorm coming on, Frank thought.

"Follow me careful," the hobo warned. "Trail's hard to see."

Frank nodded. He knew where they were going. There was always a hobo jungle near the railyards. He had never been in this one, but he could have found his way without the old man.

They brushed through a screen of scrubby pines and down a slope to a half-frozen stream trickling under willows just turning faintly greenish yellow. A jumble of old packing crates, corrugated iron roofing, and discarded bedsprings resolved itself into a human habitation as they got closer.

The jungle was a semipermanent settlement constructed of flotsam dragged in by various transients. Except for Frank and the old man, it was empty now at the end of winter, but it would fill soon enough as hoboes wandered back from Florida or California or wherever they had gone to escape the cold.

Frank found some dry kindling in one of the lean-tos and set about making a fire in the rock firepit in front of it.

"You don't look like a bum to me," the old man commented.

"Not now," Frank said. "I have been."

The old hobo nodded with understanding. "Found a place on the plush. Some female. Tried that myself once, but I just couldn't stay with it."

Frank wondered how long *he* could stay with it, even if the female was his mother. He didn't say anything, just smiled at the old man. The flames leapt around the kindling, and Frank put on a broken board and the scavenged end of a two-by-four.

"It's nice to be warm at night," he said finally.

"Well, you got that look the ladies like. I reckon you had lots of offers. Can't fault you for takin' them."

The old man seemed to feel that he had to find excuses for Frank's having left the road and gone soft. This one was a bum for bumming's sake, Frank thought. Even in good times he would have been on the road.

Looking at the old hobo, Frank had a fleeting vision

of himself in forty years: gray mustache twitching, bugs in his hair, cooking swill over a burning two-by-four, maintaining he was a free man. He dug in his pocket, found a five-dollar bill, and handed it to the old man.

"Get yourself some new pots," he said as the old man's eyebrows shot up under his battered hat. "And don't hang around here too long. It'll be the first place they look when they find that bull out cold in the yard."

"Who the hell are you?" the old man demanded. Five dollars would buy him new cook pots ten times over. Nobody just up and gave bums money.

Frank smiled wryly. "Just a philanthropist of the jungle. And you're the Gypsy's warning, pal. I owed you a fee." He turned his back on the bum and walked out of the jungle, leaving the "warning" staring incredulously at his five dollars.

Frank hailed a cab and arrived in proper style outside his mother's stone house in a quietly fashionable section of old Alexandria, Virginia, outside the District of Columbia. He hoped she didn't know he'd been hanging around the railyard. He still wasn't quite sure why he had gone; he'd just felt he had to go somewhere. Before the bull showed up, he had been within inches of getting in that boxcar himself.

He was not quite twenty-one, and he had been home for two weeks after three years of wandering. The fatted calf had been fed him; his mother and his little sister, Midge, had cried over him; and now he wasn't sure what should happen next. He could get into any university he wanted; his military school marks and his family name were sufficient for that, even though he hadn't finished his last year. Any number of friends would be glad to help him find a position on some congressman's staff. There was, his mother had said hopefully, a post available in the

Treasury Department, and the secretary had kindly offered to interview him.

Frank ducked around to the rear of the house as if the secretary of the treasury were lurking in the parlor. He stamped his snowy boots on the back steps and noticed the second tread from the bottom was split. It felt spongy under his foot. *Ought to fix that*, he thought. He glanced at the sky. It had quit snowing; it hadn't been but a halfhearted attempt anyway.

He went through the kitchen, hung his damp overcoat on the hall tree, then bounded up the back stairs to the second floor. As he shrugged out of his new clothes and into denim work pants and a red flannel shirt, he looked in the mirror and saw he had blood on his mouth, which the cabbie had tactfully not mentioned. Frank scrubbed it away with a pocket handkerchief—new—from his bureau drawer and stuffed the handkerchief in his trouser pocket. He went back downstairs, whistling, then down another flight to the basement, where he hunted up some scrap wood and his father's tools.

Frank took his finds outside, pried the loose tread up with a crowbar, and yanked out the oddly angled, jutting nails. He measured a new board, still whistling softly. The *scritch* of the saw chewing its way through the end of the plank made a harsh but, to Frank's ears, pleasant sound. A blue jay flew onto the top of the stair rail that bordered the small back stoop. It squawked at Frank, and he squawked back. Across the back alley a housemaid shaking out a dustmop from her stoop paused and looked at him. Frank smiled and waved. "Nice day," he called. "I believe the sun's coming out after all."

"Cain't be too soon for me," she called back. "I'm going to get me a parasol and a big glass of lemonade and just sit out in it, listen to the bees hum, come the spring. Been a terrible winter, cold as stone." A carriage rattled down the drive of her house to the stable at the back. "Uh-oh!" She gave the mop one final shake and scooted back in the house. Employers didn't generally hold with the help lollygagging on work time.

Frank raised his hand in greeting to the man who alighted from the carriage, and he nodded briefly in return. Frank didn't know him. His mother had said the family was new since he had left home. A lot seemed to be new since he had left home, he thought. There was his sister, Midge, nearly fifteen. She had been a little girl when he took off, and he wasn't used to her looking like a woman and not a child. He didn't think she was used to it, either. There were his cousin Janessa's twins, three years old and underfoot and staying with Frank's mother on some sort of indefinite visit while their mother and father worked at an army hospital in Cuba. There was his father, still absent, on service in the Philippines—the culmination of the recent war. The ignominious end showed every sign of dragging out for years, and the country was beginning to wonder what it had gotten itself into. Then there was the continuing uncertainty of his relationship with his brother, Peter, from whom he had parted on unfriendly terms. Peter had written an earnest but stilted letter, saying he was glad Frank was safe at home—and then spoiled it by adding he was glad his younger brother had finally come to his senses.

Frank pounded the last nail into the tread and ran his hand over the smooth new board. He felt fine as long as he was doing something that seemed useful. And he couldn't make himself feel that adding up money for the Treasury Department was useful.

He pushed his hair back from his eyes and looked at the porch railing. It had a big patch of rot. *I ought to replace it, too. Before I repaint it all,* he thought.

*   *   *

He finished just as Midge got home from school. Since Frank's return, she regarded him as her special gift and property. She linked her arm affectionately through his and wrinkled her nose at the sawdust smell. "You look just like an old handyman," she chided. "If you don't watch out, people will be trying to hire you."

Midge's brown hair was no longer in braids but drawn back into a knot at the nape of her neck, the next step before a grown-up pompadour. She had a nice country-girl face with a spill of freckles over her nose—despite her best efforts with buttermilk washes and lemon juice. She adored Frank regardless of the fact that he had blond hair and devil-may-care eyes and was better looking than she. He had been trying to convince her that a nice nature and a nice face surpassed a beautiful face and a nasty nature, but Midge was unconvinced. She wanted to look like Alice Roosevelt—or her cousin Sally Holt.

Frank grinned at her now. "I guess I'd better change my clothes. I don't want to disgrace you."

"Well, Mother bought you all those new things," Midge said practically. "You act like you're afraid to wear them."

"Can't mend a porch in a new suit."

"Why are you mending the porch, anyway?"

"It needed it."

"Oh." She paused. "Mother's home. And the postman brought a great big package." Midge eyed Frank cautiously, then muttered, "I didn't get to look at the rest of the mail. She stuffed it in her pocket."

"Well, let's go make her hand it over and see what's in the package," Frank said cheerfully, holding open the back door for his sister. "Maybe you're getting indecent proposals from boys."

Midge flushed. "I am not!"

They both knew pretty well what their mother had put in her pocket: a letter from their father.

Cindy Blake was kneeling on the parlor hearth, bent over the grate, when they came in. She turned at their footfalls and stood up, brushing off the front of her black satin apron. Janessa's twins were playing with a length of twine on the floor, trying to make a cat's cradle out of it. Though a boy and a girl, the twins looked identical to Frank since they both had ringlets and wore navy-blue dresses. Brandon would have to be five before he graduated to short pants.

"You need to dress," Cindy told Frank. "It's nearly dinner."

He sank down into an emerald-and-cream striped overstuffed settee, arms and legs protruding. The twins abandoned the twine and attempted to tug him out, each with a firm grasp on two fingers.

"We came to see what was in the mail," he said. "Mysterious packages intrigue us. And did we get any good mail? Invitations to embassy balls? Unexpected inheritances?"

Cindy's eyes momentarily flickered back toward the fireplace. "No," she said shortly. "Frank, you look like a socialist in that shirt."

"I could join them as an organizer," he said, as if the idea had just hit him.

"I am not even going to dignify that with a comeback." His mother stood looking thoughtfully down at him, while Midge sifted through the letters now spread on the rosewood end table. They were mostly invitations, some very likely to embassy functions.

The twins' nursemaid, Kathleen, appeared, in a blue sateen dress and starched white apron, and detached them from Frank. "It's their suppertime," she said, her voice thick with an Irish brogue. "You can play with your cousin later, then." Her eyes lingered on Frank. "And you're a good man to mind them like you do."

He smiled. "They're appealing little devils. In small doses. You should get the credit—you have them all day."

Kathleen smiled, her blue eyes lighting up. "Sure and you're a kind one to say so," she murmured, taking a twin by each hand and ushering them out of the parlor toward the kitchen.

"That girl likes you entirely too much," Cindy commented when Kathleen was out of earshot. "It's a good thing Janessa is coming for them next month."

Frank shrugged. "She's a nice girl. I'm just nice to her."

"She's stuck on you," Midge said, "even if she *is* older."

Cindy Blake eyed her son as if trying to fathom what other "nice" girls he had been "nice" to in the last three years. "Do not, in this house, be any nicer to her than you are right now," she said. She looked at him over her spectacles. "Frank, you have got to get yourself situated."

He looked back at her, hands spread, questioning. "I don't know how."

"Don't you want to work?" Cindy flung her own hands wide, exasperated. Her graying blond hair was puffed into a pompadour, and her afternoon dress of lavender taffeta had a fashionable bell skirt and a bodice pouched in the front above a nipped waist. Frank thought she looked like an elegant pigeon. A pigeon with too much on its mind. There were lines in her face that had deepened in the three years he had been gone.

Lavender. "When did you start dressing like an old lady?" he demanded. Only grannies wore lavender. Or widows in half-mourning.

"I *am* an old lady," Cindy retorted.

Frank made a face. "You're a clotheshorse. You were

always the most elegant woman in any room. I'll bet you're still buying your dresses from Paris. So why are you ordering them in lavender?"

"I asked *you* a question."

Midge eyed them both uneasily.

"I *do* work," Frank said. "I fixed your back stoop."

"I could hire a man to fix my back stoop." Cindy gave an exasperated sigh. "Oh, we'll talk about it later. You're going to be late for dinner if you don't go change. I will not allow you to come to the table in that."

Frank smiled cajolingly. "Only if you tell us what's in the mysterious package."

"Well, it isn't for you—you two are as bad as the twins—but it's certainly interesting," Cindy said, side-tracked by his question. She smiled back at him in spite of herself. He was her boy, her darling. At least he was home.

She picked up the flat parcel leaning against the wall. It was wrapped in unbound brown paper, plainly the source of the twins' twine. Cindy unfolded the paper and took out three paintings on canvas.

Frank and Midge leaned forward to examine them. The first was a cow of relatively normal proportions but with an unsettlingly direct stare. Above her head floated what appeared to be a winged calf, encircled by stars. The second was a landscape, a stark view of endlessly rolling hills studded with cattle. It gave the impression of a land that simply went on without stopping. The third was a portrait of a dark-skinned woman, a scarlet caste mark on her forehead. She was wearing a white lawn shirtwaist with a stiffly starched and boned collar.

"I know her," Midge said. "Isn't that Mr. Blackstone's wife? She's half Indian or something. But she doesn't wear that red spot. Peter says she's thoroughly Americanized."

"She does in this picture," Cindy said. "The artist is her daughter, India. She's just nineteen, and I imagine that may be the way she sees her mother. I like the juxtaposition of the caste mark and that very American shirtwaist. See how she looks just a little as if the collar may be choking her? That's the artist's vision, darling."

"I like the winged calf," Frank said.

"I like all of them," Cindy said, "which may upset Edward Blackstone. I think he was hoping I'd tell him they're no good."

"He's afraid no one will marry his daughter if she paints winged cows," Frank said.

"Well, something like that," his mother agreed. "He just wants what's best for her. Rather like all parents." A muscle next to her mouth twitched. "Well, I'll have to think over what I tell him," she said, stacking the paintings and rewrapping them.

"I'll go change," Frank said, deciding that vanishing for a moment was probably a good idea. His mother was staring at the grate in the fireplace again. The envelope, although somewhat charred, hung on it, still intact.

Frank reappeared half an hour later, his hair slicked down and his muscular frame clad in proper dinner attire. But the stiff front of his dress shirt made him feel as if he were a turtle, and the high collar dug into the bottom of his chin. Frank's private theory was that stiff collars had been invented to prevent people from going to sleep in church. If you nodded your head, the collar cut off your air.

Joining the others, Frank found that his mother's dinner guests—she usually had one or two most evenings as she held forth at a kind of artistic salon—dealt with the collar issue in opposite ways. The senator whose hobbyhorse was public art (to educate the masses, he declared) kept his head erect, never once dipping his formidable chin toward the waiting palisade of his collar. The sculptor—whose works would be more educational than the senator had in mind if only the masses figured out what they represented—dodged the problem entirely by wearing a soft turnover collar and a Windsor tie. Midge had been allowed to dine with the adults as a treat and wore a demure evening frock of brown satin. The senator told her what a young lady she was becoming and asked Frank what his plans for the future were.

Frank, resisting the urge to run his finger around the inside of his collar in the hope of stretching it, said he didn't know yet. He felt rather the way the woman in India Blackstone's painting looked as if she might feel.

The sculptor devoted himself to the wine and to a discussion with Cindy of *The Studio*, which Frank at first thought was a place but turned out to be a magazine. Frank vanished as soon as dinner was over, aided by his mother's habit of remaining at the table while the gentlemen drank their port. Cindy had her party well in hand. If the absence of a visible husband made her entertaining just a little racy, it wasn't enough to cause more than an occasional raised eyebrow. Frank slunk out on the pretext of escorting Midge upstairs.

The next morning he put his work pants and red flannel shirt back on and went out to paint his new porch railing. Midge came and got her bicycle out of the carriage house, then waved as she passed him on her way to school.

The back stoop was painted gray, and Frank had found a can of what looked like the remnants of the original paint in the basement. He brushed paint on the railing, whistling between his teeth.

After a while his mother came out the kitchen door

and looked down at him with mingled exasperation and bewilderment. "That's a very nice job," she said, apparently feeling that some appreciation was called for. "I'm going into the District. I'll be back later this afternoon."

"Yes, ma'am," Frank said, continuing to paint as his mother came down the steps, holding her skirts aside, and got into the waiting carriage. It rumbled away. Frank craned his head to see if he had missed any spot on the underside of the railing. Railings were troublesome.

"Hey, fellow!" came a commanding voice.

Frank gave a last careful dab to the underside and looked up.

"Step over here a minute, will you?" The man from across the alley was waving at him over his back fence.

Frank stuck his paintbrush in a can of turpentine and went through the back gate, wiping his hands on a rag.

"That seems like a decent job you've done on Mrs. Blake's steps," the man said. "Have you had much experience with carpentry?"

"Some," Frank said, uncertain where this conversation was going.

"Well, I've got a chicken coop that needs repair." The man gestured at a small structure near the alley, from which murmured clucks and squawks emanated. "There's a board gone at the bottom, and I think a raccoon's getting in. Come and see me when you've finished with Mrs. Blake."

"Sure will," Frank said, light dawning. *Why not?* "I'm actually a pretty fair jackleg carpenter if you've got any other repairs you want taken care of. Or I'll pull that stump for you." He pointed at the remains of a downed tree. "I'll need a horse, though."

"I just might arrange that. I fall over the darned thing every day. My wife's been after me to get it pulled." The neighbor shook his head. "It's hard to find good workers. You look all right. Come see me tomorrow. My name's Sawtelle."

Frank went home chuckling and finished his paint job. If Mr. Sawtelle wanted to pay him to fix his chicken coop, he certainly wasn't going to embarrass the man by telling him he was his neighbor's son and not an itinerant handyman. It would be nice, anyway, to have some money that he'd earned.

He scrubbed the brushes and his hands with turpentine, which made his knuckles sting and redden, then went into the kitchen to wash the turpentine off. His mother's cook fussed over him and tried to put goose grease on his hands.

"Thanks, Lutie, but Mother has some stuff she uses when she knits," Frank said, declining the goose grease that was the cook's universal nostrum for everything from chapped hands to a squeaky buggy axle. He went in search of his mother's elixir before Lutie could dose him with her own. His hands were beginning to burn.

Cindy kept her knitting basket by the parlor fire. Always in it was a bottle of glycerine and rosewater to smooth her hands so her fingers didn't snag the wool. Frank bent down and fished for it through skeins of pale blue and pink wool attached to half-finished sweaters for the twins. Knitting needles bristled from them like the decorations in a geisha's hair. Under the blue and pink balls were untouched skeins of russet and navy. Frank's hand froze. His mother had planned to make his father a sweater out of them. Frank remembered her measuring him for it. Three years ago.

He found the bottle jammed into a skein of navy to keep it from tipping over and leaking. He smoothed some of the lotion on the backs of his hands. Why did she keep that wool around all this time? he wondered. Why didn't she make something for Midge with it? Or give it to Lu-tie?

The hell with it.

He stuck the glycerine bottle back in the basket and closed the lid. His hands still burned. As he started to stand he eyed the grate, the charred letter still intact on it. He picked up the coal scoop and brought its flat side down hard across the grate. The letter vanished.

II

Manila, the Philippines

The side whiskers adorning General Elwell S. Otis's face twitched as he spoke, flaring out and in like gills in rhythm with the movement of his jaw. General Henry Blake watched them with deliberate concentration. If he kept his attention on the whiskers, he could probably manage to hold his temper.

"Over in another month," Otis was saying. "These natives are totally demoralized. Aguinaldo's nothing more than some kind of mixed-blood adventurer—part Chinaman by the look of him."

"With respect, sir, I have met the man, and I fear he is a force to be reckoned with," Henry said.

Emilio Aguinaldo had led the years-long Philippine insurrection against Spain and was quite prepared to lead another against America. Initially, Filipinos had been grateful for American assistance, but by the time the Spanish had surrendered Manila, the two defending forces were already at odds. Fighting had broken out in early February when it became clear the Americans were not going home again and were not going to give the Filipinos their independence. So far as Henry could tell, no headway had been made by either side since.

"Aguinaldo is very strongly supported in the islands," he continued. "Not only among the peasants but among many of the upper classes." *And we aren't going to dislodge him simply by saying we've won,* Henry thought, irritated.

"He's an outlaw," Otis snapped, and Henry longed, not for the first time, for a genie who would kindly take away General Otis and return General Wesley Merritt, who had been transferred back to the States six months earlier. Or, for that matter, any other commander without Otis's propensity for believing if you said a thing enough times, you made it so.

"These gugus will be crushed in a week or two," Otis said. "And then they'll appreciate what we've done for them. Lift them out of the filth, give them a chance at a decent life."

"Yes, sir."

"What I want to know," Otis barked, "is what your fellows were about, to let Wheaton fall into that ambush yesterday. Heavy losses, Blake. We can't have this."

"Yes, sir," Henry said again, watching the whiskery gills float in and out. "A war of this kind, in jungle terrain, is among the most difficult to obtain reliable intelligence on." He had been waiting for Otis to get to this matter; he knew it was why he had been called on the carpet.

"Well, I want reliable intelligence. And so does General Wheaton, who's lost most of two companies to these devils."

"I am going out to General Wheaton's line myself tomorrow, sir," Henry said stiffly. What could be found out was being found out. His intelligence people were risking their lives daily in the native barrios for this pompous parade-ground soldier. He ground his teeth. Otis had served with distinction in the Civil War. It seemed unnecessary for the War Office to have dug him up again.

"You're dismissed, Colonel," Otis said. He made it a point to keep forgetting Henry's promotion.

Henry traversed the elegant gardens of the Malaca-ñang Palace, muttering under his breath. Behind him in the polished mahogany halls, General Otis was no doubt compulsively piling up paperwork, the only activity he seemed temperamentally suited for. He composed long reprimands to officers who incorrectly filled out six-dollar supply requisitions. Junior officers' scuttlebutt claimed the only time Otis had left his desk was to verify person-ally the value of a dead army mule, whose loss had come to the general's attention on yet another form in triplicate. General Arthur MacArthur referred to Otis as a bottom-side-up locomotive, wheels revolving at full speed. The refrain the wheels sang, naturally, was that America was winning the war. There was only one government in the Philippines—America's—and the Filipinos must simply submit and be "good Indians." Otis delegated nothing, and nothing escaped his notice—except the one glaring obvious fact: The army was stuck in a quagmire, and the Filipinos showed no signs of being good Indians without a long and horrid battle.

Henry turned the corner to the promenade that ran along the Pasig River. Above him a balcony jutted grace-fully from the white face of the palace. The windows be-hind it were open, its multipaned shell screens tilted up to let in the breeze. The roof was red tile, gently sloping over the second story, creating a palette of white and brick red and misty green that made Henry think of small Virginia towns. In no other respect was there any similar-ity, however. The Philippines were jungle, the "wet trop-ics," inhabited by alien vegetation and stranger fauna: brilliantly plumed birds with enormous beaks; carabao, the ponderous water buffalo that pulled Philippine plows and carts; and people who were a mixture of Malay and Chinese, a little Moslem and Indian and Spanish. They spoke in eight languages and seventy dialects, and in the deep forests and on the smaller islands, headhunters and aboriginal pygmies still lived. Even the Spanish had never successfully held the entire archipelago. Manila stood for Western civilization; Manila was now going to be dragged from the Spanish Middle Ages into the American twentieth century.

Henry untethered his horse, mounted, and rode back into the city along the Pasig. The river was thick with dugouts and wicker-roofed houseboats. The smell of rice and fish wafted along the water, along with more malodorous scents. As many as seven or eight people might live on one of those fragile houseboats, and they dumped everything into the river. The Americans' first act of sanitation had been to drain and fill the vile moat that had surrounded the Intramuros, the old walled portion of the city, but the river and the canals crisscrossing Manila still smelled appalling. It was a joke in the officers' mess that a dip in the Pasig would either kill you or render you immune to all diseases known to mortal man.

Manila was the most advanced city in the archipelago. Outside the city center were the native quarters, such as Tondo, and beyond their environs the barrios, villages of nipa-palm huts on stilts. Beyond them lived the tribal peoples. And everywhere the jungle, lush, beautiful, and suffocating. It had always given Henry claustrophobia. The jungle seemed to simply swallow anything that stood too long in its path. Filthy as it was, Henry preferred the city.

He turned his horse up the Escolta, the main thoroughfare of New Manila, which was new only in the sense that it stood outside the sixteenth-century Intramuros. A streetcar rattled by in the opposite direction, drawn by a dilapidated Filipino pony. The driver blew a blast on a tin horn, which was lost in the cacophony of the street. Hired conveyances, *calesas* and *caromatas*, and wagons pulled by carabao surged around him.

Henry had an office in General Otis's headquarters in the Malacañang, a step up from his former digs in the old Fortress of Santiago inside the Intramuros, but he preferred to operate out of his rented house in the city. Living there made it less likely that he would end up being tried for attacking his commanding officer. Living was cheap in Manila, even when one ate at the luxurious Army and Navy Club. Civilians had the equally luxurious University Club, and lesser lights the American Club. Champagne and other wines were not taxed, and service was cheap. Officers' wives and daughters came out from the States and stayed in the Hotel de Oriente. American belles, enchanted by the Filipino ponies, could be seen riding gaily through the streets in traps drawn by these tiny horses and driven by uniformed natives. They attended luncheons on the flagships off Cavite and the horse races near Pasay and found it an exhilarating and adventuresome experience, much as their British sisters had felt when they first followed their husbands to India. And after all, the war was quite far away, outside the city. No one had been in any real danger since the first day, when Aguinaldo's men had burned part of Manila and snipers had gotten behind the lines. A number of Filipinos had been shot for cutting the fire hoses, the timid carabao had gone crazy with fear and run blindly into buildings, and the officers' wives had locked themselves in their rooms at the Hotel de Oriente. But everything in the city had been calm since then, and dances and parties had resumed at all the clubs.

Henry found it all rather silly, but that might have been because his own wife and daughter were not here, and he had little inclination to dance with anyone else's. Since the arrival of the women, caste barriers for these functions had been erected. The appearance of a Filipino at any event was rare. Even *ilustrados* of position and property who supported the United States were not considered social equals.

Everyone shopped on the Escolta, though: European ladies with servants in tow; Chinese; Malays; mestizas and Filipinas in native dress, elegant in long, flowing skirts of pineapple silk and blouses with gauze sleeves, stiffened so that they stuck out like inverted water goblets. They crowded the narrow sidewalk, chattering in Tagalog and Spanish, occasionally trying out their English on American soldiers. On the intersecting streets, shops with Spanish signs gave way to Chinese storefronts smelling of incense and hung with strange dried creatures and herbs used in healing.

Overlaying it all was the constant sensation of being in a Turkish bath. The temperature never dipped below sixty degrees, even on the highest mountain, and the humidity felt like a warm, moist hand around Henry's throat. Much longer here and he'd be going native, he thought, casting off even his tropical army khakis for native pantaloons and thin gauze shirts worn untucked. There was something undeniably attractive about the native pineapple cloth, Henry thought. He hadn't lived with an artist-wife without absorbing some of her eye. The designs were fresh and unstilted. Midge would like one of the skirts of pineapple silk. Surely if he sent it, Cindy would let her have it.

On impulse, Henry tethered his horse outside a shop whose Spanish sign proclaimed it to be a dressmaker's. The inside smelled of sachet and was lined with mirrors, which made Henry look jumpily over his shoulder each time he caught his own reflection. The woman behind the counter, a middle-aged Filipina with betel-stained teeth, was selling a rainbow-patterned kerchief to a pair of younger women, country girls, apparently, in town on a market day. The clerk looked at Henry and spoke to someone in the shadows behind her. Then she grinned at Henry, showing off blackened teeth. "Madame be with you." She nodded briskly, proud of this newly acquired American phrase.

Henry took a seat on a spindly white wicker chair with pink-striped cushions and waited for Madame, balancing his hat on his knee. It seemed he had found his way into an upper-class establishment. Possibly Madame would speak Spanish. English would be too much to hope for.

As the country girls left with their purchase, Madame appeared, and Henry was transfixed. She must have been a mestiza, a mixture of Filipino and another race, probably Spanish, and she was more beautiful than anything Henry in his depression could have imagined. He gazed at her as he would at a perfect emerald.

"May I be of service, señor?" she asked in lilting Spanish. It sounded like a tune to him, as if the translucent gauze bells of her sleeves held invisible chimes.

"I want a skirt," Henry said. "A silk skirt. For my daughter." He could not take his eyes from the woman. She had black, liquid eyes. A mass of black hair, thick and lustrous and probably long enough for her to sit on, was twisted into a heavy knot just below the crown of her head and held with a gold comb. He wanted to touch it. He stared so hard that it made her visibly nervous, and she looked down at the toes of her pink slippers.

After a moment she looked up again with a little more composure. "Your daughter? In the States?"

"Yes. She's nearly fifteen."

"Ah." Madame smiled. She seemed more comfortable now that they were talking about his daughter. "I have many beautiful skirts. You wait." She vanished again with that faint suggestion of tinkling bells, and Henry realized that her earrings were tiny gold chimes. Would Midge like those? Probably not. Earrings had gone out of fashion in the States. Hardly anyone even had their ears pierced anymore.

Madame came back with her arms full of gaily colored cloth. Henry noticed that the lady with the betel-nut teeth had gone. He thought perhaps Madame was the owner. Filipinas were noted for their business sense. It wasn't unusual for a father to set his daughter up in business.

She knelt in front of him on the seagrass carpet and spread the skirts out one by one: a froth of gold and crimson, tangerine and emerald, and turquoise.

"I don't know which she'd like," Henry said helplessly. He tried, unsuccessfully, to keep himself from staring at this beautiful, exotic woman. She had a mouth the color of watermelon flesh, and her eyes were shadowed by thick, feathery lashes, as delicate as a moth's antenna.

She cocked her head at him, apparently now untroubled by his interest—even appreciative of it. Or was he just reading first one false impression and then another in a perfect stranger's face? He didn't know.

"Men never know," she said, laughing, and it took Henry a moment to realize she had not divined his thoughts but was only referring to his confusion over the skirts. "That is why there are ladies to decide these things. I am Estrella Rodriguez, and this is my shop. You tell me what colors your daughter wears, and I will find the perfect skirt for her."

"She likes blue," Henry said suddenly. An image had popped into his head, of Midge at five, howling for a blue dress in a shop. He couldn't remember if she had gotten it or not.

Estrella Rodriguez began to pull blue skirts from her pile, first aquamarine, then teal, then sky blue with embroidered gold threads. "Are you in Manila for very long?" she asked, eyes still on her wares as she laid them out.

"Nearly a year now." Blue skirts flowed around Henry's feet like water.

"Do you like it here?"

"It's very beautiful."

"My father is an important man in Spain," Estrella said. "He will send for me one day. And my mother."

A twinge of pity passed over Henry. No Spanish don would send for a Tagalog wife and mestiza daughter, not now that he had gone home to Spain. If the Americans hadn't come, her father would probably still be here. "Do you have brothers and sisters?" he asked.

Estrella frowned. "Brothers. One was killed by the Americans in the fighting. The other was killed by Aguinaldo's men. I don't want to know any more about this war."

"I'm sorry."

"War is good for business—the American ladies buy many things—but it is wicked all the same. I pray to the Blessed Virgin every night on my way home, so it will stop." She smiled wryly up at him. "I expect that will do more good than asking General Otis and General Aguinaldo. Or your President McKinley."

A bite of conscience sank its teeth into Henry's neck. These people were real. They weren't the gugus—and worse things—that the soldiers and even Otis called them. Whatever their lives had been like under Spanish rule, Estrella Rodriguez's certainly had not improved.

"Do you think you could put together a whole outfit

for me?" he asked her. "Whatever a Filipina lady would wear? A skirt and a blouse with those—those pretty sleeves?" He pointed at her own. "And anything else that goes with it?"

Estrella smiled. "Of course. But I will have to look for just the right pieces. To go with this skirt perhaps . . ." She held up a rippled teal and turquoise silk. "I will have it delivered to you."

"I am leaving in the morning," Henry said. He looked at her deliberately. The mirrored walls reflected them, fragmenting them: Henry's pinched, tan face, almost the color of his khakis but paler than Estrella's; his pale hair, damp with the heat, plastered to his head, while Estrella's clung like some heavy black flower to hers. "I don't know when I'll be back."

Estrella's onyx eyes let his green ones hold them for a moment. He had the sensation of cupping something in his hand, something soft and unreliable.

"I will bring you the package tonight then," she said, looking away. She bent her head and began to fold up the skirts.

She had merely regarded him as a customer, Henry thought, his business as compensation for the war. No, something more than that had passed between them. No, it hadn't. He had been out here so long he was becoming deranged. He had been celibate so long he was in need of female company. Company only, nothing more. As he rode home, all Henry could think about was his encounter with Estrella Rodriguez. He didn't know why, but it didn't seem to him to be quite real. Perhaps Estrella hadn't been real. Perhaps she was some kind of Philippine fairy dust, and he would never see her again. Not tonight or any time. Although he thought perhaps he had seen her once before, on the street the day he arrived in Manila. But maybe that was his imagination, too.

He stabled his horse and went into the small Spanish-style house he had rented. Its walls were painted a lively pink, which irritated him, but they were thick and kept the temperature bearable inside, as did the tile roof and shell-paned windows on the upper floor. The house was furnished with raffia carpeting and monstrous pieces of ancient Spanish furniture and maintained by a cook and a houseboy, who seemed to go with it. Dinner was ready when he got there, a chicken flavored with the ubiquitous garlic and sweet peppers that were the mainstay of Manila cooking. The cook spoke only Tagalog, so Henry had grown tired of trying to convey to her that, unlike his predecessor, he didn't care for garlic and pepper.

He ate the chicken anyway, deciding he must have acquired a taste for the condiments, since that night they seemed almost bland. Or perhaps nothing seemed vivid compared with Estrella Rodriguez.

After eating, he prowled moodily through the house, making a big production of packing a field kit that he could have slung together in fifteen minutes had he been so inclined.

His houseboy, Arturo, padded after him. "Does the general want me to draw him a bath?"

Henry looked at his khakis. They were limp and sweat stained. A clean uniform lasted only five minutes in this climate. He caught sight of his face in the mirror above the cumbersome bureau. He needed to shave, too. But if he did that, how would it look to Estrella Rodriguez? And how much bigger a fool would he feel when some barefoot child brought his purchases around for a penny? Why did he think she would bring them herself?

Arturo peered at him through the gloom. Manila had no electricity to speak of, and Henry's house was lit with coconut-oil lamps. "The bath, General?" Henry was aware that he must have looked as if he had had a bad day. "And a gin rickey? I will put it by the bathtub."

"You do that," Henry said. The hell with worrying about Estrella. He was a married man, despite his wife's estrangement. He was an American. His business here was to settle political matters for the Filipinos, not to get personally involved with them. He thought of them as children, willful children wanting their independence before they were ready. Even Emilio Aguinaldo didn't understand politics as they really were, didn't understand the wider world. With Spain gone, if the Americans didn't protect the Philippines, the Germans or the Japanese would simply swallow them up.

Finished with his bath, Henry dressed in a clean set of khakis and swallowed the rest of his drink. It burned agreeably. He left the towels and the tub for Arturo to clean up and went out to sit on the veranda, smelling the wet night.

She was coming up the walk, just getting out of a *calesa*, turning hesitantly in the dusk, package under one arm, tripping lightly up the stone flags. The backs of her heelless slippers flapped against her feet. It was an oddly endearing sound.

Henry walked to the edge of the veranda. "Good evening."

"Good evening." Estrella cocked her head up at him. "I have brought your daughter's presents." She lifted her own flame-colored skirt with her free hand and climbed the steps with a curiously determined grace. Henry noticed she had changed her clothes, too.

He took the package. "Would you like some tea?" he heard himself saying. "Or a glass of champagne?" She smelled of patchouli oil. Her hair gleamed in the dusk.

She looked thoughtfully at the empty glass in his hand. "I will have whatever you are drinking."

"All right." Henry took her inside and called to Arturo to fix them two gin rickeys. He wondered if that was socially acceptable among Filipinos. An American woman would brand herself as fast if she drank gin, particularly if she wasn't married.

Estrella didn't seem to mind, and she appeared to have an excellent tolerance for liquor. She curled up on one of the hideous Spanish armchairs in his parlor while Henry inspected her choices for Midge. She had brought the teal and turquoise skirt and a length of delicately embroidered white silk, big enough for a shawl. Henry held it up, trying to decide if that was what it was.

Estrella saw his puzzlement. "That is a *pañolón.*" She set down her glass and stood up, taking it from his hand. "It is worn like this." She spun slowly in a circle, twining the white silk around her shoulders, knotting it between her breasts. "For formal occasions the pañolón is always proper. It should be attached with a pin of gold or diamonds so that it hangs elegantly." She smiled at him and unwrapped it.

Henry smiled back. "Most unsuitable for a young girl."

"Don't American girls wear gold?"

"Gold, yes. Diamonds, no. Not at Midge's age."

Estrella spun the shawl around her shoulders again. In the light of the coconut-oil lamp, her eyes shone. "In the Philippines that is what young girls do with their money, as they earn it. They buy gold. A new ring. A hair ornament. When they have enough, they will turn several rings in on a diamond. We like to wear our money. That way we always know where it is."

She unwrapped the pañolón and handed it to Henry. Then she lifted her glass to him in a solemn toast, eyes

sparkling above the edge. "To your daughter, General.
May she always be a lucky young lady."

Henry lifted his glass, too, a slightly ragged gesture.
"I'm afraid I haven't brought her very much luck so far. I
am . . . estranged from her mother. It has made her unhappy." He wasn't sure why he told Estrella that. Justify-
ing what he might be about to do, perhaps?

"That is sad," Estrella said.

Henry thought she looked slightly relieved. A twinge
of conscience there, too? Or was he simply imagining her
interest? Lately he hadn't pictured himself as a man
whom women might pursue, although actual experience
told him otherwise.

Estrella regarded him in the lamplight. "You are a
very long way from home," she said at last. "Are you
lonely?"

"Yes, damn it." Henry's fingers tightened on his
glass, and he set it down before he broke it. He hung his
head. "God, yes."

Estrella came and stood by his chair. "I think sometimes of what it will be like in Spain, when my father
sends for us." Her voice broke slightly. It was almost a
plea. "I think about what it is like to be a stranger."

She didn't hold out her hands to him, just stood
waiting. In a moment he was standing, his hands on her
shoulders and then around her waist, his face in her hair.

From there it was but a very short step to his bedroom on the upper floor. Arturo seemed to have vanished,
possibly sensing what was in the wind. The house was
warm and silent, lit only by a flickering bowl of oil in the
stairwell. They waded through the pools of light slowly, as
they might traverse a warm lagoon. Estrella's skirt, flame-
colored in the light, then black in the darkness, rustled
behind them.

In the bedroom was a four-poster bed hung with lace

curtains and mosquito netting. Henry laid Estrella on it and undid the buttons of her blouse while she watched him with eyes as dark as the night. Like most Philippine beds, the mattress was woven cane, like a chair seat, overlaid with a thin Malay sleeping mat, with a huge bolster to support the sleeper. Henry pushed the bolster out of the way and covered Estrella's mouth with his. The hell with any woman who didn't want him when he could have one who so plainly did. Quickly he stood, took off his clothes, then lay down beside her. Estrella wrapped her arms around his bare back, and her hair slid from its gold clip, flowing over golden breasts.

It was the hair he felt first in the morning. It had been a long time since he had wakened with a woman's long hair tickling his face, and at first, in the depths of groggy sleep, he thought it was Cindy's. He opened his eyes wide, heart pounding, and was snapped into reality by the sight of the sleeping Estrella. Her hair, which must have hung nearly to her heels, covered her like a curtain; she needed no nightdress but that. She opened her eyes solemnly as he stared at her.

"Oh, God." It was almost a moan. He bent his head in self-accusation.

Estrella touched a finger to his lips. "I am not unhappy," she whispered. She smiled and snuggled her face into his shoulder.

But he was. If not unhappy, guilty. The light shimmered, and Henry seemed to see another head on his shoulder, the chestnut head of Gisela von Kirchberg, his first wife. He had been engaged, unofficially, to Cindy when he had landed in bed with Gisela—and then into marriage. Estrella stirred, and Gisela faded away, but he didn't like the comparison. What was wrong with him? He had always thought himself a man in control of his life.

What was he doing here, cradling the beautiful Estrella Rodriguez?

He climbed out of bed. "I'm supposed to be in General Wheaton's camp this morning," he said. He found a clean pair of drawers in the massive bureau and pulled them on self-consciously.

Estrella didn't appear to be insulted. She slipped her own clothes on, her dark hair swinging against the backs of her calves, then piled its whole amazing length onto her head in a quick, expert knot, pinning it with the gold clip that lay among the bedclothes.

Henry fled down the hall to shave, guilty and half expecting Estrella to pursue him with anger and shouting. Either Gisela or Cindy might well have done so.

He came back to find her polishing his boots. A clean khaki shirt and trousers from the clothes press were laid out on the bed, which she had made up, and she sat cross-legged on the raffia carpet with his left boot between her knees.

"Arturo does that," Henry managed to say.

"I think Arturo should pay more attention to his work." Estrella smiled. "I think Arturo is a lazybones. He should take better care of you." She gave the boot a final swipe and stood, rising in one fluid, graceful movement, and kissed him while he looked at her, startled. He put on the khakis she had laid out for him and tried to think what to say next.

While he was deciding, she smiled at him again and said, "I will tell Cook to fix your breakfast and to put something up for you to take with you." She tripped down the stairs.

An hour later he was on the road, full of a better breakfast than Cook had ever managed before and with a feast in his saddlebags, ordered by Estrella after lengthy negotiation in Tagalog.

"I told her what Americans like," she had explained as he prepared to leave. "Your food will be better now." She had seemed unabashed speaking with Cook; unashamed of her presence in his house, possibly even a little proud of it. He was an American officer. A catch.

And how could he, after all that, tell her that he hadn't wanted a mistress, only a brief ease for a pain she couldn't cure?

He cursed himself as he rode. Estrella had kissed him good-bye, standing on tiptoe as he bent from the saddle. The sun had made her look as if she were cast in gold. She would cook him a wonderful dinner, her own cooking, when he came back, she said. She would send the package to Midge for him. At the last she had whispered in his ear, "I will wait for you."

Just as she was waiting for her father, Henry realized with a sick jolt. A horrible fear overtook him at the realization that his night with Estrella might create another mestizo daughter whose father would leave. But the thought of Estrella waiting for him in her shop—lovely, loving, glad to see him, someone who might see to his breakfast and his clothes—took hold of him. It wouldn't hurt to see her just a few times more, explaining gently that it couldn't be permanent.

The thought of Estrella remained with him as he rode through the hot mist that hung above the Pasig River. Although the road seemed clear and he passed Wheaton's sentries regularly, he kept a watchful eye on the trees all the same. Henry had known Lloyd Wheaton before—a gaunt, black-bearded man with a mustache of almost Prussian grandeur. A decorated Civil War veteran who made no bones about his dislike for Filipinos, he had once been heard to challenge a correspondent who had commented on their bravery with, "Brave? Brave? Damn 'em, they won't stand up to be shot!" Since Wheaton, now holding temporary rank as brigadier of volunteers, was still a captain in his head and was invariably on the front lines, Henry could see how this would irritate him. *We're all generals now*, Henry thought. *We've got more generals than soldiers.* It annoyed him to wonder if his own promotion, deserved and somewhat overdue, had finally come simply because it wouldn't do to have Colonel Henry Blake outranked in the field by former captains.

Wheaton's brigade had held a part of the southern line during the first outbreak of fighting, then was assigned to clear the area just south of the city where insurgent firepower had been harassing the Americans regularly. Henry had seen him looming over his crouching men in the rice paddies around Manila, urging them on in a booming voice heard clear across the bay: "Action! Step out! Do you think those brown bastards will wait to give you a fight? Catch 'em!"

Now his "Flying Column" had been sent southeast along the Pasig between Manila and the lake of Laguna de Bay to open the river to traffic. The land between Manila Bay and Laguna de Bay was a narrow isthmus, and Wheaton had soon found that the jungle was full of booby traps. Two companies fell into an ambush, and Henry imagined that Wheaton was not in a good mood.

He arrived in Wheaton's camp on the west side of the lake to find the general planning a punitive expedition. Wheaton clapped Henry on the back and took him into his private tent.

"Intelligence, hell!" Wheaton bellowed. "I'll give 'em something to remember us by, and they'll think twice next time. Have a cigar."

Henry accepted the cigar with a chuckle. Wheaton was the leading theatrical personality of the U.S. High

Command, and the correspondents loved him. His staff was reputed to like him as well—except on those occasions when he suffered from insomnia and woke them for conferences at two in the morning. Henry gave Wheaton as thorough a briefing as he could in the hope that he would not be inclined to request another in the dead of night.

"This is a different sort of enemy we're dealing with here," Henry said, "and I very much fear there is more sympathy for them in the villages than we would like to think." He wished he could get that across to Otis. "When a mayor in some barrio is friendly, you can pretty much bet that the local insurrectos have just buried their guns and melted in with the farmers. I'd say that at least half of the men who are out there peacefully planting rice and smiling are insurrectos. As soon as you move on, they'll be operating again."

"We'll see about that," Wheaton said grimly.

Henry watched Wheaton's men set out at dawn the next morning, spreading out toward every village within a twelve-mile radius. How Wheaton had decided on this number, Henry didn't know.

Dry palm thatch burns very quickly, even in the tropics, particularly if helped along by kerosene. There wasn't much in the huts to burn, but what the villagers couldn't snatch up and run with went up with the flames.

"That'll teach you gugus," a soldier said with satisfaction. "Now where are you going to hide?" He looked young to Henry, not old enough for the army, but maybe that was just because Henry was getting older. He had noticed lately that half the soldiers looked like children to him.

Another young soldier stood shaking, watching the flames eat up the village. The stilt huts first sagged and

then fell in on themselves with a roar, leaving little cy-
clones of sparks in the air. Almost all the villagers had
run, but a woman with a baby on her hip stood howling in
front of a burning hut.

"Sir," the second soldier said uneasily, turning to
Henry, "what if there's still someone in there? Kids, I
mean? Or old people who couldn't get out?"

"They were all warned when they saw us coming,"
Henry said wearily. He didn't like it either, but he supposed it had to be done.

The woman turned toward them furiously, hands
spread empty. She screamed something at them in Tagalog that Henry didn't understand, and then she fled. Behind her the stores of rice, doggedly unearthed by the
soldiers, burned to hard, black cinders.

"I wonder what she was screaming," Henry said to
the soldier standing beside him.

The soldier kept his eyes on the woman's back.
" 'What do we eat?' " he said quietly. "She was screaming
'What do we eat?' "

III

Oklahoma Territory

Something was in the air. India Blackstone could smell it on the cold, dank March wind. She was sitting on the top of a low rise, her boots tucked under her heavy corduroy skirts as she looked at the landscape she loved to paint: the remains of frozen grass, reexposed by melted snow, undulating for miles and miles toward the horizon, studded with the humpbacked shapes of her father's cattle. She could see a faint chuff of smoke from a train engine on the horizon. If she turned around, there would be her parents' house, windows as yellow as squash blossoms on this gray day. But whatever she smelled in the air seemed to be in the other direction, in the mysterious distance.

Next December thirty-first, nine and a half months from now, the future would arrive. The twentieth century, when man would remake himself, right all wrongs, and learn how to provide plenty and prosperity for everyone. Or so people said. India stared past the cattle. If not Utopia, certainly there would be change. Movement, like colors rearranging themselves on canvas.

Her brother, Winslow, appeared, striding across her living painting, coat collar pulled up. He halted at the edge of the slope and called to her, "You'll freeze your tailbone sitting in the frost like that. What are you doing mooning around out here?"

"Thinking," India said with dignity. "Do you know that it's almost the twentieth century?"

"It's only March," Winslow countered. He was fifteen, dressed in denim work pants and a sheepskin jacket, his dark hair resembling blackbirds' feathers under his Stetson. He looked like a Cherokee when he let it grow. "Besides," he said, "it won't really be the twentieth century until the *end* of 1900. You're not one year old until you've *finished* your first year."

"Well, nobody looks at it that way but you," she scoffed. "It's the way it *feels*. Next year we'll be writing dates with '1900,' not 18-something. And why aren't you in school on a Wednesday?"

"Father said I could help. He and Uncle Rob are going out to see how things look."

India had grown up on the M Bar B. She knew what that implied: See how the feed looked; see how the herd had survived the winter. That probably meant their uncle Rob and aunt would come for dinner, to talk it all over. It was a yearly ritual the Martins and the Blackstones—partners in the M Bar B—never failed to observe.

"Do you want to come?" Winslow said. "That's what I came to see."

There was a time when she would have gone in a flash, before she started seeing the cattle as their shapes and not their breathing selves. Now the only cow she wanted to look at was the one she could put on canvas; not entirely a cow, really—often a sort of herself as cow. Her father didn't know what to make of them.

"I don't think I will," India said. "I've got a painting started. I want to get back to work on it."

She didn't even have to skip school, she thought almost wistfully as Winslow disappeared, whistling, his breath coming in smoky puffs, his step light with the notion that he was getting away with something. India was through with school, educated like her brother in the one-room schoolhouse that served their part of the territory, polished with weekly music lessons in Folsom, and "finished" at a good academy in St. Louis for her final year. She could now play the piano, dance all the newest dances, speak passable French, and paint in watercolors. She could also paint in oils, which had been on the academy's curriculum only for the most advanced students. However, the subjects of her paintings were very unlike the floral still lifes and landscapes that well-bred young ladies turned out to frame as Christmas presents for their grandmothers. The art mistress at the academy had spoken hesitantly of art school in New York, and Edward Blackstone had been appalled. India wanted to go to New York, and a growing number of people were distressed over the idea. Her uncle Rob and aunt Kale's daughter, Cathy, had gone to New York, to get acting "out of her system." She was still there.

Deciding maybe she was hungry, India got up and brushed frost and mud off the back of her skirt with a gloved hand, then started toward the house. She had heavy black hair, dark currant-colored eyes, and skin that refused to stay a fashionable ivory despite any number of sunbonnets, since her mother was half-Hindu. Her mother, Ramedha, was fine-boned, and everyone had thought India would be delicate, too, but in her last spurt of growth she had acquired some of her father's angular solidity. The result was that she was tall, with the rangy yet muscular quality of a mare. In a drawing room in Atlanta, she would have been considered "coltish." Here on her home turf she was perfect. She moved with an easy fluidity, and her features were as beautiful as the little statue of Parvati that her mother kept in the drawing room. It was just that by the intensity of her nature she took up rather a lot of room.

Her long-legged stride brought her quickly home. Her boots in the front hall echoed as loudly as her father's, coming in the opposite direction. Edward Blackstone pulled a hat down over dark, grizzled hair. He kissed her cheek.

"Coming with us, Puss?"

India shook her head.

"Oh. Well, then, help your mother with dinner. Rob and Kale will be eating with us."

India wandered into the kitchen and took a cold biscuit off the remains of the breakfast dishes.

"Didn't you eat a proper breakfast this morning?" Ramedha Blackstone asked her daughter. She had just finished conferring with their cook.

"I am now," India said, gnawing at the biscuit. "I wanted to look at the frost."

"Oh."

Ramedha regarded her daughter with a mildly baffled air, having to tip her head back to do it. Peter Blake might have described Ramedha as "thoroughly Americanized," but the truth was that both Blackstones were British by birth—Ramedha's father had been an army officer —and Ramedha had never considered herself anything else. She had been raised in a British household, and only her honey-colored skin and her still-black curtain of hair spoke of her mother's race. Just now the ebony hair was pinned into a pompadour.

"I think your father was hoping you'd ride out with him this morning."

"I just didn't feel like it," India said. "Winslow went —he was happy to play hooky—but I felt I was being offered a treat to distract me."

"You sound as if we were trying to give you some nasty potion, when in fact it's much more as if you were trying to give your father one. And do come into the other room." Ramedha led her daughter down the hall to the parlor. "Your father is not trying to distract you. He wants you to be happy, that's all."

"If that were so, he'd let me go to New York without all this fuss."

Ramedha opened the draperies in the parlor and looked at her daughter. "India, dear, you know how your father feels about the idea of your living in New York, even with Cathy Martin."

Sinking onto the couch, India knitted her brows and pursed her lips. "Painters!" she snorted, a stodgy caricature. "Actors! Socialists! Heard the things that go on in these so-called art schools. Harrumph!"

"It's not fair to make fun of your father. He's not a provincial man, and he does know what he's talking about."

"Exactly," India said. "He had a good long inning. Traveled everywhere before settling in to be a gentleman farmer."

"India, don't be dramatic. We are not trying to immure you on a windswept prairie," Ramedha said firmly. "We have taken you to London and Switzerland and Paris."

"Where Father followed me around like a policeman the entire time in case I should meet with any depraved Parisian artists and run off to live with them. Or whatever he thought was going to happen."

Ramedha chuckled. "Your father has led a very cosmopolitan life. He's well aware of the snares that tempt the young and inexperienced. He fell into most of them himself."

"And so now he's going to protect me," India said irritably. "I'll bet he wouldn't if I were Winslow."

"You are a girl, darling. Girls are more vulnerable." Ramedha sighed. She had had this conversation with her rebellious daughter at least once a week ever since she could remember. When India was twelve it had been wanting to go on a cattle drive. Now it was art school. "Dear heart, with Cathy Martin's example, you can't expect us to like the idea."

"Cathy's becoming quite well known in the theater. She gets wonderful reviews."

"It's also well known that she hasn't married the young man she brought down here with her," Ramedha said primly. "It very much distresses Kale and Rob."

"Mother! I'm not going to live in sin with an actor. I'm going to paint."

"Don't be flip. And you don't know what you're going to do. I'm not implying that you are—well, that your character is lacking in any way. But girls get talked into things. Men take advantage. That's why girls are chaperoned."

"Because nobody thinks we have any sense?" India said scornfully. She stood up. "I'm going to go paint. At least I can still do that. I may be the only artist who ever becomes famous for painting cows—since there isn't anything else around to paint. If anybody ever hears of me."

Ramedha watched her stalk out and heard her rattling her easel out of the closet under the stairs. Maybe they could give India one of the upstairs rooms for a studio. There were certainly enough to spare. Ramedha smoothed her dark pompadour, feeling exhausted. Conversations with India were always exhausting. She felt as if she and her husband, Edward, were trying to hold on to a rocket that strained upward while they gripped its sputtering fuse. Maybe Edward *was* too old to understand

India, to understand changing times. He was seventeen years older than she, and she had always looked up to him, let him make the decisions—even when she had quite deliberately set out to capture him. That was feminine wiles. Women were expected to do that; men enjoyed it. But to go live in New York, by oneself, to paint professionally? That was suitable for a man to do. What kind of life would a woman who did that have?

On the other hand, what kind of life did India want? Ramedha wasn't sure her daughter knew yet. But she had turned down two proposals, one from a nice boy with money who lived in the territory, the other from a young barrister with a career ahead of him in London.

She sighed. India was delightful, when she was willing to be so. But lately she had grown moodier and had developed an aversion to the dances, picnics, and sleigh rides that were the young people's diversions. She spent more and more time outdoors, wearing a ratty sunbonnet that looked as if it had been retrieved from the ragbag, painting incomprehensible pictures her father didn't understand. For that matter, Ramedha hadn't much cared for the one of herself. It made her uncomfortable. But India said it was one of her "strongest," whatever that meant, so when they had decided to lay their dilemma at Cindy Blake's feet, the portrait had been one of the canvases sent.

What would happen when Cindy wrote back, Ramedha couldn't guess. If she said India had no talent, Edward would be pleased and sympathetic, but there was no telling what India would do. If Cindy supported the notion of art school, Edward would be upset, she herself would be pleased, but India would be ecstatic.

Ramedha shook her head. Either way, someone was going to be hurt.

*   *   *

India dragged her easel and half-finished canvas to the barn, her paints slung across her back in a rucksack. She pulled the main doors wide, letting in a flood of morning light, and stood staring at the horses. They whickered at her while their ears swiveled around and they tried to butt her with their noses. Finally she remembered the lump sugar in her skirt pocket and doled it out to them. In her mind they were not penned in stalls but streaming across the prairie grass.

India set her canvas on the easel. There was nothing in the barn that she wanted to paint; it was just the shape of the horses she had come for, the bones of their hocks and the angles of their feet. The horses on her half-finished canvas stood on a yellow prairie, heads thrown up in amazement. A yellow moon hung in an indigo sky, and floating over the prairie were the Indians.

She spread pools of flake white, raw umber, and marine blue on her palette, then crimson, verdigris, and burnt sienna. The horses watched her curiously, posturing in their stalls, showing off the arc of a dark eye, the slope of a haunch. The sound of a buckboard in the barnyard passed by her while the horses grew on the prairie. The light changed, shifted. The sun rolled westward, but India didn't notice. Nothing ever pierced her concentration while she was painting.

It wasn't until her father, her uncle Rob, and Winslow returned and someone sent Winslow to find her that she surfaced. He stood in the barn door, his hat blocking the light. He looked at the canvas, at the Indians who hovered above the horses.

"Why are those people hanging in the air like that? What's holding them up?"

"That's just where I felt like putting them. What do you want?"

"It's nearly dinnertime. Mother says to come in."

"I'm not hungry," India said absently.

"You have to. Uncle Rob and Aunt Kale are here."

"Oh." India focused on him. "Oh, tarnation. I'll have to change my clothes." She cleaned her brushes, packed her paints back into their box, then cocked her head at the canvas. "Maybe this is finished, anyway."

"How can you tell?" Winslow inquired.

"*I* can tell," India snapped. "You don't know anything about art."

"I know Indians can't fly. Those are Indians, aren't they? I suppose they could be birds."

India made a face at him. "Tell Mother I'm coming. And you'd better change your own clothes. You smell like a cow pie." Winslow departed, chuckling, and she packed her gear into the rucksack. She leaned the canvas against the barn wall and folded up the easel. Maybe it *was* finished, she thought, assessing it. It probably was. She left it in the barn, feeling disinclined to explain her flying Indians to anyone else at dinner.

Kale Martin was just driving up in her buggy and Ramedha was waiting for her when India came around the corner of the house. The men were in the bathroom, cleaning up. The M Bar B was too far out in the country for electrification, but it had an excellent water system and a storage tank, emblazoned with the company emblem, that was Edward Blackstone's pride.

"I'm just going to change," India called, walking up the steps to the porch. "How are you, Aunt Kale?" She went into the house without waiting for an answer.

They heard her slinging her rucksack into the closet under the stairs with a thud and a crash and then her clattering footfalls as she went up to the second floor. "When I sent her away to school, I thought they could teach her not to sound like a herd of buffalo," Ramedha said, sighing.

Kale laughed. "She wouldn't be India if she tiptoed. India is an original."

"That is what we're beginning to fear," Ramedha muttered.

The men came in to dinner with wet hair parted and slicked down, and India reappeared in a blue flannel dress. She took her place at the table and looked at everybody with interest. "How did the herd do over the winter? Any new calves yet?"

"Glad to see you've decided to rejoin the world," Winslow said, spearing a chicken quarter from the platter as it went by.

"We've weathered the winter very well," Edward said. "I don't think we lost more than a few head. No calves so far and a blessing, too. It's been too cold."

India nodded, listening while she devoured her chicken.

Ramedha took note of her daughter's appetite. "Dear, it is not necessary to bolt your food like a starving wolf."

"I'm hungry. I think I missed lunch."

"My sister flies in from the moon every day around this time for dinner," Winslow said to no one in particular. "We don't know what she does the rest of the time."

"That will do, Winslow."

"Has anyone seen the newspaper this afternoon?" Kale asked.

"It came in from town with the mail," Ramedha said. "I've been so busy I haven't even looked at it."

"They're saying the war in the Philippines is nearly over, but five more regiments have been sent over."

"That's because General Otis is an idiot," Edward grumbled. "I've heard no good of the man. They ought to

give the command to Lawton. He'd finish Aguinaldo's
rebels off soon enough."

"Rebels?" Rob Martin grinned. "When this country
rebelled against Britain, they were 'patriots.'"

"Not to the British." Edward chuckled. "But having
become an American, I'll concede you've made a good
enough job of it. However, we're talking about savages
here. Not the same thing."

"They aren't savages either," Rob retorted. "Unless
you count the tribes in the far islands. And even if they
were, doesn't every people have the inherent right to gov-
ern itself?"

"Certainly not. Appalling idea. Plenty of them
haven't got enough sense."

"You aren't going to trot out 'the white man's burden'
theory again, are you?" Rob waved a hand in eloquent
exasperation and nearly took the gravy boat with him.
"Sorry."

"It's a perfectly valid way of describing our duty
toward lesser peoples."

"Like my grandmother?" India asked indignantly.
"Not that I ever met her, but—"

"Certainly not." Edward was affronted. "Your
mother's mother came of an ancient and noble civilization. There is no comparison between a daughter of
Rajputana and a Filipino."

"I don't notice the British letting loose of *her* country, though," Rob commented.

Kale looked at Ramedha, and Ramedha looked at
Kale. "Kale is sorry she mentioned it," Ramedha said.
"You two have been at this ever since we got into the war
with Spain. Neither one of you is president, so what you
would do is not relevant—unless you want to write him."

"Sorry, my dear," Edward said. "If Rob would just
look at the lessons of history—"

"The lessons of history are as plain as the nose on your face," Rob shot back.

"Well, I want to go," Winslow said. "I hope the war doesn't end before I'm old enough."

Everyone swung around to look at him.

"There, now," said Kale, with a glare at Rob. "You see?"

"You'll do nothing of the sort," Ramedha said.

"All *I* want to do is go to New York," India said. "Doesn't that look better to you by comparison?"

"Now, we've discussed this before," Edward said. "And I'm sure Kale and Rob here will bear me out on *this*—"

"We've had a letter from Cindy Blake," Ramedha said quickly, deciding it would, at any rate, serve as a diversion from the war.

India put her fork down. "You didn't tell me! When? What does she say?"

"She says you paint funny," Winslow said through a mouthful of chicken.

Ramedha didn't bother to glare at him. India hadn't even heard him. "It came this afternoon. She says you have a 'strong style of forceful naivete,'" she reported.

Edward snorted. "And what's that when it's at home?"

"Well, I don't know, dear, but it appears to be a compliment."

"What else?" India demanded. "What else?"

Ramedha did not respond directly to India. She was careful to direct her report to her husband, who was looking increasingly suspicious. "Cindy says she wants to talk to India personally. She has invited her to Washington for a visit."

"Why, how kind of her," Kale said, seeming to feel that was a safely noncommittal remark.

"Certainly very kind," Edward said. "But perhaps—" He looked at his daughter. "Now, Puss . . ." India was grinning from ear to ear. "Now, Puss, of course you can go to Washington if you've a mind to. Take in the galleries. Go to embassy parties. Shake the prairie dust off your feet for a while. But I wouldn't want you to be disappointed. 'Naivete' doesn't sound very encouraging, and, well—"

"You've been hoping I'm not any good," India said, with more perception than tact, "so you wouldn't have to send me to art school."

"Nothing of the sort," Edward protested. "See here, I have a happy thought. Why don't we hire a fellow, some artist chap, to come and give you lessons. I'm sure Cindy could recommend one. Those fellows are always short of money."

India looked so despairing, Ramedha intervened. "Edward, since we agreed to ask for Cindy's opinion, we ought to go along with her and send India to see her. Perhaps she can suggest a school we will all be more comfortable with."

"I don't want to be comfortable," India said. "I want to be an artist."

"As far as I can tell, the two are mutually exclusive," Edward remarked, "but *we* would prefer that you be comfortable, not shivering in some filthy attic somewhere."

"Artists whose fathers have enough money generally aren't forced to shiver in attics," India pointed out. "Unless their fathers disown them, of course."

"That has nothing to do with the case," Edward said. "Who knows what these art students get up to? I hear things. That hotel Michael Holt lives in up there in New York is full of artists. One of them has a snake. One of them is—pardon me, my dears, if I am blunt—living with *two* women without benefit of matrimony."

"Well, then, he won't have room for me," India said —and knew immediately she had gone too far.

Her father's face reddened. Rob and Kale Martin had the look of guests wondering if they should try to smooth the situation over or pretend it was not occurring.

"That is precisely the sort of talk," said Edward in a formidable voice, "that comes of lowering one's standards and associating with people of loose moral tone. You have simply proved my point, India."

"I'm sorry," she said contritely. "I truly am. That was outrageous of me. But I'm not a baby, and I'm not immoral, and I don't know what you think I'm going to *do* up there!"

The four parents at the table looked at one another uncomfortably. No one quite wanted to bring up the phrase "seduced and ruined." It seemed a trifle too histrionic. But that *had* happened to young women who weren't adequately protected. It didn't even have to happen. If people simply *thought* it had, that was enough to damage a girl's reputation in the circles India moved in. Then there was the matter of Cathy Martin. No one knew for sure what she was doing up there, but she had brought the young actor-manager of her troupe home to meet her parents, and Rob and Kale had confidently expected an engagement announcement. None had been forthcoming. The consensus among friends and neighbors was that Cathy Martin was up in New York just going hog-wild.

"It isn't that we don't trust you, dear," Ramedha said gently.

"It sounds to me like it is," India retorted.

"We don't trust the young men, dear."

"Or the old ones either," Edward said. "I hate to speak ill of my sex, but not everyone is a gentleman, and a young girl alone . . ."

"And even assuming that everyone you associate

with behaves like a nun," Ramedha said, "your friends at home won't know that. It doesn't look nice, darling. It looks fast. I just can't bear that." She cast Kale a quick look of apology.

"All right!" India threw both hands up in a gesture of concession. "Then let me go to Cindy Blake in Washington. I'll promise to abide by whatever she suggests for me —if you will, too," she added craftily.

"I'm not promising anything," Edward said. "There's no telling what she might suggest. But I'll take it under consideration."

"I suppose that's the best offer you're going to make," India said.

"It is."

"All right." She applied herself to eating again, happily settling for gains won and letting the currently unobtainable ride for a while.

When dinner was over she prodded her father, by dint of much cajoling, into sending a ranch hand into Folsom with a telegram for Cindy Blake.

"You're in a hurry, aren't you?" Winslow said a week later when India dragged him to the attic to help wrestle her trunk down.

"I want to get plans far enough along that Father can't change his mind." India followed him down the attic stairs and through the hallway to her bedroom. She pointed to a cedar chest. "Put it on that." They settled the trunk on the chest, and India dusted her hands. "Thank you. Sometimes you're useful. Honestly, sometimes I wish I were a boy. Father wouldn't spend his whole time thinking about all the different ways I could get ruined. Boys don't get ruined. They just go around ruining girls."

Winslow flushed, and India gave him a stern look.

"And don't think I don't know what you were doing with that girl from the bakery, out behind the town hall."

"I didn't really do anything," Winslow muttered, scarlet-faced. "It was her idea."

"And someone spiked the punch at that dance—I know because I tasted it—and you were dumb enough by that time to go along with her. You watch out, Winslow. Girls get ruined on purpose sometimes, and then boys have to marry them. Particularly girls from bakeries and boys whose fathers have money."

"Why weren't you dancing instead of watching me?" Winslow demanded.

"I was bored," India said, rooting in her wardrobe. "Everything was so nicely-nice and safe. Except the punch, I suppose, and old Mrs. Lovern spotted that after about ten minutes and had it poured out. I kept thinking how much every couple looked like the dish that ran away with the spoon. All those girls with their skirts stuck out with dress improvers and all those skinny boys."

"You'd better be careful," Winslow said. "You'll get so strange that nobody'll marry you. You'll be an old maid."

"Maybe that wouldn't be such a bad idea," India said. "Old maids get away with a lot, once they get old enough."

"You don't have the temperament," Winslow scoffed. "I've seen you flirting. It's a wonder all your beaux aren't crazy. You flirt with them, and then you go off all moody and paint flying Indians instead of going to dances. If you'd married those fellows, they'd have been sorry in a month."

"Probably," India conceded. "Maybe that's why I didn't do it. Do you think this dress is good enough for Washington?" She held up a blue china silk.

"Why are you asking me? I don't know anything about girls' clothes. Ask Mother."

"If I ask Mother, she'll say no and want me to wait while she has new ones made." India folded the dress into the trunk.

Winslow grinned. "Looks fine to me."

IV

Washington, D.C., April

India Blackstone stepped carefully down the metal steps of a red Pullman car into the unseasonably cold wind blowing across the Alexandria, Virginia, depot platform. A porter gave her a gloved hand for assistance. With her other hand, she gripped a carpetbag containing necessities for the journey. Supposedly she was to be met by Cindy's son, Frank. India squinted at the males on the platform, trying to decide which of them, if any, might be Frank Blake, last seen by her when he was twelve. The whole enormous Holt-Blake clan, connected to the Martins through Rob's first wife, had come for a visit then, and India remembered Frank as a blond boy in knee pants with a face not yet formed enough to tell what he might look like as an adult. Probably he was not the lanky man in the Burberry; the hair was far too gingery. And probably not the roly-poly one in the Inverness cape, although his hair was the right color.

"Miss Blackstone?"

She turned to find a tall young man in an overcoat and fedora. "Oh," she said. "Are you Mr. Blake? I was just wondering if that was you." India gestured toward the Inverness cape.

"Certainly not," Frank said in horror. "I knew right off it was you, though. You have a look of your mother about you. Do you have a trunk?"

"Two. One has paints in it."

Frank whistled for a porter. Then he escorted her to his mother's carriage and driver, which were waiting in front of the depot. He handed India in and tucked a rug around her knees. She watched him curiously as he supervised the loading of her trunks and tipped the porter. She had heard all about Frank Blake's escapades; everyone in the family had, as had all *their* friends and acquaintances. She decided he didn't look awfully repentant. He hopped into the carriage, and they sized each other up.

"Mother says you want to paint," he said. "Professionally, I mean. The new Mary Cassatt."

"I don't paint anything like Mary Cassatt," India said. "You just thought of her because she's a woman."

"Probably," Frank admitted. "There aren't many of them."

"That's what people keep telling me. Mary Cassatt hasn't lived in the States for years. I might as well emulate someone I have a chance of meeting. No one is going to let me go paint in Paris."

"Oh, you don't want to paint in Paris. Stay at home and own your own soul."

"That's what I think," India said, looking at Frank intently. "Of course," she added, "that may just be sour grapes."

"Probably is," Frank said agreeably. "There does seem to be a certain feeling among traditionalists that it's not real art if you don't paint it in Paris. Unless, of course, you happen to come from Paris, in which case you are allowed to paint it here. Regardless, you'll have an even worse time because you're female."

"Are you always so encouraging to people?" India demanded.

Frank laughed. "Artists give me a headache. I grew up with them running all over the house. But my mother gave up her own art, probably because they wouldn't let her play, except as a gallery owner and a critic and patron. She's made quite a reputation for herself as that, but they wouldn't really let her *paint*. Not and take her seriously. That's reserved for the boys."

"And that annoys you?" India was curious.

"Well, certainly. I'm fond of my mother. And I thought she was good. Of course, I don't know much about it."

"I expect not."

Frank didn't appear to be insulted. "Well, give me your thoughts on art then, O Educated One." He grinned at her and cast about for a topic. "What do you think of the 'nouveau' artists like Beardsley and so on?"

"Beardsley's dead," India said in a superior tone. "I keep up with these things."

"I must have missed the news, up at the North Pole," Frank said wryly. "What did you think of him when he wasn't dead? And anyway, there are plenty of people working in his style, everything twined around something else. It seems as if all the girls are trying to look like those strange, slightly witchy princesses with the gauzy draperies and the flowing hair."

"Well, they can't. Those are designs. They aren't even really art. You can be influenced by the style of an artist like Monet, for instance, but you can't make it look like a three-dimensional design. And even if you could, the effect would be much too static." India leaned toward him, bunching the carriage rug between them, trying to explain. "All those flowing tresses and dresses and so forth are what make Nouveau so attractive. It's just nice design."

"You don't find it upsetting?"

India knew what he meant. "You mean the sensuality of it? My father thinks it's very decadent and says I don't understand, but I think I do." She grinned suddenly. "I studied my mythology."

"Maybe your father doesn't really know why it upsets *him*," Frank ventured.

"Oh, he understands all right. He was very well educated. He just doesn't approve of that kind of thing running around loose, even disguised with gauzy draperies."

"The horns and the cloven hooves keep poking through." Along with other things, Frank thought. He had seen some samples of Aubrey Beardsley's work that he was willing to bet India hadn't.

"Anyway," India continued, "the style has toned down some, now that Beardsley's dead. He was the bad boy of the movement."

Then again, maybe she had. "What did he die of?" Frank asked.

"Tuberculosis. He was only twenty-six."

Frank decided a change of subject might be in order. His mother would consider this an unsuitable conversation, and he was dead sure India's mother would. He couldn't decide whether India was extremely naive or extremely unconventional, but perhaps he should be careful what he talked to her about. Yet she seemed much older than eighteen, and he had gotten out of the habit of knowing how to talk to debutantes. The women he had known over the last few years had not required much conversational cosseting.

The carriage rolled down the Blakes' drive and stopped in the portico for Frank to hand India down. The driver unloaded the trunks and hefted one onto his back while the horses waited patiently. Cindy came down the steps with arms outstretched.

"My dear! How nice to see you. Did you have a tolerable journey?"

"It was bumpy," India said, "but otherwise unremarkable. My, it's pretty here." She looked around her at the old stone house with its newly leafed canopy of oaks and the first azaleas opening in the flower bed by the porch.

"Do come in and get warm." Cindy bustled her up the steps. "And when you've had a rest and a wash and met everyone, *then* we'll talk about art."

India looked as if she would have preferred talking about art to resting and washing—and probably to meeting everyone—but she went docilely inside and up to her room. The guest room allotted her was much like her own at home, except the Blake house was in the city and had electricity. And the walls were hung with original works in wild profusion, some of them by artists India recognized with surprise.

She looked for Cindy Blake's work but saw none. *That is not going to happen to me.* India repeated it twice to herself while she took the pins out of her dark hair and recombed it, then piled it into a knot on her head, the front and sides fluffed out. She looked at her traveling dress dubiously in the mirror. Was it all right? India was never sure. Dresses that her mother proclaimed ready for the ragbag always looked all right to her. It was probably too wrinkled, though. She changed into a broadcloth shirtwaist and a woolen skirt.

As she descended the stairs again, voices rose from below, and India stopped, one hand on the banister. Below her, two small children followed by a nursemaid emerged in the foyer. The children looked up, and seeing India, they shrieked and galloped up the stairs to her.

"Mama?" said one, and then his face fell. Not Mama after all. The boy retreated behind his sister, thumb in his mouth.

A girl of about fifteen appeared in the foyer, came up the stairs, and shooed the children down the stairs again to the nurse. "They're Janessa's twins," she explained. "My cousin Janessa. Poor things, they're starting to miss her badly. She's supposed to be coming for them soon, but she's working in a hospital in Cuba with the yellow fever there, so no one really knows for sure. I'm Midge. We're glad you're here."

"I'm glad too," India said when the girl paused for breath.

"It makes a houseful," Midge said. "That's always nice. My brother Peter is in San Francisco. He has a motor car company. He told me he met you in the Oklahoma Territory. Your father gave him advice on petroleum or something."

"I expect so," India said. "Yes, I remember him. He didn't look much like your other brother."

"No, Frank got all the blond hair and good looks." Midge sighed. "Peter and I have to make do with nice personalities."

India grinned. "You'll find they're more useful than good looks. But *I* happen to think you're very pretty."

"That's nice of you." Midge's expression said that India probably wasn't much of a judge. She wasn't blond and ethereal, either. "Mother's in the parlor," Midge added. "She told me to come and find you."

Apparently whatever discussion had been taking place had been abandoned. India found Cindy and Frank sitting by the parlor fire, eating muffins and drinking tea. Midge sat down on the sofa beside Frank and gave him an affectionate hug, to the danger of his teacup. Cindy was seated sedately in a blue brocade armchair, a delicate rose-flowered plate balanced in her lap. India counted the Blakes up in her head: Peter in San Francisco, Frank home now from whatever wanderings he had been on. There was no sign of his father, no mention made of "Henry will be home for dinner" or "My husband is working late this evening." India had heard rumors of an estrangement over Frank's escapades—the Martins kept track of the Blake clan's doings—but felt uneasily as if she were walking up a set of stairs with one bad tread. One didn't want to pry. Equally, one didn't want to put one's foot in it accidentally.

India would have liked to paint the family, sort them into their different combinations: Frank and Cindy in a tense balance; Frank and Midge entwined almost, Midge with her possessive grip on her brother's arm; Henry somewhere above them, perhaps, isolated in a cloud. Peter where? Peter on a far hill, in San Francisco, bowing out of the family dance.

They made family chat, and India heard again the saga of Cousin Janessa, who was a doctor and having trouble finding her niche. "I am afraid she stirred up more difficulties for herself than she intended at her hospital in New York," Cindy said. "And so it was rather a blessing when the war came along and the army needed doctors. I've loved having the twins, of course, but they miss her. I believe she'll be back in the States soon."

"What kind of difficulties?" India asked.

Cindy looked uncomfortable. "Her notions on maternity are rather modern."

"She started teaching women contraception and nearly caused a riot," Frank said. "From what I hear, the preachers were lambasting her from their pulpits."

"Frank," Cindy said sharply, "I do not feel it necessary to discuss this further."

"You brought it up," Midge said.

"I didn't mean to. I should like to be able to introduce a topic without its being carried to extremes."

"It's all right," Midge said. "I know what contraception is. It's how not to have babies." She blushed.

"You are showing off," Cindy scolded. "That will do."

India decided she wouldn't ask any more questions.

"Janessa's husband is from a fine old family in Richmond," Cindy said, apparently to convey that the absent Janessa was not a dangerous radical. "She met him at college in Virginia and then again in medical school. He has been most supportive of her desire to practice medicine."

I should hope so, India thought. It would be a disaster to marry someone who wasn't supportive. Maybe you *could* get married. It looked like a lot of trouble, though. Then there were babies, and you had to figure out how to take care of them and do your work, too. "I don't imagine I'll get married," she said reflectively.

Cindy laughed. "My dear, you are much too young to decide that."

"If I don't decide it now, I might make a mistake and do it."

"While you're thinking about something else," Frank noted.

India grinned at him. "Precisely."

Midge scooted a little closer to Frank.

"You're going to spill my tea, Pudd'n," he said mildly.

Cindy adjusted her spectacles and gazed on India. "I hope you have brought some more of your work with you, dear."

"Yes, ma'am. There are six rolled canvases in my trunk."

"Good. We'll get them out after dinner. And I do hope you're prepared for a whirlwind social life. Washington always seems to generate more invitation cards than one can possibly accept, but you might as well have some fun while you're here. And, of course, there are some that one *has* to accept. You've been sent a card for the President's reception."

"And if you're very good, you'll be taken to see Dewey's sword," Frank put in. "We wouldn't want you to miss anything."

Cindy chuckled. "People have been lining up to see the silly thing since January. It has an inscription on it in gold letters—'The Gift of the Nation'—and is embellished with gold dolphins and laurel leaves and resides in a wooden casket at the Navy Department."

"We had to go see it," Midge said. "Some old general who's a friend of Father's"—she shot her mother an uneasy glance—"invited us. They have a sign telling you they'll put you in jail for ten years if you steal pieces of the Spanish flag that's hung over it."

"Souvenir hunters are rather a problem in Washington," Cindy explained. "Last spring a policeman just barely saved one of the figures from the Rotunda doors from being pried up and carried off, and this year someone stole one of the Indians' bows from the statue of Marquette. Now the poor Indian is leaning forward on thin air."

"Rather like being at a White House reception," Frank said, "gastronomically speaking. The last time that I was forced to escort Mother to one, we bought popcorn on the way home, we were so hungry. There's a vendor who keeps his cart at the corner of the Treasury Building, I think to feed people leaving the White House."

"It's not nearly as bad as that," Cindy said firmly. "But you may eat something before we leave home if you wish because you most certainly *are* going to escort us. Your uncle Toby arranged for the invitations so that India could meet the President."

"A lifelong wish, I feel sure," Frank murmured.

"I would not leave Washington without it," India said decisively. If she had to go, she saw no reason why the irreverent young Mr. Blake should not suffer as well.

After dinner she produced her rolled canvases at Cindy's request, and Frank and Midge sat quietly while their mother studied them. Art was serious business in this house; the Blake children gave it proper respect.

India fidgeted. Cindy peered at the canvases over her spectacles, through her spectacles, from six inches away, from three feet away, and from across the room. India bit her thumbnail until she caught Frank watching her. She snatched her finger out of her mouth and sat on her hand.

"Well, my dear," Cindy said finally, and India jumped as if the painting had spoken to her, "I am still impressed with your work. Very impressed. You have the makings of a unique style. Exactly what you ought to do with it I am not so certain."

"I want to go to art school," India said hopefully.

"Yes, I know you do, and I've heard from your father on that subject, too."

India looked depressed.

"I want to show your work around and ask advice of certain people. You will have to be patient. And in the meantime, you can enjoy Washington. Spring should arrive eventually; it's never failed to, despite appearances."

"I like those horses," Frank said. "Are they for sale?"

India looked at him, startled. "I don't know. I mean, I never sold one before."

"You have now. I want those horses. As soon as I get

some money, anyway. Mother will tell you how much you ought to charge."

India wondered if he was serious. He seemed to be, but he didn't mention it again the next day, or the next, when India, Cindy, and Frank drove across the river into the District to attend the President's reception. India found it impossible at that point to concentrate on anything except whether she was going to freeze to death or not. Guests entered from the north porch of the White House into a hall studded with rows of coatracks and so packed with people that the outside doors could not be closed. Hoping to avoid the unusually cold gale blowing in from outside, bare-armed women in evening dresses huddled in the shadows of their escorts, as they waited to move into the main rooms. India stared around with an appreciation for their resemblance to her father's cattle being herded into a chute. She was almost irresistibly tempted to moo, and from the light in Frank's eye, she thought he knew it.

Against one wall, among the coatracks, was a sideboard that India thought was quite hideous, a conglomerate of jigsawed rosettes and marquetry. Atop it squatted a vast china hen on a china nest, with a look of contented obliviousness. The sideboard, Cindy explained, had been a present years ago from a temperance union to Mrs. Rutherford Hayes, who refused to allow wine to be served in the White House. Where the hen had come from, heaven only knew.

The temperature rose somewhat as they inched through the family dining room. Peering into the conservatory, India could see the U.S. Marine Band in their crimson coats. They were playing, for reasons she couldn't fathom, "The Wedding March." In the Red Parlor a firm voice said, "Single file, please," and she settled into line between Cindy and Frank and hoped he wouldn't step on her train.

Minutes later she had shaken hands with President McKinley and received a whispered welcome of some sort from Mrs. McKinley. The First Lady spoke so softly as to be unintelligible and looked ill. A row of elegantly dressed women—Cabinet wives—smiled aloofly at them from a row of blue-velvet sofas. Then they found themselves in the East Room, gaping at the national shield done in flowers, repeated in displays on each wall.

"Why on earth would anyone want to do that with perfectly good flowers?" India wanted to know.

"The devil makes work for idle hands," Frank said.

"The White House has never been known for its artistic sensibilities," Cindy said. "People present things, you know, and everyone feels obligated to keep them. Like the temperance sideboard. Flower pictures rather match the rest of the decor."

India thought the guests more than made up for the decor as a source of interest. The diplomatic corps was present, in a profusion of medals, epaulettes, and military swords. There were Germans and Russians and Austrians with imposing whiskers and wives dripping with jewels; Turks and Hawaiians and Koreans; and South Americans whose liquid Spanish and slightly dangerous air of banditry appealed to India enormously.

"He looks as if he ought to be on a book cover," she whispered to Frank, pointing at a dark man in a gold and white uniform who was chatting graciously with a very short bishop. "He looks like a jaguar about to pounce."

"Are you going to pursue him?" Frank inquired. "It's quite the thing to do. Mrs. Colgate, the soap heiress, just married the Earl of Stafford, and all the debutantes are in full cry over anything in a foreign uniform. It comes of not having our own aristocracy."

"I don't want him. I just want to look at him."

"Then let me also recommend to you the minister from Haiti for his uniform and General Shafter for his sheer vastness of plane."

India contemplated the figures in question with the appreciation of a sightseer. She recognized General Shafter, who had commanded the American forces in Cuba, from newspaper engravings, but his bulk was even more impressive in person. Beside him was the scrawniest general she had ever seen, "Fighting Joe" Wheeler, an ex-Confederate who had served in Cuba, too. Rumor had it that when the Spanish began to retreat, he had lost all sense of where he was and shouted, "After them, boys! We've got the damned Yankees on the run!" Supposedly he was shipping out for the Philippines in a few days. Just now he was drinking wine punch and complaining that it was tasteless.

Frank managed to get them each a glass of it, and India and Cindy declared it tasteless, too. So was the soggy cream bun that Frank put into her other hand. After a while even the chance to gawk at the diplomatic corps palled, and they wriggled their way out through the crowd again to fish for their coats in the by-now totally disorganized coatracks. The temperature on the porch had not improved, and a venerable congressman was heard stating in unseemly language that he would not return until summer.

As Frank had predicted, they bought hot popcorn at the corner of the Treasury Building, taking some home for Midge. "Although she'll have been better fed than we are," he muttered. "Probably warm as toast and full of Lutie's pie."

When they got home, thoroughly frozen, Midge took the popcorn greedily and linked her arm through Frank's.

"Who did you see? I wish *I* were old enough to go to the White House. Did anything exciting happen?"

"We listened to a lot of people who don't really know what they're talking about telling a lot of other people how we're winning the war in the Philippines," Frank said.

Midge made a face. "I hate the war in the Philippines. I hate the Philippines. Daddy would be home if it weren't for the stupid Philippines."

"Midge . . ." Cindy, looking unhappy, reached a hand toward her daughter. "It's not that simple."

"Well, he would!" Midge lifted a face suddenly tear-stained and glared at her mother. "Frank came home, so why can't Daddy come home? I think it's awful for the army to keep him in the Philippines so long when we need him."

"He's there by choice, dear."

"You mean *you* won't let him come home!" Midge hurled the words at her mother. "You said it was because of Frank, but Frank's home!" Her eyes were streaming now.

"Now wait a minute, Pudd'n . . ." Frank said.

"Midge, we have a guest," Cindy said.

"Oh, I don't care!" Midge flung herself away from Frank and fled up the stairs, clutching her popcorn.

"Goodness, what brought that on?" Cindy said. "India, I am very sorry you had to be imposed upon."

"Not at all," India murmured.

Midge poked her tear-streaked face over the banister. "I forgot. Mr. Gallatin telephoned you." She whirled and fled again.

Cindy sighed. "At least she's well trained. We must try to pay some extra attention to her. It's—everything's hard on her. I'm going up to talk with her. I'll speak with Mr. Gallatin in the morning."

"Gallatin's a 'noted connoisseur,'" Frank explained as his mother went upstairs. "A big art poobah. I'll bet Mother's going to talk to him about you."

"Oh." India's confidence wavered. "I wish you hadn't told me that."

Frank was scornful. "If *you* don't think you're any good, what makes you think Gallatin will?"

"I *do* think I'm good. I just find being looked at by critics somewhat daunting."

"Better get used to it," Frank suggested.

India's stomach growled, and she flushed. "And I'm hungry. How can I be sure of anything when I'm starving to death? I hope they feed the President better than they fed us."

"I believe he exists entirely on thin gruel. Let's go look in the kitchen. There must be something left over. I have work to do tomorrow. Can't work on wine punch and a cream bun."

"What sort of work?" India asked, following him. So far she had seen him actively evading all his mother's suggestions for useful employment. "Are you going to take that post in the Bureau of Printing and Engraving?"

"I'd rather be dead." Frank opened the icebox. "There's cold tongue. Do you like cold tongue?"

"I'll eat it if I have to."

"Good. I hate it, too." He rummaged further, propping the tin-lined wooden door open with his shoulder. "Here we are. Yesterday's leg of lamb." He dragged it out and set about slicing it. "There's bread in the bread box. Probably."

India investigated. There was the end of a loaf. She sliced it economically. "Well, what *are* you going to do?" she asked Frank.

"I don't know. I feel rather like a boarder here. It's odd. I know a lot of things I *don't* want to do again."

"That's not very productive."

"You think I ought to be productive?"

"I think you ought to do *something*. I mean, isn't that what we're here for?"

"You're a fine one to talk. Where's the mustard pot?"

"I don't know. It's your kitchen. Over there with the spices, maybe. That would be likely." She was beginning to be annoyed with him. Frank found it where she suggested.

"You're quaking in your little boots at the thought of having some flatulent old fool look at your pictures and pronounce on them," Frank said, spreading mustard on his bread. "Don't you *know* whether you're any good or not?"

"Of course I do."

"Then what are you going to do if he says they're awful? Go into a nunnery?"

"Of course not. But it's hard, all the same. At least I'm doing something. I'm working; I'm willing to risk failing."

"You don't sound like it to me." Frank bit into his sandwich, gnawing through the thick slice of lamb with a quick doglike shake of his head.

"I'm doing the best I can," India said irritably. He was hitting too close to the bone. "*I* don't have the option of making a grand gesture and running away. I'm much too fond of my parents to want to hurt them."

"You're also a girl. It's a handicap. Makes it harder for you."

"What exactly do you mean by that?" India demanded.

"Just that running away is more difficult for girls," Frank said innocently. The gleam in his eye betrayed a certain satisfaction in having annoyed her. "They're more vulnerable."

"You sound like my father," India said in disgust.

Frank sobered. "I wish I *had* your father. There. That's my dreadful confession for the night. What's yours?"

India looked at him defiantly. "I don't see how somebody I've only known for three days can irritate me so much. And be right some of the time," she muttered. "I *am* going to die if this Gallatin person says I'm no good. And then I won't know what to do."

"Sure you will," Frank said, encouraging now. "You'll figure it out that Gallatin doesn't matter, any more than the Bureau of Printing and Engraving does."

"Well, *I* think the Bureau of Printing and Engraving matters. I think you ought to get a job. Or go back to school. You're too educated to be a railroad bum, and you know it."

"We'll see what you say after Mother talks to Gallatin," Frank said, his mouth full. He swallowed and gave her a grin. "If you want to run away, I'll take you on the road. You could pass for a boy with the right clothes."

"Oh, thank you very much." India gave a snort of derision.

"Please don't take that the wrong way. I only meant that—" He waved his arm and knocked the pot of mustard off the table with a crash.

The swinging door that connected the kitchen to the breakfast room creaked open. Midge looked at the two of them angrily. "Isn't anyone coming to bed? You're all making so much noise I can't sleep."

In the morning, Cindy went to see Mr. Gallatin, with India's rolled canvases under her arm. "I'll be back this afternoon, and you can make some calls with me, dear," she told India briskly.

"Your heart's desire." Frank chuckled.

"I look forward to it," India said politely. "I rather enjoy anthropology."

Really, Cindy thought as she climbed into her carriage, India was a well-mannered child, if a trifle candid. A long-time participant in the Washington social gavotte, Cindy found that refreshing. What Frank thought of her, Cindy couldn't tell. He seemed to be serious about wanting to buy the painting, and she had told him firmly that it was worth at least a hundred dollars. She could only hope that lack of money might spur him to consider the several posts he had been offered.

Her carriage rolled to a stop in front of Otto Gallatin's house, and she alighted. Mr. Otto Gallatin was a Washington institution. He wrote a column for the *Post* and was feared and loathed by any number of artists as a result. But he knew art and had an eye for the artist who would be famous in ten years. The maidservant who answered his door ushered Cindy in past a mahogany table with gilded alligators for legs, into a room smoky with sandalwood incense. Otto enjoyed his eccentricities.

He met her clad in a maroon brocade smoking jacket and Turkish slippers and held his hand out gingerly, as if she might nip at it.

"I have some work I want you to look at," Cindy said, once the formalities had been dispensed with. The maid reappeared with two tiny glasses of liqueur on a tray. "The artist is quite young yet, the child of some friends of mine. I like to be sure I am not being prejudiced by affection."

"Well, I shan't be. I believe other people's babies are always hideous," Otto said. He took a pair of pince-nez from the pocket of his smoking jacket. "I shall be quite ruthless. Hmmmm." He inspected the first canvas, the portrait of India's mother, and then the cow with the floating calf.

"Quite interesting. Needs polish, but there is a vision there." He peered at the signature, "Blackstone. And where is Blackstone from?"

"Oklahoma Territory, but the family has traveled extensively."

"That shows. There is a sophistication here that one rarely sees in the genuine primitive." Otto adjusted his pince-nez with spidery fingers. He affected long fingernails, like those of a Chinese mandarin. "And what are you planning to do with young Blackstone? Bring him to see me, there's a good girl. I want to know more."

Cindy sat back in her chair and took a sip of the liqueur. It tasted of oranges. "*She*, Otto. The artist is female."

Otto stopped, one hand held delicately above the canvas, fingers arranged like a temple dancer's. He cocked his head at her. "Indeed? Very practiced work for a woman." He appeared to scrutinize it. "Of course, now that you have told me, I do see the femininity in it. Your sex never can quite escape it, you know. It would have begun to grate on me with time."

"What if I told you I was making a joke, and the artist is a man?" Cindy inquired evenly.

"What?" Otto studied her. "No, no, I can see that you weren't." He inspected the canvas again. "Closer scrutiny reveals undeniably that this is a female's work. Very promising, of course, but not a great artist. She is too much confined, you see, by her subject matter—portrait work and animals and rather pretty landscapes. They *are* pretty, you know, despite that disturbing note. She cannot get past her essential nature, which is rooted in the small and trivial, and into the wider world of men and events."

Cindy set her glass down on a marble-topped plant stand, in the shade of a funereal Boston fern. "If I hadn't told you she was a woman, you wouldn't have known."

Otto touched the tips of his fingers together, nails clicking. "Pish. Of course I would. Some might be fooled . . . if she's never seen at her showings."

"So would you advise her to pursue the study?"

"Oh, certainly. She has talent, no doubt about it. And there is a market for competent art. I merely meant that in *my* humble opinion she will never be great."

"Because she is female?" Cindy demanded, determined to pin him down. It was important.

"She lacks the wider vision. Females do, as a rule, although one hopes not to insult present company. Have there ever *been* any great woman artists?"

"There won't be at this rate," Cindy muttered. She stood and extended her hand graciously. "Thank you, Otto. You have been very helpful."

"Bring your protégée to see me, anyway," Otto said benevolently.

The prospect of turning India Blackstone loose on Otto amused Cindy briefly, but she knew better than to do it. India would never restrain herself, and Otto wielded too much power in the art world for India to insult him in any way.

The problem of India occupied her mind as Cindy returned home and collected the girl, then set out again on a round of duty calls. India seemed faintly puzzled by the necessity, and Cindy explained a general's wife had certain social requirements that could not be ignored. Having chosen to live in Alexandria rather than in the District of Columbia did not free her of the obligation to call, between three and seven in the afternoon, on those ladies of official position who had called on her: senatorial and congressional wives, Cabinet wives, and army wives. And always armed with sufficient calling cards: one from each adult female in the family making the call—present or not—for every adult female in the family receiving.

India was familiar with the custom of social calls and had, reluctantly, made numerous ones with her mother, but the draconian rigidity of the Washington system left her bemused. As Cindy consulted her list, India made up packets of visiting cards and secured them with rubber bands. Cindy said she used the hundreds that came to her house as kindling.

At each stop they were ushered through the chill air that pervaded every foyer into an equally chilly drawing room where the hostess and the ladies receiving with her, shivering in semievening dress, offered vague handshakes in which the fingers never quite touched, followed by glasses of iced lemonade or scalding tea. The weather and fashion were dutifully discussed; then Cindy and India took their leave each time to a strange chorus of "good mornings." In Washington it was officially morning, Cindy explained, until you had eaten dinner.

India studied with delight a vast hostess wearing a cerise velvet dress with a plunging neckline at the vee of which was an enormous diamond brooch. India couldn't help smiling at the thought that the woman's bosom was in danger of springing from its confinement to the possible peril of all. Then India's eyes widened, just enough to make Cindy wary, at the sight of a tea table tied up like a package with baby-pin ribbons crisscrossing it diagonally, huge bows at each corner. It was adorned with a centerpiece of Battenberg lace over pink silk and reminded India of a nursery. She half expected to find a baby in the tea urn.

"And how are you finding Washington, Miss Blackstone?" A storklike congressman's wife in a gown of grassgreen silk bent over her, peering through a lorgnette.

"Enthralling," India said. What she wanted to say was that it was better than a zoo.

Cindy took her home after that call, uncertain as to when India's tolerance for boredom and her proper demeanor, obviously a disguise, were going to slip.

She still hadn't said anything about her visit to Mr. Gallatin that morning, and India was visibly restraining herself from asking. As the carriage rolled up the Blakes' drive, Cindy took pity on her.

"Well, dear, I think I have a plan for your art. We'll talk about it over a decent tea and see if you like it."

"I'm sure I will," India said in a voice holding the proper amount of gratitude, underlaid with faint skepticism.

Cindy laughed. "My dear, you make me remember what it was like to be eighteen. Be that as it may, my considered opinion is you are beyond a good art school, frankly. Both by talent and by temperament. You have something I don't want spoiled." She paused to climb down from the carriage and gave an audible sigh as Frank passed them in the portico. He was wearing blue jean trousers and a sweat-stained shirt, and his hair was matted. He carried a crowbar under one arm and gave them a cheerful wave with it as he disappeared into the house. Cindy started to say something to him, then thought better of it and hurried inside with her charge.

India was grateful to be home and was warming her toes at the fire and watching Midge helpfully butter her a muffin when Frank reappeared. He had changed his clothes, but there was dirt under his fingernails. India could see it, and she knew his mother could see it. She waited for whatever confrontation might take place— Frank had a gleam in his eye. But instead he leaned over the tea cart and put five dollars in India's lap.

"That's a down payment. For your horses. Mother says I have to pay you a hundred."

"Where did you get that?" Cindy asked suspiciously.

"I fixed Sawtelle's chicken house for him. And pulled his stump."

"You *what*?" Cindy stared at him. "Mr. Sawtelle behind us?"

"Sure. He saw what an ace job I did on your stoop."

"You let a neighbor *pay* you to do handyman's work?" Cindy put her teacup down.

"He offered to. Called me over across the back fence. Said good workers were hard to find."

"You didn't tell him who you were?"

"If I had, he wouldn't have hired me," Frank said practically. "That stump was an awful nuisance. It didn't want to let go, and the horse wasn't up to it. We had to borrow a mule."

Cindy put her hand to her forehead. "My God, I'll never be able to look at him again. He's bound to find out who you are. How could you do a thing like that?"

"Mr. Sawtelle would have had to hire *somebody*," Midge said in her brother's defense.

India watched the exchange appreciatively, but kept quiet. She put the five dollars in her pocket. She had never sold any work before, even in five-dollar increments.

"Not my son," Cindy said icily. "We are on social terms with the Sawtelles."

Frank buttered a muffin and leaned against the mantel. "Don't worry," he said a little stiffly. "I got a job with the fellow we borrowed the mule from. He sinks wells for people. Out in the country. He says he witches them, and he'll pay me to sink the shaft. I'll be gone all day, and I'll be sure to slink back under cover of darkness."

Midge stared at him. Her face said plainly: What on

earth was the matter with Frank? A chicken coop was one thing, but digging wells? People in this family didn't have jobs like that.

Frank grinned at India, but there was a twitch at the corner of his mouth. "I'll have my horses paid for in a month. Don't you sell them to anybody else."

"I won't," India said faintly.

She wondered if Cindy had forgotten about her.

Finally Cindy stood up. She gave Frank a penetrating look but said nothing further to him. "Well, dear, I told you I had a plan," she said briskly to India. "I have been to see the great Mr. Gallatin, and he thought your work was excellent and wanted to know more about you until I told him you were female. At which point he stopped seeing vision in your work and noticed that your talent was confined by your essential female nature."

India looked indignant.

"That decadent old coot wouldn't know decent art if it bit him," Frank said.

"Otto isn't going to give up that particular prejudice," Cindy said, "and I don't intend to offend him. But he confirmed what has been troubling me. You have a hard row to hoe, young lady."

"I don't care," India said stubbornly.

"Of course not. You're young. But it would be a mistake for you to stay here, or in New York, and contend with men like Otto. For one thing, you'll spoil your style trying to prove you're not confined by femininity. For another, the first time some professor tells you any such thing, you'll start a row and get thrown out."

India bit her lip. "I won't. I promise."

"Yes, you will," Frank said.

"I didn't ask you," India retorted.

"What you need to do," Cindy went on, "is to find a location that will give you suitable material to work with, and paint until you have enough good work for a collection worth showing. It will be a few years, but when you do, I will see that it gets shown."

"Go where?" India asked, perplexed.

Cindy went to one of the glass-fronted bookcases that lined one parlor wall. "A long time ago I went to Arizona," she said, bending down. She pulled out a leather-bound portfolio and smacked it on the hearth to dislodge the dust. Frank and Midge watched her curiously, the way children do when they are suddenly confronted with their parents having had a past life, an existence before them.

"It wasn't a happy journey," Cindy said. "I went out there to join my first husband. Reed was stationed at Fort Peck."

"Is that when he was killed, Mama?" Midge asked.

"Yes." Cindy sat down and seemed to be looking through some mist at a face long forgotten. Abruptly she opened the portfolio. "But I did a lot of drawing while I was there. No paints, I'm afraid, which rather spoils the point of my showing you these—it's the color of that land that strikes one first. But at the time I was more interested in drawing *things*—people and events. Still, it will give you some sense of the scope of the place—far beyond the kind of thing you've been painting in Oklahoma." She spread out a pair of sketches of a solitary rider in the desert.

India studied them. "It's very open, isn't it?" she murmured.

"Yes." Cindy carefully chose another and laid it out. She kept her hands on the rest. "It's the distance that strikes one first—the distance from where you are to anywhere. And the color. Blood-red stone and blue, *blue* sky and brilliant green that comes and goes, bang, like a stereopticon slide, each spring. It's extraordinary."

"And you think our little da Vinci ought to go there

and paint?" Frank asked. "What else is in there?" He
reached for the portfolio.

Cindy kept a grip on it. "Work I had published once.
By subscription."

"Well, let's see it."

Cindy hesitated, then seemed to come to a decision.
"I knew you'd want to if I dragged these out. I suppose it
doesn't matter." She opened the portfolio again and
spread the published drawings on the tea table. Midge
moved the muffins and teapot out of the way.

"Oooh, look!" Midge stared.

The prints told a continuous story, the saga of an
attack on an army supply train, its near annihilation, and
its ultimate rescue by a column of cavalry. They were
numbered and had obviously been published in sequence.

"High drama," Frank said. "I'll bet you made a mint
off these. Is that why you wouldn't show them? Too dime
novel? I *like* them."

"At the time, they were . . . medicine," Cindy said.
"That was the raid my husband was killed in. I was
there."

Midge gasped.

India stared. She had had no idea that Cindy had
even been married twice, much less this. The dying
cavalrymen, the attacking bandits, seemed to leap off the
page. These pictures had been done from bitter memory.

Frank looked at his mother with respect. "And you
could draw it all afterward?"

"I had to. I kept having nightmares. It wouldn't go
away until I got it on paper. It was very strange, like a
kind of conduit that went from my brain to the paper. It
was like pouring water out of a pitcher. The images
weren't in my head anymore. After that I could get on
with things."

"What was he like?" Frank peered at the drawings as if trying to pick the ghostly former husband from them.

"What if he had lived?" Midge said, suddenly struck by that notion. "We wouldn't be here!"

"You'd be different," Cindy conceded. "Reed was nothing like your father."

"What was he like?"

"He was very brave," Cindy said, looking at the drawings. "Not that your father isn't," she quickly amended. "I was with an army supply train, coming out to Fort Peck to be with Reed. We were attacked by comancheros—bandits—who wanted the rifles we were transporting. Winchesters. They were new then. We would all have been killed if Reed hadn't brought a relief column from the fort." Cindy's eyes glazed over. She was looking backward again, into a time the other three couldn't see. "I had a pistol with one bullet in it. I was about to use it on myself—the comancheros weren't men a woman would live through being captured by. And then Reed came, just like in the dime novels—" She shot a glance at Frank. "Only the hero didn't survive the rescue. He was killed. And I packed up and left Arizona."

"I'm sorry," Frank said. "I didn't know."

"Why haven't you ever told us this before?" Midge demanded.

"Maybe because it hurt," Cindy said.

"Oh," Midge said softly, sorry she had asked the question.

Cindy gathered the drawings, laying them carefully one on top of the other. *Such a long time ago,* her mind said. *Why did you bring these out?* But she knew. Because she had married Reed still bitterly, obstinately, in love with Henry, even though Henry had left her for the German woman. For Gisela. She had been so ashamed of that, of not loving Reed the way he had loved her. She had done her utmost to be a good, dutiful wife, to make it up to him for that. She had gone out to Fort Peck to be with him, and he had been killed.

"Does Daddy know all about it?" Midge asked.

"Oh, yes." Cindy stared at the drawing on top. "Your father was never jealous of Reed." He never had cause to be, she thought. He knew. When she had finally married Henry, she had been almost grateful that poor Reed was dead. If he hadn't been, would she actually have left him for Henry, when Henry was available? Cindy would never confess that guilty fear to a soul, but she had always feared she might well have left. Whatever had linked her and Henry had been strong enough for that. Was it still? Cindy flinched, both inwardly and with a visible outward twitch.

"Well!" she said abruptly. "I haven't done any work like this in donkey's years. I was quite a well-known etcher in my day, but"—she gave India a long look—"I had nowhere the talent that you show."

"That's because you quit," Frank said. "That's because all you ever tried seriously were etchings of famous places or battles or quaint characters. Magazine illustration stuff. And I *do* mean that. You never let yourself go."

"I didn't want to pound my head against a brick wall. And it was really just a stopgap, I think. Something to take my mind off Reed. And you're impertinent."

"Yes, ma'am."

"Do you think I should go to the West?" India asked. "It's very stark and beautiful. But I wouldn't know where to stay."

"I do," Cindy said, grateful for the return to India's plans. "Michael and Eden Holt are in New Mexico right now, in Taos. I know they'd be glad to let you stay with them. Eden seems to run a very relaxed household. And the country around Taos is said to be spectacular."

"What the heck are they doing in New Mexico?" Frank asked.

"Mike's making a moving picture about the passing of the cowboy. Or at least that's what Eden said in her letter."

"That makes cowboys sound as if they're becoming extinct," India said. "Like the passenger pigeon. But Oklahoma's full of them."

"Well, Mike says that's what's happening," Cindy said, smiling. "He's a romantic, I think. But the West *is* filling up, is being built up. Eden says Mike wants to catch the essence of the real thing—all the men who've been glamorized in pulp fiction—before they're gone for good. She says they met a writer who's apparently some sort of expert on cowboys and the West, and he's given them introductions to a lot of people."

"Well, if he wants cowboys, I still say he should come to Oklahoma," India said.

"Oklahoma's not the Wild West," Frank said. "No romance. No trail drives. No outlaws."

"I see." India dismissed him and gave his mother her attention. "I'd like to go there. But I don't know what my father would say."

"He'll be glad it isn't New York," Frank remarked. "No lecherous male artists to lure you into their garrets."

"Quite a number of artists have gone to Taos to paint," Cindy said. She eyed Frank. "Extremely respectable souls, all of them. You can stay with Mike and Eden, and Frank will escort you out there. I think your father will approve."

"What?" Frank looked at India with suspicion, as if he had been suddenly given a large, unwieldy package.

"Frank?" India regarded him as if Cindy had suggested that she take a wheelbarrow or an umbrella stand. "What on earth for?"

"Because you cannot possibly travel without an escort," Cindy said firmly. "Your father *would* have a fit. It is a much longer trip than the one out here—and through wilder country."

"Hard to get much wilder than Washington," Frank commented. "Mother, you didn't even *ask* me."

"She doesn't need to ask you," India retorted. "I can certainly take care of myself as well as *you* could take care of me."

"Well, I've been taking care of myself in stranger surroundings than you could dream of," Frank said, affronted, "and I don't feel like baby-sitting a pigheaded female barely out of finishing school. I have better things to do with my time."

"Absolutely," India scoffed. "There are wells to be dug. Are you going to learn dowsing, too?"

"I wouldn't sneer at dowsing. I watched the fellow. It was pretty amazing. He even let me put my hand on the rod."

"The human mind is very suggestible."

" 'There are more things in heaven and earth, Horatio, than are dreamt of in *your* philosophy,' " Frank retorted. "Do you always rule out everything you can't personally explain—with your vast experience? Do you rule out the supernatural entirely?"

"Only the freelance sort. Although I admit you might be good at it. Have you thought of that for a calling? You could start your own, like Madame Blavatsky."

"That's enough!" Cindy said briskly. "You are the next thing to related to each other through your mutual connection with the Martins. That makes Frank a suitable escort, and there isn't anyone else to do it, which will have to be good and sufficient reasons for you both. Unless, of course, India, you do not want to go to Taos."

"I'd go to Taos with a baboon if I had to," India said.

"Not that I meant that personally," she added airily to Frank. "It just seems to me unnecessary. I wouldn't be a nuisance to Frank for worlds."

"You already are," Frank said grumpily. He seemed to have grasped from his mother's expression that this was not a chore he could weasel out of. He brightened. "It would be fine to see old Mike again, though."

"Exactly," Cindy said. "I knew you'd be glad to do it."

"I didn't say that."

"You will when we present our travel plans to India's father," Cindy said. Her eyes showed relief. Frank was restless here—that was what all this idiocy of digging wells came of. She had been afraid every morning that she would wake and find him gone. At least this would give him something to do, even if it meant leaving home. Also, Mike might give him a job. And she would know where he was. She patted his hand affectionately, holding on just a moment too long.

V

The engine puffed out clouds of steam onto the station platform, wreathing India's boots and the hem of her traveling skirt. She assiduously studied the windows of cars, the other passengers, the conductor's hat, reluctant to intrude on Midge's farewell to Frank. Midge clung to her brother, her face red and tear slicked, and with angry hiccups she made him promise he would come right back home again.

"Midge, dear, that will do," Cindy said uneasily. Midge had been distraught ever since the plans had been made for Frank to escort India west. For the last three days she had been barely civil to India.

"You have to come right home. On the next train," Midge sniffled into the front of Frank's overcoat.

"Well, Pudd'n, maybe not the *next* train. I want to see old Mike."

"The next train," Midge said stubbornly. "You're supposed to be home. Everything was supposed to be all right when you came home, but it's not, it's horrid!" She shot India a look of intense dislike. "Daddy didn't come home, and now you're going away again!"

"Honey, you don't own me," Frank said gently. "You don't get to do that."

"But you're coming back right away, aren't you?" She held him tighter, her face turned up to his, pleading.

"Well, pretty much," Frank hedged.

"All aboard!" the conductor boomed over the shriek of the train's whistle.

Frank detached Midge from him, and he and India climbed into their Pullman car. After they were seated, they looked out their window to wave. India gave Midge a smile but didn't get one in return.

"I feel rotten that she's so upset," she muttered as the train pulled out.

"She's had a rough time. But it's not really you. She just thinks it is because I'm taking you out West."

India gave him a baleful look from under the brim of her black felt hat. "You aren't 'taking' me. I'm not a poodle. You are *accompanying* me."

"Oh."

India relented. "I feel very adventurous. Don't you?"

Frank grinned at her. "Adventurous is riding on the rails *under* the car. Or on the roof."

"Don't give yourself airs. Being a bum is nothing to be proud of." She looked a little wistful, though. "I've never really been out West. What's it like?"

"Well, I bummed through it, understand," Frank said as he settled into the blue plush Pullman seat and stuck his legs out comfortably in front of him. He looked sideways at India. "So I didn't see the nice side of the tracks. Except maybe to look for a handout." He waited for her to be shocked.

She looked at him expectantly. "Did you get one?"

Frank laughed. "Usually. If a woman came to the door. It's usually a woman. You go to the kitchen door."

"Well, I hope you won't be bored on this trip," India said serenely.

Four days on the train would be enough to bore anyone, but they had both brought books, and when those palled, they argued. Art was a useful subject, one for which it was easy to take opposite sides, and politics was almost as serviceable.

"Statistically speaking," Frank said on the second day out, "when ninety percent of the wealth is concentrated in the hands of ten percent of the populace, and thirty percent of the populace goes to bed hungry at night, you have a formula that, practically speaking, demands revolution as its only natural outcome."

"Thirty percent?" India was startled. "I can't believe it's as high as that."

"A number of studies have been done," Frank assured her.

India looked at him with suspicion. "Which studies? By whom?" When he didn't answer, she narrowed her eyes. "You're making that up."

"I'm quite sure there have been studies. There's always someone with a theory on anything."

"Including you," India said indignantly. "I'm not going to argue with you if you're going to make things up."

"Why not? I'm pretty sure I'm right. I'm just giving my position a little more verisimilitude."

"Well, that's cheating." India looked haughtily out the window until the scenery began to depress her. The lush new green of the eastern woodlands had been broken by the gray air and looming triple-decker apartment buildings of Appalachian coal towns. And by the rubbish-strewn backside of the city they were passing through. Since no one wanted to live by railroad tracks, only the poor lived there.

"That ought to back up my statements," Frank said as the train slowed on its way through a dismal corridor of unpainted shacks with dingy laundry flapping in barren dirt yards. A barefoot child digging a hole in the dirt beyond his stoop paused long enough to watch open-mouthed as the train went by.

"It does nothing of the sort," India countered. "You're talking about percentages, which is a mathematical fact, and one shantytown outside one city doesn't back up anything at all."

"You're supposed to be an artist. Where did you get this passion for hard fact?"

"Arguing with you. We can't both be making things up at the same time."

"Why not? 'It is through Art and through Art only that we can realize our perfection; through Art and Art only that we can shield ourselves from the sordid perils of actual existence,'" Frank said. He waited to see if she recognized the quote. "Oscar Wilde," he said, when she didn't.

"Well, Oscar Wilde doesn't know anything about the poverty rate in America, either," India insisted. "Anyway, it was the sordid perils of actual existence that we were talking about." She gestured out the window. "Good socialists don't go around quoting Oscar Wilde, for heaven's sake."

"I don't know that I am a good socialist. Their faith in the essentially unselfish nature of the average working man is possibly misjudged."

"I wish you'd pick a side and stay on it," India muttered.

The train stopped long enough at the next depot for them to get a meal, then roared on toward Kansas City, where they would change for Denver, and then in Denver for Santa Fe. The land shifted gradually to flat farm country. They crossed the Wabash by moonlight, which prompted Frank to sing "The Banks of the Wabash" in loud, sentimental tones until India made him stop. They crossed the Mississippi at St. Louis, determinedly staying awake to see it because Frank insisted that it was a sight no one should miss.

"I've seen it," India said sleepily. "Lots of times."

"You're too young to be jaded," Frank observed.

India retreated into her lower berth and pulled the curtains shut in his face, wrestling with her stockings and corset and managing finally to get her nightgown on over her head in the coffin-sized enclosure. Above her in the upper she could hear Frank restlessly trying to read by the moonlight and the dim ceiling lamp in the car—and swearing and thumping his pillow when it proved impossible.

The next day they steamed into Kansas City, where the stockyards along the tracks laid a barnyard odor over everything, even inside the cavernous halls of the Kansas Pacific depot. A newsboy was peddling papers with a blaring black headline: DENVER MAIL ROBBED!

Frank bought a copy while an official-looking minion of the Kansas Pacific tried to chase the paperboy away. "Bad publicity," Frank commented to the agent at the ticket window.

India took the paper from under Frank's arm and peered at it. "Passengers Stripped of Valuables," the subhead ran. "Payroll Seized."

"I assure you that the miscreants are being apprehended," the ticket agent said. "Naturally our passengers will be compensated."

"The ones who weren't shot," Frank said cheerfully.

The ticket agent was clearly disapproving. "No passenger has ever been shot, sir."

"Well, then that's all right." Frank pocketed the tickets and took India's arm. "Come along, Cousin. You have time to compose your nerves before our train leaves."

India paid him no attention. She was too busy reading. Robbers unknown—although they were rumored to be the notorious Butch Cassidy's gang—had blocked the tracks and held up the train at gunpoint.

"Now, you don't get that in Oklahoma," Frank said, guiding her to a bench so that she didn't walk into something while reading. "That's the Wild West."

"Oklahoma has robbers," India said, defending her home territory against charges of dullness. "They don't usually rob trains, though," she conceded.

"The average criminal is more intrepid in the West," Frank said. "It's all the fresh air, I suppose."

"Aren't you worried that we might be robbed?"

"No. These gangs don't usually try another one so soon. They wait for the railroad to relax again."

"They don't look very relaxed to me," India said, watching a trio of burly men in overcoats lumber past. They wore brass badges and carried shotguns slung across their backs. A conspicuous bulge at the side of each coat indicated the presence of pistols as well.

"Good thing," Frank said. "Gives them something to do besides roust 'boes off the rods."

"Do you think it really was Butch Cassidy?"

"Butch Cassidy hasn't got time to rob all the trains he gets credited with."

"Well, maybe it was," India said hopefully.

A conductor came through, calling their train to Denver, and they picked up their belongings. India's trunks were supposedly ticketed straight through.

They settled themselves in their new coach, an elegant affair with carved paneling and chandeliers, and peered through the window as the train pulled out. The country grew as flat as an ironing board and was planted with countless fields of corn. India dozed, too hypnotized by the endless rows fanning past the window even to argue with Frank.

By the next morning the train had begun a long, slow

climb, switchbacking into the Rockies. Traces of snow lingered in shaded crevices as they went higher, and the engine labored and huffed. India and Frank were in the last Pullman before the baggage cars, and India looked out her lower-berth window to see the train snaking ahead of them, sending clouds of steam into the air, white against the crystal-blue sky and the pine trees. She was just pulling on her corset, wrestling with it and with unwieldy layers of petticoats, when the train slowed with an agonized shriek and a swaying of the cars. A stout man in a smoking jacket blundered into her berth and caromed out again as the train swayed the other way. India snatched her camisole over her head and was pulling her shirtwaist over that when Frank's feet swung over the edge of the upper berth and bounced against her curtains, cracking her in the chin.

"Ouch!" she yelped. She wriggled into her skirt, hooking it up in front regardless, and peered through the curtains. Frank was in the aisle now, tucking his shirttail in. India climbed out and tugged her skirt right way around. A woman in a closed berth was demanding loudly that someone tell her what was going on, and a male voice from above her kept saying he didn't know. The porter, making up the berths of early risers, peered out a window apprehensively. The train slowed still further, and the railroad agents they had seen in the station came pushing their way down the aisle.

"Just stay calm, ladies and gentlemen. Please keep your seats." The agents moved on through the car. "No, ma'am, there won't be any trouble. Please keep your seats." They vanished through the door at the other end. India noticed they had their shotguns with them.

Frank was trying to fold the berths back up, kicking at the mechanism and cursing it under his breath. The porter was being detained by the woman demanding to know what was going on. India helped Frank wrestle the upper berth into its compartment and convince the lower to metamorphose into seats again.

"What do you think it is?" she asked. They couldn't see anything unusual ahead, but the train was still slowing.

"I don't know, but those railroad cops think something's happening," Frank replied. "If this is a robbery, just do what they tell you."

"*What?*" India said indignantly.

Frank spun around, his nose three inches from hers. "My mission, for which I did not volunteer, is to get you to Taos without damage to either your person or your virtue. I am not going to risk either for the sake of whatever silly jewelry you think you can't live without."

"But—"

"If you indulge in any ill-judged behavior, I will tie you up. This is *not* some dime novel. These men are serious."

"And of course I'm too stupid to know that," India said between gritted teeth. "Why do you always presume you know everything I'm thinking?"

"Because you were the one who was fairly squeaking with excitement over Butch Cassidy."

"This is different!"

"You bet it is." Frank turned toward the window as a sign flashed by them. India barely caught its message—a crude skull and crossbones and thick black lettering declaring: THE TRACK IS CUT ONE MILE AHEAD.

Frank grabbed India's arm and sat her down in the seat. "Nice of them not to just derail us."

The train was still slowing, and they could hear the scream of air brakes and the thud of boots on the roof above them. The woman wanting to know what was going on had apparently found out. She was praying hysterically in her berth, while a man who was no doubt her husband kept trying to get her to dress.

Then the train stopped, and there was the sharp crack of gunfire. India pressed her nose against the window. Near the head of the train, horsemen with bandannas over their faces were coming out of the trees. Ahead of the engine on the curve she could see a jumble of ties and track. If the train had slammed into that, she realized, they would have tumbled over the mountainside. The thought made India shudder.

Everyone in the car was opening the windows to see what was happening. A spatter of gunfire came from the front of the train, and the passengers pulled their heads down in a hurry. Ahead the railroad police were shooting it out with the bandits. India scrunched down and tried to watch without getting too near the window.

"Lord forgive me for my sins!" The praying woman seemed to be hitting her stride. "Forgive me my tasks undone, not leading my husband in a better way to give up horses and drink."

"Hush up, Hettie, and get your clothes on." The husband sounded embarrassed.

A tall man in a Prince Albert coat stood up and pulled a derringer from his coat pocket. "Are we men or mice?" he demanded. No one answered. "We must band together and not allow these desperadoes to have their way."

Frank got up, too. "Are you aware that we have a carful of women and old folks here? If you were planning a showdown, I'd be more inclined to just cut my losses and let them have my pocket watch."

"Young man, I happen to be carrying a great deal of money, and I can ill afford its loss."

A gray-haired woman who came approximately up to Frank's nose stood up and glared at the man in the Prince

Albert. "If you are carrying a great deal of money, the chances are that you will be able to find more of it," she snapped. "I find this is especially true with people who brag about it."

Another outburst of gunfire put a stop to the conversation. India could see the mounted men firing at the front of the train. The railroad police returned fire, and one of the robbers slumped in his saddle and fell over his horse's withers. But another dismounted and ran for the cab, pulling himself up the ladder hand over hand. There was sporadic gunfire, and another bandit raced around from the far side of the engine, whooping. It looked to India as if there were at least fifteen of them.

The man who appeared to be the leader was shouting orders. Another burst of gunfire crackled around the engine, and then the cab door opened, and the engineer and fireman came down the ladder.

"Oh, no," India breathed. Exiting the mail car at the front of the train were a half-dozen railroad police, their hands in the air, except for one whose left hand clutched his right arm. Blood dripped between his fingers onto the dirty snow by the track.

Two horsemen peeled off from the rest and rode along the Pullman cars, one on each side, their rifles leveled at the windows. "All right, ladies and gentlemen, just sit tight and you'll be attended to," one of them called. "No one's going to get hurt."

The man in the Prince Albert coat lifted his derringer undecidedly. India felt Frank rocket from his seat and turned in time to see him snatch it from the man's hand. Frank stumbled in the aisle, thudded into the lap of a startled drummer, who sat clutching his sample case, and pitched the derringer out the window.

"Wise move," said the man on the horse. All they could see of him were his eyes, bright above a blue bandanna. "Now, while I'm inspecting the mail car, a couple of my associates are gonna come on board and take up a little collection for the widows and orphans we support. I hope you folks'll be generous. We don't want anybody accidentally hurt."

"Lord forgive me all my sins!" the praying lady whimpered from her berth.

"You put in a good word for me too, lady," the bandit said.

"Hettie, for the love of God get your clothes on! They're boarding!"

The bandit turned his horse and galloped toward the engine again, leaving the passengers looking after him. The horseman on the other side of the car stayed put, just outside Frank and India's window.

India tugged at the sapphire ring on her middle finger. "Father gave it to me," she whispered to Frank. "For my eighteenth birthday. I'd hate to lose it."

"You can put it in your corset if you want to," Frank said. "If you want to take the chance of their looking for it there."

"They might look anyway," India said. "Just to be sure they didn't miss anything. What difference would it make?"

"Because if they pat you down and find something, they're likely to decide there's more and strip you completely. Of course if you don't mind that—"

"You're horrid!" India snapped, still in a whisper.

"Look, you moron, these aren't Robin Hood and his merry men. They'd be perfectly happy to peel all your clothes off and leave you in the snow if they thought you had money in your drawers."

"Don't you mind being robbed?" India fumed. "It's so degrading."

"Of course I mind," Frank said grimly. "But it isn't

the first time, and sometimes you just have to take it. Sometimes you get the bear; sometimes the bear gets you."

India wasn't comforted by this thought. She stuck the ring down her bodice.

Suddenly screams and protests came from the cars ahead of them.

"What are they doing?" India whispered to Frank.

"They're robbers. What do you think they're doing?"

A gunshot punctuated the protests up ahead, followed by a shriek.

The little woman with the gray hair turned to the other passengers. "If any more of you dang fools have guns, the rest of us would appreciate it if you'd just throw them out the window to that fellow out there right now, and save him the trouble of shooting you in the car."

"They're down to the third car," Frank said, looking out the window.

"I wish they'd get it over with," India muttered. "Waiting for them is worse." She looked at Frank. "When were you robbed before?"

"In a hobo jungle," he replied, watching the outlaws' progress. "A man I was supposed to be palling with took the only thing I had that was worth anything: a gold signet ring. Then someone else stole it from him. Knifed him for it. Tried to pin it on me and nearly got me lynched." He glanced at her, then looked out the window again. "It wasn't a wonderful experience."

India blinked at him, trying to envision that other life he was so matter-of-fact about. She couldn't quite. She sat quietly, watching the man on the horse outside the window.

There was a stirring in the next car and a burst of laughter from one of the outlaws.

"They'll be up here in a minute," Frank said.

Everyone looked uneasily at the car door. A moment later, heavy footfalls sounded on the iron platform outside. Then the steel door banged open, and two bandits came in, wedging themselves in the aisle back to back. Each had pistols drawn and cocked, and one held his hat in his hand, upside down, like a church collection plate. His bare head displayed a cap of sweat-stained dark curls. His nose and mouth were covered with a bandanna.

"Just put your valuables in here, and we won't have to shake anybody down." He assessed the man in the Prince Albert. "Don't hold out on me, bub."

The other outlaw, who seemed older, had his slouch hat pulled low over his eyes and the rest of his face covered with a greasy bandanna. He walked backward, keeping his pistol leveled on the passengers. His other hand held a sack. When his partner's hat was filled, the contents were dumped into the sack. No one was inclined to challenge them.

The younger man jerked open the curtains of Hettie's berth. She had stopped praying. Wrapped in a shawl, she meekly stuck out her head, covered with curling papers, and put a watch and a brooch in the hat. "My husband carries the money," she said, sniffling. Her husband reluctantly parted with his wallet.

The little gray-haired woman handed over her earrings and the contents of her pocketbook, glowering all the while. The drummer opened his sample case and shoved it under the bandits' noses. It proved to contain ladies' underwear.

"I don't think anything will fit you, pals," the drummer said smugly.

The younger outlaw gave a whoop and scooped up the contents. "I got a gal," he said happily. "I'm gonna make her a happy woman."

Frank and India, who were standing at the back of

the car, watched uneasily as the bandits approached the man who had had the derringer, but after a moment of indecision, he reluctantly pulled a money belt from under his shirt.

India bit her lip. She could feel the sapphire ring, tucked into her bodice; her rapidly beating heart seemed to be causing the ring to pulse against her skin. She dropped her eyes to her chest and then looked up again quickly. Had the bandits noticed? Why did people always want to look at things they had hidden? To see if they showed, she supposed. She took Frank's hand and squeezed it, until he said in her ear, "You're going to break my fingers."

The outlaws made their way down the car to them. The older bandit covered the other passengers with his six-shooter, clutched in a dirty hand with a big gold ring on the forefinger. Probably stolen from one of the cars ahead, India thought indignantly.

"Well, now, ma'am, what have you got for us?" The younger man sounded almost cheerful, as if robbing people were a lark. Their sack brimmed with rings and watches and pink silk underwear.

India glared at him. She tugged her other ring off and took the gold earrings out of her ears. Frank handed over his watch and his wallet, while India dug in her pocketbook and took out fifty dollars.

"You're right generous, ma'am." The younger outlaw's eyes crinkled; it was obvious he was grinning. "But I'd sure like to know what you stuck down your dress."

"What?" India glared at him again, this time with outrage.

"Mostly ladies don't keep looking at their chest unless they think something might be wrong with it. And being as I can't see a thing wrong with yours, I reckon you got something in there 'sides your camisole." He handed the hat to his partner and snatched her shirtwaist.

"I don't!" India said. "Truly!" Outside she could see the other outlaws remounting. They must have gotten what they wanted from the mail car. Maybe this one would give up if she could stall long enough. A line from a dime novel surfaced in her mind as probably appropriate to the situation. "Take your hands off me, you cur!" she cried, backing away from him.

It didn't do any good. The outlaw tightened his grip on her shirtwaist and grabbed her breast. India shrieked and slapped at him.

From outside came three gunshots and a piercing whistle. "I got to go, lady." The outlaw reached his hand down under her collar.

"Give it to him, India, damn it!" Frank barked. "Just give it to him!"

"I won't! I—" India found herself backed against the door of the car. The outlaw had his hand on her breast again.

Frank wasn't even thinking about helping her. He was staring at the older outlaw still covering the young one's back.

Another whistle sounded. The younger bandit seized India's collar and ripped downward. The thin cotton lawn tore, and he stuck his hand in her camisole.

"No!" India tried to bat his hand away. "I'll get it. I'll give it to you. Leave me alone!" The man withdrew his hand, and she scrabbled frantically for the ring. "There!" She reached past him and threw it into the hat. "Now, go *away!*"

Thudding hooves sounded outside the car, and a horseman rode up with the bandits' mounts. "Lady, you're lucky I don't have time to look some more." He grabbed her breast again, apparently just for amusement,

and squeezed. Then he and his partner were down the
steps and on their horses. He upended his hat to tip in the
last of its contents into the sack held open by the older
man; the rest of the gang was already headed into the
trees.

"You son of a bitch!"

India didn't even realize Frank was the man who had
shouted until he had shot past her out the door and
launched himself at the older man, dragging him from the
saddle. They rolled on the ground, thrashing in the
railbed cinders while India watched out of a window, horrified. The hat and the sack fell, too, as the younger outlaw drew his pistol and tried to aim. His gun wavered
while the men on the ground rolled left and right. He
turned his horse toward the wrestling men, leaned down,
and snatched the fallen sack. Then he galloped bare-
headed after his cronies, his hat bobbing along by the
rails, scattering the last of the loot.

India screamed as the outlaw wrestling with Frank
managed to get his pistol out; she screamed again when
they rolled nearly under the car. India leaned out the
window, hanging almost upside down, and could see only
flailing legs.

"Somebody help him!" she shrieked.

Nobody seemed inclined to. Under the car, Frank
got a grip on the outlaw's wrist and bent it backward
against the rail. The man writhed under him and kneed
him in the groin. Biting his lip, Frank slammed the bandit's wrist on the rail. The grip on the gun loosened. Frank
pushed harder, leaning with his other hand on the man's
throat. The man's fingers opened, and Frank snatched the
gun and raised it, but before he could aim, the man's fist
was in his face, and the gun spun away.

Frank slid back and scrabbled for it. The outlaw was
getting away, running for the horse still pacing uneasily

along the length of the train, reins dangling. Abandoning the gun, Frank pulled himself out from under the car, scrambling to his feet to race after him. The man was nearly on his horse when Frank caught him and yanked him to the ground again. The bandanna had slipped down around the outlaw's neck, and his hat was gone, revealing his balding crown. He was no match for a man in his twenties, not without a gun. Frank got him by the throat again and pounded his head on the ground. He punched him hard in the jaw, and the outlaw slumped, groaning.

Frank sat on him and, with diligent concentration, tugged at the gold ring on his finger. Everyone in the car had flooded out and was looking in the grass and gravel for what might have spilled from the sack. Frank paid them no mind until India came up, the outlaw's pistol in one hand, and stood over him, her other hand on her hip. Frank finally worked the ring loose and put it on his own finger. Then he looked up at India and the gun.

"You know how to use that?"

"Yes." She looked very much as if she were thinking of using it on him. "What in the name of God are you doing? That wasn't even the right man!"

"You never know where someone'll turn up," Frank said pensively. Still sitting on the outlaw, he pulled his belt off and wound it around the man's hands. He looked with satisfaction at the gold ring on his finger.

"Whose is that?" India demanded. "He was already wearing it."

"I know. That's why I went after him."

"I assumed you went after him because of what he did to me," India said icily. "Except this is the wrong man."

Frank looked at her. The front of her shirtwaist was held together with a safety pin. "I told you not to stick that thing down your bodice," he said.

"Oh, look, dearie." The little gray-headed woman trotted up. "I found your nice ring, lying in the grass. Isn't it a mercy?" She handed it to India and looked at Frank curiously. "Did he risk himself just to save your ring? What a devoted young man!"

"He is, isn't he?" India said sweetly.

The railroad agents came purposefully down the line, their expressions irritable. "Which one of you's the fellow that caught one?" They looked at Frank, atop his captive. "That be you, sir? The Kansas Pacific appreciates it."

The outlaw groaned. Frank stood up, and the railroad agent prodded the man over with his toe. "On your feet." The other two hauled him up.

India regarded the man with curiosity. His face was seamed and his chin overlaid with graying stubble. Most of his teeth were missing. He didn't look like a man who had profited by his trade, and she had a momentary twinge of sympathy for him, caught and abandoned by his comrades.

"We got two men dead up front," the railroad agent said, and her sympathy vanished. The railroad bull snapped a pair of handcuffs on the captive and handed Frank back his belt. "That was quick work, young fellow, and well thought out, not to endanger the other passengers. If you ever think you might want a job with the railroad, you come and see me." He gave Frank his card, then pushed the man toward the steps of a car.

"Thank you," Frank said solemnly, but he broke into a stifled howl of laughter before the men were even out of earshot. He spit on the ring and polished it on his coat, which was mud stained and split down the back, with pieces of cinder and gravel clinging to it.

"Maybe you would like to explain just exactly what you were doing?" India hissed, jamming her own ring back on her finger. "And don't tell me you were defending my honor, because I won't believe a word of it."

Frank shrugged. "I never said I was. You go sticking that ring down your front after I told you not to, your honor's on its own as far as I'm concerned. I went after *my* ring."

"That one?" India scowled at him with patent disbelief.

"I told you. I lost it in a jungle. Well, surprise, surprise. Guess who turns up today, riding with the big bad outlaws? The son of a bitch who knifed Bill and took my ring. A lot of those hoboes were blacklisted railroad men." Frank waved carelessly at the stand of pines the outlaws had disappeared into. "Old Butch or whoever that was might have figured he'd be useful."

"Not enough to wait around for him," India noted. She looked thoughtfully at Frank. "Blacklisted?"

He nodded. "In the strike of ninety-three. Lots of the guys who struck went on the bum afterward."

"Well, why would he keep the ring all this time?" India persisted.

"Maybe it was a rainy day stake. Why don't you go and *ask* him?"

"I'm just trying to figure things out." India sniffed. "*You* aren't making any sense."

"Well, figure it out on the train."

The other passengers were climbing reluctantly back into the car, herded by the railroad cops, one of whom told them, "If there was anything left here to find, folks, you would have found it. The head office will be happy to hear all claims at your destination."

Frank sniffed. "They'd better pray. The railroad never pays a nickel."

"How do you know?" India asked, exasperated. "You just don't like the railroad. And how on earth do you know for sure that's *your* ring?" She followed him up the steps into the Pullman car and grabbed his hand to look at the ring. It had a wide, flat seal carved in the top, with "Hargreaves Military Academy" on a banner above it, and "Pro Patria" below.

"How many bums do you know who went to military school?" Frank asked. He settled into his seat.

"I know one."

He sighed. "Woman, on the Day of Judgment you'll want the Lord's credentials." He pulled the ring off and handed it to her. It was engraved inside the band: "Francis Leland Blake, 1896."

India stared at it. "How could you be so sure?"

"I just was. When someone nearly gets you lynched, you remember his face."

"He had on a mask," India pointed out.

"Will you just let it *be*?" Frank snapped. "I remembered his walk, I remembered his eyes, I remembered something. I was *right*, wasn't I?"

"They'll probably hang him for those two men that got killed. But he didn't do it. I gave his gun to the railroad men, but it hadn't been fired."

"In a holdup?" Frank said with derision.

"If he was just a bum, he probably didn't shoot very well." India knew that wouldn't matter to the railroad. Anyone who took part in a holdup in which someone was killed would be held responsible. Even more so in this case, since they hadn't caught anyone else.

India wondered if that might be bothering Frank, too, even though he said gruffly, "Well, he killed somebody. He killed a friend of mine. If they want to hang him for these guys, too, it doesn't matter to me."

"A friend of yours?" India demanded. "I thought you said this 'friend' stole your ring in the first place."

Frank turned in his seat to look her right in the eye.

"You don't know beans about life on the road. A lot of things happen that you wouldn't like to know about. A lot of things happen that you probably don't even know people *do*. Whatever he did, Bill was a pal of mine at the time, on my terms and his. This guy stuck a knife in him while he was sleeping off a drunk. Then he tried to make it look like I did it."

"How could he do that? Why would you have?"

"I was young. They thought I was Bill's— They assumed things. Some of those road kids get pretty desperate."

"I don't have any idea what you're talking about," India said, baffled.

"That's exactly what I mean. You don't know as much as you think you do, so quit pressing me. It's not part of my mission to introduce you to the seamy details of life in the jungle."

The train started forward with a lurch, and Frank leaned back to stare moodily out the window, turning the big gold ring around and around on his hand.

VI

India left Frank alone the rest of the way to Denver, too annoyed to talk to him. In Denver they watched as the outlaw was taken off the train in handcuffs. Meanwhile, the passengers besieged the Kansas Pacific office. Frank and India didn't bother since she had gotten her ring back and Frank was convinced the railroad would make no compensation anyway. Besides, she had in the meantime revealed to Frank that she had more money stashed in one of her trunks and would get it once they reached Taos. A reporter for the Denver paper, tipped off by another passenger, trailed Frank through the station, attempting to extract the heroic details of the bandit's capture.

"How did you feel, sir, as you wrestled the villain to the ground?" The reporter's black eyes gleamed, and he scribbled furiously in his notebook.

Frank didn't answer him.

"I'm told you rescued the lady's ring, sir. What urged you to perform this feat of gallantry?" He turned to India. "Might I look at the ring? An heirloom, I expect?"

India had buttoned her traveling coat over her ruined bodice and wanted nothing more than to find the ladies' lounge and change—and rid herself of the feel of that man's hand on her breast. She glared at the reporter, but he appeared to be undiscouragable. She peeled off her glove and let him see the ring, since Frank didn't seem willing to talk to him, and he obviously wasn't going to leave until someone did.

"It was a present from my father," she said sweetly. "It means a great deal to me."

The reporter wrote that down. India thought fleetingly of the trial of the knave in *Alice*. Certainly she expected Frank to try to take the reporter's head off at any moment. She spied the ladies' lounge and said firmly, "You must excuse me. I am still quite overcome. Mr. Blake is, too," she added.

Frank stalked on without a word, and India ducked into the lounge, hoping he wouldn't do anything drastic. When she emerged, he was sitting on a bench, reading the railway timetable.

"What did you do with him?" she demanded, but he didn't answer.

She didn't bother pressing him.

By the time they got to Santa Fe, Frank seemed contrite. As the engine steamed into the desert depot, India pressed her nose against the glass, watching the blanket-draped Indians on the platform.

Frank nudged India's arm and gave her a rueful look as they got off the train. "I expect I've been a pig. I'm sorry."

India thought about it. "I'm nosy," she said finally. "I'm sorry, too."

Because Taos lay at the base of the mountains in difficult country, no rail line to it had ever been attempted. A stage line ran the seventy-five miles north, its next departure scheduled for the following morning.

"If he ain't broke another wheel," the ticket agent told Frank and India pessimistically.

Frank saw that their luggage was collected and rede-
livered to the stage office, and India counted her trunks.

"You're like a cat who thinks she's lost a kitten,"
Frank said. "There aren't but two."

"I have my paints in them," India said, as if that
explained everything.

"You could chain them to your wrist."

The stage duly arrived that evening while Frank and
India were dining at the depot Harvey House. The vehi-
cle appeared to be intact, so they went to the Hotel
Grande and asked to be called at six the next morning,
then went to their respective rooms.

The following morning India got up, dressed, and
stumbled downstairs, yawning, to an early breakfast—
gobbled hastily because she had forgotten to wind her
watch, and it had stayed six-thirty for twenty minutes.

Once the stage set out, it was impossible to sleep,
even if she had wanted to miss the scenery. The old Con-
cord coach swayed and lumbered, bouncing its passengers over every rock and mudhole. An elderly Mexican
beside her kept his eyes closed, but India refused to believe he was actually sleeping.

"He couldn't be," she whispered to Frank. "If he's
not pretending, he must be dead. *Oh, look at that!*" She
abandoned him for the view.

The stagecoach made its way northward through the
canyon of the Rio Grande. Huge igneous rock cliffs tow-
ered over them as they climbed steadily. India stared at
everything: at piñon pines clinging to the canyon walls; at
yucca plants pushing tall spires of white blossoms up from
spiny leaves; at a thin coyote padding along the road who
turned to stare at the coach, then vanished with a silent
scramble into the sage. He had a face not doglike but

indelibly feral, and India wished she could catch him just long enough to memorize it.

Coming up on a plateau into a purple and incarnadine sunset, billowing like fire across the sky, they reached Taos. In the distance the houses looked like boxes scattered along the foot of the mountain, their tan mud walls soaking up the crimson sky.

Mike and Eden Holt met them at the stage depot. He was a tall, lanky man with red hair and a raffish red mustache, wearing blue denim jeans and a faded plaid flannel shirt. His hair was covered by an old Stetson hat, which he swept off at India's arrival. His wife was slender and willowy—the kind of beautiful blond that Frank's sister, Midge, longed to be—with a practical look about her. She eyed Frank with a balance of appraisal and amusement as she held out her hands to India. "Welcome to Taos."

Mike was pounding Frank on the back. "Do you know how much trouble you got me into? And I think you've grown about a foot. Adventuring seems to suit you."

"It certainly does," Eden said, inspecting him. "Frank stayed with us in New York," she added behind her hand to India, "just before he had his blowup with his father and headed off for parts unknown. We were held to blame for that. Unsuitable companions."

India thought they looked like fascinating companions.

They gathered her luggage into a pony trap that Mike drove himself and set out through Taos. India was too excited to look in any one direction for more than a moment. Her eyes wandered, taking in a jumble of adobe buildings where buttercup light was beginning to blossom in narrow windows. A bell pealed softly from a Spanish-looking church. An Indian woman in a red-and-yellow patterned blanket walked along the dusty street, followed by two speckled hens and an elderly man with a turquoise band around his black hat. A grocer's shop was just closing, the cat in its window yawning and stretching its feet out splay-toed atop a pile of squashes.

Mike and Eden's house lay outside the old town, half a mile along the Pueblo Road amid pastureland dotted with browsing horses. It was a sprawling adobe, flat roofed with the characteristic beams protruding from its mud walls. It looked elegant to India and completely indigenous, as if it had somehow heaved itself up from the ground. To one side grapes grew up a weathered arbor above a flagstone courtyard. Inside, the house glowed with the same soft light India had seen in town, which she recognized as oil lamps. There was no electricity or gas in Taos. The house was pleasantly warm—although the night was cooling rapidly—and was furnished with heavy dark chairs and sofas offset by colorful Indian rugs. Everything looked softly polished. A fire of pine cones glowed and snapped in the big parlor, sending occasional melon-colored sparks over the red-tile hearth.

Eden took them up a narrow staircase to the second story, exclaiming over Frank's unwilling account of their adventures; India had told on him. "Those gangs get more outrageous all the time. The railroads are going to have to do something if they expect people to come West. They don't mention train robberies in all their fancy prospectuses," she added indignantly.

The second floor offered another piece of flaming sky visible through a window. From here you could walk out onto the roof. The house was built on a number of levels, a flow of blunt angles stair-stepping away from a central core.

India's room had a brass bed with an Indian blanket on it, and whitewashed walls adorned with a heavy wooden crucifix. Through the window she could see the mountains.

"We thought you might like this room for a studio," Mike said, opening a connecting door. He walked with a slight limp, a souvenir of the war in Cuba. "It has north light and a cupboard for your things."

"It's wonderful," India said. The studio room had three big windows and a polished-wood floor. The walls were the same creamy white, and another crucifix hung over the cupboard.

"We rented it furnished," Mike explained. "You could take some of those down if they're too oppressive."

"I rather like them," India said, looking at the carved crucifix. It was an original piece and by an artist who had some talent. "They seem to belong here."

Frank was given a room down the hall for his stay— no one seemed to know how long that might be—and he and India were instructed to come and meet the rest of the household after washing up. There were bowls and ewers in each room, but alas, Eden informed them, no indoor plumbing. The privy was out back, in a little vine-covered house of its own.

India washed her face and hands and put on yet another clean shirtwaist and a red skirt, which seemed to suit the house. An Indian maid brought her a pile of fresh towels, but India couldn't understand a word she said. A few minutes later she heard her across the hall, chatting volubly in Spanish with Frank.

"Just California Spanish," he said when she met him in the hall. "I worked the oil fields there for a while." He had changed, too, into a clean shirt and a linen suit. He looked considerably more formal than he had ever been in his mother's house, and India wondered if that was sheer perversity.

The group that was gathered over sherry in the cool,

dark parlor proved even more fascinating than their hosts. Mike introduced them one by one.

A woman of India's age, with smoky dark eyes and a cloud of dark, thick curls, was presented as Rochelle Blossom, and while India pondered that improbable name, the woman said, "In Michael's moving pictures I'm Rochelle. To you I'm Rachel. Rachel Poliakov." She had a thick Russian accent, which India thought was exotic. She found it hard to visualize Rachel in a movie about cowboys, however, and raised her eyebrows involuntarily.

Mike caught India's surprised look. "I'm going to call this next one *The Prairie Flower.* Rachel's a chameleon. It's extraordinary."

"No, it's because I don't talk," Rachel said placidly.

The next guest was Mike's assistant, Herb Lumb, who doubled as cameraman, set rigger, and the man in charge of whatever needed doing. He had a long, lantern-jawed face and dark half-moon eyebrows that gave him an expression of gloomy surprise.

Rachel and Herb were also living with the Holts, India gathered. And then there were three visitors who had come to dinner. One, a middle-aged man with a pleasant face, was introduced as Owen Wister, and India gathered he was Mike's writer friend. Mike introduced Gibson and Fayette Millirons, who, he said, owned a cattle spread just to the north. Mr. Millirons was heavyset and wore the remains of his hair slicked down with brilliantine. Mrs. Millirons seemed to be younger and had a taste for gaudy jewelry. She had strawberry-blond hair that India was sure was dyed. There was no getting around it, India thought; Fayette Millirons was common. But she had a sweet face, and she seemed genuinely glad to meet India.

"It's not like I get to see another female for days on end, and now *three* women to chat with, well, it's a treat."

She looked at Frank with interest, too. "Are you a moving-picture maker like your cousin?"

"No, ma'am. I'm afraid not."

Fayette looked disappointed. Mike's business apparently enthralled her. "I've seen the pictures he made in Cuba three times. We don't have a moving-picture palace out here, of course, but we set up in the town hall and hung a sheet. Everybody turned out for it."

Mike chuckled. "Not everybody. The local artists' colony thinks I'm vulgar. Entertainment for the masses. Are you going to snoot me, too, India?"

"Certainly not."

Eden's cook, a round woman with gleaming black braids, announced in Spanish that dinner was served. They settled around a long table in an even longer dining room. "This house was part of a monastery at one time," Mike explained. "I believe this was the refectory for the brothers."

India looked at the food being served with interest. The main course was a dish made of green chilies and pork, eaten with a round, flat piece of bread folded up like a napkin, as a sort of scoop. The bread was a tortilla, Mike said.

"Watch out. The chili verde's hot," Eden said.

India grinned. She liked peppers. She was going to like it here.

"How far along are you with your chronicle, Holt?" Owen Wister asked. "Have you had any luck in getting the local cowboys to talk to you?"

Mike chuckled. "I didn't—until we set up the projector and showed the film of Cuba. Now they all want to have me take their pictures. I brought a still camera out, too."

"Good," Wister said. "I do believe we're seeing the last of a uniquely American phenomenon."

"Oh, now, Owen, I refuse to believe that." Fayette Millirons pouted at him. "You make us sound like— like . . ."

"Like an extinct species? Not you personally, my dear. The ranches will continue to exist. But the railroad will replace the cowboy. The ranches will get smaller— they won't need so many men. The cities are coming. There will be farmhands, not cowboys, in another twenty years." Wister smiled sadly. "You will grow civilized and die."

"Oh, Owen, that's just the most awful thing I ever heard anybody say. Anyway, we *are* civilized. And proud of it."

Wister nodded. "Precisely."

In the morning Frank and India watched as Mike's camera was loaded onto its wagon. Mike was experimenting with a new style of camera that used larger film and, so he said, produced clearer pictures. It was of monstrous size and weight and had emblazoned on its side the trademark of the Eden Motion Picture Company: a tree silhouetted against a rising sun. It was called a Biograph, and Mike had bought it from its inventor, W.K.L. Dickson, who had jumped ship from Thomas Edison's company not long after Mike did. Mike still had his old Vitascope as well, in case the Biograph should prove too cumbersome. Most of the Biograph Company's own pictures were shot in their rooftop studio in New York. The camera hadn't been designed to be lugged about in a wagon, and Dickson had said so. Dickson didn't usually sell his camera either, but Mike had been willing to pay a hefty price out of the sale of his Cuba films.

Frank noted that several purposeful-looking men were standing around the wagon, six-guns evident on their hips. "How much is that thing worth?" he asked

Mike. "And would anyone really try to steal it out here in the middle of the desert?"

"It's worth a fair amount," Mike said, lashing it down. "But it isn't bandits I'm worried about. Not the kind that operate out here, anyway. I paid a fat price for this thing to stay out of Edison's patent wars, but I can't say it's been entirely successful. Edison wants to keep a grip on the motion picture business, and he's been suing the pants off everybody else, claiming he owns the rights to the Latham loop. That was the breakthrough that made projection possible, so essentially he wants to own the world. He's after anybody else who's trying to shoot moving pictures." Mike tied off the rope and tugged it experimentally. "He's put a lot of smaller companies out of business."

"With lawsuits?" Frank eyed the gun-toting guards.

"No, the lawsuits are all tangled up in court and look likely to stay that way. The writs have nuisance value. I've had to hire a lawyer. But Edison's private detectives have a tendency to take a shortcut with a sledgehammer. I had a visit from two of his thugs in New York, and if my studio hadn't been on top of the Chelsea, I'd have lost my camera."

"I'd like to have been there," Frank murmured. The Chelsea Hotel was inhabited largely by artists, and, just on general principle, they tended to close ranks against outsiders who tried to assert their authority.

"Pyotr and a couple of friends who had been there all night drinking vodka just picked Edison's detectives up and walked them down the stairs as if they'd been packing crates," Mike said. He glanced around at the desert, flowing in a fiery rainbow of red, green, and ochre toward the pueblo where the Taos Indians lived. "I can't count on that out here."

"Can you count on these fellows?"

"So far as I know. I pay them to count on them."

Frank inspected them carefully. Two were young and looked as if they might come from the pueblo. One was balding, with a thick sandy beard and a plug of tobacco in his cheek. An ex-prospector, Frank guessed. The fourth appeared to be a mixture of every race that had ever come to Taos—European, Indian, and Negro. He had tanned skin and curly black hair, fancy new boots, and his belt had a wide silver buckle.

"These boys double as crew?" he asked. "That's a lot of muscle just to stand around and look tough."

Mike sighed. "They're supposed to."

"Give me a job," Frank suggested. "That's why my mother sent me out here. She thinks you'll give me purpose in life."

"What do you know how to do?" Mike asked. "Besides give your mother gray hair."

"Lift heavy objects. Gunsling. I was sheriff of Dawson City for a year."

Mike stared at him.

"Gotcha," Frank said, grinning. "I truly was. And I'm a lot less conspicuous than Dick Daring over there." He pointed at the man with the silver buckle.

"José? He's a cocky devil, but I haven't had any more pilfering by the locals since I hired him. We attract attention like a circus parade, and half of them seem to think I'm a rich gringo here to supplement their supplies of groceries and ammunition. Stuff was disappearing hand over fist."

"They don't have much," Eden said, coming to stand beside them. "It's not an easy country."

"I like my charity to be voluntary," Mike muttered.

"It's beautiful, though," India said. "Can I just follow you around for a while and get ideas?" She had a sketch pad under one arm.

"Sure." Mike grinned at her. "Shooting a motion picture is a lot slower process than you think. You're going to get bored."

"Take a parasol," Eden said. She was staying behind to fix lunch—her most useful contribution, she claimed.

Mike hitched a donkey to the camera wagon and climbed into the pony trap, while the crew followed on horseback. Herb Lumb was in charge of the camera wagon. He perched like a morose stork on the driver's seat, a Mexican sombrero pulled low over his sunburned nose.

Just as they were setting out, three cowboys arrived in a cloud of dust: Mike's borrowed subjects from the Millirons ranch. They pulled their mounts to a halt with a flourish and swept their hats off to India and Rachel, then squeezed into the pony trap with Mike and Frank. The cowboys eyed Rachel with longing and with some self-consciousness. She was dressed for her part in a calico dress and an apron, her hair pulled into a loose knot at the nape of her neck and soft tendrils framing her face. When they started out again, the cowboys' horses pranced and jigged, tossing their heads; the cowboys were showing off.

The drive to town was a short one. Herb stopped the camera wagon in the plaza at the heart of the old town, and the film crew set up while the populace came out of shops and adobes to stare at them. A half-dozen children scooted over and sat down in the dirt in front of the camera wagon—plainly their usual place.

Rachel climbed down and inspected her made-up face in a hand mirror. To India the actress looked almost ludicrous, with her dark eyes ringed in black and her mouth painted blood red. But Rachel had explained how the camera tended to lose features in the same way they vanished under stage lights, making it necessary to exaggerate them.

India wondered what she would look like, made up like that. As if she had on a mask, she thought. Could you just move into the story, if you had on the right mask? she wondered. Mike's moving pictures always told stories. From the very beginning, when other companies were just filming trains rushing by or people sneezing comically, Mike had known what the public wanted, Eden had said proudly. The first picture he made had been called *The Homecoming*, and in it Rachel had been an immigrant girl who found her true love in America. The audience had loved it. "Eaten it up with a spoon," Eden quoted Ira Hirsch, who used to own a magic lantern show and was partners with Mike in the moving-picture business. A nontraveling partner, the one who kept the books, Ira Hirsch had lived in New York all his life and wasn't about to go to the Wild West.

This new picture in some ways was like *The Homecoming*. It had a heroine who had to choose the right man. ("The public wants romance," said Ira. "Art you can give them if you sneak it by.") And it had a brave hero, in the person of one of the cowboys. But Mike had held forth at dinner the previous night that this picture was to be more: a chronicle of a vanishing life.

India was enthralled with the idea of painting Mike filming that life. Right now they were filming a scene set in the plaza: The cowboy hero was baffled because the girl had begun dating a rich man she knew to be wicked. India sketched the actors, ignoring everyone else around her until a voice over her shoulder said, "Well, my dear, you really do have talent there. They look so real!"

India looked up to find Fayette Millirons, wearing an elegant dress and holding a lace parasol over her shoulder, watching the work. Fayette waggled her fingers at Mike when he looked their way.

"How nice to meet you again," India said, feeling unaccountably hostile. "Have you come to watch, too?"

"Oh, I'm quite a fixture on the set," Fayette said gaily. "Michael even took some film of *me*! I tell Mr. Millirons he'd better watch out, or I'll run off and be a motion picture actress."

Does Eden know you're here? India thought.

"Every woman in town is just green with envy," Fayette said.

A small girl who had come out of the grocer's shop stood toeing one boot with the other and staring at Rachel with rapt absorption. "They'll show this at a big theater in San Francisco," she said under her breath, possibly mimicking a discussion she had overheard. "All the swells will come out for it, and the mayor will have his top hat on. There will be pink cakes afterward."

India thought that Fayette Millirons and some of the other women in Taos might have had the same vision. But it looked like work to India. It was work making pictures of any kind.

When the camera was set up, the cowboy hero guided his horse back out through one of the narrow passageways between the shops and houses that ringed the plaza. Mike shouted, and the cowboy galloped in again, raising a cloud of dust that boiled around his horse's hooves and set Herb Lumb to hacking.

"You get grit in this thing, you ain't going to be in the business long," Herb complained. He was obviously unhappy about filming in the desert.

Fayette coughed delicately and waved her handkerchief in front of her face.

"All right," Mike said. "We'll try it a little farther from the camera. Mac, pull up just before you get past the well. But let the dust settle first." Fayette smiled at him as if that were for her benefit. "And you kids watch out," he added. He came over to peer at India's sketchbook and grinned at the images on the paper. "I like the gesture with the arm. You make me look like a magician. Is that why the top hat?"

India grinned back and nodded.

"Of course he is," Fayette said. "An absolute genius."

India decided that that was so far from what she had meant, it was easier to pretend Fayette wasn't there. She took stock of the plaza instead.

The rear walls of the houses encircling the plaza were joined, creating a rectangular fortress, protection that the Spanish settlers had found necessary some two hundred years earlier, Mike had explained. From outside, the old town looked like a fairy-tale castle, its adobe walls glowing golden in the sunshine. Inside it was less glamorous but more interesting. Donkeys wandered in and out of the plaza, and everyone from the parish priest to the saloon girls came to get water from the central well. Women did their marketing with big woven baskets on their arms, in shops that sold rice and pinto beans, cornmeal and coffee, and chili peppers. The smell of frying tortillas hung over the plaza. Tourists came to Taos, and for them there was Indian silver and turquoise, a bookstore, and stalls of Pueblo weaving. The Taos Indians lived almost exclusively in Taos Pueblo, two and a half miles to the north of town. The town of Taos had originated when the Tiwa Indians had asked the Spanish, politely but firmly, to stop hanging around the pueblo and find their own spot.

"They were marrying the girls and teaching the boys bad habits," Mike had explained over last evening's dinner. "The pueblo elders knew a bad influence when they saw one."

A lot of the pueblo Indians seemed to work in town, India noted. She looked at Mike's Indian crewmen with

interest. One of them had struck up a conversation with
Frank and José—he of the silver belt buckle. The other
one caught her watching him. India blushed and looked
away.

The countryside had not been what she had expected
of desert—somehow she had had the Sahara in mind.
Here there were mountains with snow still on their north
faces and canyons and valleys painted green with spring
growth, emerald against the red stone and the russet of a
shrub India didn't recognize. There were ranches in all
the surrounding valleys, Mike said. Then to the north was
the Taos Mountain with the pueblo at the foot of it: adobe
houses built onto each other in a maze, a mysterious warren of rooms, a portal into another kind of life. More than
anything, India wanted to go inside the pueblo.

VII

"The pueblo has been there since before the Spanish came in the sixteen hundreds," Eden said when she came out on horseback from the house with two luncheon hampers for the crew slung over her pony. "They've survived the Spanish, and they're managing to survive us. Although sometimes I wonder what they think, what they make of the tourists and artists. And heaven knows what they make of Mike and me. Johnny and Paul don't say."

India helped her unpack the hampers. Eden's pony was saddled with a western stock saddle and a Navajo blanket, and Eden wore a divided skirt and hand-tooled boots, which India thought dashing. She nudged Eden and gestured at the two Indian crewmen. "Are those Johnny and Paul?"

"Yes. They've worked for Mike since we got here. They're very gentlemanly boys, always polite. And they work hard. Paul doesn't speak any English, only Tiwa and Spanish, so I can't talk to him. Johnny speaks English, but I think I make him nervous."

The crew started clustering around Eden's hampers as she unwrapped sandwiches and apple turnovers and tortillas with a filling that India couldn't identify.

"Eden's such a good cook," Fayette said to no one in particular. "She takes such good care of Mike. Every genius needs a good cook behind him, doesn't he?"

"Honestly," India said softly to Eden, "how do you stand her?"

Eden gave Fayette a thoughtful look, then said, "Fayette's one of those women who wants to be somebody's muse—and unfortunately her husband hasn't given her much scope. So she collects acquaintances who are creative types. She's collected that nice Owen Wister, and she's trying to collect Mr. Blumenthal."

"Albert Blumenthal, the artist?" India asked, diverted. "Is he hard to collect?"

"He's moderately hard to collect, I suppose. He doesn't have much patience with poor Fayette because she really doesn't know anything about art. Of course, he thinks Mike is on the same level with a carnival or a dime show, and he's said so quite rudely. I think it annoys Mike, but I can't be sure."

"He didn't sound as if it did."

"No, but he wouldn't."

"Are there many artists here?"

"Several, all from the East. They all wear blue serge suits and bowler hats. You can't miss them."

India chuckled, but she thought about those other artists. She hadn't told anyone but Frank how much Otto Gallatin's comments had stung. She was curious about these men, possessed of an urge to see what they were doing, what they were making of this crystalline air that seemed to magnify everything and bring it nearer so that each grain of sand, each leaf on the cottonwoods in the plaza leapt out of the air at her. What would they do with the luminescent moon that, in midday, hung suspended in a turquoise sky over the red mountains to the south?

While the crew ate lunch, India prowled along the plaza, peering into shop windows. The bookstore offered Navajo silver jewelry and framed watercolors of the desert among its wares. She went inside. It was a tiny postage stamp of a shop with floor-to-ceiling shelves of books, mostly local history and the newest popular novels interspersed with religious tracts and other inspiring works. A middle-aged Indian with a smooth, bronze face and a red-and-yellow patterned blanket around his shoulders sat on a stool behind the oak display case that supported the cash register. Displayed inside the case was a squash blossom necklace, laid out on a red scarf.

The man behind the counter watched India with silent interest, as if puzzling over her.

"Who does the watercolors?" she asked, gesturing toward the front window.

"Mr. Blumenthal," the Indian said. "And anybody else Dorothy lets put their pictures out there. Since Mr. Blumenthal come, we have many artists."

Since they found out tourists might actually pay money for paintings, India thought. "Who is Dorothy?"

"She owns the store. I just work here. Who are you?"

"I belong with them." India waved a hand at the film crew in the plaza. "I'm staying with the Holts. They're my cousins. Sort of. I'm an artist, too. I came here to paint."

"You don't look like you belong to them." He inspected her dark and angular features. "Navajo, maybe."

India was not at all sure that was a compliment since she didn't think he was Navajo. "My grandmother was Indian," she said, "but the other sort. From India. A princess of Rajputana," she added, embroidering a little. "That's my name, in fact—India Blackstone."

The Indian looked more dubious than ever. He produced an atlas of the world from a dusty shelf and said, "Show me."

India complied. She opened the atlas and, after consulting the index, pointed.

"Hmmm," said the man. He looked at her with renewed interest and slowly held out his hand. "I am Luis Flores. I tell Dorothy to look at your pictures."

India shook his hand. "Dorothy does what you tell her to?" she asked, amused.

"I live here longer than Dorothy. Dorothy knows I know things."

"Ah." India pointed at the squash blossom necklace. "Who made that?"

"Navajo. Pawn from the trading posts. Nobody redeems it, so Dorothy buys."

"Do you live at the pueblo?"

Luis nodded, but to her disappointment didn't elaborate. "I think your cousins leave now," he commented.

India looked out the window. "Oh, heavens!" She pulled the door open. "Thank you for talking to me!" A quick wave and she was gone.

Eden was astride her pony. "We wondered where you had gone. Did you meet Luis?"

"Yes, I rather liked him. I had to show him India on a map to prove it existed. He said I didn't look like I belonged to you, and I must be a Navajo."

Eden chuckled. "The Pueblo Indians don't like the Navajo much. They're ancient enemies. Did you convince him of your bona fides?"

"I think so. He said he would 'tell Dorothy' to look at my pictures."

"She will, too, if Luis says so. He's an elder in the pueblo and a force in Taos. He found us Paul and Johnny. He's Johnny's uncle. You may see him again tonight. We're invited to a party at Dorothy's. Sometimes the Indians will come to things like that, and sometimes they won't."

"Who else will be there?"

"Heaven knows."

*   *   *

India began to understand Eden's assessment of Dorothy Brattow's guest list when they climbed out of the pony trap in front of the high adobe wall that encircled Dorothy's garden. Through its gate India could see a throng remarkable for its heterogeneity, to say the least. There were several Indians, solemn in their enveloping blankets; Spanish families; two Anglo men in blue suits; a priest in a clerical collar; the Millirons and their guest Mr. Wister; and any number of children of various races shrieking across the lamplit patio.

Dorothy Brattow had been in Taos only a year, but she planned to stay. The weather suited her lungs, which had been dangerously close to consumptive in the East. Therefore, she considered it her job to keep herself amused here, and she collected every interesting person who crossed her path. Dorothy herself was weathered and wiry. She wore a black skirt and a blue silk shirtwaist that set off a heavy necklace of Mexican silver. After firmly shaking India's hand, Dorothy handed her a glass of sherry. India had worn her red skirt and decided that for once she had dressed in the right thing.

She and Frank looked around with appreciation, and she knew they were thinking the same thing: Why be at the White House when you could be here? Dorothy's garden was lit by votive candles sunk in sand inside oiled paper bags, and the effect was fairylike and magical. The sky overhead was cobalt blue and pierced with stars. An old Peace rose climbed a trellis above a blue-glazed bird-bath, and rush-bottomed chairs were gathered in groups of three and four around the garden. An Indian girl of about twelve was passing trays of sherry and small pieces of spicy chicken fried in cornmeal.

Mike was mobbed, India noticed, by the curious, and he was laughing and drinking sherry and gesticulating expansively with his free hand. Fayette Millirons stood proprietarily at his elbow, which India found irritating. Eden, however, did not seem to be bothered by Fayette's attention to her husband. She had drifted off with a gentle smile at Fayette and was talking to the priest. She appeared to be telling him a joke, and he threw back his head with a sudden roar of laughter.

"A particularly egregious display," a voice said beside India, and she turned to find a short, round man in a blue suit at her elbow.

India raised her eyebrows in question.

"Our resident P.T. Barnum is holding court," he said with hauteur.

"Do you mean Mike Holt?"

"Ah, I see he has swept you into his net already," the man said ruefully. "Welcome to Taos, in any case. You must be a newcomer since I haven't seen you at Dorothy's before. I am Albert Blumenthal." He proffered his hand, and India noted that his fingernails were rimmed with paint.

"India Blackstone." She gave her hand gravely. "I've heard of your work. I was hoping I would meet you."

Mr. Blumenthal grinned. "Dear lady. I saw you from across the garden. I should greatly like to paint you. You have a look of New Mexico about you, although *not*, I think, the pueblos."

India again explained her background for Albert Blumenthal.

"British," he said. "How interesting. And what brings you to Taos? I can't imagine it is for your health's sake. You'll forgive me for saying this, but you don't look in the least consumptive."

"Actually, I am visiting relatives. Mike Holt." She cocked her head to see how he took that.

Mr. Blumenthal smote his forehead dramatically and then bowed low. "Ah! Dear lady, pardon! Purely a professional judgment, you know, and nothing against Mr. Holt himself. I daresay he is an admirable cousin."

"You don't like the moving pictures?" India asked.

"My colleagues and I"—Mr. Blumenthal nodded at two other men, one in a blue suit like his own and the other in a more romantic garb of soft-collared shirt and red bandanna—"have given our lives to art. It doesn't sit well to hear a magic-lantern-show proprietor describe himself as an artist."

"Did he?"

"Not until I asked outright," Mr. Blumenthal admitted. "He was drawing considerable attention. My colleagues and I wished to know what his pretensions were."

His colleagues, taking note of him in conversation with an interesting woman, began to drift their way.

"I found it rather promising," India said. "I think there's much that can be done with it, not at all like a magic lantern. Perhaps what we're seeing is the birth of a new form of art."

Mr. Blumenthal snorted.

"Ah, a pretty lady who can talk art," one of the colleagues said. He jabbed Mr. Blumenthal in the ribs. "Why do I never meet the pretty ladies who like art?"

"Even if misguided," murmured the third man into his bandanna.

"You met Mrs. Millirons," Mr. Blumenthal noted.

"I shall defer to Mr. Holt," the man in the bandanna said acerbically. "Blumenthal, introduce us."

"Miss Blackstone, this is Mr. Bennington, and this is Mr. Cattrell. Miss Blackstone, gentlemen, is a cousin or some sort of connection of Mr. Holt, and she isn't trying to live it down. She thinks perhaps he has found a new medium."

"Ladies are invariably generous," Mr. Cattrell said, grinning.

"Nonsense," India said. "How much attention have you paid to what film can do with light and shadow? For that matter, with making its subject actually move?"

"Then where is the skill involved?" Mr. Bennington demanded. "Where is the genius if the medium does it all for you mechanically?"

"It's what you do with the medium." India took a small triangular sandwich off a passing tray and gesticulated with it. "I am certain I have not been painting as long as you gentlemen have, but I *have* been watching Mike."

"Ah. She *paints*." They looked at one another solemnly.

Mr. Blumenthal smiled at her. "What is your medium? Watercolors? You must ask Dorothy to put some in her shop window. Landscape watercolors do very well here with the tourists."

"You ought to know, Blumy," Cattrell said.

"I have a living to make," Blumenthal said loftily. "If I want to dash off trivial pretties to put the tortillas on the table, I will." He smiled at India again. "More often I send my work to my gallery in Chicago. My serious work, you understand. But you must show me what you do," he said encouragingly.

"You must show *all* of us," Cattrell said. "We aren't going to let Blumy get ahead of us."

"I haven't had a chance to do any work since I got here," India murmured. "Just some sketches of Mike and his crew this afternoon."

"All work and no play makes Jill a dull girl," Mr. Bennington said as a fiddle and a guitar struck up a tune from the other end of the garden. "Come and dance with me, and leave art alone for a while. It's no career for a nice girl, anyway."

Mr. Bennington led her across the courtyard. "Art is

a tiresome and tyrannical mistress, but worse, she's a female. Female artists have the devil of a time getting on with her. Too much competition."

"*Au contraire,*" India said. "Females quite possibly understand better than males what she likes." She was aware that she sounded snappish.

"Touché." Mr. Bennington swept her into his arms, and they waltzed across the flagstones. "Then you must show me your work."

"I will when I have been here long enough to accomplish anything," India said, sweetly now.

"Tut, tut, Miss Blackstone, you are holding out on us."

"Certainly not." India slid from his arms and took a gold pencil from the beaded bag that dangled from her wrist. Not seeing any handy paper—and sufficiently goaded—she scratched a quick caricature on Dorothy's garden wall: Three men, two in suits, one in Byronic disarray, all peering earnestly at a desert sunrise, brows furrowed, lips puckered. Above them she wrote in swift capitals: BUT IS IT ART?

Mr. Bennington roared with laughter, but he looked as if his collar had grown too tight, and he eyed her warily.

Just then Frank came up and bowed over India's hand. "Will you dance?" he inquired.

As India excused herself, she noted Bennington's relieved expression. The musicians had struck up a polka. She picked up her skirts and bag with one hand and let Frank sweep her down the garden.

"Who was the chubby party you were cavorting with just now?" Frank asked.

"Mr. Bennington," India said. "He paints. Along with Mr. Blumenthal and Mr. Cattrell. They seem to form the Art Committee of Taos."

"Why don't you like them?"

"They condescended to me."

"A fatal move," Frank agreed solemnly. He spun her around a trio of chairs, somewhat off the designated dance floor, and they whirled in and out among the candles. Mike galumphed past them with Fayette Millirons in his arms. Fayette's chest, ballasted with ropes of pearls, was heaving from exertion, and she looked as if her corset might be too tight. India hoped it was. She saw Eden dancing somewhat more sedately with Mr. Wister, and Dorothy Brattow was insistently teaching Luis the polka. He clearly didn't want to polka and very patiently kept not understanding until Dorothy gave up.

"Shall I take you back to your beaux?" Frank asked when the tune ended and they halted.

"I wish you'd go dance with Mrs. Millirons," India muttered.

"And detach her from Mike? She's got no time for me. I'm not artistic enough."

"You're handsomer," India said hopefully.

Frank glared at her with pretended affront. "And so you'd throw me to the she-wolf just to save Mike's skin? It won't work, you dunce. Fayette really is interested in the artist first and his outer beauty second. Heaven knows where she gets it. It must be frustrating for her, married to old Millirons. Mike says she tried to get her dear hubby to take painting lessons. It was the only row they've ever had."

India looked darkly at Fayette Millirons, but she had drifted on to dance with Owen Wister, and Mike was talking to Herb Lumb, who looked as somber as ever. Mike slapped Herb jovially between the shoulder blades, then went to get another glass of sherry. A curious knot of admirers followed.

India glared at Fayette again.

Frank took India by the wrist. "Come on, you witch. If you don't want to dance with the art committee, I'll show you something wonderful I spotted."

They slipped through the garden gate, leaving the party behind them.

Fayette Millirons had competition. Eden, being not quite so oblivious as India had thought, found that a certain satisfaction.

"Tell us, Mr. Holt—how *do* you choose your actresses? Is there a certain something a woman has? A certain . . . *allure* you look for?" The wistful blond lowered her lashes and shot an electric look at him from beneath them.

"I was accounted quite an actress when I was at school," a round-eyed woman, touching the rose pinned into her pompadour, said. She moved a half step in front of the other. "I played Ophelia," she informed Mike proudly. "I can still remember all my lines. 'There's rosemary—' "

"There *aren't* any lines in Mr. Holt's moving pictures, dear," the blond said. "One must convey emotion with body language." She smiled at the other sadly. "Not a talent that *everyone* possesses, as I am sure Mr. Holt will tell us."

Really, thought Eden, this was funny.

"It depends on whom the camera likes," Mike said. "And there is no accounting for the camera's tastes. It is capable of making a lovely lady look like a pigskin purse and quite a homely damsel look like an angel. I just let the camera choose. That's how I found Miss Blossom."

"Just think of having your face shown on a screen in some motion-picture palace in San Francisco." The round-eyed woman sighed.

"It will be such fun to see how one looked on film," said the blond. "*Just* for fun, of course."

I'd better rescue him, Eden thought. *Film's expensive, and he's had three glasses of sherry.* She trotted across the patio, chuckling, but before she came even with him, Fayette Millirons stepped in front of her and slid her arm expertly through Mike's, detaching him from the other two women.

"You must come and eat Dorothy's wonderful lamb that's been cooking all this time. I've fixed you a plate. You can't live on music and sherry *all* night," Fayette teased. She turned him toward the house, where double doors stood open to the dining room, and appeared to see Eden for the first time. "I'm just going to feed him for you, dear," she said with a smile. "These men of genius are such a trouble. It takes more than one woman just to see they're taken care of."

"There," Frank said. "See?" He put an arm around India's waist and steadied her as she bent over the well in the plaza. The water blazed back up at her, alive with stars.

"It's like looking into a hole in the sky," India said.

"I thought you'd like it. It gives me the feeling I could lean down and dip them out."

She turned and studied him thoughtfully. "What *are* you still doing here, anyway?"

"Mike's promised me a job; I'm getting the urge to go on the bum again; I'm here to see you. Take your pick."

India sniffed derisively. "You sounded like a wasp in a bottle when your mother wanted you to come out here with me."

Frank turned the big gold ring on his finger. "Maybe you're a lucky piece for me." His eyes looked directly into hers for just a moment. Then he kissed the tip of her nose.

"Maybe I just think I should keep you out of trouble. Your father worries about artists with no moral compass, adrift on a sea of iniquity, luring you into their vile lairs."

India thought of Mr. Blumenthal and Mr. Bennington, even Mr. Cattrell, and folded her arms suspiciously.

"*I* worry that you'll be seduced by some cowboy," Frank went on. "José was asking me about you. He was quite plaintive when I told him you were the boss's cousin."

"You discussed me with José?"

"Did you have your eye on him?" Frank asked, unrepentant. "I said you were a woman of forceful attitudes, but I didn't say you were a shrew. Paul and Johnny hung around the edges of the conversation and looked wistful."

India burst out laughing. "One of them doesn't even speak English. Thank God." She tilted her head back and looked up at the stars. "This is an amazing place. Very good for making you feel a speck of dust in the celestial scheme of things and immensely aware of God's power at the same time."

"Lots of people would find that unnerving," Frank commented.

"I don't."

Frank tilted his head back, too. He was wearing his white linen suit again, and he seemed to give off a smoky shimmer in the darkness. He put an arm around her waist again—but he was only being companionable, India thought. Or was he? She looked at him out of the corner of her eye, seeing new possibilities, aggravated that she couldn't read him the way she could the boys who courted her.

You're here to paint, she told herself crossly. *You need Frank Blake like a hole in the head.*

Footfalls sounded behind them. India turned and saw Herb Lumb looming out of the dark.

"Mr. and Mrs. Holt have gone along home," he said. "The boss sent me to tell you."

"Gone home?" India said. "What in?" She, Eden, and Rachel had ridden together in the pony trap.

"Mrs. Holt took Mr. Holt's horse," Herb said carefully. "Mr. Holt took yours," he told Frank. "He didn't seem like he was coming back, so I suppose you'd better come in the pony trap with the gals."

"We aren't ready," Frank said firmly. "And I think Rachel was having a good time. You tell her we'll collect her when the party dies down a bit more."

"What I thought." Lumb looked relieved. "Give Mrs. Holt a while to get settled," he added cryptically.

"They've had a fight," India said when Lumb had trudged back through the garden gate.

"Mike was soaking up the sherry and the admiration pretty steadily," Frank said. He put his arm around India again and said into her ear, "Let's put that on our list of reasons not to get married."

Goodness yes, India thought. Why would anyone get married, if even nice Mike and Eden couldn't get along?

VIII

"Nice Mike and Eden" were having the first serious fight of their four-year marriage. Eden had climbed off Mike's horse and was furiously unsaddling it in the corral when Mike thundered up on the gelding he had lent to Frank. The horses came with the rented house.

Mike tried to take the heavy stock saddle from Eden as she staggered to the tack shed with it. "Give me that. You'll get your dress all dirty."

Eden snatched it away from him. "I can carry a saddle," she gasped. "Go away!"

"Why did you take off like that?" Mike demanded. "I would have driven you home if I'd known you wanted to go."

"I seemed to be superfluous," Eden said between her teeth. "And far be it from me to disturb you while you and your genius are being ministered to."

"Aw, come on, Eden. You know I don't take that seriously."

Eden grunted as she heaved the saddle onto its rail.

Mike followed her out of the shed. "I thought it was kind of funny," he said hopefully while she unbridled her horse.

Eden smacked the horse on the rump, and it trotted down the paddock. Mike's gelding snorted at him. He untied its girth while Eden glared at him. The front of her taffeta dress was smeared with saddle dirt and horse hair.

"Eden, honey—"

Eden switched the bridle in her hand, and the heavy bit clacked against the fence rail. "I wasn't inclined to stay at that party and be made a fool of by you any longer!"

"Now just a minute. *I* made a fool of *you*? *I* took *your* horse and rode off at a dead gallop in a gown all bunched up around my waist and my stockings showing?"

"I feel quite certain that no one noticed me," Eden snapped. "They were all much too interested in you."

"Herb Lumb noticed you and came to tell me you'd taken off. He looked like a puzzled moose the way he usually does. He tapped me on the shoulder in confidence and whispered in my ear until everyone in the room noticed."

"I suppose I should have said no *female* noticed me," Eden said, "being all too busy feeding you lamb off their forks. But since you managed to bring my unseemly appearance to their attention, they can have a good laugh over it."

"*I* didn't bring it to their attention," Mike said. "And Herb was not so indelicate as to mention your stockings. That was Dorothy. She was afraid you might take cold."

"Don't you even *bother* talking as if all this is funny and it doesn't matter," Eden fumed. "It isn't funny, and it matters to me!"

"I didn't say it was funny." Mike pulled the gelding's saddle off and started for the tack shed.

Eden was following him now. "It *was* funny at first," she said. "All those women falling all over themselves, imagining themselves the toast of some picture palace. Glamour! Champagne! If the poor things only knew— and Rachel never bothered to disillusion them. Even when that idiot decided she was going to be your muse, I could stand it. She was spreading it around anyway. But this was too much! I do *not* need someone who 'truly understands art' to take care of my husband's intellectual needs while I do the cooking. And I do *not* subscribe to the notion that the man of genius needs a damned harem to keep him satisfied!" Eden was furiously trying to hang the bridle on a too-high peg and scream at Mike at the same time.

"Oh, Eden." He took the bridle and hung it up for her.

"I could put up with it until she got that proprietary look in her eye. Staking her claim and feeding you lamb. I'm fed up, Michael! I have had all I'll stand for!" Eden balled her hands into fists, and her blue eyes shot sparks at him.

"What do you want me to do?" he asked contritely.

Eden stared at him. That wasn't the answer she had expected. Protestations of innocence maybe. Laughing assurances that it all meant nothing. That no one had noticed Fayette Millirons publicly staking her claim to Eden's husband.

Instead he said, "I'm sorry. I guess I was kind of caught up in it. It never happened to me before."

"Well, you certainly seemed to get your money's worth out of it," Eden said.

Mike leaned against the tack shed wall and folded his arms. "I don't suppose it has occurred to you that the shoe is now on the other foot?" he said gently. "Ever since we got married, I've watched other men practically slaver over you."

"Mike!" Eden was horrified. "You *know* I never even give them the time of day!"

"No, but you know they do it. You can't pretend you don't notice."

"Of course I notice. I'm not an imbecile. But *you* never said anything."

"Oh, hell. I married you so young. It seemed like you ought to have a chance to be the belle and have men flirt with you. A chance to know how pretty you are," he said softly.

Eden lowered her eyes. She dug her toe in the dirt of the tack shed. "I didn't flirt with them. Not exactly."

"Not exactly?"

"I never let anyone act like he *owned* me, in front of you!" Eden flared.

"I know. And I guess I did. I didn't mean to. I was hungry. It seemed like a good idea to go eat."

"You were full of sherry," Eden said with the trace of a smile.

Mike nodded. "What do you want me to do?" he asked again.

"What do *you* suggest?"

"I think I should make it clear to Fayette Millirons that I *have* a wife. Also that I have a muse and don't require another one." He put his hands on Eden's shoulders. "You've spoiled your pretty dress."

Eden looked down at it ruefully. "It'll clean. Probably."

Mike pulled her into his arms and kissed the top of her head. "You know I don't want somebody else. You're all I want. I guess if this moving-picture business grows, I'll have to watch out for that. You'll have to help me wade through the rapids. I don't want to be rude to anyone."

"You can be rude to Fayette Millirons," Eden said. Her face against his chest muffled her words.

"Well, maybe just a little." Mike nuzzled her hair. "Do you want to go inside? It's getting colder than the North Pole out here."

*   *   *

When the rest of the household came home, uncertain of what they might find, all was quiet. Mike was not asleep on the parlor sofa, which they took to be a good sign.

India slipped up to her room and thought about marriage while she undressed. If a woman married, she seemed to lose all autonomy, all definition of herself as an individual. And was laid open to being made a fool of. But if she didn't marry, where did she find companionship? And certainly the physical act of sex was intriguing—although nice girls weren't supposed to know anything about it. Nice girls did, though, in theory at least. Particularly nice girls who lived in the country. It wasn't an experience that India was prepared to forgo indefinitely—not until she found out whether she liked it or not. Of course, if you were married and you *didn't* like it, you didn't have any choice. India had listened enough to the whispers of her mother's friends and the speculations of her own to be queasily uncertain about the subject.

She suspected Frank knew a good deal about it. And when he had put his arm around her, something had happened. But she didn't want to speculate about it. *I need to get some sleep,* she thought. *And forget about these silly ideas.*

At dawn she woke to the shrill notes of some desert bird, got up, and stood stretching at the window. The air was chilly and as crisp as apples. From Mike and Eden's room, which shared a wall with hers, she heard sounds that she couldn't quite identify but which she knew, without knowing why, she ought not be listening to. She pulled her wrapper on and padded downstairs and outside to the little privy in the back. The air smelled of sage, and the noisy bird that had woken her was rocketing about in the sky above her. On the way back to the house, she mentally made a note of the things she wanted to borrow from Eden: saddlebags and a divided skirt.

The house was soon bustling, with everyone eager to get to work on the film. India declined to accompany Mike's crew, even though Frank gave her an amused look. She was not avoiding him; she was going to paint today. She said so. Firmly. The smile that curved Frank's mouth deepened as she saddled one of the pinto ponies.

"Don't get lost."

"I won't get lost. Eden says just to look for the mountain." She mounted up. "And the horse knows how to get home."

"Don't fall off."

India kicked the pinto's flank and trotted off, back straight, not bouncing at all. She had been riding since she was two—and in a stock saddle to boot. Let Frank put that on his needles and knit it.

She rode toward the pueblo, drawn by its mystery and the antiquity of its walls, as if there might be spirits there, ghosts of the ones who had made the white men move on, away from the pueblo, and dwell elsewhere. She kicked the pony into a gallop.

She had gone a fair distance when she came up even with a wagon. The lone passenger was a familiar one. She reined in, sending up a small cloud of dust.

Albert Blumenthal tipped his derby to her. "Going to paint the pueblo?" he inquired genially, noting the folding easel lashed behind her saddle. "Everyone always paints the pueblo first."

"I'm just exploring," India said, deciding instantly not to paint the pueblo until she could find a piece of it that Mr. Blumenthal hadn't painted. She waved and gave the pinto his head, veering off from the road down a track that looked inviting.

The trail might have been just a deer track; it was

hard to tell. It meandered through sage and scrub, past clumps of startling scarlet wildflowers. A blue-green lizard sunning itself on a rock vanished in a quick emerald streak when the horse's shadow crossed it. Farther along the trail was a pile of speckled feathers. India climbed down and looked at them, lifting them gently to find that they were still attached to a shred of skin. Some coyote's meal, perhaps. She had heard them yipping in the early morning air. She fluffed the feathers with one finger, then tucked them into her saddlebag.

The trail continued on, into a stand of sycamores beside a cold stream. India dismounted and put a halter on the pinto so that he could graze. She set up her easel facing away from the stream, toward Taos Mountain where the sky and the land flowed over each other in stripes of red and blue and green.

By the time she packed up her paints, the sky had turned russet. The pinto was asleep under the sycamores, tail swishing automatically, an equine metronome. India discovered she was ravenous, ate the sandwiches that Eden's cook had packed for her lunch, washing them down with gulps of cold coffee, then rode toward home. She held the reins in one hand and the wet canvas, in a frame she had devised for the purpose, dangling from the other.

Coming out onto the Pueblo Road, she encountered Luis Flores and his nephew Johnny heading home. They reined in their horses and raised dark hats politely.

Luis craned his neck to see the canvas. "You don't paint the pueblo," was his comment.

India couldn't tell whether he was surprised or possibly offended. "I'm dying to paint the pueblo," she said in a flash of inspiration. "But I thought the people who live there mightn't like it. And I didn't know who to ask for permission."

"You ask me," Luis said, as if that should be obvious. "Hold up your picture."

India held it up obediently, curious as to what he would say. The reds and greens and blues of the countryside were broad bands that looked like beadwork. In the foreground was the shred of feathers, intricate in its detail as if the living bird itself still resided in that scrap. In the sky above it, flying on bird wings, was the coyote.

Luis didn't seem surprised by the flying coyote. "The ears are wrong," he said simply. "Johnny will show you a coyote in the morning."

India looked at Johnny. He was studying the canvas intently, his long black braids that usually swung with his every move as still as the feathers.

"Can you really find one, just like that? Or do you mean a stuffed one?" India asked.

Johnny jerked his head up. "I'll find you a live one. But I like this coyote fine, even with dog ears." His voice was mellifluous and supple. "You don't paint like those other ones."

"No. I paint the way I like to."

"Your cousin, Mr. Blake, says that your name is India. That is a fine joke."

His mouth moved in what she thought might be a smile. The Indians hardly ever smiled, she had noticed. When they did, it was subtle. You had to watch for it.

"It wasn't intended to be a joke," she said. "India is the country my mother's mother was from. The country that Christopher Columbus was looking for when he found this one by mistake. A silly mistake to call your people Indians really, but I suppose it stuck."

"White men's mistakes have a way of doing that," Luis commented.

"Anybody's mistakes do that," India said practically. "I find they're much more tenacious than good judgment."

Luis gave what might have been a snort of amusement.

"Tomorrow, just before dawn," Johnny said, "before Mr. Holt needs me, I will show you coyotes."

The two young men raised their hats again and rode on. India looked speculatively at their backs and then at her canvas. Coyotes! She couldn't wait to tell Frank she was going to be shown coyotes.

Frank was unimpressed. He had seen coyotes, he said, more than he wanted to, while working ranches in California. "I'll admit to a sneaking fondness for them, though. They're almost smarter than people."

Coyotes were out again that night, under the moon, possibly having a party, India thought. A shrill, yelping chorus ended in a long, quavering howl that seemed to bounce off the mountains and skim across the high valley. The sound made the hair on India's arms stand up, a physical sensation of peculiar excitement. "What are they doing?" she asked.

"Hunting," Frank said.

She went to bed and dreamed of coyotes, two-legged ones, dancing around her bed.

Waking early, India dressed quickly and quietly. She found Johnny waiting for her by the corral, his horse and the pinto pony she had ridden the day before both tethered to the fence. It was still dark, and cold, and he wore a sheepskin jacket with the collar turned up over his chin and his hat pulled low on his forehead. The dew that would evaporate with the first sunlight was clinging to the horses' ears.

"This way," Johnny said after she had mounted up. She kicked her horse into a trot behind his, and they turned off the road to follow some trail that India wasn't really sure she could see. They passed by the backs of farms, lamps just beginning to glow in their windows, and saw a man with milking pails stumbling sleepily to his barn.

"How do you know where to find them?" India asked.

Johnny eyed her over his shoulder. His face looked content, as if he were giving her some present. "I know where they like to hunt." That faint interior smile again. "They like chicken."

They rode on to the edge of a meadow, where suddenly Johnny drew rein. He held up his hand for silence as India came up beside him.

"There," he whispered. "Special for you." His eyes danced. "No wings."

India looked where he pointed and saw them trotting along the far edge of the meadow—three of them, gray as the dawn light, shaggy and bushy-tailed, their ears pricked. Bigger ears than she had thought. They trotted one behind the other, nose to tail, purposeful. There was something feral in their shapes; you would never take them for dogs.

"What do they eat?" she asked.

"Anything but rocks," Johnny replied. "The next farm's an egg ranch. They've got a big dog now, but the coyotes keep track of the place anyway, just to see if the dog's still there. Sometimes they'll bring a bitch in heat and lure a dog off."

"I heard them hunting last night."

"Me, too. They sounded mad, like they missed. They hunt just about anything; rabbits, mice, quail, frogs, snakes. Insects, even. Cats, too; maybe somebody's little dog. Two or three of them will work together to bring down larger prey, like a deer, running in relays to tire their quarry out or waiting in ambush while another chases it toward them. They even eat fruit. They eat the windfalls in the orchards."

The coyotes had reached the end of the meadow, and while India watched, they seemed to melt into the brush as the rising sun pooled out over the meadow. One moment they were there and the next they weren't. India envisioned them in their burrow, sleeping curled around one another, bushy tails just covering their noses. She turned to Johnny to thank him and found that he was watching her, not the coyotes.

She smiled at him. "Thank you."

"I like what you paint. The way you picture this land."

"It's beautiful land."

"Too many people think so, maybe. Uncle Luis says."

India took that to mean too many white people. She rested her elbow on the saddle horn and put her chin in her hand. "Do you mind us being here?"

"*I* don't mind. I am modern, not like my uncle."

"Your uncle seems pretty modern to me. He invited me into the pueblo."

"Not quite. But he will if you ask him."

"Is there a proper way to ask?"

"Bring him a present. He likes tobacco."

"I wish he'd let me paint him." She looked thoughtfully at Johnny. "I wish you would."

Johnny looked uncomfortable. "I don't know." He gathered up his reins. "Your cousin will be waiting for me."

"Have you had any trouble?" India asked as they rode back. "Mike must be worried if he's got four men just to guard that camera."

"No trouble so far. It is a disappointment to José. He would like to shoot at someone."

"Where is José from?" India asked. "And that other man."

"Hawley's been here for years. He thinks he'll find gold. When coyotes really get wings, maybe. He works sometimes long enough to get a stake together again. José, he grew up here. His mama's a Navajo. I don't know about the father. He's long gone. Some kind of cowboy. José's a hotshot."

India chuckled. "He looks like a hotshot."

They rode in silence back to the house. Mike was loading his camera wagon when they got there. "Thank you for the coyotes," India said to Johnny.

The next day she went out again, and the day after, caught by the landscape. Sometimes she went with Mike and painted his crew, but more often she simply rode the pinto until she found something she liked. She painted the stark red mountains—the Sangre de Cristo, in whose lap the plateau of Taos sat—and the farms of Ranchos de Taos. Often when she was packing up her paints she would discover Johnny was there, just quietly watching.

"I will show you a place," he said once, and took her the next day to a canyon hemmed in by stone walls, out of which grew the wildflowers that paint the high plateau every May. After that he began to bring her things he thought she would like: a king snake that stayed in a box long enough for her to paint his mysterious stare, a handful of green stones washed by the Red River, an owl's feather.

As Johnny had suggested, India bought a can of tobacco and took it to the bookstore for Luis. To thank *him* for the coyotes, too, she said.

"You want to see the pueblo," Luis said. He thought a moment. "I take you."

India would have thought he'd have Johnny take her, but perhaps it had to be an elder who escorted you. "When, Luis?" she asked, anxious to pin him down. "When?"

"Now."

Johnny came anyway. Luis frowned at him, but Johnny just looked straight ahead as if he hadn't noticed, wasn't paying attention. India thought it deliberate, that there was some silent argument going on between them.

The pueblo rose in two sections across an intervening river, five stories high on its north side. Stair-stepped adobe walls glowed with the patina of age and the burnishing sun high above the blood-red mountains. The "Blood of Christ" was what Sangre de Cristo meant. The Spanish had named the mountains to suit themselves, no matter what the Indians had called them previously. A Spanish mission stood at the pueblo entrance, and the Taos Indians were Christians. But, India had discovered, they blended Christianity with their own older, deeper religion, their tie to the spirit world and to the earth that gave them life. Their Catholicism sat rather lightly on them.

The pueblo had square rooms with flat roofs rising like upended nesting boxes, connected with doorways and ladders. Lines of drying clothes flapped in the breeze like bright flags, and children chased each other up and down the terraces.

Luis took her up the ladders to the door of a dwelling. He frowned at Johnny, but Johnny came along anyway. Inside, the room was smoky, the scent of pine logs and cornmeal in the air. It was dark, too, as if the red light playing on the outer walls wouldn't venture in. India was glad enough to go outside again, onto a wide, flat roof from which she could see across the river into the terraces of the south pueblo. The wind that whipped the laundry blew her divided skirt around her ankles and the wide brim of her straw hat down over her ears.

A ladder protruded a length of three rungs from a hole in the ground below them, and she peered curiously down into it. "What is that?"

"*Kiva,*" Luis said. "You don't know anything. And no, you cannot go in there."

"I do know," India said. "It's for religious ceremonies. Men only."

"Indians only," Luis said.

India looked wistfully at the ladder.

"No," Johnny said firmly. It was the first time he had spoken.

"I wasn't going to pester you about it," India said. "Thank you for bringing me here. It is a magical place." She watched the light wash the walls, warm as honey. A child peered at her from behind a pair of red long johns. "May I come back and paint here? If I don't go inside anything?"

"Since you have the manners to ask permission, yes," Luis said. "Don't paint people."

"Only imaginary ones," India promised. "Only gods and . . . spirits." She almost said "ghosts" but decided that would be a mistake. They took ghosts seriously, she had found. If you grieved for the dead too much, they might hear your grief and come back to you, Johnny had told her. It was a danger. It had happened to people, who were very happy for a few days—until the returned one's body began to rot. Maybe Johnny and Luis felt that portraits were too close to ghosts. She sighed and wondered if she could memorize their faces well enough to paint them later, elsewhere.

Johnny gave India his hand to help her down the

stairs. Then he tightened her pony's girth for her. "I'll take you home," he said, quietly solicitous.

"No," Luis said firmly. "I will take her home. Your mother needs you."

"You'd better watch out," Frank said sagely. "You shouldn't be stringing that boy along."

"What?" India looked up from rapt contemplation of the king snake in its box. He was just beginning to take shape on her canvas, coiled around the Sangre de Cristo Mountains. "What boy? Johnny? I'm stringing him along?"

"Yes, you are. He follows you around like a puppy. He holds your horse; he shows you wildflowers; he brings you snakes."

India wiped her forehead, under the brim of her straw hat, leaving a smudge of crimson lake along her right eyebrow. "That's not exactly a box of chocolates."

"It's what he thinks you'd like. Now he takes you out to the pueblo. The Indians don't take white people to the pueblo. They go anyway, but the Indians don't take them."

"Frank, what are you still doing here?" India abruptly demanded. "Aren't you supposed to go home?"

"Mike gave me a job. Fourth assistant gunslinger. Old Hawley went off back up the mountains looking for El Dorado."

"Well, keep your eye on Mike's camera then, not on me," India said. "Luis took me to the pueblo because he likes me. Johnny had nothing to do with it. I think they like my name. They think it's funny. And what makes it your business, anyway?"

"Look," Frank said in an exasperated voice, "you breeze on out here with your paints and set up camp. You're not Spanish, and you don't look like any white girl they've ever seen. You look just enough like an Indian to get a foot in the door. And when you're through out here, when Mike packs up, you're going to breeze back out again. You'd better discourage Johnny now."

India pointed a brush at Frank's nose. "The same way you've been discouraging the señoritas in the cantina in Taos? Or that woman who's visiting Fayette Millirons—who's got a husband in Kansas City? Unlike Fayette, her interest doesn't appear to be purely in art."

"She's a grass widow," Frank said mildly.

"She's ten years older than you!"

"Now who's trying to run whose life?"

"I just think you could do better," India said. "She giggles."

"She doesn't have any illusions of commitment, either. Which is more than I can say for poor Johnny. He's fallen in love with you, you idiot. God knows why," he added.

"Don't be a dog in a manger," India said airily.

"Hah!"

They glared at each other, uneasily aware that some feeling seemed to be there, on both sides. Neither was at the moment willing to contemplate *what*, exactly. They came from the same world, which made it a different proposition from a casual flirtation with a thirtyish grass widow or the silent adoration of an Indian boy. Any step they might take toward each other carried the danger of permanence.

"I am not stringing Johnny along," India said finally. "I have never given him the least reason to expect anything but friendship. I don't suppose you can say the same thing," she added. How far had he gone with the grass widow? It was unfair that men could do whatever they felt like while women were supposed to remain in well-behaved ignorance.

"Your snake's getting away," Frank said blandly.

"Oh!" India grabbed the king snake and tucked him back into his box, trying to coax him to coil around the warm rock she had provided. By the time she had him settled to her satisfaction, Frank was gone. "Of all the nerve," she muttered to the snake.

India finished her painting in a temper, which didn't seem to do it any harm, and was pleased with herself by the time it was finished. She stuck her brushes in a glass filled with the last of her linseed oil; the flaming sunset beckoned her to ride out in it and get some more. Mike and Eden—and Frank—wouldn't be back for an hour yet. A ride to the trading post half a mile away would be better than sitting under the grape arbor thinking of things she should have said to Frank. She liked the trading post, anyway. It was run by a pair of Navajo brothers and was pleasantly exotic.

India saddled the pinto and rode off. When she got to the trading post, she tied the pony to the rail outside and climbed carefully up the steps. One had a broken tread; all the locals had it memorized.

A fair number of Navajo were scattered in and around Taos, and India was beginning to know them. They were intrigued by her in the same way the Taos Indians, who were Tiwa, were. She looked as if she might be Indian but never quite like their own particular tribe.

The trading post sold dry goods and harnesses; hoes, rakes, and shovels; and foodstuffs, coffee, and candy, all in large quantities. People who lived a long way out didn't come in very often. In a glass-topped case was the pawn jewelry, necklaces, rings, and belt buckles, left as surety for credit. Leo Horseman nodded from behind the counter. He was a tall, lanky man with a wide mouth and a shock of thick, black hair. At India's request for linseed oil he produced a five-gallon barrel.

"Heavens, is that the smallest you have?" She looked at it dubiously.

"People out here don't paint pictures with it," Horseman said. "They paint barns with it."

"I could pour you off some in a can," his brother, Joe, said.

"Would it make it harder to sell the rest?"

"Naw, I just charge a little less." Joe, shorter and stockier than Leo, produced a coffee can and filled it. He put a scrap of oilcloth over the top and tied it with a string. "That'll get you home all right."

"How much?"

"Three cents."

India counted it out, thanked them, and left, carefully avoiding the missing tread. As she mounted her pinto she glanced back. The Horsemans were watching her, their heads together in a low murmur.

Casa Rosario was a cantina on a side road that wandered through Ranchos de Taos, a village to the east of the old city. It was seedy and smelled of frying lard and boiled chicken. India would have been uneasy had she known she was the subject of conversation there, too.

"You been in the sun too long," José said with disgust to Hawley, the old prospector whose place Frank had taken. "I can't bust up his camera, *estúpido*; I'm hired to guard it. Then I get fired, I can't watch nothing."

He seated his black hat, adorned with a band of silver conchos, more carefully on his head. His black leather vest was embellished with silver buttons. Hawley thought he looked like a magpie, bright and cocky. The prospector scratched the pale stubble on his chin. "If he ain't got a camera, you don't have to worry about him poking around all over."

"He has another one," José said. "And it's not Holt we need to worry about right now—he hasn't gone far out of town yet. It's that Johnny Rojas taking the Blackstone girl all over like he was trying to sell her the place. And that Blake fellow doesn't like it. *He* may start going with them, and he's likely to snoop if they don't fall on it themselves. I told you it wasn't a good place."

"You picked it," Hawley said, unwilling to let José rewrite events because they'd gone wrong. "And anyway, nothing's amiss yet. The Indians don't take people out there. They're afraid of it. Navajo are more afraid than Tiwa. Don't know why it doesn't bother you. Must be your daddy's blood." He studied José's face. "What the hell *was* he, anyway?"

"Shut up."

Hawley downed his whiskey and rattled his glass on the table. A Spanish barmaid wearing an apron in which she had plucked a chicken brought him another shot.

"You'll get too drunk to ride," José warned.

Hawley ignored him. He slurped the shot, and it dribbled down his chin. "You're the one made me quit the job," he said resentfully. "Want to send *me* down to the border, like as not get me shot. It's *your* fault Blake's still here. He's got my job."

"It seemed where you'd do the most good at the time," José said. "And Blake would still be here if he wanted to be. He's cousins with Holt. They're *all* cousins."

"Kin to everybody," Hawley grumbled. "Like you. Well, I just hope your mama's sister's husband's uncles, or whatever the hell they are, don't get me shot by the *rurales*."

"They'll meet you in Hermosillo, and just stay away

from the rurales; they got no quarrel with you. That's why I can't go."

"The rurales got a quarrel with everybody, what I hear. Not just big-britches Indians who think they're gonna start some kind of revolution."

José shrugged. "You don't want to, don't go. I can find plenty of others."

"Like hell you can," Hawley said. "Tiwa don't like Navajos so well, and you ain't even a whole Navajo. Who you gonna find to go down and talk to Yaqui Indians for you?"

"Push me any further and you'll find out." José snatched the shot glass out of Hawley's hand. "And you won't get any more drinks, either. Just get yourself down there and tell these people the cargo's safe. I'll meet them in Juárez with the next shipment."

"You got rocks in your head. That cargo might as well be live rattlers, and you got some eastern lady painter wandering around out in the desert with a lovestruck Indian showing her the sights." Hawley grabbed his glass back and downed its contents.

"I'll worry about her later," José said. "I have to talk to my family. I told you that."

"You got more aunts and uncles and cousins than any man I ever saw," Hawley growled. He stood up. "But you'd just as soon get *me* shot."

José sat down at the table and stuck a fork in the tamales his mother put in front of him. "Hawley's gone," he said.

His mother looked at him. "I don't like this. Only because Mary asked, I let you get mixed up in this."

"Mama, the Yaqui need the guns. Díaz and his rurales are trying to kill them all."

"I don't like that that's our trouble. I don't like that Mary marries away from our people."

"You did," José said bluntly. And wouldn't his life have been simpler if she hadn't? He knew his mother could read the unspoken words on his face.

"I was young," Rosa Horseman said. "Stupid. Stupid like you. I didn't know anything. My father warned me. Uncle Joe and Uncle Leo warned me. But they are like fathers to you now."

A real father would have been preferable. A real father who wasn't a cowboy drifter with so many strains in his blood he didn't *have* a people, who couldn't settle to be part of his wife's people. "Uncle Joe and Uncle Leo agree that we do this," José said.

"I don't like it," Rosa said flatly. "And I don't like it where you put those guns."

"Hawley says people are afraid of it," José said.

"Maybe you better be afraid, too. There are . . . things out there. It's not a clean place."

"Reservation superstition," José scoffed. He washed his tamale down with water and looked for another one. "I don't believe in that anymore."

"You better believe in it. You bring something back to this house, we all pay. We sicken and die. You believe."

"It's not even a Navajo place. Let the Tiwa worry about it."

"The Tiwa will worry about *you*," Rosa said darkly, "if they find you been there."

José looked uncomfortable. "That's what I got to make sure of. That they *don't* find out."

IX

Washington, D.C., May

"When is Frank coming home?" Midge Blake leaned over her mother's desk, between Cindy and the light, and accidentally bumped against the desk.

"Darling, don't do that." Cindy put her pen down on the blotting paper. "Don't loom over me like that. And for heaven's sake, stop jostling the furniture."

"Well, when is he?" Midge backed off a scant few inches. She seemed to feel that if she was not staring into someone's face, they were not listening to her.

Possibly true, Cindy thought with a sigh. She capped the pen and gave her daughter her full attention. "I don't quite know, darling. Michael has given him some sort of job, and he seems happy there. I think we should give him a little time. It's been hard for Frank to come home after all those years."

"He's not home!" Midge said, almost wailing. "He went away again!"

Cindy tried to think of what to say. "Dear heart, Frank is a grown man. No matter what he had done before, by now he would be old enough to be out of his mother's house and living on his own. You can't keep him

by you forever. Peter moved away long ago, and you
didn't act like this."

"It isn't the same," Midge said stubbornly. "I love
Peter, but he's not like Frank."

"You can't hang your whole life on Frank," Cindy
said, troubled. "You're nearly fifteen. In a few years you'll
be married and moved away yourself. People grow up, my
darling."

"Father won't ever come home then!" Midge blurted.
"That's why you quarreled with Father—over Frank. You
told him it was his fault Frank left, and you didn't want
anything to do with him until Frank came back. You
thought I was too young to understand, but I wasn't. And
now Frank's back, and you have to let Father come home,
and you're breaking your word!"

"That's enough." Cindy stood up. "I know how you
feel, but things aren't as simple as you think. And you
cannot tie your father to Frank."

Midge glowered at her. She swung the toe of her
black boot against the leg of the writing desk.

"You'll break that," Cindy said with another sigh.
"You need something to occupy you while school is out
for spring break. The Willoughbys have invited us to
come to their farm for a picnic after service Sunday. You
and I and the twins and Kathleen. They have the most
wonderful little farm just a few miles out of the city—
you'd never know it was there—with horses to ride and
chickens and geese and ducks and a new litter of pigs."

"Mother!" Midge's voice was scornful. "I'm not a
child."

"Well, the twins are," Cindy said. "And I need you to
help spell Kathleen. There are too many bulls to get trampled by and ponds to drown in out there. Someone will
have to watch each of them every minute, and my knees
aren't up to chasing four-year-olds." She rubbed her left

one ruefully—the first touch of rheumatism. And how had she gotten old enough for that?

"Well, I suppose if I have to go . . ." Midge muttered.

Cindy played her ace. "There's a litter of kittens, too."

The Willoughby farm lay just south of Alexandria in the northern Virginia horse country. Hugh Willoughby, a retired professor of chemistry from Georgetown, had been a gentleman farmer as well for most of his life, and Emmeline Willoughby was a plump woman with the placid nature required by such a husband. She greeted them in the driveway with the information that Hugh was down at the barn chasing pigs in his Sunday suit.

"One of the hired hands left the pen open—and Hugh didn't even bother to change his clothes. You'd think those pigs were children."

The twins stared around the farmyard with delight. A rooster stalked solemnly by, his tail held at a lordly angle. A table with a red-checkered cloth rested under an immense oak a few feet from the paddock fence. Three horses looked across the fence at them.

"I've had the ponies saddled," Mrs. Willoughby said, "and I thought we could take the little ones out on a lead. I know Midge rides beautifully, so I have something a little livelier for her." She smiled at Midge.

"Lovely," Cindy said. "What a treat. We don't get out in the country very often, but I was raised on a ranch in Oregon. Midge loved it there."

Midge tried to look discontented, but it was hard.

Hugh Willoughby came up from the barn, mud streaked and smelling of pigpen. He laughed and pantomimed a reluctance to greet them in his condition, then went off to change. When he returned, he had a wicker basket of kittens in one hand, a calico tabby cat following closely behind him.

"They're just about weaned," he said, looking mischievously at Cindy.

"Oh, Mother?" Midge asked hopefully as she and the twins bent over the basket.

"We'll see," Cindy said, amused. One minute Midge was fifteen heading for twenty and the next she was ten. If a kitten was all it took . . .

She took a deep breath and looked around her. She had an urge to run giddily through the horse pasture, through the flocks of ducks and geese, to stick bare toes in the cool pond. She felt younger than she had felt in many years.

The twins, tired of being told how to hold the kittens, spotted a flock of white ducks around the rim of the pond and ran after them with Kathleen in pursuit.

"Midge, dear, go and help her. Those children need a nurse apiece," Cindy added to Emmeline. "Their mother is coming for them at last, I think. The house will feel very empty, but it's time. They need her." Her voice conveyed the unspoken thought that it was high time Janessa remembered she was a mother. When the twins first came, before Frank had returned, Cindy had wished she could keep them forever. Since then, they had rather begun to make her feel her age. And she wanted to travel with Midge, take her to Paris and London, help her out of the somewhat gauche stage she was passing through.

After the twins had fed the ducks, ridden ponies, and seen the pigs, Emmeline Willoughby brought out chicken and peach cobbler, lemonade and a frothing pitcher of fresh milk. "Straight from the cow," she said cheerfully.

"Oh, Emmeline, what heaven," Cindy said. She didn't actually like milk and drank lemonade instead, but it was the *idea* of it. Midge gulped down a glass and grinned at her, a white rim of milk around her mouth as if she were five.

"From a *cow*?" one of the twins, Lally, said suspiciously.

"Sure, me darling, and where do you think milk comes from?" Kathleen asked, holding a cup out to her.

"Bottles," said Lally, screwing up her mouth.

"Oh, you city child." Cindy laughed.

Brandon sipped at the cup. "It tastes funny," he pronounced and put the cup down.

"Never mind," Emmeline said. "There's lemonade."

"Well, *I* like it," Midge said. "I'll have some more, please. And I have my kitten all picked out."

Kathleen drank Brandon and Lally's glassfuls and told them to think of the poor babies in the tenements who didn't have milk at all, much less fresh milk from the farm. Midge's kitten, a gray tabby with a white nose, climbed up her skirt to investigate the chicken. Somehow, without Cindy actually consenting, the kitten had moved in. Perhaps it was a good idea, Cindy thought. Mice had taken up residence behind the baseboards in the kitchen. A cat would give them a surprise. Cindy detached it from Midge's bodice and upended it. It was female.

"You'll have to teach her to catch mice, dear," Cindy said. "Make her earn her keep." The kitten squealed and tried to climb into the chicken. Cindy handed it back to Midge.

Lunch was quickly devoured. Feeling sated, elbows on the table, chin resting on laced fingers, Cindy took in the view. It had been a nearly perfect day, she decided. But the light breeze was getting stronger, and there were thunderheads in the south, moving closer. *It's going to pour in about half an hour*, she thought. Kathleen was already packing up the twins' things, one eye on the sky.

"I'm afraid we had better head back," Cindy announced reluctantly.

A small basket was found for the kitten to travel in, and then they piled into the buggy, declining the Willoughbys' invitation to wait out the storm.

"With luck we'll keep ahead of it," Cindy said. "And no one ever melted in rain." With a final good-bye, she clucked to the horse, and they headed down the drive.

They didn't outrun the storm, though, and by the time they were halfway home, Cindy was wishing she had listened to the Willoughbys. The rain came suddenly in torrents, and the wind whipped around them, buffeting the buggy and coming in under the wholly inadequate canopy. A flash of lightning lit the sky behind them, and rather too soon on its heels a clap of thunder rumbled like an avalanche. The twins shrieked and hid their faces in Kathleen's lap while Midge's kitten mewed dismally in its basket.

Lightning crackled again, thunder crashed, and then ahead of them as well as behind they saw the lightning's jagged imprint on the sky. Kathleen shrieked and then clapped her hand over her mouth.

"It's all right," Cindy said with more confidence than she felt. "We aren't very tall. It'll hit a tree if it hits anything. And we have rubber tires." But she shook out the reins and let the horse go faster, hoping he wouldn't lose his nerve entirely and bolt. They were all soaked to the skin.

They made it home without being struck by lightning, a fate that Kathleen had grown steadily more certain lay in store for them. Wearily, they staggered, sodden, into the house.

"Get these children dried off," Cindy told Kathleen. "And yourself, too. Midge dear, you come with me."

Lutie lit the oil stove in Cindy's bedroom, and they

stripped in front of it while the maid clucked and talked about hot broth and flannel next to the skin. The kitten was dried off and fluffed up and given a pillow for her bed, although everyone was quite aware that she wasn't going to sleep on it; she was going to sleep with Midge.

Lutie, having been informed that the kitten was to catch mice in the kitchen, looked at her dubiously. "And leave 'em half eaten back behind the stove, most likely. What're you going call her?"

"Diana, I think," Midge said. "To encourage her, since she's supposed to hunt. But only mice," she told the kitten sternly. "No birds. Not even starlings. And absolutely no cardinals." Diana put her head on Midge's chest, covered now with a dry chemise newly warmed in front of the stove, and purred.

To Cindy's relief the twins survived their soaking without so much as a sniffle. Janessa had wired that she would be there in five days, with month-late birthday presents for her children. Cindy had planned a party for the occasion—the twins were enthralled at the notion of two birthdays—and she would have hated to present them to their mother sniffling and dripping with colds. But Kathleen had developed a chill, and as a precaution Cindy and Lutie took over the care of the twins. When Midge began to feel clammy and complained of a sore throat, she was ordered into bed as well.

Thank goodness Janessa was coming, Cindy thought as she bustled between the twins and Midge's room, where Midge was tucked up in bed with Diana on her chest. She was better than a hot compress, Midge said, speaking carefully because her jaw was beginning to hurt.

Cindy peered down Midge's throat and saw nothing more than some redness and swelling. She was eating all right. If Midge had her appetite, there probably wasn't much wrong with her.

"Do you want me to call Dr. Amos, darling?"

"No!" Midge sounded horrified. "It's just a cold. And anyway, Janessa's coming tomorrow. She can look at me." Midge folded her arms stubbornly across her chest.

Cindy knew what the problem was. Midge was fifteen, and Dr. Amos was a man. The prospect of his seeing her undressed and thumping her bare chest was embarrassing. Midge wasn't above being caught kissing a boy in the barn, Cindy thought ruefully, and even letting him put his hand on that same chest, but being coldly examined in broad daylight by Dr. Amos was different. She kissed Midge's forehead. It felt less clammy.

"All right, darling. We'll wait for Janessa."

Cindy returned to the birthday preparations, seeing if there were enough gold paper hats and tin horns left over from the last party. The twins pattered after her happily, doubly excited by the second celebration and their mother's promised return from the hospital in Cuba.

Janessa Lawrence leaned wearily against the Pullman seat and watched the farms and pine woods of Virginia flash by the window. The force that had pulled her between the twins and Charley, the twins and her work, was still tugging, but she knew she would have to ignore it for a while. Yellow fever wasn't going to be cured by letting her children grow up without her, and Charley's research was too important to him. She couldn't ask him to come home, and she couldn't stay.

The train pulled into the Alexandria station. Janessa found that Cindy had sent her coachman to meet her. The drive was a short one, and as Janessa stepped down from the carriage under the portico of Cindy's house, the twins broke from a knot of shrieking children and flew across the lawn.

"Mama! It's our birthday!" They flung themselves at her. "Again!"

"We're five!" Brandon hugged her around the knees, making her stagger.

"No, we're not. We're still four. We had cake!" Lally jumped up and down, butting her head against Janessa's leg. "Mama's staying here," she said gleefully to Brandon. "Mama's home."

"Well, not quite, darling," Janessa said, kneeling. "I'm staying with you, but we're going home to our house in New York."

"With Daddy?"

Janessa sighed. "Not yet." She looked around the yard. "Where's Midge?"

"She's laid up," Cindy said as she came around the corner of the house. "She's got a bad throat. We all got soaked a few days ago. I wanted to call Dr. Amos, but she insisted on waiting for you. She's at the age where she's shy with men."

"I'll take a look at her as soon as I'm settled. And I can detach these barnacles." Janessa cuddled her clinging children, smiling, rubbing her nose against Lally's. As much as she already missed Charley, she was delighted to be with her children again.

A half hour later, when she came downstairs after examining Midge, she was no longer smiling. Janessa looked at the children shrieking on the lawn, at the crumbled cake and the sunshine glinting on their gold paper hats. She closed her eyes for a moment. *Oh, Lord, it isn't fair.* She opened them again, stepped purposefully onto the lawn, and found Cindy.

All Cindy had to do was look at Janessa's face to know that something was wrong. "Oh, no, what is it? She's worse." It wasn't even a question.

"It isn't a cold. I'm afraid it's diphtheria. And these children had better go home." And what about her own? Janessa looked with fear at Brandon and Lally cavorting in their gold hats.

Cindy's face lost its color. She flew into the house, leaving Janessa to move among the mothers, whispering the news, offering reassurance. She snatched the twins and looked at their throats but saw nothing. However, Kathleen—Kathleen was ill, too, Cindy had said.

When the last child had left, hand in hand with a panic-stricken mother, Janessa made a phone call to Dr. Amos, gave the twins over to Lutie, then went to see Kathleen.

"I'm so sorry, Dr. Lawrence," Kathleen said. Her voice was snuffling and bubbly, and she winced when Janessa pressed the glands under her jaws.

"Hush, dear." Janessa looked down Kathleen's throat. Like Midge's, it was red and swollen, and grayish white patches on the inflamed surface were rapidly thickening into a membrane that clung to the back of the throat.

Cindy came to the door, her hand to her mouth. "I would never have left her alone," she whispered. "She said she was feeling better."

"She may have. But this comes on quickly. I've telephoned Brice Amos and asked him to bring some antitoxin. Also, I need someone to go to the telegraph office. We'll have to send the twins to Charley's mother in Richmond. And I want Charley to come home." Janessa, trying to think, ran a hand through the pompadour that had come unpinned and hung over her eyes. "Everyone in the house should have antitoxin."

Almost as soon as Janessa had spoken, Dr. Brice Amos arrived. He looked at her weary face and said briskly, "How are you, Janessa? You look dreadful."

"I've been in Cuba," she replied. "It isn't a finishing school."

Standing at the side of Midge's bed, they prepared the antitoxin as they spoke. Brice's having once jilted Janessa had long ago been patched over, largely because Janessa would not now have married him had he asked—but it left them wary of each other.

"Have you traced the path of infection?" he asked in a low voice. He bent over Midge. "All right, dear, this will prick a little."

Midge nodded without speaking. Dark circles rimmed her eyes, and her face was pale. Her pulse was thready.

"I just got here," Janessa said.

Brice looked at the kitten curled purring on Midge's chest. "If I were you, I'd start with that," he said grimly.

Midge clutched the kitten. "No!" she whispered.

Janessa closed her eyes for a moment. "Cats can be carriers, dear."

"Then why is Kathleen sick?" Midge demanded. The congestion in her throat made it hard to get the words out. "Diana hasn't been with anybody but me."

"Where did you get her, dear?" Janessa asked gently.

"At the Willoughby farm." Midge wrapped both arms around the kitten.

"There have been no local cases that I know of recently," Brice murmured.

"What else did you do at the farm?"

Midge took a deep, bubbling breath. "Rode horses. Looked at the animals. Had a picnic."

"What did you eat at the picnic?"

"Chicken. Cobbler. Milk."

"Who had milk?" Brice pounced on this piece of information.

"Just Kathleen. Besides me."

"Not the twins?" Janessa tried to keep her voice even.

Midge gave her a faint smile. "They said it didn't taste good out of a cow. Kathleen drank theirs."

Oh, poor Kathleen.

"It could still be the cat," Brice said. "Ten to one the cat drank milk. Better to drown it and be certain."

"No!" Midge wailed.

"Haven't you any brains?" Janessa hissed at him. "We'll have to go out there, and if you can't keep your thoughts to yourself until we get back, I'll kill you."

They gave Kathleen a shot of antitoxin before starting for the Willoughby farm. Cindy, having been given a shot herself, was left as nurse. Janessa held her hand for a moment as she left, telling her, "Midge is calling for Frank. Send for him. And for Henry."

When they got to the farm and explained what they were doing there, Emmeline Willoughby ordered a hired hand to fetch her husband. "Oh, no," she whispered. "Oh, *not* our cow!"

Hugh Willoughby came at a run, his expression bleak. "I know exactly which cow it was. We just bought her. She's a good milker."

"Is she pastured with the rest of your herd?"

Hugh nodded. "Oh, dear Lord."

"We'll have to see the cow," Janessa said. "And the rest of the herd has to be tested. You two and all your hands need a shot of antitoxin, and you have to get that cow away from the rest right now."

"She's in the barn," Hugh said. "We were just getting set for evening milking." He put his hand on Janessa's arm. "Little Midge is sick?"

"I'm afraid so. And my children's nurse."

"Ah, God. I'll have the cow put down, poor old

bossy, as soon as you say to. But I'll tell you whose herd ought to be tested: the devil who sold her to me. I got too good a price. I ought to have known."

He rattled off the seller's name, and Janessa wrote it down, saying, "If they think their herd's going to be condemned, sometimes they'll sell them off fast before the health service can get to them. Where did you buy her?"

"At an auction," Hugh said. Brice groaned. "South of here," Hugh added.

"We'll track the seller down," Janessa said grimly. "And any other cows he's sold."

Emmeline Willoughby twisted her hands in distress. "I'll never forgive myself."

Janessa put a hand on her shoulder. "You'll have to scrub out the whole barn and house with carbolic, especially the kitchen. Anyone who has had contact with milk is at risk." The calico tabby twined around Janessa's ankles, and she remembered her other problem. She picked the cat up and stroked it. "They can be carriers, too," she said. "Like the cows. They don't get sick, they just carry the bacillus. This is a nursing mother. Have you been feeding her milk?"

"Of course." Emmeline stroked the tabby's head. She thought for a moment. "But not from the new cow!" she said triumphantly. "We were lucky. We didn't put the new one in with the herd until this morning. We—" She sniffled and dabbed at her eyes. "We always keep them separate until we're sure the old ladies won't bully the new one. I always feed Tabby a dip out of the bucket from the main milking."

"It's just a *cat*," Brice muttered under his breath.

Janessa turned on him. "Even if this one is a carrier, the kitten shouldn't be. If you take that kitten away from Midge right now, you'll— You just be *quiet*."

"We sent the milk to market, though," Emmeline

Willoughby said. "And had it for the picnic because the cream was so nice!" She began to cry.

"Has this morning's milk gone off yet?"

"Yes." She was clearly horrified. "The whole batch!"

"All right. We'll stop it if we can. And I want a blood sample from this cat. I'll let you know the results."

Janessa opened her bag while Brice rolled his eyes to indicate his opinion of testing cats instead of drowning them.

He commented further in the buggy on the way back to town. Janessa ignored him and counted up in her mind the things to be done: Notify the local authorities; test the milk of every cow in the Willoughbys' herd in the hopes that they wouldn't lose their entire dairy; find the source of the infected cow, and track all the cows from *her* herd; if possible, jail the seller for marketing diseased animals— if it could be proven that he knew. And hope to forestall an epidemic. But no, she reminded herself, she didn't have to answer that bugle. She wasn't in the Hospital Service now. Her job was to pull Midge and Kathleen through. Someone else would do the rest.

"That whole herd will have to be put down," Brice said, interrupting her thoughts.

"Not if they don't test positive."

"Ridiculous amount of work. Who's going to test all the cows?"

"I am, if nobody else will," Janessa snapped. "Haven't you got any sympathy for those poor people?"

"My job is to prevent disease in humans," Brice said in a reasonable voice. "Not to save cows and cats."

Further conversation was confined to the prognosis of Midge and Kathleen. Janessa knew Brice was worried about them.

They returned to find Cindy frantic. She flew out the door when the buggy drew up. "Oh, she's worse!" Cindy moaned. "They both are. We got the twins on the train to Charley's mother in Richmond, with Lutie. They'll be fine with her. Charley wired. He'll be here late tomorrow. Oh, please, come look at Midge!"

Janessa ran up the stairs. Midge was lying on her back, propped against pillows to help her breathe, with Diana clutched to her chest. Her eyes opened feebly at Janessa's approach, and when she saw her, she tried weakly to put the kitten under the covers.

"It's all right, darling. We aren't going to take her away. We've been out to the Willoughbys', and we think she's okay. I'm going to take a little of her blood to be tested, just to be sure. After I look at you. Can you open your mouth?"

Midge opened, gagging. The membrane across the back of her throat was thicker and yellowish. She rubbed at her nose, trying to rub away the bloody, dreadful-smelling discharge.

Janessa prepared another syringe of antitoxin for Midge. It was too early to tell if it would help. Janessa was miserably aware that its effectiveness decreased with each day that it was administered after the onset of the disease.

"Can you eat soup?"

"I tried," Midge whispered.

"Try some more. You have to have food."

"What about Kathleen? Mama won't tell me."

"We're going to look at her now. And I'm going to have some more soup sent up. And some juice and water."

Cindy hurried into the room past Janessa and Brice and took Midge's hand. Janessa gave her shoulder a reassuring squeeze; then she and Brice went to check Kathleen.

"We may have to go into that throat," Brice murmured on the stairs as they climbed the half flight to Kathleen's room.

"That's what I'm afraid of," Janessa whispered back. If the false membrane in the throat extended too far, it could block the air passages and choke the victim. But cut away, it left gaping red, raw passages that only grew a new membrane immediately, and raised the risk of other infections setting in.

Next to Kathleen's room, the twins' room stood open and darkened. "I didn't even get to explain to them *why*," Janessa said, conscience stricken. "I packed them off to Richmond just when I'd got back to them."

"Best thing you could have done," Brice said brusquely.

"You don't understand. I've been gone nearly a year, with just a few visits."

"Damn fool thing for a woman," Brice muttered. They went into Kathleen's room, and he bent his head over her. She was barely conscious, mouth open, breath bubbling in her throat, her nostrils closed by thick discharge. Hattie, the little maid sitting with her who had had diphtheria as a child, said, "I tried to clean her nose, but it's so thick, it won't come out."

"Never mind," Brice said briskly, getting to work on it. "Has she been able to take any food?"

"Not since midday."

He worked as he talked, skillfully clearing Kathleen's nose and filling another syringe with antitoxin. This was what he was good at, Janessa thought: cool, efficient medicine and sympathy for his patients—on his own terms.

Charley Lawrence arrived as promised, nearly at midnight the next evening, and found Brice just leaving.

"What's he here for?" he demanded.

"He brought me the report on the infected herd,"

Janessa said wearily, "and he's been looking after Midge and Kathleen. Kathleen's weakening, and we're afraid we're going to have to open Midge's throat. Oh, Charley, hold me!"

He gathered her in his arms. He was still in his Hospital Service uniform, the gold-braided cap askew over one eye. The rough blue wool and the heavy buttons scratched Janessa's cheek.

"You have to go to Richmond right away," she said into his chest. "I've sent the twins to your mother with Lutie, but Cindy needs Lutie here desperately, and they have to have someone they know with them. They know your mother, of course, but I mean someone they've *lived* with. And she's not prepared for two four-year-olds. You *have* to go."

"Of course I'll go," Charley said. "I'll go tomorrow. Slow down, you're babbling."

"You have to go *now!* What if you took it to them with you?"

"There aren't any trains tonight. Janessa, you're blithering. How long have you been on your feet without sleep?"

"I don't know. Charley, the babies— "

"You're going to bed," Charley said firmly. "I'll clear out in the morning."

"Antitoxin," Janessa said. She looked around wildly for her bag.

Charley dragged her upstairs by the wrist. "You're going to bed. I'll give it to myself."

X

In the morning Charley decided that Janessa ought to go to Richmond and he should stay with Cindy.

"Certainly not." Janessa forced herself to wake up from deep sleep. "I'm much more likely than you are to carry it to Richmond. And anyway, you won't work with Brice."

"Considering that you once wanted to marry that society's darling, it's possible that I don't care for the idea of your working with him, either."

Janessa yawned. "I wouldn't marry Brice if they paid me. Charley, he irritates me to death, but he's a good doctor. You'd probably punch him in the nose."

"I might," Charley admitted. "Despite the fact that if he hadn't treated you abominably I wouldn't be married to you myself, I still feel the urge to defend your honor. Besides, I don't like his looks. He's sleek."

"Charley, get out of the house. Now. Please. I'm terrified for the twins. Please just go."

"And I'm terrified for you."

"I won't be any happier if you die of diphtheria than if I do," Janessa assured him. "Charley, *please!*"

He gave in, primarily because he was out of ammunition. "Have you scrubbed everything with carbolic? Are you airing the rooms?" he asked as she hustled him out the door.

"Yes! I know my job! Just *go!*"

Cindy was shouting into the telephone. Peter had been notified and Frank sent for. Now she was trying for the first time in two years to reach Henry.

"No, madam," the clerk's voice came over the line in the slightly triumphant nasal tone in which "regulations" were always stated. "I cannot release the whereabouts of overseas personnel."

"I'm his *wife*," Cindy said through clenched teeth. "Our daughter is gravely ill. I *must* reach him."

"You can write to him in care of the War Office here in Washington."

"And how long will it take you to forward it?" Cindy asked, exasperated. "I want to *wire* him!"

"You can wire him personally, madam, at whatever return address he has given you."

"I don't *have* a return address!" Cindy snapped. "I want to speak to your commanding officer!"

The clerk sounded pleased to pass her along, but the maneuver gained her no further information. "General Blake is in intelligence, ma'am," a patient voice informed her. "We cannot release his whereabouts."

"I'm his *wife*," Cindy said again.

The colonel on the other end sounded sympathetic but wary. "Mrs. Blake, if the general hasn't seen fit to apprise his family of his whereabouts, he must have a reason."

"He did apprise me! I—I burned the letters."

"Oh." The colonel let a tactful silence fall. "If you will give me the message, Mrs. Blake, I will attempt to have it sent by cable. That is the best I can do."

Cindy gave it, then hung up the telephone with shaking hands. She buried her face in her palms as much to still her trembling fingers as to stop the sudden flow of tears. Why had she burned Henry's letters? Was this a judgment on her for refusing to reconcile with him? Cindy had never felt God operated in that way, but she was too terrified to discount what she knew a great many people would believe to be divine retribution.

"I'm sorry!" she whispered in a frenzied, fervent prayer. "Please, let me find him."

And how long would it take for the War Office to cable him? If *they* even knew where he was exactly. Often they didn't; she knew that from previous experience. How hard would they look for him? Would they just wait until he surfaced? Who would know where he was? Edward Blackstone! Something from Edward—

Cindy ran to her desk and scrabbled in the drawers. There had been a long, chatty letter from India's father, thanking Cindy for her sponsorship of his daughter, regaling her with odds and ends of family news, worrying about India's future, telling a few good stories, asking if Cindy was certain that India would not be exposed to detrimental influences. Somewhere in there had been . . .

Cindy found the letter, put her spectacles on her nose, and scanned Edward's sprawling hand.

We had a letter from Teddy Montague—Lady Theodora—not so long ago. Do you remember her? Lady explorer. British. Takes off for who knows where at the drop of a hat. Fine woman. I don't mind saying I've been in a tight spot or two with her and glad to have had her there. She's in the Philippines just now. Dashed silly place to be while there's a war on, if you ask me, but that's Teddy. I don't quite know whether I ought to mention it or not—don't want to bring up a painful subject (keep hearing scuttlebutt and don't know how things really sit with you and Henry)—but thought perhaps you'd like to know. Teddy says she saw Henry there, before the Spanish pulled out. He was in Emilio Aguinaldo's camp, and so was she. Must have been a lively time. Just before the balloon went up, he had her thrown off the island. She was quite annoyed about it, although I gather it was for her own safety. So it appears that Henry is in the thick of things. Of course, I'm sure you knew all that. But just in case you mightn't have had word . . .

Cindy put the letter down. The news that he was in the Philippines was no help. But Teddy Montague . . . Teddy might very well know where to find him.

If she could find Teddy.

She ran to the back door and shouted for the boy who groomed the horses.

"Take this to the telegraph office. As fast as you can go." She scribbled on a sheet of notepaper: TO EDWARD BLACKSTONE, M BAR B, OKLAHOMA TERRITORY. DESPERATELY NEED TO FIND HENRY. WHERE IS TEDDY NOW?

No use worrying about saving her pride. It didn't matter what Edward thought, any more than the operator who had undoubtedly been listening in on the telephone. "Wait for an answer," she called after the boy, then went back upstairs to sit with Midge.

The sickness seemed to cling to the air in Midge's room.

"Daddy?" Midge opened her eyes.

"We're sending for him, darling."

Midge's hands stroked Diana's fur over and over again, automatically, unceasingly. The kitten purred bliss-

fully. Diana had a warm body to sleep on; of course she
was happy, Cindy thought. You couldn't expect a cat to
understand. Did the stupid little thing know how close it
had come to being drowned? Janessa was right, though—
that might have pushed Midge over the edge. *Why my
baby and not a cat?* Cindy thought furiously then, agonized by Midge's gray skin and hollow eyes.

The stable boy came back with a wire from Edward
Blackstone: LONDON, I THINK. He gave an address.

Cindy sent the boy off to the telegraph office again,
with a wire for Teddy Montague: URGENT. MUST CONTACT
GENERAL BLAKE. DAUGHTER ILL. PLEASE CABLE WHEREABOUTS.

Night crept through the windows while she waited,
one hand on Midge's arm as if she could somehow tether
her daughter to life by her touch. Even if Henry came, it
might be too late. If it wasn't too late, it would be unnecessary. By the time he sailed home from the Philippines,
Midge would have recovered—if she was going to. Cindy
closed her eyes, squeezing back tears, assailed by a vision
of calling Henry home for a funeral. If she did, she did. It
was his grief, too. He had a right to it. And she had a right
not to bear it alone.

Finally the boy came back, and Cindy snatched the
yellow envelope from his hand. It wasn't from Teddy.
DON'T KNOW GENERAL BLAKE. VERY SORRY. MY SISTER IS IN HONG
KONG. SCOTTISH HOTEL.

Cindy moaned; Midge didn't even hear it. Was she
mad to try to find Henry this way? Wouldn't a sensible
person just leave it to the War Office?

Cindy answered her own question. "I don't *trust*
them," she whimpered. Quickly she wrote another telegram, this one to Teddy, and gave it to the boy. "One
more try. Please?"

The boy looked at his mistress's tear-splotched face,

trickles running down the lines beside her mouth, and at Midge's chalky one, and fled, terrified.

Near dawn, Janessa came in, her face taut. "Kathleen's failing," she whispered to Cindy. "I've wired her aunt, the only family she has, and sent her the fare."

"Oh, no." Cindy looked at Midge to see if she had heard. She gave no indication of it. Whether to be relieved or frightened by that, Cindy didn't know. Midge's hands were still now, laced across Diana's fur but not moving.

Janessa detached the kitten and put her in Cindy's lap. She bent over Midge and felt her pulse, then cocked an ear and listened to her slow, bubbling breaths. "Has she been having more difficulty?"

"About the same. Kathleen—is it her lungs?"

"No, it's her heart. The membrane hasn't advanced very far, but her body just won't stand up to the disease. I doubt her heart's ever been good. She had a hardscrabble childhood. I think her mother was malnourished most of the time and so were the children."

Cindy looked at Midge; Midge who had had her diet supervised, her hours of fresh air and sunlight monitored, who had been vaccinated for smallpox, inspected for toothache, and had had her every baby cough attended to. Tears of sheer terror rolled down her mother's face.

"No word from Frank?" Cindy whispered.

"He's coming," Janessa said. "He wired yesterday. Don't you remember?"

"Yesterday," Cindy murmured.

"*You're* going to bed," Janessa said promptly. "And this just came for you." She pulled an envelope from her apron pocket. "I hope it's what you want."

Cindy pulled it open. It was a long, extravagant cable

from Teddy Montague. Cindy's first thought was "How can she afford it?" She stared, trying to make sense of it.

> NO IDEA WHEREABOUTS GENERAL BLAKE. HAVE
> PUT DOGS ON HIS TRAIL IN PERSON OF MY ASSISTANT
> PAUL KIRCHNER. PAUL VERY GOOD AT THAT. WILL FIND
> HIM AND PUT HIM ON SHIP FOR STATES IN SACK IF
> NECESSARY. TELL DAUGHTER HE IS COMING AND GET
> WELL. THEODORA MONTAGUE.

Blankly, Cindy handed the paper to Janessa. Janessa read it and gave an involuntary chuckle. "I've met Lady Teddy. And Paul Kirchner. If she says they'll find him, I'd put my money on them and not the War Office."

"It will take weeks for him to get here," Cindy whispered.

"I know," Janessa said and rested her hand on Cindy's shoulder. She noticed how very sharply Cindy's collarbone stood up. "I'll sit with Midge. She'll very likely sleep till late morning. Go and sleep yourself. I'll call you if there's any change. As soon as Lutie gets home we'll have her to spell us."

She pushed Cindy out of the room and sat down by Midge's bed, trying to count again the things to be done: Kathleen's aunt to be met at the station later that afternoon, Frank the day after tomorrow. . . . Kathleen wouldn't last until day after tomorrow. Charley would be in Richmond by now—Lally and Brandon would have him, at least. Janessa pictured him and the twins, out of harm's way, wrestling on the wide sweep of his mother's lawn.

Janessa closed her eyes. There were too many people clinging to her. It made her head swim. Charley and the twins, Midge and Kathleen, the Hospital Service, and her Women's Hospital back home in New York. Cindy. And now Eileen Riley, Kathleen's aunt, was arriving. She was a nurse in the Hospital Service, so she knew what was what. But it wouldn't make it easier.

Lutie arrived at lunchtime, all businesslike, and Eileen Riley in the late afternoon, her clothes rolled into the shabby black leather bag she always took on assignment. Janessa met her at the door, answering the question in her pale eyes.

"She's still holding on. I keep hoping, but she's so weak."

Eileen followed Janessa up the stairs, looking around with a certain amount of awe. The Blake house was far grander than the small one Janessa and Charley rented on Staten Island. "No wonder she wrote such happy letters from here," was all she said.

Janessa took her into Kathleen's room and sent Hattie to her own to sleep. "This is Kathleen's aunt, Miss Riley. She'll be staying. She's a nurse."

Hattie nodded wearily and crept up the stairs to her room.

Eileen sat gently on the edge of the bed. "Ah, my poor love. She's my sister Mary's daughter. Poor Mary. It's a blessing she's dead and gone herself and doesn't know." She stroked Kathleen's hand. "I'll stay by her. You have the child to see to."

"There's broth in the bowl on the table," Janessa said. "If you can, get her to eat. If you want more or you want it heated, just ring that bell, and Lutie will send it up. Supper will be in an hour or two, and someone will come and spell you. I won't have anyone eating in the sick rooms. It's taking too much of a chance, even though we've all had the antitoxin."

She returned to Midge's room, monitoring herself as she went. Throat sore? Glands tender? Sniffles? No.

None. Next she looked at Cindy's throat and pressed her fingers under her jaw. Cindy sat dully and didn't protest.

Midge's breath was labored and thick with the mucus that clogged her throat. Her nose was crusted almost closed, and she breathed open-mouthed, struggling for air. Janessa set about cleaning her nose while Midge whimpered and batted at her hands. She stuck a tube with a rubber suction bulb on it down Midge's throat.

"You have to lie still, honey. You have to let me get this stuff out." Midge gagged as the tube drew the mucus and some of the membrane from her throat. Janessa wiped the tube on a cloth and inserted it again. "These rags have to be burned," she said over her shoulder to Cindy.

"How is she?" Cindy whispered.

"The membrane is shedding small pieces," Janessa said, struggling with Midge. "That's a good sign. And she's a strong girl. But someone has to be with her every minute."

"I'm so scared. She sounds as if she's choking to death."

"That's the danger. We have to keep her throat clear. If the membrane grows any farther down, we may have to cut it out. But it grows back so quickly that unless we can arrest the disease, it won't help."

"I should have known," Cindy whimpered. "I thought it was just a cold. We got caught in the rain. I'll never forgive myself."

"Don't start that," Janessa said briskly. "You couldn't have known, and you won't do Midge any good. Just *stop*! I mean it. We don't have time for that!"

Cindy flinched, but she brought her self-recriminations to a halt. She sat instead by Midge's bedside, cleaning her nose and clearing her throat as she had seen Janessa do. Cindy sat with Midge for hours, repeating the process. Then suddenly, despite everything, Midge couldn't draw a breath. It was late at night; Cindy had lost all track of time. Midge made a terrible wheezing noise, and she opened her eyes wide, panic-stricken. She struggled to sit up, her hands grasping at her throat.

"*Janessa!*" Cindy shouted into the hallway. She grabbed the suction tube and forced it down Midge's throat while Midge fought with her in fright.

"*JANESSA!*"

Cindy cleaned the tube on the pile of rags that lay beside the bed and forced it down Midge's throat again. When she pulled it free she could see pieces of the membrane clinging to it. Midge coughed and gagged and spit up more. But she took a deep whistling breath, and her color began to come back.

"Here, spit it out." Cindy held a clean rag under Midge's mouth. "Cough it up."

Midge's shoulders shook with a racking cough, and more came up. Cindy held her daughter's shoulders and stroked her hair. She heard flying footfalls in the hallway, and Janessa appeared, white-faced, at the door.

"I couldn't breathe," Midge whispered. She seemed terrified.

Janessa looked down her throat. "The whole membrane's loosening," she said in a voice of exhausted relief. There was a catch at the back of her throat that made Cindy look at her sharply. But Janessa went on, with a smile for Midge, "You started to breathe it in. You'll be all right now. Just be careful and cough it up as it comes."

Janessa stood up shakily, and Cindy went to the door with her. "Is she—? Is this the turning point?" she whispered.

Janessa nodded. She leaned wearily against the door-jamb in the dimness of the hallway. "I think so. She's not out of danger, but it's a good sign."

"You sounded . . . The way you spoke in there, I was afraid—"

"Kathleen's dead. I was with her when I heard you call. She—she just gave out. It was very sudden."

"Oh, poor Kathleen." Cindy wiped her eyes. "She was such a good girl, so good with the twins."

"I have to go back," Janessa said. "Eileen. I have to see to Eileen."

Someone to see to, she thought as she went back down the hall. Always someone to see to. How well had she seen to Kathleen, always so good with the twins? How would she tell them? She stopped, leaned her forehead against the cool plaster of the wall, and let the tears run down her face. How could you see to everybody, all at once?

Eileen came out of Kathleen's room. She had turned out the light. "How is the child?"

"Better. The membrane is loosening."

"I'm glad for that."

"Oh, Eileen . . . I am so sorry." Janessa turned a stricken face to the nurse.

Eileen nodded slowly. "Life is hard and not easily mended. I wish she could have married and had babes of her own." She paused. "I'd take it kindly if you'd help me with the arrangements. I don't know the city or a soul in it, but she must have a funeral mass."

"Of course."

"And right away, too. We won't take any risks of infection. She'd understand that." The nurse knew what was needed and spoke with the certainty of her profession.

"Yes, of course," Janessa said again. "Can you—can you sleep till daylight?"

"I'll sit up with her awhile. And say the rosary for her. There's no one to say it but me."

"You teach it to me," Janessa said, "and then there will be two of us."

Kathleen's funeral mass was said in the small parish church where she had attended mass for the past year. It was smoky with incense, and the sun coming through a stained-glass window depicting a kneeling Christ colored the altar in red and blue light.

Cindy was at home with Midge, too terrified to leave her, but Lutie had come, as had the two maids and the stable boy. The Willoughbys were there as well, their sorrow evident on their faces. Brice Amos had come, something he would not have done if Janessa had not telephoned him and given him no excuse. And much to her pleasure and Eileen's openmouthed astonishment, Theodore Roosevelt, the governor of New York, appeared just before the mass.

He shook Eileen's hand gravely. "Sheer chance I happened to be in Washington. Grateful that I was. Your niece was a fine woman with the children. Mrs. Blake allowed her to help me out more than once when we've been in town. Always been grateful. We have quite a brood, you know. Tragic thing." He sat down several rows behind Eileen and Janessa.

The Latin words of the mass were incomprehensible to Janessa, but Eileen knew them by heart and seemed to find comfort in them. Her head was bowed under her black bonnet, and she twisted and twisted the beads of her rosary between her black-gloved fingers. Janessa tried to concentrate on the prayers, whatever language they were being said in. She felt bereft and adrift without Kathleen, but her mind would not stay on mourning. It roved through a catalog of questions and ached immeasurably for Charley. *I must be completely unnatural,* she thought, *leaving my children for this long, but they don't*

*seem to have taken harm from it. I'm home now. What do I
do now?*

Someone slid into the pew beside her. "You're supposed to count off prayers on that thing, not mangle it," a
masculine voice whispered.

Janessa glanced at her hand and found that she had
been wrapping her borrowed rosary around and around
her knuckles. She looked at the speaker in the dimness,
for a moment puzzled before realizing it was Frank Blake
—older, more muscular, not at all the boy she remembered.

"I just got in," he whispered. "Mother sent me along
here. Poor little Kathleen."

The funeral mass ended, and the coffin was carried to
the waiting grave in the Catholic cemetery. Janessa found
Frank beside her, one arm out to steady her. "You look
like you'd blow away in a high wind," he said.

"I may," she said. *How unlike me.*

Frank took charge of packing Kathleen's belongings,
with a grieving Eileen who seemed more comfortable
with him than with Janessa's formidable aunt, and of putting Eileen on her train. That evening he sat in Midge's
room, letting her hold his hand, telling her silly jokes,
reading to her when she was restless. Even Cindy, who
was sitting with him, could find no fault with her son.

"Have you told Father?" was the only thing he asked
about Henry.

"I've sent for him," Cindy said softly. "They're trying
to find him. It's . . . you know he may be anywhere.
Frank, you and he—"

"Will have to get along," he finished.

"I want Father." Midge's voice was still a croak. She
looked woefully up from the pillow. She clutched the kitten under one arm. She had taken Kathleen's death badly,

and now, slightly on the mend, was afraid to be alone for more than an instant.

"You will have him when we find him, Pudd'n," Frank said. "But you'll be fifteen before he gets here. What do you want for your birthday? A black velvet gown? A tiara? The head of John the Baptist?"

"Frank!" Cindy said, shocked.

But Midge chuckled. "I'll never be a femme fatale," she said wistfully. "I don't think Salome had freckles."

"No, but she had a nasty nature," Frank said.

"And I have such a sweet personality." Midge made a face.

"I'll tell you a secret," Frank said. "Young India Blackstone isn't pretty either, not by all your women's magazines' standards. But she stands out in a crowd. And all the men want to dance with her."

"Oh, her." Midge looked suspiciously at Frank. "I don't want to talk about her. I don't want to look like her, either."

"Time for the patient to sleep," Janessa said, sweeping Frank out of the room.

He came back the next day with an armload of birthday presents, leading a procession of Cindy, Janessa, Lutie, and Hattie singing "Happy Birthday" and bearing a cake aflame with candles.

The whole household was different since Frank had come, Janessa thought. He had eased the air of strain and tension. How much it took out of him to do it, she had no idea. The night before she had caught him in Kathleen's room, sitting with his head in his hands. He hadn't been in love with her, Janessa was certain, but she had been with him, and he knew it. Now he gave everything he had to keeping Midge—someone else who loved him—afloat.

He brought out several presents and watched gleefully while she unwrapped them: a pearl choker (he must have spent every cent he had earned in Taos, Janessa thought); a book of jokes; and a rhinestone collar for Diana, who immediately tried to claw it off over one ear, writhing in circles on the floor.

"Mama, why didn't the maid give the goldfish fresh water?" Midge grinned at her mother over the joke book.

"I have no idea, darling."

"Because they hadn't drunk up what she gave them yesterday!"

Frank and Midge howled with demented glee while Cindy smiled at them. Midge leaned over the edge of the bed and scooped up Diana, who had got her paw stuck in her new collar.

"Maybe you should keep it for state occasions," Frank suggested.

"For when I have visitors," Midge said with a sigh. "If I ever do."

"You can't have visitors until you aren't contagious," Janessa said.

"But when's that going to *be*?"

"Soon, I hope." Janessa was resolutely noncommittal.

Something in her expression seemed to strike Frank. Leaving Midge opening a box of chocolates from Lutie and a handkerchief, hand embroidered, from Hattie, he pulled his mother to the door.

"What is going on? Why is she still contagious? She looks a hundred percent better."

"We don't know," Cindy said, keeping her voice low. "Janessa's been testing her, and the infection is still there somewhere. We thought the cat . . . but—"

"The cat wouldn't keep Midge infected, not after she's gotten over it. It might infect other people, though."

"I know. It was just a last-ditch thought. But Janessa's tested the cat."

"Then where's it coming from?" Frank demanded. "Poor little soul, she's about worn out."

Cindy's temper snapped. "You do not get to come home and criticize the way things have been handled in your absence! Although I suppose I should get used to it. Your father is bound to do the same thing."

"Whoa!" Frank said. He pulled her into the hall. "You're so wrought up over Midge and over the idea of having to face Father again that you're just about crazy. And I'm not such a puttyhead that I'm going to get into this argument with you. Now, back off and tell me how serious this lingering infection business is."

"I don't know!" Cindy moaned. "Janessa won't talk about it, but she's worried. Doctors never tell you anything, even ones who are family!" She rested her head against Frank's chest and sobbed.

Time to corner the doctor, Frank thought, and stick needles in *her* until she talked to him. He lurked outside the back porch until Janessa came down, as he knew she would, to burn the dirty rags in the incinerator. It was just dusk, but already warm and misty. An early summer, Frank thought. A mockingbird in the hedge was running through his repertoire. Just then Janessa came down the steps, and Frank lifted the incinerator lid for her.

"I want a consultation," he said mildly.

"Throat sore?" Janessa demanded. "Neck tender?" She reached for him.

"Not in the least," Frank said, sidestepping. "I'm in the pink. What's Mother telling me about a lingering infection in Midge?"

"It's hard to say."

"Don't dodge." Frank took a match from his pocket,

lit it, and dropped it into the incinerator. The rags curled as the flames ate them.

"I'm not," Janessa said indignantly. "Frank, I don't *know*, and I can't bear to tell your mother that. There's a pocket of infection somewhere. She could have a relapse. We're not out of the woods yet."

Frank groaned. "I don't think I could stand it if something happened to the baby."

"You're doing her more good than anything. Just having you here makes her so happy it helps her get well."

Frank groaned again. "I can't stay. Not once she's well. Not if my father comes home. I want him to, mind you, for Midge and my mother. And me, I suppose. I don't want him on my conscience. But I doubt we can coexist."

"You don't have to live here, for goodness' sake," Janessa said. "Just show up periodically and be filial."

"Have you ever tried to be filial to my father?"

"Not since the recent unpleasantness," Janessa murmured. "I always got along well with him before then. I was very fond of him."

Frank sat down on the steps. "I suppose I'm exaggerating. I really think it's just me. I was supposed to be the one who'd fulfill all his hopes and expectations, and when I didn't, there was hell to pay."

"He didn't react that way to Peter? He wanted Peter to go into the army, too."

"I know. But Peter hated it so. And there was always me. I was such a good little soldier. Father put all his bets on me."

"What happened?"

"I found there was more out there in the world. I discovered it rather suddenly and behaved rashly. I wasn't to cross the threshold again until I came to my senses."

"Well, you'd better figure out what to do about it," Janessa said grimly. "Your father *has* to come home. Your sister may die, and not one of the three of you will ever forgive yourselves if you've been squabbling like children when it happens."

XI

Manila, The Philippines, June

General Henry Blake trotted, whistling, up the walk to his house, past a trellis bright with scarlet bougainvillea. The shell-paned windows on the upper floor stood open to let in the evening breeze, and the inside looked cool and inviting. Even the pink walls didn't annoy him as they used to. They seemed pleasantly eccentric, like Manila itself.

Estrella glided out of the shadows as he came through the front door and put a gin rickey in his hand. He sank down on a huge Spanish chair of dark oak, and she knelt and pulled his boots off. A pair of raffia slippers lay on the floor beside the chair. Henry brushed Estrella's cheek affectionately. Exactly how she had moved in Henry was not quite sure. Suddenly she just seemed to be there, a beautiful convenience.

"I have to leave again tomorrow," he said heavily. "I don't know how long I'll be gone."

"You never know," Estrella said cheerfully. "Or you don't tell *me*."

"I can't tell you. You know that."

"Mmm-hmmm." She nodded as she picked up his boots, then set them in the kitchen to be polished by

Arturo, who had now been taught to do it properly. Returning, she stood behind Henry, kneading his aching shoulders. "It doesn't matter," she said softly. "I have the shop to keep me busy. I will be here when you get back."

This isn't fair to her, Henry thought, feeling guilty. He had that thought about once a day, but it didn't change anything. And why would any man who had Estrella to wait on him hand and foot, and to light his nights, want to send her away for a wife who didn't answer his letters? For Estrella's sake? For her own good? She wanted to be here, that much was plain. He had told her it couldn't be permanent; she knew that.

So it was all right, and he could have someone to love him and see to his meals and keep him from loneliness. It was all right.

Estrella came and sat on the carved arm of his chair, and he pulled her into his lap, burying his face in the patchouli scent of her hair. She laughed, a liquid murmur like water. "Disgraceful Enrique. What if Arturo comes in?"

"Arturo knows when he had better not come in," Henry said. He ran his hands along her thighs, under the whispering yellow pineapple silk. Her stiff gauze sleeves brushed his nose. The house was growing dark, lit only by the flickering coconut-oil lamps.

Estrella hopped from his lap and tugged at his hands. "Come. Everything is ready for your bath. And dinner is ready when you want it."

He followed her up the stairs and stood docilely while she unbuttoned his khakis and stripped them off him. A tub filled with cool water sat in the middle of the bedroom, and he stepped into it, luxuriating in the feel of it and in the notion of Estrella watching him. That had made him uneasy at first—in America one wouldn't think it quite nice. Shocking even. In Manila, in the warm, soft

night and the slow undulating shadows of the oil lamp and
with Estrella waiting, a towel over one arm, it seemed
permissible. Like the raffia sandals, Henry thought with
an inward chuckle, as close to going native as he would
ever get.

He scrubbed himself, enjoying the cool water and
the fleeting sensation of being clean. In Manila's muggy
temperature, even now in the "dry" season, he would be
sweat-stained again with the slightest movement. He
scrubbed soap through his pale hair and upended the can
of fresh water over his head, spluttering as he did so.

Then he stood, and Estrella brought the towel and
wrapped him in it. As he stepped out onto the raffia floor
mat, a sea breeze sighed through the opened windows,
fluttering the mosquito nets on the bed. Henry dropped
the towel and reached for Estrella's blouse, tugging at the
buttons. She slid out of her filmy clothes, her body a cool
yellow flame in the oil light.

Over her shoulder Henry could see stars beginning
to come out, blurred by the mosquito netting. He had a
sense of being in a foreign country that was different from
the one he had reluctantly inhabited a month ago. Estrella
was a strange land unto herself, but she was also the Philippines, tutelary goddess of whatever had lured the Americans there and proved so reluctant to let them go.

Estrella turned in his arms, drawing his mouth down
to hers. She, too, was caught here, Henry thought, in the
net that had caught the Spanish—her father among them,
a virtuous don who had taken a Tagalog wife on the as-
sumption that here he would stay, then found himself
called home to Spain, where a Tagalog wife was unaccept-
able. Henry felt Estrella's soft breasts against his skin, and
his bones turned to water, much as the Spanish don's
must have done.

*   *   *

At full dark, with the moon slanting watery bars of light through the window and the bowl of oil nearly burned out, they pushed the mosquito netting aside and arose.

"Dinner," Henry said. He grinned. "Now I'm hungry. I could eat a horse."

Estrella looked at him oddly.

"An American expression," he explained, laughing. "It doesn't translate, I suppose. Eat a horse." He said it in English. "It means I am hungry enough to eat anything."

"Eat a horse," Estrella repeated thoughtfully. She was learning some English from him and proud of it.

They tiptoed down the stairs, laughing like truant children at what Arturo must have thought of them before he had presumably gone home to his own house in Tondo. On Estrella's instructions, the cook had left a dinner waiting: the ubiquitous chicken but without the peppers and garlic, seasoned instead with just a little soya sauce. A dish of papayas and honey sat beside it, both covered with cloths to keep the flies out. The cook hadn't seen what harm a few flies did, but Estrella had had a loud argument with her in Tagalog, and now cloths were put over the food.

Henry ate ravenously while Estrella served herself a daintier portion, moving the oil lamp so that he could see his plate without the flame being too close to his elbow or its flicker shining in his eyes. He was used to servants who took care of him but not to being waited on by his lover. There was an intimacy about this that was almost more sensual than sex. And there was something comforting about it, too, a refuge in being taken care of that he had not found before. Henry Blake was the one who took care of people, not vice versa. And yet here was Estrella, not taking charge but taking care, seeing to his wants, finding no fault, just loving him. *I have earned this,* Henry thought, putting aside his qualms. *I deserve this, and I will have this.*

Estrella took his plate after he had eaten. "When do you leave in the morning?"

"Early," Henry said and groaned. "Dawn. And that means out of the house by dawn."

"I'll put up something to take with you, then. Cook won't be here that early." She looked thoughtful for a moment, then added, "I will tell her and Arturo not to come back until I send for them. They are a waste of your money when you are not here."

"What about you?"

"I have a house," Estrella said. "I have the shop, too. When you find General Aguinaldo, come to the shop and tell me, and I will come back and send for Cook and Arturo."

"What makes you think I am looking for General Aguinaldo?" Henry's voice rose sharply.

"All the Americans are looking for Aguinaldo," Estrella said.

"Not at every moment," Henry said firmly. "Estrella, you cannot pry into what I am doing when I'm gone. It's official army business. I cannot tell you."

Estrella hung her head. "I know. It is only that I hope always you don't find him."

Henry looked at her with a faint unease. If her sympathies were with the rebels, it made her a dangerous mistress for an officer in intelligence. Until now she had maintained a careful unconcern with politics, wanting only for the fighting to end. "Estrella . . ."

She looked at him sadly, her long black hair flowing down her back, her pineapple-silk wrapper askew over one shoulder. The playfulness had gone out of her face like a candle blown out. "I am afraid that when your army has captured General Aguinaldo, there will be no more need for you here."

Henry let his breath out carefully. "I wouldn't worry. I'm likely to be here a good long while. General Aguinaldo isn't the only fly in our ointment." That didn't translate either, he saw by her expression. "He is not the only difficulty we have to contend with. It's more than likely that I will be assigned here for quite some time." *Where else do I have to go?*

Estrella's face lit again. "You would stay? After there is a peace?"

There won't be peace for a long time, at the rate we're going. "I think it will take us a while to get to peace." And what after that? Would he really stay here? Why not, damn it, with a woman who wanted him?

Henry stood, gently closed his hands around Estrella's wrists, and pulled her up from her chair to him. "But tomorrow I have to go away." He kissed her. "So let us make sure"—he kissed her again—"that I remember why I want to come back."

With any luck, this time they would have Aguinaldo. Henry crouched beneath the spiky form of a papaya tree and peered through the thicket. Lieutenant Estep beside him wriggled like a man who suspects a bug has gone down his shirt and dare not make any noise about it. Emilio Aguinaldo was supposed to come to this barrio to confer with the headman, who had been supplied with enough money to render him a "civilized" Filipino in the Americans' view. He was the "bait" to entice Aguinaldo.

Behind the thickets on all sides of the barrio was a company of soldiers, carefully watching the dirt trail by which Aguinaldo was supposed to come. They had been there since morning and were restive in the noon heat, but no one knew when the rebel general might appear.

In the meantime, the barrio went about its business. Women and children scooted up and down the ladders that were the only access to huts raised five to ten feet off the ground. The men seemed to have comparatively little to do and strolled up and down the rutted dirt street that ran through the village or sat in solemn conversation under a nipa palm. Crops grew here merely by scratching the ground, there were fish in the river, and rain was plentiful. The women did the work of preparing the food, leaving little to be done unless one had acquired a taste for European luxuries, a rarity in the barrios. No wonder the Americans complained that the natives they hired worked only when they felt like it. It was difficult to civilize a population that believed it was lacking nothing.

A faint sound whispered through the jungle from the distance, and the men in the thickets tensed. The headman stopped in his stroll, drew himself to an imposing height, and so carefully refrained from looking at the bushes that Henry groaned.

He stood in the dusty street, listening to what might be faint footfalls, when suddenly, from the bend where the track wound away into the jungle, a stray goat erupted.

The villagers went whooping after it, and one of the headman's cronies returned hauling the goat by a rope around its neck. Henry and his cursing soldiers subsided again into the thicket.

Aguinaldo didn't come until nightfall. Suddenly hoofbeats sounded on the road, and a small group of rebels came trotting into the barrio.

"Wait," Henry whispered. "I don't see him."

"There," Estep said, pointing into the dusk beyond the headman and his delegation. "Isn't that him?"

"Maybe. No, it's too big for Aguinaldo." Henry had

an uneasy sensation, one he had learned to trust long ago. "We're going for them now," he said. "No matter."

He raised his hand, and the thickets burst open, filling the street with soldiers. They fired on the rebels while the headman fled. Stumbling, legs cramping after so much time in crouched hiding, Henry saw the rebels retreat, fading among the stiltlike houses; at the same time he heard the guns behind him.

"Regroup!"

The Americans dived for cover, firing as they went, pursuing their unseen foe. While they had been waiting for Aguinaldo, someone had been waiting for them. Henry swore, hacking his way through the knotted jungle, machete in one hand, pistol in the other.

"Damn their eyes, I can't see them!" Estep shouted.

The jungle crackled with gunfire, punctuated by half-seconds of absolute silence. Everything that lived in the jungle, birds and monkeys and wild pigs, and everything in the barrio was frozen, cowering. A bullet went past Henry's ear like a bee. And how the devil had they got wind of the plan? There was no use asking, Henry thought. The headman would only spread pious hands in protest. Henry could make an example of the village, as Wheaton had done, but he hadn't the stomach for it, and it would only drive other barrios into the rebel camp.

They lumbered on through the jungle grass and the creepers that gnawed at their ankles. Henry nearly fell over a dead rebel. They had gotten one of them at least, he thought with vicious satisfaction. But a dead man would have nothing useful to say.

"I want them alive!" he shouted, and Lieutenant Estep sent the word through the ranks.

They might as well have been trying to catch the wild pigs. The barefoot rebels in their tattered clothes blended into the jungle like the hot mist that hung in the air. They came on two more dead and a third who had climbed a tree and lay along one of its limbs, dripping blood. He was picking off the Americans, and they couldn't get near him, so they shot him down. He fell with a crash at Henry's feet, mute.

At nightfall they turned back toward the village, cursing and sweating, and made camp. Henry sat moodily over a tin cup of boiled coffee and reflected that he could have been at home in Manila, with Estrella ladling cool water into a bathtub for him. The village headman, perhaps with the idea of making amends for the ambush gone awry, presented him with a large leaf in which six huge white grubs with brown heads were wrapped. Henry looked at them with revulsion.

"I don't want those," he said in Spanish.

The headman looked hurt. "Very excellent," he said.

"I don't want them!"

The headman shrugged. Perhaps the American general didn't know what they were for. He took one by its head and bit off the rest. He swallowed happily and rubbed his stomach.

Lieutenant Estep spit out his coffee.

"Take those away from here!" Henry roared. He got a grip on his own stomach, figuratively speaking. "It's all right, Lieutenant," he dryly told Estep. "We are not required to be polite to the old devil this evening and eat his offerings. Although I'm told they're considered a delicacy. They live in the sago palm and eat the palm heart. They're quite sweet to the taste."

"How do you know, sir?" Estep asked suspiciously.

"So I've been told. I have no desire for firsthand knowledge. In the pure spirit of research, however," he added wickedly, "one of us really ought to try them. They may be a valuable food source." He cocked an inquiring eye at the lieutenant.

"No, sir!"

They heard a scuffling in the darkness, and Henry snapped his head around. Two of his men stepped into the firelight, dragging another between them. The prisoner was a youngish man in khaki shirt and trousers, none too clean, and a battered straw hat. He grinned at Henry and, as soon as the soldiers let go of his arm, doffed his hat, revealing a cap of straight, fair hair.

"Says he was looking for you, General. Caught him sneaking around the village."

"Sneaking is the only sure way not to get shot these days," the young man commented.

"What the hell are you doing here?" Henry snapped.

Paul Kirchner's face sobered, and he ceased joking. "I have a message for you, sir. From the States. It's private." He glanced at the soldiers and the lieutenant.

"I know him," Henry growled. "Leave him with me. If you don't mind excusing us, Lieutenant?"

"Certainly, sir." Estep rose with alacrity.

Henry turned on Paul. "What the hell are you doing in these islands? What message?"

"Teddy sent me to hunt you up," Paul said. "Your wife tracked us down in Hong Kong and cabled for help. I don't know why she couldn't find you, but she was frantic. Your daughter's ill."

Henry froze, motionless, the cup still in his hands. "Ill with what?"

"It's diphtheria, sir. That's all I know. You can't get much into an overseas cable. They're too expensive. I gather the War Office may have been giving your wife the runaround."

"She had my address," Henry murmured. But she hadn't kept it, of course. Undoubtedly she had thrown away his letters. She must have; she had never answered them. And the package for Midge, if it had even arrived yet, would have no more than a shop name. *Estrella!* The name came into his head like a blow, like a fist striking him. Oh, God, Estrella.

He stood up, shouting for Estep. It didn't matter that it would take him longer to get home than it would for his daughter to recover or die. He had to go.

Ten minutes later he was riding through the blackness toward Manila with Paul Kirchner beside him astride the scrubby native pony he had tethered in the jungle. Henry gave Paul the key to the house in Manila and was outside General Otis's office in the Malacañang Palace by dawn.

"Army communications are extremely efficient," Otis said reproachfully when he found Henry still pacing there some three hours later. "We received word. I was personally holding it to be sent on to you as soon as you returned."

"As soon as I returned?" Henry's hands balled into fists, and he forced himself to unclench them.

Otis made a tutting noise and appeared to be counting the stacks of forms on his desk. "Naturally we can't recall a man in the midst of an important mission over domestic matters." He straightened the edges of each stack. "But here you are now. I shall want your report on Aguinaldo first, of course, and then we can discuss your domestic situation."

"There is no report on Aguinaldo because we didn't get him, sir, I regret to say," Henry said stiffly. He was not going to be put off by Otis's churning through his endless papers. He felt on the edge of explosion. "May I ask, sir, why I was not advised immediately of my daughter's illness?"

General Otis's side whiskers bristled in irritation. "You were in the field."

"My daughter has diphtheria!" Henry barked. "I request leave to go home, sir."

Otis glared at him, then tried to soften his approach. "I understand your concern, General Blake. Most understandable. But you are needed here. I'm sure your wife will manage splendidly, and, in truth, you know you can't help the child. It's a long voyage back," he added.

"Precisely why I must start immediately," Henry countered. He found, somewhat to his surprise, that he didn't care if he was leaving a job undone, didn't care what ruse was tried on Aguinaldo next, didn't care if someone else finished his work. It was a sensation he had never experienced before.

"Request denied," Otis said, settling a stack of forms smartly down on his blotter, edges neatly aligned, with military precision. "We can't have senior officers charging off for the States. Never get this job done."

Henry's head felt much as it had during his bout with measles as a child. He'd had a high fever, and the world had seemed very far away and not particularly important, except for a glass of lemonade, which he had wanted fiercely, demandingly, insatiably, *right then*. He felt that way now about going home. It had come as swiftly as the burning thirst for lemonade, and he approached it with the same single-mindedness.

"Then I resign my commission."

"You can't resign in time of war!" Otis looked shocked and as thunderstruck as if the forms on his desk had metamorphosed into beetles and flown off.

Henry stood in front of him, the feverish feeling still in his head, and said simply, "Court-martial me."

Otis pounded his fist on the desk, but Henry had walked out. "You will come to your senses, General Blake!" he shouted after him. "To your senses!"

*   *   *

Henry thought he had twenty-four hours. Otis didn't believe he would really do it. Military transport was out of the question. He would have to go to Hong Kong by way of whatever had gotten Paul Kirchner to Manila, then sail on a commercial liner from there. He rode through Manila, thinking, and handed his reins to Arturo when he arrived at his house. He peered at him. "What are you doing here?"

"Miss Estrella, she say you may need me," Arturo said.

Estrella! Henry bounded up the front steps. He flung the door open and found her in the parlor with Paul Kirchner. Paul's expression was carefully blank.

"Estrella, why are you here?" Henry demanded, taking off his hat.

Estrella leapt up and took his hands. Her voice had an unaccustomed note of pleading. "I saw . . . I saw Señor Kirchner's pony, so I thought perhaps you were—were home, and I . . . and Señor Kirchner told me, and oh, Enrique, please, take me with you!"

Paul fled into the next room.

"Take you—" Henry looked blankly at her. "But I can't."

"Oh, please, Enrique! I would be so good. I would be no trouble. A little house in Washington. I could have a little house in Washington." Her eyes gleamed with the thought of it, of her little house in that important city.

"Estrella, I'm married."

She hung her head. "I know."

Henry saw her eyes fill with tears, and his heart twisted. "My wife and I are . . . estranged. But I can't have a mistress in Washington, I—" But a great many men did. Was he one of them? Or was it only all right to have a mistress in Manila? In Manila, where it didn't count?

"I would be so good," Estrella said again. "I would never trouble you." Her eyes flashed suddenly. "My father was *married* to my mother, and he didn't take her. He didn't take *me*. 'I will send for you,' he said, but he *didn't!*" She was wailing like a child now. "Oh, please, take me! I won't ask anything else."

Henry put his hands on her shoulders, looked into her wild, pleading eyes. "Oh, my God. You mustn't— You are not a 'trouble.' It isn't that. You've made me very happy. But I have to go home for a while, and I can't make a place for you there. You wouldn't like it, you know. Everything would be strange, and you wouldn't know anyone." *And no one would speak to you, and you would be looked down upon instead of being a respected businesswoman.* How could he tell her how cruel his countrymen could be?

"I would like it if you were there," Estrella said.

She didn't get angry and throw things as Gisela would have done; she just pleaded like a child. He hated it that she abased herself so.

She seemed to sense that she was making him turn away. "I will go upstairs now," she said in a small voice, "and wait for you."

Henry groaned. He wanted a cool bath, but the thought of letting Estrella draw it for him made him flinch. He went into the dining room, where Paul Kirchner was discreetly waiting, and took a bottle of rum out of the cabinet. He poured himself a substantial shot and swallowed.

"Early in the day, General," Paul said mildly.

Henry gave him a look that advised him not to remark on his drinking habits. Paul shrugged and poured himself a finger's depth in the bottom of a glass. It was going to be a long afternoon.

"How did you get here?" Henry asked abruptly.

"Steamer from Hong Kong. Nasty boat. I don't advise it."

"Not much choice." Henry tipped the rest of his drink down his throat. "Military transport is out of the question. I resigned. Deserted, actually, I think. Otis didn't accept the resignation."

Paul looked at him with respect. No wonder he was drinking at one in the afternoon. "The *Zafiro* sails again in the morning," he suggested. "I don't think the captain much cares who's on it."

"Good." Henry put his glass down. "I'm going to my bank. Hold the fort here, will you?"

Henry vanished, leaving Paul to wonder what that meant he was to do with the woman upstairs. Avoid her if possible, Paul decided. Getting into the thick of Henry Blake's amours was not something he wanted to do. Since venturing upstairs didn't seem a wise idea, he stretched out on the hard, dark oak settle in the parlor and put a stiff horsehair cushion under his head. It was certainly as comfortable as the jungle floor and with fewer insects. If it came to that, it was marginally better than the Scottish Hotel in Hong Kong that served as the headquarters for the always cash-strapped Lady Teddy. With that thought amusing him, he went to sleep.

At around five Henry returned. He glanced down at Paul, who opened his eyes on Henry's arrival and then deliberately closed them again. Gritting his teeth, Henry climbed up the stairs.

Estrella was sitting at Henry's desk, very quietly, studying the street. He knew she had been watching for him. She didn't say anything, merely looked at him with such a luminous stare that his resolve crumbled. Just once more. It really wouldn't make any difference.

She was in his arms like a quick candle flame, kissing

him, touching him, small delicate hands opening the buttons of his khaki shirt as if by magic. He quivered and pulled her to him in the bed and lost himself for an hour in her skin and hair.

But afterward nothing was different. Afterward he still had to go home. Estrella kissed him, smiled, and began to pack his bags for him, her expression excited and hopeful. She folded his shirts neatly, polished his shoes, and wrapped them in a cloth to keep the fresh polish from soiling his trousers. She moved gracefully, like an exotic bloom on a slender stalk. What if he took her with him?

Henry pulled his clothes on, another instant desire overriding all others: *I want her with me.* He fled before she could ask him again, for in a weak moment he knew he might answer yes.

Paul was downstairs, cooking rice on the stove with no difficulty, when Henry came down. "I'm hungry," he told Henry. "You ought to eat, too."

Henry ignored the suggestion and poured himself another shot of rum in the dining room. "When does this ship sail?"

"Daybreak, probably," Paul said.

"Oh, God." Henry downed the rum and poured some more. He put the bottle on the kitchen table and sat down beside it, his head in his hands.

"You'd better have some rice," Paul said and placed a steaming bowl in front of Henry. "The China Sea's no fun with a bad head."

"I don't know what to do," Henry whispered.

Paul was certain it was not an admission Henry would ever have considered himself likely to make, particularly not to the likes of Paul Kirchner. "She's very beautiful," he said carefully.

Henry opened the bottle again. "She loves me. She's

very good to be with. She's always there when I want company. She doesn't carp at me. No matter what I do, she thinks I'm right."

"Very alluring," Paul murmured. "Particularly if somewhat different from one's wife. Not that I have a wife, but I see the difference."

"My *wife* doesn't answer my letters," Henry said bitterly.

"Oh," Paul said noncommittally. He wondered how much rum the general had drunk to make him so confiding. He measured Henry with his eyes and decided that if he had to, he could carry him aboard the steamer.

Henry looked up defiantly. "We quarreled. We quarreled with our son over his future. He defied us and left home, and I told him not to come back until he was willing to respect our wishes and the way in which he had been brought up. Then my wife turned on me and held me to blame for his leaving."

"And you didn't."

"I don't know anymore," Henry said mournfully. The rum and Estrella seemed to have shaken his confidence. Or maybe just shaken out old doubts.

"Where is she?" Paul asked softly, meaning Estrella.

"Upstairs. She's waiting for me to decide. She won't come down unless I call for her."

"Godlike," Paul commented. "One assumes your wife does not accord you this deference."

Henry didn't answer.

"She wouldn't, of course," Paul said thoughtfully. "Real families can't afford that."

Henry looked up from his glass. "And what does that mean?"

"I'm working on it," Paul said. *I have you over a barrel, Blake. You can't court-martial me, and you need me to get you out of Manila. So you have to sit there and listen to me.* "I left home because my mother wanted me to be her instead of me. I haven't regretted it once. I don't know how she feels. She's probably fine. It was very important to her to be right."

Henry glared at him. "Why am I listening to philosophy from a young wastrel like you?" he demanded.

Paul raised his eyebrows. "Because I'm happy in my life and you're not?"

Henry snorted. "Happiness is not the sole requirement in life. There's duty. . . ." His voice trailed away as it appeared to occur to him he was in no position to remark on this trait.

"Certainly," Paul said. "The trouble with duty is so many people seem to equate it with being right. If you're in the right, you must be doing your duty and vice versa. The trouble with being right is it means somebody else has to be wrong. It's hard to find people to accept that assignment when you hand it out."

Henry opened the bottle again. He looked more miserable than any man Paul had ever seen.

Paul took his glass and went quietly back into the parlor. He drained the last sip and stretched out again on the oak settle. Experience had taught him that when there was nothing to do, it was a good idea to sleep. It passed the time and conserved strength for whatever was going to happen next.

Henry peered into his glass as if he might find in its depth a more agreeable voice than Paul Kirchner's. But the rum had nothing to say except to promise a headache in the morning. How had he found himself in this fix, taking up with a woman he couldn't, and didn't even want to, marry? He didn't even have the heat of youth for an excuse.

He knew how. Because, as Paul Kirchner had so sardonically pointed out, Estrella made him feel godlike. To her he could do no wrong. A very handy hole to hide in, not to have to confront the fact that with his family he had been dead wrong on a number of counts. That and the fact that Estrella was beautiful. Henry had felt, as his wife had aged into bitterness, the world somehow owed him that.

He closed his eyes despairingly. The upright Henry Blake. The incorruptible Henry Blake. He had to get out. Cut the tendrils clinging to him and get out. He couldn't shake the terror of doing to the daughter what the father had done to the mother. He stood and bounded up the stairs.

Estrella was sitting at his desk again, his packed trunks at her feet.

"Are you pregnant?" Henry demanded.

"What?" She stared at him, startled. "No."

"Are you sure? Are you positive?"

"Yes," she said quietly, reassuringly. "I know."

Henry let out a breath of relief. He pulled money from his pocket and pressed it into her hands. "For you, for the shop, for whatever you need." The color had gone out of his face. "I can't take you."

Estrella stared at the money in her hands. She didn't protest; she seemed to know the finality of his decision. "You will come back," she said after a moment. She looked at him for reassurance. "After your daughter is better."

"I don't know. Maybe not." Not after what he was about to do. If they court-martialed him, it would be in the States.

She got up and went slowly down the stairs, head up, skirt rustling, the way she had gone up them two months ago. Henry watched bleakly as she stepped into the street and waved at a passing *quelis*. He turned away as she stepped into it.

Henry sailed in the morning on Paul's steamer, a dilapidated craft with a draft shallow enough to cross the sandbar into Manila Harbor and maneuver up the Pasig River. With the monsoon blowing, she rolled heavily, churning her way through the two-day voyage to Hong Kong. No soldiers barred Henry's way at the pier, and there had been no communication from General Otis. There would be one waiting for him when he got home, Henry expected, when Otis found out he had really done it.

Paul asked Henry what he intended to do about that, and Henry, uncharacteristically, said he had no plan. He would see what happened, he said, looking uneasily at the sky. He was feeling the effects of the rum and the rolling boat, and the wind seemed to blow a mist around him. It might almost be possible to see a face in it, he thought, his stomach heaving, but whether it was his mistress or his wife or his daughter, he couldn't tell.

XII

Washington, D.C., July

"I know she seems better," Janessa Lawrence told Cindy Blake angrily as they sat in the parlor of the Blake home, "but she's not! She can give this disease to everybody she comes into contact with."

"There is a pocket of infection," Brice Amos said gently, his best professional manner shielding the patient's mother from too harsh a description, his voice a calm flow in contrast to Janessa's ragged torrent of words. "A pocket of infection in her throat. It is a fairly simple operation to remove it."

"Simple!" Cindy said. "You want to cut into my daughter's throat, and you tell me it's simple!"

"I assure you she will be completely anesthetized, and all antiseptic procedures will be observed." Brice smiled gently, his leonine head bent graciously in Cindy's direction. "It is, unfortunately, absolutely necessary. Dr. Lawrence has perhaps not fully explained—"

"Of course I've explained," Janessa said testily. "We've been arguing about it all morning."

"Sometimes it is best when the physician is not a member of the family." Brice gave Janessa a nod that she chose to interpret as condescending, and she glared at him.

"Will you do the surgery, Dr. Amos?" Cindy asked.

"Naturally. I've dealt with several of these cases, as I believe Dr. Lawrence has also."

"One," Janessa said shortly. Brice's gallantly deferential manner irritated her, but the real reason for her mood was that she knew Brice was right: physicians should not treat their own relatives. The sheer terror that she might somehow bungle the operation and Midge might die overwhelmed her. And Cindy was right: Midge appeared healthy. It hardly seemed right or fair that she should need surgery now. And Henry was on his way home. He had cabled immediately from Manila as soon as Paul Kirchner had found him. That was a month ago. He would be here soon. There had been another cable from Hawaii and one several days ago from San Francisco. What if he came home to find that they had saved Midge from the disease and then . . . ?

Janessa thought about Midge. She knew how frightened her niece was. Midge was feeling well enough now to be afraid of the anesthetic, afraid of not waking up again, afraid of letting someone cut a hole in her throat.

"I recommend we tackle this early in the morning," Brice was saying. "No sense in letting the little lady worry herself over it any longer."

Janessa pulled her attention back to Cindy and Brice's muted conversation. She nodded her assent.

Brice patted Cindy's hand. "I'll be here at the crack of dawn and we'll see to things." He stood and showed himself out.

"He's a good surgeon," Janessa said when he had gone. "The best in the District."

* * *

She told herself that again when Brice came in the morning and they scrubbed together with carbolic soap, washing themselves and every available surface in the spare room set aside for the operation. Midge, lying on a long table in the center of the room, looked up at them with frightened eyes.

Brice's nurse, crisply efficient in a white starched apron and stiff-white mob cap, set up the ether and smoothed the girl's forehead with one hand. "Now, you're not to worry. You won't even know what's happened until you wake up with some stitches in your neck. It'll hurt then, but it will be all done, and you're a brave girl. I know because I've been told."

"Janessa," Midge whispered, "where's Frank?"

"He's downstairs. With your mother and Peter." Peter had come from San Francisco, worried about the length of Midge's illness, and Midge had been glad to see him. But it was always Frank she asked for. Frank, who could soothe her fears and make her laugh. She had quit asking for Henry; he was so close that Janessa thought Midge was somehow afraid to ask, lest she break some spell and he not come.

The nurse put the ether cone over Midge's nose while Janessa and Brice pulled on surgical gloves. "It's funny," Janessa whispered. "When I was in medical school, some of the older doctors were still complaining about antiseptic procedures. I wonder what it would have taken to get them into gloves."

"Possibly if an angel with a flaming sword had come and urged it on them," Brice murmured, and Janessa, smiling, remembered why it was that she had once wanted to marry him. "Barring that," he went on, serious now, "one simply has to let the oldest generation die out. There's a limit as to how far people will change."

He looked across at Midge. "Is our patient asleep?"

The nurse nodded. "Good." Brice turned to Janessa. "I'll ask you for assistance if necessary, but the less you involve yourself, the better."

"Certainly," Janessa said briskly, remembering also why it was that she had thereafter been disinclined to speak to him for fifteen years.

The operation took even less time than Brice had promised, and Janessa felt a vast surge of relief as she went downstairs to tell Cindy. It had been a textbook procedure, and Brice had been brilliant. Even she had to admit that.

Cindy was sitting with Peter and Frank, twining and untwining her fingers endlessly. Half the lines in her face seemed to smooth out with Janessa's news.

"May we see her?" Frank asked.

"Certainly. She's groggy, but you seem to exert a calming influence on her. Heaven knows why."

Frank chuckled and took Peter upstairs with him. Cindy leaned back against the sofa. "I'm just going to wait until I have my breath back." She looked uneasily at the cushion beside her, upon which rested a parcel in brown paper with many exotic stamps. "This just came," she said. "It's from Manila. It's for Midge."

"A birthday present, I expect," Janessa said, looking at it. "You know what overseas post is like. Henry probably mailed it months ago."

Cindy continued to stare at the parcel.

"It hasn't got a snake in it," Janessa said. "Just take it up to her."

"He'll be here today," Cindy said.

"I expect he will."

"What am I going to do?"

"What do you want to do? Do you want to let him back in your life—or just in the house?"

"I don't know," Cindy said. "It seems like too much trouble. I'm tired, Janessa."

Janessa bent over her and kissed her forehead. "Wait and see what happens, then. You don't have to straighten everything out the first night." She looked at Cindy thoughtfully. "Uh, what have you—?"

"I've put him in the spare room. The one the twins had."

No conciliatory gestures there, Janessa thought. She sighed. Brice and his nurse came downstairs, and she let them out. She wanted to go to Richmond and be with her own husband and children. With luck she could leave in a few days. Midge would be on the mend, Henry would be home, and Henry and Cindy could work out their row without houseguests to observe it.

As if on cue, carriage wheels crunched in the driveway, and Cindy snatched up the parcel and held it to her as if it were a shield. "You answer the door," she told Janessa.

Janessa went briskly toward it, but it didn't require answering. Henry Blake was not going to use the knocker on his own front door. He opened it and stepped in. "Good morning, Janessa," he said wearily.

"Good morning," Janessa said, startled by the wear and tear on his face. *Good Lord, he's old!* she thought. The cabbie was piling bags in the front hall. Henry tipped him, then took off his hat. He tossed it onto the halltree, and it caught. He gave a faint grin. "Where's Cindy?"

"In the parlor. I'll have your bags taken up." *Before you put them in your old bedroom.*

Henry and Cindy stared at each other across the parlor. *She looks dreadful,* he thought. She still had the parcel from Estrella's shop clutched to her chest. Henry saw it and winced. "That's for Midge," was the first thing he said.

"It just came. Did you think I wasn't going to give it to her?" Cindy fairly flung it away from her onto the sofa.

"Midge is—she's all right?"

"Yes. There was lingering infection, but—" Cindy explained it to him as Janessa had explained it to her, carefully, as if she were a nurse speaking to an agitated parent.

We don't know how to talk to each other, Henry thought. "May I see her?"

"Of course. The boys are up there now."

"Boys?"

"Frank's home. Come along. I'll take you up."

She swept out of the room. After a moment of sheer panic, Henry followed her.

"Janessa! Mother!" Feet clattered in the hall as Frank came racing down the stairs. He looked at his father, said, "Good God!" then turned to his mother. "Where's Janessa? Midge can't move her legs, and there's something funny about her eye!"

Cindy flew up the stairs with Henry behind her.

"Janessa!" Frank shouted again.

She came running from the kitchen and up the stairs behind Frank.

Midge lay in her own bed again, the incision in her throat stitched closed, and tried to look at her father, but her right eye slid slowly to the side. "I can't make my feet move," she whispered.

Henry snatched the sheet back to see if he could determine what was holding them down. Janessa dashed into the room and looked carefully at Midge's wandering eye.

"Can you move anything? Wiggle your toes?"

Midge's jaw clenched as she tried. "No."

"How about hands? Arms? Can you swallow?"

Midge lifted hands and arms, swallowed, nodded.

"What is it?" Cindy whispered.

Janessa took Midge's hand. "It's an aftereffect of diphtheria." She spoke to Midge. "Sometimes it affects the whole side of a patient's body. Sometimes it affects the soft palate and pharynx so you can't swallow properly. It almost always goes away again."

Midge caught that. "Almost?"

"Nothing is ever certain, sweetheart," Janessa said lightly. "But this is pretty certain. You just have to rest and give it time."

"Did the surgery do this?" Cindy demanded.

"Not directly," Janessa said firmly. "And it had to be done. It may be that it would have come on anyway. We don't know what causes this effect."

"Well, why don't you?" Henry sounded as if she could have looked it up and hadn't bothered.

"Because nobody knows but God!" Janessa snapped. "Now, all of you clear out. Midge needs rest. Uncle Henry, you can spend ten minutes with her because you just got here."

They trooped downstairs, white-faced. After a few minutes Henry followed them, leaving Janessa with Midge. The four of them stared at one another. No one knew what to say.

Lutie stuck her head out of the kitchen. "Lunch on the table," she announced. "Mr. Henry, I made you a cherry pie like you like. You came at just the right time for them cherries."

Frank held his hand out to his father. "I didn't say hello properly."

Henry shook his son's hand carefully.

"I'm glad you're here," Frank said. "It'll do Midge good."

They sat down at the table. Cindy picked up her fork,

and the men followed suit. No one seemed to have anything to say.

Eventually Peter broke the strained silence. "Did you have a pleasant voyage?" he asked his father.

"Parts of it were less unpleasant than others," Henry said. He eyed Cindy dubiously. "Have there been any messages for me here from the War Office? Or the army?"

"No," Cindy said, tight-lipped. "Not even to tell me you were coming."

"They wouldn't, I imagine, under the circumstances."

"What have you done?" Peter asked with a faint smile. "Deserted?"

"I rather think so."

Cindy stared at him. "Are you serious?"

"I was not given leave. That may be how General Otis will take it."

"Henry, how *could* you?"

"I was under the impression that it was important I come home. That you particularly wished me to do so."

"Midge wished you to do so," Cindy snapped. "No one suggested you throw your career— Surely General Otis would have—"

"Damn my career," Henry spat. He viciously sliced the cold ham on his plate.

Cindy's fingers tightened around her glass.

"Midge will hear you," Frank said quietly.

Everyone knew that if they squabbled, Midge might get worse. Janessa had said stress might be a trigger.

They stared at one another bleakly. *We might as well all be strangers,* Peter thought. *No, we* are.

After lunch Henry found that his trunk and bags had been deposited in the spare room. He made no comment but changed out of his traveling clothes and went to sit with Midge, the only person in the household he was certain wanted to see him.

Janessa had brought Midge her present from Manila, and she lay propped against her pillows with the blues and greens of the pineapple-silk skirt arranged across her lap, the closest she could come to wearing it. Diana was curled in the empty box, blissfully asleep in tissue paper.

"Mother says that when I'm better, we can have a party and I can wear it," Midge said, trying to smile. But her face was white, and her right eyelid trembled. Her eye had slid clear to the corner. "I *am* going to get better?" she asked, looking for reassurance. She was still young enough to believe that if an adult told her something, it would happen.

Henry didn't feel as if he had any reassurance for either of them, but he gave it anyway. "Of course you are. You'll be downstairs in no time."

"I want to go down now," Midge said fretfully. "I hate it up here."

Henry smiled. "It just so happens that Janessa has given her permission for exactly that. For only half an hour at first, mind, and not until day after tomorrow if that incision is looking well. But downstairs you shall go." It wouldn't matter, Janessa had said. All they could do was wait. He took her hand and held it until she drifted into sleep.

Two days later Henry carried Midge down, bundled in her best nightgown and wrapper, and installed her in the parlor, a hassock under her immobile feet. The rest of the family looked at Henry in the way they had developed, as if he were a ghost that had had the ill grace to appear, an apparition they did not know what to do with.

"I'm going out for the afternoon," Henry said abruptly.

Peter appeared to take pity on him. "Would you like some company?"

"Not this time. But next. Thank you." Henry smiled at his elder son.

He carefully kept his eyes from Frank. Frank looked like a bum. His hair needed cutting, and he was wearing a frayed shirt with no collar—a disgraceful way to dress in front of his mother, Henry thought. Furthermore, he was reading a socialist newspaper. A jolt of anger ran through Henry every time he looked at him.

Henry left before he lost his self-control, going instead to plague someone he could beat. He had decided a frontal attack on the army seemed the best plan, possibly because he didn't have a leg to stand on in terms of military law. Accordingly, he marched into the office of the War Department and let his temper loose in there.

"Disgraceful runaround my wife was given! Unconscionable treatment of an American officer! Appalling lack of support for our own troops! Incompetency of the highest degree! I am reporting directly to you and cannot advise strongly enough a change of command over there and a careful look at policy here!"

Russell Alger, the secretary of war, looked at him with bemusement. "We've had a request from General Otis to court-martial you, General Blake."

"Possibly because he knows what my recommendations with regard to him are likely to be," Henry snapped. "I was sent over there to take charge of military intelligence. No amount of intelligence will serve to suppress that insurrection as long as the high command appears to have mislaid its own and continues to dance about like a maiden afraid to step in a mud puddle." He looked aggrieved. "However, if you doubt my assessment, you may consult with General Wheaton or General MacArthur. Sir."

"They have made their views known." Alger sighed. He didn't appear to feel he was any match for General Blake. "The President respects your judgment enormously, General Blake," he offered.

"My judgment is that we are sinking in quicksand!" Henry said. *And if you ever get me back over there, it will be because you shipped my dead body back.* Then his mind cringed. *Oh, Estrella.* "I request your permission to return to my daughter, sir. I have a great deal of leave due me."

"Ah, yes." Alger looked at him slyly. "The problem seems to be that you were expressly forbidden to take it just then."

"My daughter is recovering from diphtheria," Henry said. "She nearly died. My house is in chaos, my wife is distraught, and General Otis deliberately sat on the message to me until I found it out from other sources. If this is the way my country treats its officers, you can have my resignation!"

"I'm not certain that you can resign while you are being court-martialed," Alger said, smiling slightly.

Henry glowered at him and tossed his head back irritably. "I will welcome the forum to make my views known!" he barked.

Alger sighed. "I should hate to see it come to that," he said truthfully. "I should not like to lose a good officer —by either means." If they court-martialed him, a furious General Blake might have no qualms about informing every civilian newspaper of his opinion of General Otis. It was hard enough to keep the lid on the junior generals' dissatisfaction as it was. And the country was already growing dispirited about the war, having seen no progress. "I am sure there is some way around this difficulty." He looked at Henry hopefully.

Henry folded his arms. "That is up to General Otis."

"Not entirely. Nor do I intend to be blackmailed by my generals in the field, much less by generals who have left the field when they were not supposed to. You are aware, General Blake, that I could charge you with desertion?"

"It would make Otis happy," Henry retorted. For some reason, he didn't seem to care whether the army court-martialed him or not. Six months ago he wouldn't have considered disgracing himself in such a way. Why didn't he care now? He felt like daring them to do it.

Alger seemed to sense that. "I am not interested in making General Otis happy, any more than I am in making you happy, General Blake. You have both caused me a great deal of difficulty at a trying time."

"Perhaps you should let me resign." Henry felt like pushing the issue.

"You have had a lifelong career in the army, haven't you, General Blake? So did your father, as I recall."

"It is a tradition in my family," Henry said stiffly.

"Well, then, perhaps you simply need a vacation from it and not a divorce," Alger said mildly. Henry flinched at the last word, and the secretary looked at him curiously. "A rest, General. You have been in the field a long time." Henry seemed ready to argue. As far as Alger could tell, the general was prepared to argue with anything said to him. Alger put his palms flat on his desk and pushed himself up, holding Henry's glance. "General Blake, I am going to put you on extended leave. Indefinite leave. I do not intend to accept your resignation of your commission until such time as I think you are rational enough to do so. Nor am I going to permit a court-martial, despite overwhelming temptation. You may consider yourself under orders not to discuss the situation in the Philippine Islands *or* your impressions of General Otis's command with anyone, most particularly not with journalists. Do I make myself clear?"

"You do, sir," Henry said.

"If I read your opinions on how the war ought to be conducted over my breakfast in the morning, all bets will be off. You will find yourself before a military tribunal faster than you can say Jack Robinson."

"Yes, sir." Henry saluted crisply. It was what he had come for, what he had obliquely blackmailed Alger into doing. Why didn't he feel more satisfied? Where was the hot, fierce triumph he always felt when he made someone do what he wanted?

He thought about that on the ride home but didn't come to any conclusions. As Henry's carriage drew up to the portico, Peter and Frank were throwing a football back and forth on the lawn. Henry regarded his sons as he got out of the carriage. Even in a cotton pullover and knickers, Peter contrived to look like a banker who had just left the boardroom for his appointed bout with healthful exercise. Frank, in a pair of work pants and an old shirt with no collar, looked like the rags-and-old-iron man. Henry swerved away, and Peter tossed the football to Frank with an easy throw, then took his father's arm.

"Come and shoot the breeze awhile, Dad. I need to take the Blake out for a run. I don't think anybody's looked under the hood since I was here last."

He steered Henry toward the carriage house, where one of the first products of the Blake Motor Car Company usually resided under a protective tarpaulin. It was out of its dust cover and sitting proudly in the drive. The horses gave it no more than a passing snort. They were used to it. The rest of Alexandria was generally more excitable.

"Your mother doesn't drive it?" Henry asked quietly as he got into the passenger's seat. He hated the thing. He wouldn't have put it past Cindy to drive it just because of that.

"She says it gets grease on her clothes," Peter said. "Frank's taken her out in it once or twice, but I don't think she's really interested." He sighed. "Frank might be if he could stick with one thing long enough. He's got the aptitude. Better than I do, maybe, in terms of mechanics." Peter chuckled. "In terms of keeping a business afloat, he thinks I should give it all to the workers. He asked me what I paid them by the hour, then told me it wasn't enough."

"He's a damned socialist," Henry said.

Peter turned the crank under the Blake's grille and hopped in when it sputtered to life. The engine purred, and the little silver Diana on the hood gleamed jauntily in the sun. Peter donned a duster and goggles and handed a similar outfit to his father, saying, "I just gave it the once-over, but you really ought to drive it soon." He steered the Blake down the drive, past Frank, who stood on the porch watching them, the football tucked under one arm.

Peter turned the motorcar down the cobblestoned street, bouncing along until he came to a dirt road and turned onto it. "Nice day for a country drive," he shouted through the cloud of red dust that the Blake raised.

Henry coughed. "Delightful."

"When are you going to bite the bullet and sit down with Frank?" Peter bellowed through the roar of the car's engine.

"This your idea of a quiet chat?" Henry bellowed back.

Peter laughed. He slowed the motorcar until they barely crawled along. The dust subsided, and the dragon-flies and june bugs swarming in the warm air circled them instead.

"I don't know how to sit down with Frank," Henry said abruptly. "I don't know him anymore."

"He's appallingly like you. Much more than I am."

"Don't even bother to try that. I don't buy it."

"You have to come to terms with him if you're going to live with Mother." Peter raised a questioning eyebrow. "Assuming you still want to. I've always been under the impression that you went into intelligence because you didn't have the patience to deal with the army's passion for regulation. You might cut Frank the same slack." He glanced at his father. "By the way, what happened at the War Department?"

"I'm on indefinite leave. And under orders not to discuss it."

Henry stared at the red dirt road slowly unwinding in front of them. It was getting hot. And overcast. A light wind blew through the trees overhanging the road, turning the silver undersides of their leaves to view. It would be simpler if you could just turn people over the same way and see what drove them, Henry reflected.

Peter kept the motor car moving at its snail's pace while they talked about anything other than Henry's relationships with his son and wife: of the weather in Manila, of the modifications in the Blake for 1900, of Midge's boredom and how they might amuse her.

"She's the glue," Peter said. "Poor little thing. She's the force that's keeping us all in the same house and civil to each other. I wonder if it was worth it to her. It's what she's wanted so desperately."

Henry looked at him, appalled. "Are you implying that your sister wanted peace in the family so desperately that she contracted diphtheria to get it?"

"Not on purpose. Not knowingly. But it makes you wonder."

Peter turned the Blake into a side lane and sent a

cow rocketing to the other end of her pasture. Another turn, and cautious navigation through a herd of pigs, and they came out on the main road again. They headed home.

Frank was gone when they returned; no one knew where. He vanished periodically when he thought he might get caught alone with his father. *Wait until Midge is well* was the unspoken caution that surrounded them all.

Janessa pronounced Midge much improved. Midge said furiously that she wasn't improved if she couldn't move.

"You're not contagious any longer, darling," Janessa said. "That means you can have visitors. The Roosevelts are in town for a week, and Alice sent a note round. She wants to come see you."

"She does?" Alice was her cousin Sally's friend, a beautiful and mercurial creature who made Midge feel drab.

"Certainly. And she sent you a basket of pears." Janessa held it up for inspection.

Midge looked at the beribboned pears with amazement.

Alice followed the pears the next day, in her father's carriage. She wore an elegant blue crepe de chine dress and a blue taffeta toque and looked bewitchingly grown-up. Henry had been half-afraid her father would come with her and want to talk about the war he had enthusiastically helped to start. But Theodore stayed home. Apparently this was Alice's visit.

She settled herself next to Midge and accepted Cindy's offer of a cup of tea. "I heard you have had a dreadful time," she said, cocking her head at the invalid.

"It's been awful," Midge said. "I'm so bored. Thank you for the pears. I ate two yesterday. I love pears."

Alice smiled. "You mustn't waste being ill, you know. Since you're going to live, you must take advantage of the opportunity."

"What do you mean?"

"Oh, it's your chance to be a whole new person." Alice grinned conspiratorially. "Once you go back to school, you can be anyone you want to be. Not satisfied with the old Midge Blake? *Whsst*, she's gone, she's been ill; this is the *new* Midge Blake."

Midge giggled. "I wouldn't have the nerve."

"Oh, you ought to try it. I do it all the time."

They chatted for nearly a half hour, and then Alice stood, saying she didn't want to tire Midge out. She left in a flurry, like a pale-blue tornado.

"That girl's a menace," Frank said after Alice had departed. "She ought to run for office instead of her father."

"She said something very interesting, though," Midge said. "She said that because I've been sick I have a chance to be a whole new person when I go back to school. Maybe she was joking, but I hate being me. Could I really be somebody else?"

"You can be anybody you want, Pudd'n," Frank said.

"What about Alice? Could I be Alice?"

"You don't want to be Alice."

"Oh, but I do! I want to look grown-up like Alice." Midge lowered her eyes. "I want the boys to look at me."

"Alice is a darn sight too grown-up, if you ask me."

"Well, I didn't. And don't you think she's pretty?"

"Yeah," Frank admitted. "She's a stunner. Heaven knows she didn't get it from her old man. But it's what she does with it that gives men goose bumps. *You* can do that. It's just confidence."

"Very well," Midge said airily. "When I go back to school I shall be Marjorie, not Midge. I shall pin my hair up like Alice's, and no one will be allowed to call me Pudd'n." The tears slid suddenly down her cheeks. "That is, if I can ever walk again."

"You'll walk again!" Frank said fiercely. "You'll walk again, damn it." He sat down on the edge of her chaise longue and cradled her. "You'll dance the quadrille, and all the boys will fight over your dance card." He hugged her tighter.

"It's time for her to go upstairs," Janessa said from the doorway. "It's been a big afternoon."

Frank scooped her up in his arms and took her upstairs. He kissed her forehead. "Good afternoon, Marjorie Pudd'n," he said with a smile.

Henry was in the hallway when Frank came out. Father and son looked at each other, taken aback.

"Hello," Frank said. "She's resting."

"Any change?" Henry might have been consulting with a doctor he didn't know very well.

"No. Janessa says it's too early. A week at least."

"Oh."

They stood looking at each other, balanced almost on the balls of their feet as if waiting for some clash, some combat. They were trying to figure out who owned the house, Frank thought. Cindy had given him his father's place, he realized. Now that Henry was trying to come back into it, it was awkward. Cindy was keeping Henry at bay, in the status of a guest. Or trying to. Henry was fighting back in various ways. He gave orders to the cook and the stable boy; he had begun collecting the bills from the mailbox and paying them; he had ordered a new lawn mower.

"Midge is glad you're home," Frank said. He folded his arms and leaned against the newel post. He was as tall and muscular as Henry now. Maybe a little more so. "I am, too."

Henry didn't answer that. "When did you come home?"

"Last Christmas."

"Why?"

"It seemed like time. The war. I thought you'd be in the thick of it and Mother might need me."

"You never thought of joining up yourself?"

"Nope. Damn fool operation. Tim thought so, too."

"Tim went," Henry said. He couldn't help himself.

"As a correspondent. Tim's a journalist; that's his bread and butter."

"At least your cousin has a job. What did you do?"

"Helled around. Rode the rails, worked a circus, dug gold. Learned to be a carpenter."

Henry's mouth twitched. "I don't think any purpose will be served by rehashing our previous differences," he said carefully.

"Good. Let's stop now," Frank agreed.

"We have to make peace for Midge's sake. That's why I came home."

"Just for Midge?" Frank knew he was pushing it. "What about Mother?"

"My relationship with your mother is my business."

"You've got a lot of years invested," Frank remarked. "She told me all about you, the two of you. It would be a shame to waste that."

"I don't wish to discuss it!"

"Certainly, sir." Frank held his hand out. "Shall we try to give each other a chance? I've no wish to be estranged."

"Very well." Henry extended his own hand, and they

shook gravely. Then they stepped back without the faintest idea what to do next.

Cindy came down the hallway, stopping when she saw them. It was only the faintest pause, and then she walked on. "There you are, Frank." She linked her arm through his. "Come and look at the yardage I've bought for Midge's bedroom and tell me what you think of it. I'm going to redo it all for her." She swept him down the hall.

Looking over his shoulder, Frank could see his father stiffen. *I have to leave,* he thought.

"Now, dear, take a look at this." Cindy shook an ivy-covered chintz out on the big double bed in her room—the bed she used to share with his father. "Tell me what you think."

I think I have to leave.

Four days later, ahead of Janessa's schedule, Midge wiggled a toe.

"Look! Look, it *did* move!"

"Yes, it did!"

The family gathered around her, gleeful, hugging and kissing Midge and one another. Henry even kissed Janessa, a quick peck on the cheek. Cindy kissed Frank, flinging her arms around him.

Midge creased her brow, trying to move more. She beat her fists on the chaise longue in frustration.

"Take it easy, honey. It'll come," Frank said.

"I want it now!"

The months of pent-up frustration poured into her efforts. In the morning she could bend her knee. Diana, who had begun to regard Midge as a permanent warm cushion, looked startled.

Janessa pronounced her out of danger, and Peter, who had been uneasy as to what his company might be doing without him, telephoned the railway for a ticket home. Frank knelt down by Midge.

"Pudd'n, I have to go, too."

"What? *No!*" Midge wailed.

He shrugged. "Old Mike gave me a job, and I ran out on him. When you're all well, maybe I'll take you out there for a look at the country. It's mighty pretty. But right now you have to rest up, and I—" He looked at his father and mother, standing next to each other, not touching, like china figurines. "And I have to leave."

XIII

Taos, New Mexico, July

The train rattled its way across the country under a canopy of smoke from its stack and a high, bereft wail from its steam whistle. Frank Blake watched the cornfields go by from the windows of the parlor car. He had thought about riding the top deck or bedding down in a boxcar for spite, or for the hell of it, but he hadn't. He was a good citizen now, back in a country where people had true names and families to define them and purchased railway tickets to their destinations. He had left his father's house again, but he hadn't left that "civilized" country. Maybe he wouldn't be able to leave it again. Maybe he was going to have do whatever it was he was going to do within its boundaries. He thought about that as the train rolled westward.

He wondered what India Blackstone would think of the notion and tried to explain it all in his mind so that he could explain it to her. It came out muddled. India knew what she wanted; damn it, why didn't he? Why the itchy foot and the urge to rebel—yet knowing he never could, or wanted to, permanently sever himself from his family or from his background?

He gave up on it. He'd see the West before it was

gone, and then maybe he'd find whatever else he was looking for.

Frank arrived in Santa Fe and boarded the stage for Taos, feeling sorry for himself in an indefinable way and eager to tell India about it. Mike Holt's buggy was waiting to meet him at the Taos depot, but India was nowhere in sight. Neither was she at the Holts' sprawling adobe house a half mile from town.

"I don't know, dear," Eden Holt replied vaguely to his query after greeting him. "She's gone off somewhere with Johnny Rojas." Eden, in a fine cloud of cornmeal, was learning to make tamales from her cook and looked distracted. "She'll be back at dinnertime. She always is. How is poor little Midge?"

"She's doing better every day," Frank replied, unreasonably annoyed to find India not there when he wanted her. "Is Mike out with the camera?"

"Yes, but I don't think you can find him. He's gone off into the country with Rachel and Herb. He took Paul and José with him and said he didn't need Johnny, so he probably has plenty of crew. He said he'd put you to work tomorrow."

"All right."

He wandered aimlessly back outside, leaving Eden being patiently told by her cook, "No, no, señora," then learning once again how to roll up a tamale.

Frank stood in the yard, feeling sullen. It was as hot as the devil, and it didn't look as if it had rained much while he had been gone. The corral was so dry a cloud of dust rose every time the lone pony moved its feet. India had apparently taken the pinto wherever she was going with Johnny Rojas. And where *was* she going anyway? He had warned her about not leading Johnny on; didn't she have any sense?

*   *   *

The horses picked their way along another of those paths that only Johnny seemed to see. He looked over his shoulder. "Are you okay back there?"

"I'm fine," India called. "Wonderful!" She looked around her at the burning blue sky scalloped at the horizon by mountains. "It's a wonderful morning."

"Even without breakfast?" Johnny's lip twitched, his usual indication of mirth.

"I overslept," India said with dignity.

"I told you I would be there at five. You should believe me."

India yawned and stretched, lifting her arms over her head, the reins hanging on the pinto's withers. "I will next time."

It had been worth getting up, just to see this morning, India thought. Above them a hawk circled on the updraft, and a quail and her chicks scooted across the path and froze in the shadow of a rock. Bees hummed in the air, a low, persistent note; the farmer whose land they were passing kept hives. They were nearly out of any country that India recognized, farther afield than she had yet been.

Her saddlebags were loaded with her paints and a roll of canvas. Johnny wouldn't tell her what she was going to see, only that it was a present. His uncle Luis didn't know, she suspected. Johnny had been very circumspect. Was it some forbidden ceremony? She doubted that he would go that far, but you never knew. Whatever it was, she wouldn't turn it down. Despite Frank's dire warnings, she and Johnny had become friends over the past month or so. Part of what Frank had had to say might have been right, she suspected. But if Johnny felt more than friendship for her, that was beside the point. She had already turned down two proposals of marriage. Not loving

Johnny back wasn't any different from that, which was what she would tell Frank if he said anything else on the subject.

By eleven it was hot, and she had no idea where she was. Johnny halted the horses under a shady stand of cottonwoods, where a small creek bubbled along. "Lunch?" India asked hopefully.

Johnny nodded. "I don't want to have to carry you if you faint," he said as he unslung the canteen from his saddle horn. "You are too heavy."

"I never faint!"

"Anglo ladies always faint."

India unpacked the hamper that Eden's cook had sent with them and handed Johnny a packet of cornbread and tamales wrapped in a napkin. "I wouldn't want you to faint either," she said dryly.

They ate quickly and then rode on, India's curiosity growing by the minute. She again asked Johnny where they were going, but he just shook his head and said solemnly, with that faint twitch of his lip, "It is a surprise." Thinking that he was laughing at her, India suppressed any further outward evidence of curiosity.

Instead, she studied the countryside. They were riding through a dry riverbed that narrowed steadily into a canyon, sides gradually rising. The rock was pale red sandstone, pink in the sunlight, the cliffs dotted with gray-green shrubbery. Johnny looked uneasily over his shoulder once or twice, not at her but to the side, and she wondered again if he was taking her somewhere he shouldn't. Once he stopped and looked at some sign on the trail and clucked his tongue in what seemed to be irritation.

Slowly, as the sun climbed to noon, the canyon walls narrowed claustrophobically; the trail ended abruptly at the sheer rock face of a box canyon. India drew in her breath and stared.

It was a city, embedded high in the rock, old and dead and silent. And yet it spoke. It seemed to India that it hummed like the bees. Tier after tier rose up in the cave that opened in the cliff face, a prehistoric tenement that might once have housed hundreds. She could almost feel people still there, sense a face at one of the narrow windows, an Indian padding swiftly across a rooftop. The sun bathed the sandstone and old adobe in a light rose pink. India opened her mouth and whispered, "Petra."

"My people built it. Long time ago," Johnny said.

"There's a city in Jordan," India said. "Carved from rock. It reminds me of this one. I've seen pictures. A poet called it the 'rose-red city half as old as Time.'" She sat staring, watching the faint shadow of a hawk against its walls.

"Nobody knows about this," Johnny said. "Just Indians."

"But if I paint it, they will. They'll know it's here. You said it was a present for me to paint."

"If you don't say where. Indians all know anyway. It isn't sacred. Not exactly." Johnny looked thoughtful. "Just haunted, maybe. Maybe there are ghosts. The Navajo don't like it. They are very afraid of ghosts."

"But you're not?" India lifted her eyebrows at him.

"Not if I don't make them angry," Johnny said. "To let you paint it—you don't bother them; you know how to act around Indians. But white people—if word gets out, we get scientists." He made them sound like disease carriers. "Measuring and digging things and asking foolish questions." He scowled, furrowed his brow, licked the tip of an imaginary pencil. "'How often do you bathe? Do you bring your children up communally? Do you practice magic?' Pah!"

"Does Luis know you brought me here?"

Johnny looked away from her. "No." He made it sound casual. "It is not Luis's business. I bring you here for a present. Because I think you like it." He glanced at her quickly.

"I do like it. Oh, I like it enormously. I have never seen anything like it. It *is* magical."

"You like it to paint?"

"Oh, yes!" India slid from the pinto's saddle and began unbuckling her saddlebags.

Johnny smiled—a real smile this time. "Then you paint," he said, satisfied. "I wait."

It occurred to India that what Johnny had given her was truly a love offering, but she was not going to turn it down. Refuse the gift and lose these glowing, magical walls leaning out from rose-red rock? The clean angles of the walls, leaping from the cliff face? Leave without painting it and forsake the ghosts that still moved within those rose-pink walls? Never.

She set about making her palette while Johnny hobbled the horses and found himself a seat in the shade of a piñon tree. He sat cautiously, like a man who thinks there might be ants, but India doubted it was that. He was watching for something. Or someone. Not guiltily, as if they might suddenly have to flee the wrath of tribal authority, but watchful, as if there might be someone else around of whom he did not approve.

No matter. India forgot everything in the salmon-colored light flowing along the walls of the cliff house and running like water through every fold and crevice. She squeezed the paints out: cadmium and flake white, vermilion, burnt sienna and yellow ochre, ultramarine for the sky. She began to put the ghosts in almost before she had delineated the walls to enclose them. They were just the faintest brush strokes; she couldn't, of course, point to them, but she *knew* they were there. This time they didn't hover in the sky but abided where they had lived their lives in the distant centuries. The sky had life of its own, bursting in the present: a hawk gliding, caught in the instant it began to swoop on a quail frozen in terror at the cliff's base.

When she put down her brush after an hour, not finished but just needing to breathe, Johnny came over. He hadn't once looked at her work while she was painting but apparently assumed it was fair to inspect it when she stopped. India wondered what he thought of the ghosts. She knew he could see them; she could tell by his face. But he didn't say anything about them. "Foolish quail," he said. "The hawk will get it."

India shrugged. "Hawks have to eat. Hawks live for the moment." That was the counterpoint to the eternal rose-red walls and their ghosts. The hawk of the moment. "I want to come back," she said. "There isn't enough time in one day. Is it all right if I come back?"

"If you can find it. Or I bring you. But the cliff house belongs to Pueblo people, not Navajo!"

"I don't know any Navajo," India said, puzzled by his intensity. "Well, the Horseman brothers at the trading post a little. But—"

"Someone's been along the trail. Navajo pony. I don't like it. They have no business. These are our people." He gestured at the cliff house. "Not Navajo. The Navajo call them Anasazi—Enemy Ancestors. So you don't let Navajo show you the cliff house. You go with *me!*"

"Of course. It was your present to me. I wouldn't let someone else give me the same present."

Johnny relaxed. "I just don't like them out here," he muttered, a little shamefaced.

"Tiwa don't get along with Navajo?" That had been the impression she had gotten from both sides.

"Pueblo people were here first. Hopi and Zuni, Tiwa, Acoma. Then the Navajo come, say that their Changing Woman showed them the country to be theirs."

"I can see that the Tiwa wouldn't like that."

"There were wars in the old days, before the white man. Now—" Johnny shrugged.

The white man hadn't left much to fight over, India thought, embarrassed by her own ancestors. Johnny looked embarrassed, too. He had gone to sit under the piñon tree again. This was the most conversation she had ever had out of him about anything that mattered to him.

She worked on the painting until Johnny got up from the shade again and said it would be night before they got back if she didn't quit.

"Oh, all right. I'll come back tomorrow," India said, regretfully cleaning her palette. She looked wistfully at the high city. "I want to see inside. Can I climb up?"

"Not without me," Johnny said firmly. "And I have to work for Mike tomorrow. You fall and break your neck or get bit by a rattlesnake and I'll probably lose my job."

"Probably." India laughed. "Then when? We can go up, can't we?" If she could only look at it from down here, it would break her heart. She wanted to be inside, in the heart of the house, to paint it from the inside out when she had finished with its surface, to dive through all the onion layers to its core.

"I knew you would want to. You want to get in everything, turn it inside out, see the seams."

"Well, how on earth are you supposed to know things if you don't do that?" India asked.

"You can't hold everything upside down and shake it," Johnny countered.

"I don't!" India was indignant. "Well, I try not to."

"You've been good," Johnny allowed. "With Indians. But you want to."

India sighed. "Of course I do. I want to know everything. It seems like a waste of life not to find out things."

"You have too much energy." He made it sound as if it were a condition of the blood that ought to be treated.

India repacked her saddlebags and hooked the sling around her wet canvas.

As Johnny was mounting his pony, he said, "I'll bring you back the first day Mike doesn't need me. We'll take a ladder."

India's eyes lit up. "Oh, Johnny! Bless you. I can't wait."

Johnny watched her wistfully as she swung into the saddle, tucking in the folds of her divided skirt. Then he looked thoughtfully at the trail again. Finally he shrugged. If he told his uncle about the Navajo pony's hoofprints, he would have to tell his uncle what he was doing out here. Luis had already warned him away from India. "She is a good girl," he had said. "But she is not *your* girl. Don't break your heart, and don't do anything stupid."

Luis wasn't the only one who wouldn't approve of the outing. Frank was waiting for India when she rode in at dusk with Johnny. The two men looked at each other with careful disinterest; then Johnny lifted his black hat solemnly to India and rode off down the Pueblo Road, his dark braids bouncing with the pony's trot.

"When did you get back?" India asked, sliding down from the saddle and leading her horse to the stable. "Does this mean Midge is all right?"

"She's better," Frank said. "On the mend. I had to get out of there."

"Had to?" India wrinkled her brow.

"Where have you been?" Frank demanded.

India's eyebrows shot up. "What?"

"Where did you go off to all day with Johnny Rojas? And what was Eden thinking of to let you? Has everybody lost their minds?"

"Just you, apparently," India commented. She undid the pony's girth.

"Anything could have happened to you out there."

"With *Johnny?*" India's snort of amusement was audible.

"He's in love with you," Frank said stubbornly. "That makes men do strange things."

India cocked her head at him thoughtfully. "Like the urge to stick their noses into other people's business without offering a good reason."

"What's that supposed to mean?"

India dragged the saddle into the tack shed, and Frank followed her. She thought she knew what was bothering him. It might be dangerous to bait Frank with Johnny, but she felt disinclined to let that stop her. She watched him as he stood in the doorway, arms folded, the sunset flaming behind him. It created an aureole around his head that made her think of fire rather than halos. Crossing her arms behind her back, she leaned against the saddle on its bar. "What gives you the right to care who falls in love with me?"

Frank took two steps into the tack shed and without warning put both hands on her shoulders and kissed her, hard.

India found it an entirely different sensation from the peck on the end of her nose by the village well. She remembered, without being certain why, the murmured sounds she had heard coming from Mike and Eden's room. Frank's body, which seemed to be all hard angles, was pressed close against her, and his mouth covered hers.

Just as she was about to put her arms around him, Frank stepped back. "Damn," he whispered. "Poor old Johnny."

"I never kissed poor old Johnny," India said indignantly when she had her breath back.

"You didn't kiss me. I kissed you."

"I was going to kiss you."

"I know." Frank looked at her seriously for once. "Maybe I've got some sense left."

India eyed him speculatively. She wanted to kiss him again, but maybe that wouldn't be a good idea. "If Midge isn't well yet, why did you come back?" she asked, needing to change the subject.

Frank ran a hand over his face. "There was something strange going on between my parents. I didn't want to leave Midge alone in the middle of it, but I was making it worse."

"How?"

"I don't know exactly. But my mother's been giving me my father's place, shutting him out." He eased out the door. "Sex is very strange chemistry. You're too young for it."

"I'm nineteen!" she shouted to his retreating back.

XIV

Washington, D.C.

Midge tugged at her mother's fingers. "No, Mother, stay. We can all be together." She smiled at her father, firmly attached to her other hand. Outside it was raining, a gentle summer evening patter that had cooled the air and made the bedroom feel cozy instead of stifling. "Let's play cards. The three of us. This is perfect." Midge smiled and stretched her legs, wiggling her toes with delight.

Cindy looked at Henry across the bed. Their eyes didn't quite meet. "Well, perhaps just for a little while," she said, carefully enunciating the words. "Since you want us to." She bent and got the deck of cards from the bottom shelf of the nightstand by Midge's bed. A white folding bed tray was propped beside it, and she placed it carefully across Midge's lap. "You'll have to shuffle, darling."

"Cassino?" Midge asked.

"All right." Cindy settled herself in the small armchair by Midge's bed. Henry scooted his own chair close to Midge's other side.

Midge dealt, and they all consulted their hands and the cards in the center. Midge sighed happily. "Now that

Daddy's home and I'm getting well, we can play cards every night the way we used to."

Henry turned up a six and took one from the pile.

"*Can't* we?" Midge asked, smiling—although a pleading note had crept into her voice.

"I'd better watch out," Henry said. "You're getting old enough to beat me."

"I'm working on it. If only Frank was here, we could play partners, Frank and me against you and Mama. Then we could beat the socks off you."

Her parents were silent, turning over their cards. Midge looked from one to the other. "When I'm well, we could go camping together. As long as Daddy has leave, we can have such fun!"

Cindy put two cards on the table. "Building fours," she said. "Darling, I don't know. Your father will probably have a busy schedule. . . ." Her voice trailed off as she studied the cards.

"How can he have a busy schedule when he's on leave?" Midge demanded.

Henry smiled at her. "You don't know what the army's like, dear. They can be quite unreasonable when it comes to any plans one might be making."

"It's not fair! I want us to be together. We used to *do* things together. I think the army's awful."

Henry and Cindy glanced at each other, then away. "I'm sure your father will have time for you, dear," Cindy said.

"Of course," Henry said stiffly. "Whatever the . . . *army* decides, I won't miss a chance to beat you at cassino." He leaned forward and kissed her forehead.

"Did you hear that, Mother?" Midge tried to pick up the conversation, push it, poke it into a semblance of family banter. "I'm going to devastate him now, but I'm going

to let you come in second just to punish him for brag-
ging."

"All right, dear."

It was hardly a response at all. Midge looked at her
mother, bewildered. They used to laugh over cassino and
old maid, brag and threaten each other. "This is fun," she
said adamantly. "I'm so happy."

They played until the cards were gone, and Midge
laboriously counted up the scores.

"Are you tired, darling?" Cindy asked. "Do you want
me to do that?"

"No, I will." Midge looked pale and stubborn. "Can
we play again?"

"Do you really want to? I think you should rest."

"Maybe you and Daddy could play, while I rest. You
could play pinochle," Midge offered. "I know you like
that."

"You aren't obliged to entertain us," Henry said.

"I'm not. I mean, I just want you to—to—"

"I'll tell you what, dear," Cindy said smoothly. "Why
don't you show your father how far you can move your
legs? I was very proud of you this morning."

"I think I'm too tired." Midge closed her eyes. "It
doesn't feel right now."

Paling with concern, Cindy stood up. "Let me look."

Janessa tapped at the open door. "Bedtime," she announced.

"She says her leg is worse again," Cindy said anx-
iously. She looked over her shoulder at Janessa, her hand
moving up and down Midge's shin.

"Let me see." Janessa politely but firmly elbowed
Cindy aside and took Midge's knee in practiced hands.
"Bend it here for me. That's right. No, hold it."

"I can't," Midge said.

Janessa looked sharply at her and back to the knee. It

flopped in her hand. Henry leaned over the bed from the other side, his hand stroking Midge's forehead. "You have to try, sweetheart. Hold my hand and try again."

Midge's fingers gripped his like a vise. She lifted the knee a little bit. Cindy edged back past Janessa and took her other hand.

"Good girl," Cindy whispered. "Can you move the other one?" She looked at Janessa, frightened.

Midge lifted her right knee. It wavered. Tears slid down her cheeks. The knee collapsed. "I can't do any more," she whimpered. She looked at the window, the rain sliding softly down the pane. It seemed depressing now, damp and chilly. "Maybe I'll be better in the morning."

"I'm sure you will be," Janessa said briskly. She pulled the blanket up over Midge and tucked it in with hospital efficiency. "We'll get you up and try walking. It's about time."

"But it's gotten worse again!" Cindy said.

"Aren't you running the risk of her straining it?" Henry asked. "I don't think that's a wise idea."

Janessa looked at them and jerked her head toward the hallway. "Midge needs to sleep now," she ordered. She strode out and waited, plainly intending to stay there until they came out, too. When they did—carefully apart, as if they were strangers—Janessa shut the door behind them with an angry pull that managed at the last minute not to make a noise. "I won't have this kind of goings-on with my patient," she hissed.

"Anyone can see her knee is worse," Henry said. "I'm her father. I have a right—"

"Get away from that door," Janessa whispered. "If you want to argue with me, do it in the parlor." She marched down the stairs, and Henry followed, Cindy behind him.

"Now, see here!" Henry said in a rising voice to Janessa, who was halfway through the parlor doorway.

Cindy pulled the door shut. "You might want to keep our quarrels private," she commented between gritted teeth.

"You were the last one through the door," Henry snapped.

Ignoring him, Cindy turned to Janessa. "I want a complete evaluation of Midge's condition from you. I'm concerned about this relapse. Do you think we should have a specialist?"

"I intend to call one in this afternoon," Henry said.

Cindy rounded on him. "You are not in charge of this decision!"

"This is my house," Henry said curtly, "and I am still the head of my family."

"You forfeited your family. I sent for you as a courtesy. Because Midge wanted you here."

"Stop it, you two!" Janessa said.

"For all the good you are doing her." Cindy ignored Janessa and continued lashing out at her husband. "Endangering your career and her future in that cavalier fashion."

"You sent for me!"

"I had no choice!"

Janessa looked at her aunt and uncle in exasperation. "I'll give you an evaluation," she said irately. She tried to push them apart with her presence. "If you don't change your attitude, you will turn that child into a permanent invalid. There is nothing the matter with her knees."

"What are you talking about?" Cindy asked. "She couldn't keep them bent for thirty seconds."

"She could earlier," Janessa said grimly, "before she tried to play cards with the two of you."

Cindy looked at her, stricken, and then angrily at Henry.

Janessa was trying to rally her tact. These were, after all, her aunt and uncle, older than she. She wrapped her doctor's dignity about her. "If you continue to be at odds with each other, you will damage her chances of recovery. That's put as nicely as I can manage it. She wants the family together. You've made it quite obvious that that is not the case."

"I've never permitted a quarrel to take place in front of her," Cindy protested.

"Great Caesar's ghost, you don't need a quarrel!" Janessa flung up her arms in vexation. "The air is practically poisonous in any room the two of you are in together. Of course she's having a relapse! That's the only way she can get you to stop throwing vitriol at each other and pay attention to her."

"Do you mean she's faking it?" Henry demanded. "I felt that leg. It was limp."

Janessa lost her tact. "Of course she's not faking it, you puttyhead. Not intentionally. But if being bedridden was the only situation that got you what you wanted, you might find it easier to let it happen. She'll stay sick as long as that is the only thing that will keep you both focused on her. And keep you from savaging each other."

They both stared at her now, as if they had gotten the message and were prepared to kill the messenger.

Let them snap each other to bits, Janessa thought. *How did I get caught up in this?* "The longer she stays in that bed, the more her muscles will atrophy," she snarled. "You had better come to terms with each other fast." She spun on her heel, wrenched open the door, and marched into the hall, wondering angrily if she had done any good at all or simply set the stage for a final explosion in which the entire family, not only her aunt and uncle, would be bruised and battered.

She went into the dining room and sat at the long, bare table with her forehead in her hands. *Oh, Charley,* she thought, *will this happen to us someday? Does marriage invariably come to this?* Across the hall she could hear the explosion somewhat muffled by the again-closed parlor door. She felt furious herself, ready to snap at anyone because love didn't seem to be enough.

Henry and Cindy faced each other across the parlor rug, across the homely details of a knitting basket and the morning paper. They stood, fists clenched. Both their faces were red, splotched with anger. It seemed to each that the other looked ugly, deformed.

"You never cared about the children!" Cindy shouted at him. "You never cared about me! All you *ever* cared about is the army, your everlasting precious *job!*"

"The children were *your* job to raise!" Henry shouted back. "If you'd paid as much attention to them as you did a parcel of lisping artists who wouldn't know what a real job was, Frank wouldn't be the disgrace he is!"

"*I* managed to refrain from mixing my work with my personal affairs," Cindy spat at him. "I was mistaken. You did care for something else: that German tart you couldn't resist falling all over your boots for."

"Gisela was my wife," Henry said coldly.

"Not while you were climbing into her sheets in such a hurry. *I* was your fiancée while you were doing that!"

"I thought we'd buried all that. It's like you to rake up everything you can think of, things that were settled years ago."

"Settled to *your* satisfaction. You got your piece on the side! You got your rich wife with a title! Then when she died, you managed to come back here and actually persuaded me to marry you. I must have been crazy!" Cindy screamed.

"I think you are! You weren't exactly untouched when I got back, either. You hopped into the marriage bed with Reed Kerr pretty fast. Why were you in such a hurry?"

"I don't have to listen to this. I don't have to listen to *you!*" Cindy marched to the other side of the room. Then abruptly she spun around, a finger leveled at Henry's face. "Why should I have waited for you? You were dandling that German *whore* on your knee—"

"You are speaking of Peter's mother!" Henry thundered. "Don't you—"

"Peter isn't here!"

"It's just like you to bring up—"

"And I raised Peter for you. When were you ever home to do it?"

"That was your job. You're the mother."

"Yes, a mother, not an unpaid serf! You expected me to raise perfect children for you and trot them out to curtsy and bow whenever you decided to come home. From the army. From your job." She marched across the floor again and glared up at him. "From your goddamned job!"

"My job put food on the table! My job bought this house!" Henry bellowed. "Your job was to run it. But you had to have your art." He had seized on that as his injury. He mimicked a swooning, insipid aesthete. "Ran around all over the city with fancy boys in velvet coats and made me a laughingstock."

"That's ridiculous! You never objected at the time."

"I wanted you to have an outlet. You were unstable. Your mother thought it was your first husband's death."

"That is ridiculous! My mother never said any such thing."

"You are doing it now," Henry said. "Losing control. I think you need to see a specialist."

"You keep quiet!" Cindy screamed. "You smug, patronizing *bastard!*"

"That is precisely what I mean." Henry's tone was maddeningly calm. "You wouldn't be using that language if you weren't out of control."

"You never spent enough time with me to know what's normal. You were never home for more than a day at a time."

"Well, it didn't appear to bother you!" Henry roared, his pitch now matching Cindy's. "I offered to take you with me—*tried* to take you with me—whenever I had assignments that wouldn't be dangerous for you and the children. You only came once. You couldn't be bothered. You had to hang a show with some slimy— How many of *them* have you slept with?"

"How dare you! And what would they want with me? I'm old enough to be their mother, most of them, by now. And I never was pretty—at least not like your Gisela. I don't know what you wanted with me! And I'm not pretty now!"

"You look like hell now. You didn't used to. Are you going to blame me for that? Or for your having decided to just go ahead and curdle? You invested so much hate in me it made you ugly."

"You're ugly, too," Cindy said, tears suddenly spilling down her face. Angrily she wiped them away. "You look mean; your face is pinched."

"I'm not surprised. When I married you, I thought I was getting back what we'd lost. I thought I was getting the sweet girl I left."

"I grew up!" Cindy shouted.

"You haven't grown up yet!" Henry shouted back. "You've put me through hell. You and the rest of your family. You deliberately set out to corrupt Frank, to serve I don't know what—your brother's damned pacifist opinions."

"Wonderful. Let's drag the whole family into this. They're your family, too. I should never have married you. There isn't any place to get *away* from you!" That Henry had been adopted by Cindy's mother and her second husband had made the whole situation too close for comfort.

"Maybe you'd have done us both a favor! I wouldn't have had to watch you fawn over the children and spoil them. You took Peter away from me, too. You made sure he wouldn't go into the army. Was that because you hated his mother or because you hated me?"

"I hate you both!" Cindy spat. "You never cared what you did to me."

"How did you know?"

"The evidence at hand. She wasn't the only one either, was she?"

Henry flinched. Cindy didn't miss it.

"I take it you've enjoyed the Philippines," she said acidly.

"I haven't had a wife!" Henry snarled. "I've had a millstone around my neck, whose house I have to pay for and whose gowns I have to buy and who won't let me in the same room with her much less in the same bed. Why should I be faithful?"

"I can't imagine. You never were before."

"And you've been trying to spite me for it ever since. You saw to it that Frank turned into a wastrel. He was my pride, and you turned him against me!"

They glared at each other, beyond reason or caring, dredging the depths for something else to hurl. "I nearly lost my daughter," Cindy said, her voice as brittle as glass. "I don't have the energy to expend on your sensitivities."

"Go ahead!" Henry yelled. "Throw it in my face! I left her, and she got sick. Do you think I haven't beaten myself with that often enough? Do you think I need you to do it for me?"

"She didn't get sick because you left," Cindy said, her eyes narrowed and her face contorted. "Don't give yourself that much credit. You aren't that important."

"Midge thinks I am."

"Midge drank infected milk. I'm the one who should have seen what it was. I should have thought about diphtheria. I'll never forgive myself for waiting so long, letting it get worse. Don't you dare tell me about yourself. *I* know what I did!"

"You don't know beans. What the hell do you want to blame yourself for, anyway?"

"Because it's my fault."

"It's not. You heard Janessa. It's my doing."

"She didn't say that's why she came down with it."

"I'll ask her."

"No, you won't. Leave her out of this!" Cindy screamed.

"I know what I'm talking about!" Henry screamed back.

They fell silent, temporarily out of ammunition.

Then Henry slumped against the wall. He bent his head. "God damn you, Cindy, can't you let me alone to be sorry? Must you have your pound of flesh, too?"

Cindy's face was white. Her hands and knees shook. "I don't want—" It seemed an effort now to talk. "Your going didn't make Midge sick," she said dully. "Not in that way, anyhow."

Henry looked at her bleakly. He, too, looked spent. "You didn't make her sick, either." The words were flat. "And you couldn't have known what it was."

Cindy shook her head. They looked at each other

across the chasm of the parlor rug, trying to find some path that at least would allow them to speak. The quick flame of their anger had consumed nearly everything. There wasn't enough left to build another fire. Tomorrow maybe, when they had slept, they could tear at each other again, but not now.

Would they? Cindy thought. Would they simply go on flaying each other day after day until there was nothing left of either of them? Henry's expression was so miserable, his face so scored with sadness that her eyes overflowed again and her voice caught in her throat. "It's not fair," she said. "Why did this happen to us?"

"I don't know," Henry said, baffled. "I've never known. I didn't know . . . how it happened with Gisela."

"She just swept you off your feet?" Cindy said, a bit of acid left in her voice.

"I wasn't—I wasn't very old. I listened to my pants instead of my head. You weren't there and she was. But you *were* just as pretty."

"I wasn't. And I'm not now."

"I didn't fall in love with you because you were pretty," Henry argued.

"But once you were living with Gisela, you wouldn't come back—until she died."

"I couldn't," Henry said. "I was trapped. She'd had my child. And damn it, I did care about her. But not ever the way I did about you."

"That doesn't make any sense," Cindy said, exasperated.

"No."

"Why can't we let this go? Is it Frank, or is it Gisela we've been fighting over? Was there someone in Manila, too?"

"Yes."

"Was she prettier than me?"

"She was younger. Yes."

"Are you going back to her?"

"No."

"Why?"

"Because I'm too tired."

Cindy looked at his face. Henry was nearly fifty. It was odd how she saw him almost always as the boy he had been, and then there would be quick, shocking flashes of a face creased with lines and eyes sunk far under their brows. Was that how he saw her, or did the old woman stay always on the surface? She was afraid to ask.

"Did we make Midge sick somehow?" she whispered. "Is this our punishment for hating each other?"

"Do we?"

"I don't know. I thought we did. I can't be indifferent to you. I tried, but I can't. Hating you seemed the best solution."

"Because of Frank." It wasn't a question.

"I think so."

"Now that he's back?" Henry pressed.

"I don't know. He came back for you. Because there was a war. He thought I would need him."

"That doesn't sound like he came back for *me*."

"He came back *because* of you. Can't you let him in?"

"He is in," Henry said stubbornly.

"Into *your* world. Into whatever you've shut him away from."

Henry sighed. "I don't know. Would it make a difference with you?"

"You would do it for me and not for Frank?"

"I've cursed myself over and over because I couldn't keep Frank on the right path." He paused. "Because I lost him."

Cindy sighed. "You never could bend."

"I never tried," Henry said abruptly. His voice broke. He put out a hand to her and then drew it away again.

"Oh." Cindy stared at him, reading the misery in his face. She stepped across the parlor rug as if it were a canyon in the floor that might yet swallow her up. She held out her own hands.

He took them, and she thought he would break her fingers he held so tightly. She looked into his face and saw that it was wet with tears. Henry never cried. She stared dumbly. The tears slid down his cheeks. She put her head against his shirt. "What went wrong?" she asked with a sob.

"I thought it was Frank," Henry said in a now-uncertain voice.

"So did I," Cindy said against his chest. "But if something wasn't wrong to begin with, would we have pulled apart like that over Frank? What's wrong with us?"

Henry released her hands and held her around her waist instead. "You mean, why aren't we perfect?" he asked with a little snort of laughter. "I thought we were supposed to be, too."

"I'm tired," Cindy said. Her knees shook again.

"Sit down." Henry led her to the sofa, sat her down on it, put his arms around her. "Is it all right if I hold you?"

She nodded. "I'm sorry I said I hated you. That was wicked."

"You did hate me. But I'd rather you hated me than didn't care."

"Oh, I cared." Cindy gave the same weary laugh that Henry had. "I burned your letters. I didn't just throw them out, I made a ceremony of it. If I hadn't been so old and respectable, I'd have danced around the fire."

"Like a witch. I can just see that."

Her arm crept around his neck. "Where did our sense of humor go?" she said finally. "We got to where we couldn't laugh. We got self-righteous."

"You may have had some reason to be," Henry said quietly.

She let out a long, slow breath. It was the closest he had come to saying he was in the wrong. She couldn't find any joy in rubbing his nose in it. She felt achingly sorry for him.

"You didn't do wrong by Midge," he said into her ear. "You have to get hold of that. And she's going to be fine."

"Janessa said—"

"Janessa." Henry gave a weary, irritable grunt. "Janessa had better go home and look after her own children. Midge will be fine."

"Henry, I couldn't have done without her. She saved Midge's life."

"That doesn't mean she's responsible for her forever. Or us. She can go and lay down the law to her husband." Henry yawned. He rested against the back of the sofa with Cindy leaning on him. His bones felt heavy yet liquid. He didn't know where the anger had gone, but he didn't want it back.

Cindy lay against him like a dead weight, her eyes closed. No one had lit the lamps, and the sky was darkening outside, dimming the parlor with it. The shadows seemed to cling to them, hold them down, as tired as they were.

"I don't suppose it matters," Henry said, "but I didn't stop loving you when I was with Gisela. I think that I was fool enough to think I could somehow have you both. Keep you in memory, anyway."

"It matters," Cindy murmured. "I don't suppose it

should, but it matters." She didn't tell him how she had felt about him while she was married to Reed. Let him guess about that. She yawned and pressed her face against his chest, too hot for comfort on a hot night, but she felt cold now, chilled by her weariness.

What will happen to us now? she wondered, but she was too tired to ask. And she didn't think he knew.

They sat in stillness, eyes closed, dozing in the shadows. Once he shifted an arm that was going to sleep, and she moved to sit up. He pulled her back down.

The sky outside darkened, and stars came out. The insect chorus swelled in the althea bushes outside the window, cicadas and katydids yammering into the hot darkness. Finally the cicadas went to bed. No one had knocked at the parlor door, for no one had had that much nerve. Cindy woke, half-sat up, and looked around blearily. It was full dark outside, a sliver of a moon giving the room its only light. Henry was snoring. His mouth hung partly open, and his face looked relaxed, the lines smoothed out of it with sleep. She touched his cheek, and his eyes opened.

Cindy moved stiffly off his lap. "Come to bed."

Henry nodded. He stood, gingerly, wincing at creaking joints. "I'm an old man," he said ruefully.

She nodded, held out her hand. He took it, and they went into the dark hallway and up the stairs. In the upstairs landing he stopped, waiting, watching her. She opened their bedroom door and led him through it.

XV

Cindy woke at ten, the light streaming through the east window full in her face. She heard birdsong outside and noises downstairs. There seemed to be a tactful silence in the hallway outside her bedroom door, as if everyone was carefully keeping their distance.

She looked down at Henry, still sleeping, his face still relaxed as it had been last night when unconsciousness had smoothed his age away. His hair had gradually darkened from the straw color of his youth and now was lightening again into gray. His skin was burned brown to the base of his neck and then from his elbows down, but his chest and legs were pale. The Philippines had marked him only in the parts that showed, Cindy thought, but had left the core as it had always been. Or was it? Cindy watched him curiously, tracking the slow rise and fall of his chest, the faint sibilant whisper of breath between his lips. Was he the same? And had she ever known him clear to the bone anyway?

This seemed to be a new guise he had come home in, or perhaps it was only that she hadn't seen it before, hadn't given notice and thus reality to the signs of age—in him any more than in herself. She marked them now: the loose skin at the throat, the spidery blue veins down the sides of his thighs, the roll of skin around the waist. They were a satisfaction to her, symbols of what tethered him here to her now.

She looked down at herself, at the sagging breasts beneath the lawn nightdress. She'd nursed two babies; you couldn't keep a young woman's figure forever, not even with a corset. And her hands—the veins stood out and the skin was etched with tiny lines. She spread one before her, made a fist to see the skin tighten and then loosen again when she relaxed her hand. How odd only to look young when you clenched your fist. But she had done that for a lot of her youth: clenched her fist.

Henry stirred beside her, and she watched him wake up, his mouth moving, murmuring something. He rolled toward her, draped an arm across her lap, then tightened both arms around her. She sat against the pillows with his head in her lap, his arms around her hips.

She held her breath, daring him to call her by the wrong name. He opened his eyes, and his grip on her tightened. He turned his head so that he could look up at her. His green eyes were shadowed beneath his brows, and the faded scar that ran down his left cheek stood out nearly as white as her nightgown against his tan.

"Good morning," he whispered.

"Good morning," she said solemnly.

"I was afraid you might hate it when you remembered I was here."

"Is that why you have such a strong grip on me?"

"Yes." He loosened it just a little, and she slid down in the bed again. He propped himself on his elbows above her. "You *are* pretty," he said quietly. "You have always been beautiful to me."

"I know," she whispered. She touched the scar and the ridges of his face. "What will happen to us now?"

"I don't know," he said. He put a hand on her breast almost imploringly, and she pulled his face down to hers.

They had tried the night before to make love. But still keyed up with their anger and worn out with its aftermath, they had been unable to seal their pact, to make themselves married again: The physical responses had refused to waken. Now was the time, Cindy thought. Now. And afterward, perhaps then, they would know something about their future.

They slept again, wrapped around each other, drained, sated with relief beyond bearing. They woke again, somewhat sheepishly, at, according to Henry's pocket watch on the bedside table, two in the afternoon.

Cindy sat upright, fumbling for her glasses. "Oh, my goodness!"

"Slow down," Henry said.

"What will they think?"

"I don't care what Janessa thinks, and Midge won't know. Relax. Stop fluffing your feathers like a hen."

"*Someone* had better set some standards in this family." Cindy's mouth twitched with amusement. "However, I don't really care just now if everyone thinks I'm completely depraved," she said with satisfaction, climbing out of bed.

Henry swung his legs over his own side of the bed and reached to the floor for his drawers. The room no longer looked like her own, Cindy thought; it was no longer her private retreat of anger and grief. It was theirs again. His pocket knife and his watch chain and his shirt studs on the dresser had taken their possession of it. His trousers on the cedar chest and his shoes on the floor gave evidence of residence, of male habitation as strong as the scent of saddle leather among the perfumed cushions. He pulled his trousers on, oblivious to their symbolism in her world.

Cindy pulled her knickers on and picked her corset

off the rug where it lay. Henry came around the bed and hooked it for her, the way he always had when they were alone. He pulled her tangled hair aside and kissed the back of her neck. "I don't know what's going to happen now," he said truthfully. "I'll try my damnedest. But you'll have to let me find my own way with Frank."

"I know." She looked at him woefully. "It breaks my heart to see the two of you estranged."

"You can't force us back together."

"I know that, too." She brushed her hair and swept it into a practiced pompadour, securing it with a handful of tortoiseshell pins.

Henry took her hand. He grinned. "Then let's scandalize Lutie by asking for breakfast."

Lutie was properly scandalized and took much pleasure in it, frying bacon and muttering, "Past two in the afternoon!" She squeezed them fresh orange juice and set two places in the breakfast room, demanding to know what the world was coming to.

"My question exactly," Henry murmured. "Cindy, what am *I* going to do now?"

Cindy hesitated. "Do you mean with your work? Do you mean with the army?"

"They won't court-martial me. You can relax."

"Well, they'd be fools!" Cindy said indignantly.

"I am on extended leave. Indefinite leave. I tried to resign."

Cindy stared at him, bacon frozen halfway to her mouth.

"Well, it was mostly temper," Henry said. "At the time. Now, I don't know."

"Don't know what? Whether you want to go back?"

"I could retire. I have enough pension. We would be comfortable."

"I would," Cindy said frankly. "Would you?"

"To stay home and rave at the editorials in the evening paper and work on my memoirs? I don't know. That's what I don't know. Not to have the job—" *To know I'll never go anywhere with purpose again. Nevermore the excitement, the sense of being that alive . . . oh, Estrella!* The thought was a fleeting wail in his mind; he closed his ears to it and looked at his wife. Her graying pompadour framed a face that seemed to have softened since the previous day. Her spectacles sat low on her nose, and her blue eyes looked out at him from their nest of fine crow's feet. They were still so blue, he thought.

"Right now," he said carefully, "I want nothing more than to stay here, with you and Midge. I might even grow a garden." He smiled. "Maybe get some bib overalls and chew tobacco."

"Horrors," Cindy said, laughing.

Henry contemplated his immaculate hands and shirt cuffs. He was a fastidious dresser even when an assignment didn't demand otherwise. "The only trouble," he said seriously, "is that I don't know how long I might feel that way. Not about you and Midge, but about not working."

Cindy nodded. "I understand. Is there any middle ground? Do you *have* to be in the field? Men younger than you are running the show in Washington. Wouldn't they kick you upstairs?"

"They might. I might not like it."

"*They* might not like it," Cindy said with asperity. "You might be as restful as a caged wolf."

"I feel restful now. Lazy. Maybe I'm just tired."

"You are dead tired," Cindy said in a tone that brooked no argument. "So am I. I lived on anger for so long, I feel like Midge, as if my muscles won't work. Let them leave you on extended furlough. They won't bother you if you don't bother them. Give yourself time. Stay home with us and see if it galls you."

"All right. I'll try it. At the moment I feel oddly content." Henry looked around the breakfast room as if seeing it for the first time. Maybe this *was* going to work.

"I want to check on Midge," Cindy said. "Despite Janessa's theories." She stood up as he finished his eggs, and he followed her upstairs. There had been no peep from Midge's room, but when they went in, they found Janessa sitting by the bed and Midge with an impish grin on her face, picking up playing cards with her toes.

"Where have you *been?*" she said reprovingly, but her eyes were dancing.

So much for marital privacy, Cindy thought. But if it did Midge good—

"Look what I can do," Midge said. She waggled her toes, which were clutching the ace of spades. "Janessa says I can probably try walking tomorrow."

"Really?" Cindy asked.

"I think so," Janessa said. "The sooner she's up, the better." The look that she gave her aunt and uncle was bland and careful. Cindy tried but couldn't detect a hint of I-told-you-so. Janessa must be dead tired, too.

"What about you, dear?" Cindy asked. "You've been a godsend, but you haven't even seen your own babies."

Janessa gave them an assessing look. Cindy could feel Henry bristling beside her. She knew that whether Janessa had been right or not didn't make Henry delighted to have his paternal obligations outlined to him by his niece.

"If Midge is really out of danger . . ." Henry said.

Janessa laughed. His thoughts were far too plain on his face. "She is. And I agree; it's high time I went to Richmond and collected my own kith and kin. I was thinking that this morning," she said with a sideways glance at the two of them. "As soon as I see Midge on her feet."

"I think she'll surprise us," Henry said, kissing his daughter's forehead, "how soon she's up and around." His expression said that he certainly hoped so.

The next morning Janessa stood on the depot platform wreathed in a white cloud of steam from the train engine as she said her good-byes to her aunt and uncle. *It's time,* she thought. Her uncle would never make the house his again, his and Cindy's, as long as she was there. Frank had been right to go, and now she had to go, too. Between them, they had filled the hole left by Henry for too long. To come home and find yourself told how to conduct your marriage by your niece and to find your son in your place—literally, the first night at dinner—well, none of that was conducive to a proper homecoming for the head of the family. Janessa just hoped that Henry could hang on to what he and Cindy had managed to achieve if she got out of their hair.

Not my business now, she thought, giving Cindy one last kiss, then stepping up the iron stairs into the car. *I have my own fish to fry. Oh, Lord!* Janessa took her seat and leaned her head back against the stiff horsehair cushion that was only marginally softened by its plush cover. Her uncle would have to figure out his questionable future without her help. She and Charley had enough to work on.

All the questions hovering in the air around her and Charley had only been postponed by diphtheria. Nothing was any more certain than it had been. Less so—Kathleen was gone. Had Charley told the twins? she wondered. He'd better have. *I'm not going to do that, too.* She felt unreasonably annoyed at having shouldered the burden for so long in Cindy's house, despite her having ordered

Charley out of it and off to Richmond. *I've gotten illogical,* she thought. *Cross and illogical. Maybe if I sleep I'll be reasonable by the time I get to Richmond.*

She closed her eyes with determination and dozed, a half-sleep into which strange dreams intruded. The twins pulled at her skirts, and all the male doctors from her hospital in New York shook their fingers at her. Charley faded in and out like Alice's Cheshire Cat, never solid enough to grab. He was metamorphosing into the preacher who had preached a sermon against her for advocating birth control when she abruptly woke up. The train was pulling into Richmond. She didn't feel any more reasonable. On the contrary, she was annoyed with Charley for taking the fool's side.

She staggered off the train to find him waiting for her, and whatever annoyance she had harbored in her dream state vanished. She put her head against his coat and heaved a deep sigh. "Oh, thank God."

Charley inspected her. "You look worn out. Mother says, 'It's our duty to put you to bed and wait on you hand and foot until you have roses in your cheeks again.' That's a direct quote."

Janessa chuckled. Miss Lida, as Charley's mother was called by everyone who knew her, was given to high-flown sentiment, but she meant every word of it.

"Nan's champing at the bit to see you," Charley said. "She and George are coming to dinner." Nan Eames, Charley's sister, was Janessa's college roommate from more years ago than either of them cared to count. "The twins are fine," he said before she could ask. "Fat and sassy."

"Do they know about Kathleen?"

"I told them. I don't know how well they've grasped it. They were very solemn, but they seem to still be looking for her."

"We have to decide what we're going to do," Janessa said. "About a nurse. And what to do now. And—"

"Tomorrow," Charley said firmly. "You've been thinking about what we ought to do all the way down here on the train. I can tell by looking at you. You need to get some perspective."

"Why?" Janessa asked suspiciously.

"Because I have some ideas, too," Charley said mildly, "and I'm not going to expound them to anyone who looks like she was just pulled off a lifeboat."

Miss Lida flew out the front door and greeted Janessa in a flutter of gardenia cologne and lace shawls. She always wore two or three, for decoration more than warmth. Vernon Hughes came after her, shook Janessa's hand with pleasure, and shouted for a stable boy to carry her bags upstairs. He was Miss Lida's second husband, a northerner who had married the young widow after the Civil War and made enough of a place for himself in Richmond that that was no longer held against him. In fact, he had just been appointed a state appellate court judge, to the great satisfaction of his wife. She referred to him as "the judge" whenever she got the chance.

The twins shot out between Vernon and Miss Lida, with a black girl in a starched apron on their heels. "This is Belle, Louise's daughter," Miss Lida said. "She's been helping with the twins."

Janessa scooped Lally up. Brandon was hopping up and down, trying to climb her leg for his turn. She smiled at Belle. "Thank you. I'm sure they've been a handful."

"No, ma'am, they're good children, just lively. Ain't you, Pestiferous?" Belle detached Brandon and hugged him. "Your mama got time for you both. Don't you be in such a hurry."

"They can come up with me while I unpack," Janessa

said. What would Belle think of New York? she wondered. Probably she'd hate it.

Janessa spent the afternoon playing with Brandon and Lally. It didn't matter how tired she was. Four-year-olds didn't understand adult weariness. They always went at full speed, throttle wide open, until they collapsed, sometimes with their faces in their dinner plates.

After the twins had been fed and put to bed, Nan and George Eames came over. The adults gathered on the veranda with sherry and mint juleps and iced tea, waiting languidly for Louise to call them to the table.

"This is heaven," Janessa said. She sipped her sherry and looked lovingly at Charley. Nan sat beside her in the porch swing, talking delightedly about having a party for them.

"Now, you can't go away when you just got here. I can't put together a party in less than a week, and that's only if Mama lends me Louise." Nan was already counting up a guest list on her fingers. She had Charley's brown hair and round, slightly snub-nosed face and seemed to have settled happily into married life and motherhood. Her three children were eight, six, and three, and she dutifully sent Janessa photographs every Christmas.

Janessa always felt like the goblin's changeling among the Hugheses and the Eameses and the other Lawrences who inhabited Richmond. Janessa's mother had been a Cherokee, so her skin was dark. She had also inherited her mother's high cheekbones and sharply defined features. Those features, combined with her father's blue-gray eyes and hair that was light brown, made Janessa feel as exotic as a wild snakeroot in the daisy bed. From the time she was eight and had gone to live with her father, she had grown up a well-off rancher's daughter, but that hadn't kept her from finding herself unwelcome in some circles. Her Cherokee blood had had a lot to do with why Brice Amos had jilted her. There had never been a hint of prejudice from Nan and Charley's family, but wherever she went, Janessa was conscious that she was different and that some people didn't like that difference.

"A garden party," Nan was saying happily, oblivious to her sister-in-law's musings. "If it's not hotter than the Bad Place—it's been just awful lately—and if it doesn't rain."

"And how do you plan to predict either one, my dear?" George inquired genially.

"I don't. I always have two battle plans. Any good general knows that. Mama, *may* I borrow Louise?"

"Well, of course," Miss Lida said. Janessa wondered how Louise would feel about being "borrowed," but she suspected Louise was used to it. Miss Lida and her daughter traded their servants' services as blithely as they traded dress patterns and lent the good silver punch bowl back and forth for parties. It was just the sound of it that grated on Janessa's nerves—as if they still owned her. Miss Lida *had* owned her mother, Dolley, now retired with a little cabin of her own and an ample supply of snuff and bacon, sent by Miss Lida weekly. It was complicated.

Janessa waited until the next morning to confront Charley about what they should do. And then it didn't seem the right time, what with the twins bouncing around their parents' bedroom like rubber balls. Maybe when they took their naps. But during naptime Janessa then found herself helping Miss Lida polish the silver punch bowl and cups for Nan's party, instead. She had to admit she was reluctant to bring up the problem. There didn't seem to be any solution that someone wouldn't hate.

Eventually it was Charley who brought it up, sitting in the porch swing with a twin on either side and Janessa ensconced in a chaise longue with a pitcher of iced tea on a lacquer tray beside her. She had on a dress she hadn't had any chance to wear since she had bought it: a thin, rose-flowered silk with row after row of embroidery running across the bodice and the bottom of the skirt. She had picked a rose out of Miss Lida's garden and stuck it in her hair, its end concealed in a little glass vial. After a year in a sweltering, filthy hospital in Cuba, capped off by a case of diphtheria that had terrified the entire family, she felt almost sinfully luxurious. She heaved a sigh indicative of that, and Charley, who knew her well, read it accurately.

"This has gone on long enough," he said. "We are going home. After a suitable visit here, of course."

Janessa started to sit up. "Charley, you can't—"

"I can do anything I damn well please," Charley said mildly. "And you lie back down. What do you think you're doing?"

"I can't argue lying down," Janessa said. "I was afraid you'd do something like this."

"And so you got yourself all kited up to argue with me and do your duty?"

Janessa bit her lip. "It's all very well for me to go home—I was planning to. The twins need me. I couldn't leave them with Cindy any longer even if Midge hadn't got sick. But your job—"

"I imagine the government can get along without me for a while."

"But yellow fever—" Janessa pulled herself up and swung her legs onto the porch floor. "Charley, I have to sit up. I can't discuss this lying on a chaise like an odalisque."

He grinned. "I rather like you as an odalisque."

"Charley, yellow fever is your life's work. You won't be happy if you leave Cuba now."

"How do you know that?"

"You'll never find such a good laboratory setting to study it in New York. I won't have you give that up for me."

"How do you know I'm giving it up for you? Maybe I don't find Cuba the tropical paradise I was led to expect."

Janessa snorted. Cuba was disease-ridden, dirty, devoid of any sanitation system, and hotter than an oven. None of this had bothered him before, not with a hospital full of yellow fever cases to study. "Charley, it's your passion; it's an obsession. I've watched you. It's the whole focus of your work."

Charley's eyes held hers. "Janessa, I was unduly delighted to be sent for, despite the reason. When I got your wire, I packed up, saluted, and left—without a qualm. I missed you already. And I was afraid Brandon and Lally weren't even going to remember me." He looked down at them, then back at Janessa. "I'm not sure now that they did at first. I won't have that."

"How do I know you're not just doing this for me?" Janessa demanded.

"Is there some reason I shouldn't do it for you? You're my wife."

"I don't *want* you to do it for me." She flung up her hands. "I want you to do what *you* want. I want you to be happy."

"By being totally selfish?" Charley asked. "You don't offer yourself that option."

"Well, no."

"Then stop trying to foist it off on me. Sometimes you have to reorder your passions. I'm putting my passion for you and the children ahead of my passion for microbes. That's my privilege."

"But do you really *want* to?"

"I want to be where you and the children are."

"More than you want to work on the fever?"

"The two are just incompatible at the moment."

"Charley, I need to know if you are doing this for me."

"Well, you aren't going to. It's not an either/or proposition. Janessa, will you just relax?"

"I can't relax," she muttered.

"That's why we're going home. Now, lie down, while I swing the tads."

Dubiously, Janessa lay back on the chaise, while the porch swing creaked back and forth, in and out of the shade of Miss Lida's wisteria. She didn't argue with him anymore, but she was restless, crossing and recrossing her ankles, straightening the flower in her hair, fidgeting with the iced tea glasses on the lacquer tray.

Nan's party was a barbecue. She had decided that the twins ought to meet their Richmond cousins—and in any case, her own children had protested loudly at the idea of a grown-up event from which their own interesting selves would be excluded. At two in the afternoon her lawn was full of shrieking children, their nurses trailing them to see they did nothing too dreadful, and adults, in white summer suits and fluttering silk gowns, ignoring any offspring who didn't collide with them directly. Belle had charge of Lally and Brandon and was carefully dabbing the drips away from ice cream cones. Nan's coachman sat on the porch, turning the crank on the churn so that the children could stay sticky all afternoon.

Janessa had a new parasol with rose-colored ribbons that matched her new dress, and she twirled it as she walked across the lawn. At the far end, Nan's cook and two assistants were turning a whole pig on a spit, mopping their brows while the guests stayed well away from the fire. Louise circulated with trays of champagne punch, sherry, iced tea, lemonade, and julep cups. Janessa drank punch and thought about the disgusting cantina, dubbed the Cockroach and Banana by the American medical staff, where she and Charley and the others would occasionally go and drink rum and quinine and hope that nothing poisoned them. *Vive la différence,* she thought dreamily. If it weren't for Charley's work . . .

She couldn't help chewing at that thought, feeling somehow it was a requirement that she give up what she wanted so that he could have what *he* wanted, despite his never having asked her to. She knew she was an oddity, an "unwomanly" woman, and felt compelled to make sure Charley's work came first so that he wouldn't regret having married a woman who worked, too. She eyed him across the lawn. He was talking to George Eames and Dalton Darby, the new partner in George's carriage works. Darby was a big man in his thirties. They were howling with laughter over something. Charley certainly didn't look as though he wanted to be in Cuba.

Her children scooted across the far end of the lawn with the rest of the herd. They tumbled in the grass together, and Lally's ice cream cone went down the front of Brandon's white dress. Belle panted after them, righted them, promised more ice cream, and handed them off to another nursemaid while she went in search of something clean for Brandon. Lally howled over her spilled ice cream and kicked her brother.

Janessa headed toward the house, thinking she might help find another garment—Nan's children must have something Brandon could wear. The men under whose feet the children had rolled hadn't appeared to notice them. Charley was still chortling with George Eames, and Darby was strolling toward the house behind Belle. Janessa assumed he was looking for a bathroom, judging by the cups of julep he had drunk, but when she came into the cool dimness of the downstairs hall, she heard a furious scuffling behind the parlor doors.

"Don't you do that!" Belle's voice was angry and a little frightened.

"Nobody's going to hurt you, you silly wench," Darby countered. The parlor doors were glass, thinly curtained with lace. Janessa stood rooted for a moment, staring at the shadowy figures on the other side. Darby grabbed Belle by the buttocks, bunching her skirt between her legs, trying to run his hand up between them.

Belle batted at his hands and tried to back away. "I tell you, don't do that!"

"Who do you think you're sassing, gal?" Darby grabbed her wrists with one hand. "I told you, I ain't gonna hurt you." He put his other hand on her breast and squeezed hard. "You be nice to me, I might be real nice to you. Buy you a present."

"I don't want no presents. You hurtin' me."

Darby took his hand off her breast, and Janessa hoped she wouldn't have to barge in and make a scene that would enliven the party in a way that nobody would want. She hesitated, biting her lip, while Darby tried to cajole Belle in a tone of cheerful self-satisfaction that made Janessa's skin crawl.

"I might buy you a *nice* present. You aren't saving it, I know that. None of you black gals save it."

"Don't you call me a black gal!" Belle said furiously. "We're colored people."

"Well, pardon me." Darby chuckled. "I reckon I could show you *colored* gals a good time."

"I don't go with white men." Belle tugged her wrists away from him and stood rubbing them.

Darby leaned closer to her. "You think you can go

around strutting it all afternoon, waving your tits and your backside, and then get coy? I know what's going on, so come here and give me a li'l." He grabbed her buttocks again, pulled her to him, and tried to kiss her.

Belle turned her head and tried to push him away. Janessa wondered why she didn't just hit him, then realized she couldn't. Darby was white, and Belle was afraid of him. *This has gone on long enough,* Janessa thought. She tapped on the glass doors and called, "Belle! Belle, did you find something for Brandon?"

She had the satisfaction of seeing Darby jump back, nearly pushing Belle from him. "Yes, ma'am," Belle called. "I'm lookin'." She didn't come out.

Janessa yanked the door open. "Why, Mr. Darby," she said in mock astonishment. "Whatever are you doing?"

"Just talking to Belle," Darby said with as much dignity as he could muster. "That one's got a sassy mouth. You'll be sorry if you keep her on." He stalked out. Belle looked at the floor.

"Why didn't you yell?" Janessa demanded.

Belle's eyes flew up and widened in recognition that Janessa knew what had happened. She looked frightened again. "I come in to find Brandon some clothes. Honest I did."

"I know that," Janessa said reassuringly. "Why didn't you yell for someone to help you when that man cornered you like that?"

She saw a spark of anger in Belle's eyes. "Nobody goin' to take my word against his."

"Then why didn't you come out when you heard me call?"

Belle looked at the floor again. "I figure maybe you believe him, too. Maybe I lose my job."

"Oh." Janessa digested that.

"Girls make trouble, get the menfolks upset, they get fired," Belle said.

"I didn't barge in because I didn't want to embarrass you," Janessa explained. "Or Mr. Darby, either," she admitted. "He's the host's partner. I just wanted to get you away from him. The devil! I'll have a word to say about him to George Eames later, I can tell you!"

"Oh, no, Miss Janessa, don't you do that! Mr. Darby just come up with some story, and they fire me sure."

"Miss Lida wouldn't."

"Either that or he make up his mind he goin' have me come hell or high water 'cause I didn't want him. White men, they like that."

"Just white men?" Janessa inquired with a twitch of her mouth. Belle was well named. Dalton Darby couldn't have been the only man who'd lost his fool head over her.

Belle chuckled. "Naw, not just white men. But colored men, I can punch them if I feel like it."

Janessa thought about that. She'd had men take the same attitude with her, because of her Indian blood, but she didn't live with it every day the way Belle did.

"I expect you're right about Miss Lida," Belle said. "But one of these days I'm goin' get me out of here and go north."

Janessa sighed. "You may not find it any better up there."

"I'm goin' to try," Belle said stubbornly. "You could do worse than take me with you. I'm a good nurse, and the children like me. I wouldn't cost you much."

Janessa thought about Richmond-bred Belle in New York. "It's crowded. More people than you can imagine."

"Any colored people?"

"Oh, yes."

"They got laws say they can't vote?"

"Well, no. But it's not easy for them, either. I'm

ashamed to say it, but Yankees aren't much less prejudiced than southerners. They're just two-faced about it."

"I take my chances," Belle said resolutely. "Find me
a man to marry up there who's got a chance to make
somethin' of himself."

"It's dirty."

"You see Miss Lida's house," Belle said. "You ain't
seen where I live when I ain't livin' in."

"Well, let me talk to my husband."

"I done talked to him," Belle said. "When he tell me
he goin' to take you and the children back on up to New
York."

"When was that?"

"Back before you get here. While you were in the
District, tending that diphtheria."

"Oh, did he?" Janessa murmured.

"He say he'd talk to you."

"Oh, really?" Janessa started to laugh. Her stomach
and head felt light with relief. Charley had planned this
for weeks. It wasn't her own haggard face that had done
it. It was his gift to her. And here was Belle, the perfect
nursemaid, presenting herself to Janessa like a present.
Why on earth was she trying to turn them down?

She looked at Belle. "All right, then." She hoped it
would be a while before Belle discovered that more of her
vulnerability stemmed from being female than from the
color of her skin. Maybe she would find a good man, a
man as good as Charley, and she wouldn't have to learn
that lesson.

XVI

Taos, New Mexico, August

Luis had been watching what he was astute enough to consider his nephew's courtship of India Blackstone, and he didn't approve of it any more than Frank Blake did. But since India herself appeared to be oblivious to it, Luis kept his peace. She didn't seem interested in anything but painting, and Luis found her view of the world enlightening. She saw things more like an Indian than a white woman, he thought. She put the elements of her pictures where they belonged symbolically, rather than where they "ought" to be. It didn't disturb him when people floated in the sky or appeared to be conducting their business underground. He wasn't sure what she did with those paintings. A few small desert scenes had appeared in the window of Dorothy's bookstore, where they sold well, and Mr. Blumenthal and Mr. Bennington and Mr. Cattrell were condescendingly approving of them. But the large canvases never appeared. She sent them to somebody in Washington, Johnny said.

"Maybe just as well," Luis said. "Since you decided to show her the cliff house."

"Everybody knows about the cliff house," Johnny remarked.

"Everybody who is an Indian."

"She won't tell.

"So far. You never know."

Johnny looked uncomfortable. "Somebody else is going out there already."

"Who?" Luis demanded.

"Navajo, I think. Navajo pony, anyway. I never see anyone, but they keep going. Carrying something."

Luis narrowed his eyes. "And you don't know what, and you never look for it."

"I've looked for it," Johnny conceded, "but I haven't found it. I don't want to tell India, so I can't look too thorough."

Luis folded his arms. "And you take her in the cliff house. Exploring."

"I'm not afraid. We don't do any harm. We give the old ones respect."

"What I want to know is what the Navajo is doing," Luis said. The Navajo had an ingrained fear of ghosts and the dead. What would it take to get one inside the cliff house? "I don't like it that you take India Blackstone there so that white people know about it—and even more I don't like it that Navajo are there. And I don't like you falling in love with some woman you can't have."

"I'm not," Johnny said gruffly.

Luis sniffed. "Tell that to your mother. She says you don't eat. You're mooning about. You get up late in the morning. You'd better look out Michael Holt doesn't fire you."

"He hasn't said anything. I wasn't late but once."

"He feels sorry for you, making a fool of yourself over his cousin."

Johnny grinned slyly. "He wants me to show him where the cliff house is. India won't. I won't. Not to put

on film. Film is too real, like photographs. But he wants
to. So he won't fire me."

"You don't know about white men. If I don't know
how they think, as old as I am, you don't either. Much less
white women. Your mother made a mistake letting you
learn English." Luis glared at his nephew. "If you
couldn't talk to her, you wouldn't get into such trouble."

The ponies were coming up the canyon under a
white moon, José's in the lead. His uncle Leo and his
uncle Joe rode behind him, and he could feel their disapproving bulk at his back. It wasn't his fault that that stupid
Tiwa kept bringing the Anglo girl out here, José thought,
but he didn't say so. He already had, and they had said it
didn't matter whose fault it was; he worked for the Holts,
and he should have figured out a way to stop it. They
were his mother's brothers; they could get away with saying things to him that nobody else could, including the
three Yaquis who rode in solemn procession behind Leo
Horseman.

The Yaquis were hard-edged men with the look people get when pushed to the wall. They had insisted on
coming tonight to see for themselves that what they had
been told was done had been done. They had reached the
stage where they trusted no one because it had been
clearly demonstrated to them that they should not.

José thought about the money they were paying him
and the pleadings of his mother's sister, Mary. For his
mother and his uncles, Mary was what mattered—and
what the Mexican *Presidente* did to her husband's people.
For himself, it was the money. He had more kinds of
family than he needed, none of them really his.

It didn't matter. The money was good, and it was a
chance to strike a blow at governments in general, at all
the places that shut him out. The Yaqui had been fighting

for years with the forces of Mexican Presidente Porfirio Díaz. Now it might be because of him, José, that they would win. That would make him a person who had mattered. That could not be taken away from him.

"How much farther?" one of the Yaquis asked suspiciously. His voice was low, but it carried in the still night.

"Soon," Leo said over his shoulder. "There is time to get in and out in dark."

"Always in dark." The Yaqui who spoke said the words quietly, but there was a bitter edge to them. The Yaqui had reason to be bitter, José thought. Díaz's government was interested only in annihilating them, removing them completely from their land, which was wanted by others. His rurales burned and drove them out, murdered and scattered them like a farmer burning out a nest of wasps. But the Yaqui were tougher than Díaz knew, and they kept fighting back. With a big enough stockpile of guns built up, they might even win.

These three Yaquis had come to confirm that the guns were where they had been told they were, that José and his uncles had taken the risks they said they had. A cache of guns was no more legal on Indian lands in the States than it was in Mexico. Even if the United States could be certain an armed insurrection wasn't brewing on its own territory, it had no interest in upsetting the status quo in Mexico just now. The Yaqui would get no sympathy in the States from the white man's government.

The ponies picked their way over the rocks at the canyon bottom and whickered as they came near the cliff house. They had been there before; they got a feed of grain at the canyon's end. Leo Horseman drew his pony up beside his brother, Joe. "You take them in," he told José.

"No, you take 'em." José pushed his hat back on his

head and gave his uncle a cocky grin. Let the old man deal with that.

Leo refused to be drawn. "I tell you, I don't go in there. You pick this place, you go in. Maybe the *chindi* don't get you."

"They've had centuries to blow away," José said with disgust. "You act like an old woman."

The Yaquis listened, pretending they didn't hear. This was family business, not theirs.

José dismounted, and they unloaded the crates from the backs of the pack ponies. The cliff house loomed silently above them, a stone ghost town. Leo Horseman thought there were ghosts in it; José just worried about what live people might be in it. José picked up a crate and strapped it on his back. Then he beckoned to the Yaquis, and they followed him, crates on their backs, too, up the steep path of carved handholds and then up a ladder, which he pulled from a crevice on a ledge below the cliff house. The stone looked nearly black in the moonlight, and the men were just darker shadows going up the cliff face. They came out on a flat ledge, and José beckoned them through a doorway. They pulled the ladder up after them, using it to go up and down the levels of the cliff house, moving carefully in the darkness, feeling a slight wind on their necks that might just be the desert breeze or might be the chindi. If it was the chindi, José thought, he didn't care. They were too thin and old to hurt him. They hadn't hurt him so far. Or maybe he just wasn't any good to them, with his father's blood in him.

They ducked through a low passage into what had been a storeroom for the people who had built this aerie. A faint, musty scent clung to the air. These walls, like the rest, were earth and stone plastered over with adobe, now crumbling back to dust. In one corner a pile of stone lay beneath a buckled wall, the mountain behind it having shifted its weight over the centuries.

José unstrapped the crate and set it down, then lit a lantern and put it by the rock pile. Methodically he began to lift the stones away. The Yaquis put down the cases and helped him. When the rocks were cleared, they could see that another, newer doorway had been cut into the wall and the earth behind it hollowed out. It was only a small doorway, one a man could go through on hands and knees, and the rough edges of wooden crates were visible inside in the lantern's circle of light.

"There's room for these and more," José said. "Help me get them in."

The Yaquis looked dubiously at the low doorway.

"The ceiling's higher inside," José said. "But I wanted a doorway I could hide. It was a hell of a job to dig it out and then to cart the dirt away. I earned my money just digging." He gave a sideways glance at the Yaqui who was his aunt Mary's husband and whom he had always known by that name.

"There will be more," Aunt Mary's Husband said. "When we are ready to take the guns south, there will be more."

"And when will that be?"

"When it is time. When there are enough of us armed with enough guns. When we can take the rurales and Díaz by surprise."

Mañana, José thought. He wondered if these Yaquis, once they had actually stockpiled enough weapons for a revolution, would have the nerve to start one. Maybe he would go south and fight in it if they did.

He got on his hands and knees and crawled through the low opening, straightening up inside so that the doorway framed only his legs and belt buckle. Aunt Mary's Husband crawled in after him and looked at the cases. He didn't say anything, but José could see him counting them. When he was through, he lifted two cases down off a third and pried the third open with his knife. The rifles were there, packed in oiled cloth.

Another Yaqui crawled through the doorway and stood. He was tall, but with something wrong with his back so that he hunched like a turtle. He stared at the rifles for so long that José grew impatient.

"Let's get those inside," José said, pointing at the cases waiting with the third man in the outer room.

"You push them through," Aunt Mary's Husband said.

José shrugged. He ducked back through the low doorway and slid a crate toward Turtle Shell. The lantern in the doorway sent their shadows dipping and flapping up the walls. It was cold in the cliff house, and the musty smell made José's nose itch. He felt the tingle along his spine that came of doing something dangerous. He liked that tingle; it gave him the same pleasure that the silver buttons on his black vest gave him or the muscles of a fast pony. He and the third Yaqui bumped the crates through the door one by one. The scars on the other man's hands whitened as he gripped the crate.

After these four crates were stacked, they climbed back down the ladder and the steep path to get the other four boxes they had left at the cliff base. José could see his uncles sitting on their ponies and the red glow of a cigarette end in the dark. Leo took a drag off the cigarette, and his face flared briefly over his cupped hand. They waited silently while José and the Yaquis picked up the four crates, never coming any closer. José looked past them into the night, a quick circular sweep of vision that wasn't lost on the Yaquis.

"You look over your shoulder too much," Turtle Shell said as he hefted the crate onto his back.

"I keep my eyes open," José snapped.

"Who are you watching for?" Turtle Shell asked.

"Nobody. How the hell should I know? I'm watching." Turning, José slowly climbed the path, the stones shifting precariously under his feet, the ever present wind in his ear. No one would come here at night, unless the Tiwa boy and the Anglo painter were looking for a place to be alone, and José didn't think so. It irked him that the Yaquis had caught him looking.

They reached the ledge, hauled up the ladder, and made their way back over the rooftops and through the tumbled rabbit warren of rooms to the storeroom.

"I'll look at *these*," José said before the Yaqui could push them into the hidden room. He took out his own knife and pried up a corner while Turtle Shell glared at him.

"We have enough to do to fight the rurales," Aunt Mary's Husband said. "We don't have time to cheat you."

"When family business becomes everyone's business"—José jerked his head at Turtle Shell—"then a man is businesslike. With respect to the husband of my aunt."

Aunt Mary's Husband nodded, but Turtle Shell glared at him again. The third man, Scarred Hands, didn't say anything.

They stowed the cases and began to cover up the doorway with the rocks again, sealing in the rifles and whatever else might have scurried into the storeroom to live with them. It took over an hour to heave the stones into place. By the time they were finished, the men were filthy and sweating. Scarred Hands sat on a rock, puffing.

José waited. It would be insulting to take notice of his gasping, but he felt the immediate superiority of the young and strong for those whose bodies have begun to fail them.

The others waited, too, and when Scarred Hands

stood up, they followed their circuitous trail past disintegrating walls and crumbled doorways to the cliff face. Once they disturbed a tarantula and once a lizard, but nothing else moved. They descended the ladder and the cliff path, and José found himself drawing a deep lungful of air at the bottom. Uncle Leo saw him, and José turned his back. There was nothing in the cliff house to trouble him; it was just that the air was thin up there.

Scarred Hands knelt in the sage that grew against the cliff wall. He straightened slowly. "Someone has been here." He held out his hand, palm up, with a twisted paint tube balanced on it.

Turtle Shell snatched it from him. He whirled to face José. "Who is this?"

José shrugged. "Nobody important. Nobody who will look for guns."

"You said no one came here! Who have you been selling us out to?"

José's face flamed with anger. He slapped his hand on the hilt of his belt knife.

Uncle Leo quickly brought the lead ponies up. "If we don't leave, it will be daylight on the trail," he warned. "Time enough to sort things out by a warm stove, with coffee. Rosa will have coffee."

Aunt Mary's Husband said something to Turtle Shell in Yaqui, instead of the Spanish they had been speaking with each other. Turtle Shell got on his pony. Aunt Mary's Husband and Uncle Leo rode so that Turtle Shell and José were separated by two ponies. Uncle Joe and Scarred Hands came behind with the pack ponies.

It was nearly dawn by the time they got back to Rosa Horseman's hogan. Smoke was rising from it, and she stood in the doorway with a pail of water in her hand. The ponies were tied outside, and she gave them a drink from the pail. Inside, the six men made the hogan uncomfortably small. Rosa came in and looked at them, then turned back to the stove, listening but not interfering.

Turtle Shell threw the dried paint tube on the table.

"It's an Anglo woman," José said. "She goes to paint the cliff house."

"You showed it to her?" Aunt Mary's Husband demanded.

"Do I look like a fool? It was a boy from the pueblo. He works for my boss. She is my boss's cousin. He thinks he's in love with her."

"They will find the guns," Turtle Shell said between his teeth.

"They aren't looking for guns," José said, exasperated. "She goes to paint. The boy goes to sit and stare at her. Hawley's been out there and watched them."

"Hawley is an old drunk," Leo Horseman commented.

"He can see what goes on under his nose."

"Hawley is a white man," Turtle Shell said. "I didn't like that."

"Hawley didn't like you either," José said, remembering the old man's grumbling about being "stared down by Injuns as if I was a bug." "Hawley likes money and whiskey. And he knows I'll slit his belly open if he double-crosses us."

"There are too many Anglos in this," Turtle Shell said. "One of them will sell us to the rurales if they find out we have guns. Even if they don't. The rurales will question them, and they will tell."

"The rurales! The rurales! Everyone run from the rurales!" José said with disgust. "The guns are to *fight* the rurales."

"Not until we are ready," Aunt Mary's Husband said. "I don't like all these white people mixed in either, especially not this woman who paints. She will want to see inside the cliff house."

José didn't answer.

"She has been inside, hasn't she?"

"I told you, Hawley watched her. She won't dig through those rocks."

"A white woman may do anything."

"If she tells other white people about the cliff house, there will be many white people inside it in a very great hurry," Rosa said quietly from the stove. "You should move those guns."

"That's risky," José said. "The more we move them around, the more we come to someone's notice."

"Then we find a way to keep her out," Turtle Shell said. "Fast. *Any* way."

"I know this woman," Leo Horseman said. "She comes to my trading post. The Tiwa like her, too. I hear the Tiwa boy made her say she won't tell. If she says she will not tell where the cliff house is, she will not tell."

"What difference does it make, if she finds the guns?" Rosa said. "She will tell someone if she finds the guns, or the boy will. And then there will be trouble for us, and you will lose the guns." She looked at José. "Move the guns."

"No. Kill the Anglo woman," Turtle Shell said flatly.

Leo Horseman smacked his fist on the table. "That cannot be done."

"It can be done easily."

"No!" Rosa said. "No. That is wrong. And it will make trouble for us all if a white woman is killed. You have lost your mind."

"You can have the Tiwa boy," José said. "But it doesn't matter. I tell you, they are not looking for guns. They are not going to move a rock pile just to see the dirt behind it."

"I will do it," Turtle Shell said, "if you do not want to."

José's eyes narrowed. Turtle Shell's face was long and bony. He looked sullen and bitter and ready to bite anyone who got in his way. Aunt Mary's Husband and Scarred Hands didn't say anything; they just watched the two of them. José hooked his thumbs through his belt, but not so tightly that he couldn't quickly get at his knife. "Let's get something straight here. This is *my* country. *We* have to pay for what *you* do here, and you don't do anything that *I* don't say you do. Are we understanding each other now?"

"I hired you," Turtle Shell said quietly. "I don't take orders from you."

"You take orders from me this side of the border." José flashed Turtle Shell a feral, cocky smile, and his thumbs came out of his belt loops. One of them stroked the hilt of his knife.

"You have sold us out!" Turtle Shell said in a quick explosion of fury. He pulled his own knife and lunged. José had his knife out, too. It gleamed in his fingers, catching the light from his mother's cooking fire.

"No!" Rosa shouted, but she had more sense than to get between them. José and Turtle Shell circled each other around the fire. Joe and Leo Horseman looked at Scarred Hands and Aunt Mary's Husband, assessing the danger. If they killed each other, it would be bad. If they were separated, the bad feeling would fester and come out again. José jumped at Turtle Shell, kicking embers up from the fire, sparks outlining his snakeskin boots. His knife came an inch from Turtle Shell's ear, but it didn't connect. Turtle Shell moved faster than a man with a deformed back should be able to. He struck back at José, and blood welled up across the arm of José's shirt.

"Nobody sold you out!" José snapped at him. "You are stupid! *Estúpido!* I am going to kill you!"

"How much did they pay you, thief?" Turtle Shell demanded.

"And how much did you think you could cheat us out of?" José snarled. "Using my mother's sister to trick us into storing your guns. You were going to cry 'cheat' and not pay. Now you want to kill an Anglo woman to make it stick, let us take the blame." He dodged around Turtle Shell and got the blade up under his guard. Turtle Shell reeled back, trying to hold on to his knife, his armpit dripping blood.

"Enough!" Rosa cried.

José wasn't sure whether she was afraid of what the other Yaquis would do to him or whether she just didn't want a dead body in her hogan. Both maybe. He glared at Turtle Shell. He wanted to kill him.

Turtle Shell swayed toward him again, one last try, his knife out.

"No!" Leo shouted. Aunt Mary's Husband and Scarred Hands grabbed Turtle Shell from behind. José felt both his uncles grabbing him by the arms. He twisted indignantly, but they didn't let go.

"You don't kill him," Uncle Joe said.

José glared at them. He bounced a little on the balls of his feet.

Aunt Mary's Husband and Scarred Hands were speaking in urgent tones to Turtle Shell. He let them tie a rag that Rosa gave them under his arm, but he didn't say anything. He glared at José.

"Nobody sells out anybody," Leo Horseman said. "I know this Anglo woman; she is not interested in you. You have been fighting so long you think everyone is an enemy. There will be no more talk about selling out and no more insults to my nephew's honor."

Aunt Mary's Husband nodded. "He is my nephew, also. But my people have good reason to be suspicious."

"Not here," Leo said firmly.

"Agreed," Scarred Hands said abruptly. He looked at Turtle Shell and said something else in a fierce, low voice. Turtle Shell stiffened and stalked out of the hogan.

José pulled his bandanna off and wrapped it around his arm. "He had better leave that painter woman alone," he said to Scarred Hands, to make sure they knew he had won. "Or he won't need those guns."

Scarred Hands looked at him. "Better you see he doesn't have reason. He is stubborn. And I am not his chief."

XVII

Taos, New Mexico, September

"What would it take?" Mike Holt teased India. "A lifetime supply of cerulean blue? The head of Albert Blumenthal? I could make you a star." He put his arm around her shoulders in sharkish fashion and grinned behind his mustache. "India Blackstone, the desert princess. Direct from the great theaters of Europe."

India chuckled. "I'm not going to tell you where it is, you fiend. You'd film it and exhibit it to anyone who would pay your money-grubbing soul a nickel, and then these nice people would have their pueblo full of archaeologists and anthropologists trying to drag their ancestors' bones off and put them in museums."

"If there are bones in that cliff house, they're probably the remains of someone's dinner. They don't bury their dead indoors."

"You know what I'm talking about," India said severely. "And I won't show it to you, so you might as well give up."

"Ungrateful brat. You'd better not let old Blumenthal see those canvases."

"I have no intention of it. He'd just sneer anyway." Her eyes had a wicked gleam. "Besides, I took care of him. I told Fayette Millirons that he thought she had an artist's soul."

Mike gave a snort of laughter. He had been paying attention to Fayette only in an analytical sort of way since Eden had raked him over the coals. Human nature interested him. He thought that Fayette might show up in one of his moving pictures one of these days.

Frank Blake came up, looking like a gunslinger, a holster on his hip. "Are we ready to roll, boss?"

"Looks like it," Mike said. Herb Lumb was tying down the camera case while Paul and Johnny loaded the rest of the supplies in the wagon. José was pacing around the yard, watchful eyes on the horizon.

"He doesn't need two hotshots," India whispered in Frank's ear. "He already has José."

"If you ask me, José looks like he thinks somebody's after *him*," Frank remarked. "Or maybe he knows something we don't know. His mama's a Navajo. She lives around here. They hear stuff."

"Such as?"

"Mike got a letter yesterday from Ira in New York. It seems Edison's Pinkerton thugs busted up somebody's camera and knocked out all his teeth last month."

"Honestly!" India was incensed. "Over a moving picture camera?"

"People will fight over anything that makes money. Lord God, but you've had a sheltered life."

"Just because I haven't worked in an oil field or lived in a hole in the snow doesn't mean I don't know things," India said peevishly. "But over photographs?"

"These photographs are going to be *big* money. You can say you knew old Michael when."

"Let's roll!" Mike shouted.

India swung into the pinto's saddle. She was abandoning the cliff house for today to follow the camera crew.

Laden with picnic hampers and jugs of wine, they were heading for the Millironses' ranch. Eden was coming, too. Rachel Poliakov sat in the buggy, a silk kimono over her gingham dress, painting her face. Johnny had made India a wreath of wild grape, and she wore it jauntily around her hat.

India felt wonderfully gypsylike, trooping behind the odd caravan. Her saddlebags, loaded with paint and sketch pad, bounced behind her on the pinto's flanks, but she hadn't bothered with an unwieldy canvas. The day felt festive, like a holiday. Everyone seemed to be in that same mood. Johnny had stuck a red blossom in his own hat, and Frank was whistling Beethoven's "Ode to Joy" as he rode. José was as dashing as always, the sun glinting off the silver conchos on his hat and the silver buttons on his vest. His face still looked wary, though, India thought. But that was what Mike hired him for. Still, Frank didn't have that look. She caught José watching her and flushed, assuming that he had felt her watching him.

When they reached the gates of the Millironses' ranch, they found Fayette and her husband waiting in a buckboard heaped high with more picnic supplies. Fayette bounced on the wagon seat and waved while Gibson Millirons watched her indulgently. Mike was going to film the start of the fall roundup—if a cow didn't run over the camera, Herb Lumb said gloomily—and then they were going to dance and party under the stars. Fayette had commandeered two of her husband's ranch hands to clear a patch of its rocks and sagebrush stumps and to spread it with straw.

Mike's cavalcade wound through the stone gates—an affectation since no fence was attached to them—and headed for the foothills, where the cowboys were already bringing in the first straggling cattle to be penned and sorted. José let his pony fall into step beside India's.

"Buenos días," he said cheerfully. "Those are pretty flowers in your hat."

"Thank you," India said, somewhat surprised by his attention. He didn't seem to have anything else to say; he just trotted his pony beside hers so that she rode between him and the buggy.

Johnny Rojas rode on the other side of the buggy, watching José intensely. *Oh, Lord,* India thought, *maybe Frank was right. This is awkward.* To make conversation, she called to Fayette, "This is a beautiful place, Mrs. Millirons. How many acres do you have out here?"

"A whole section," Fayette replied. "But the cattle cover a lot of ground. There's no telling where we'll find some of them."

"Too much fence going up," Gibson Millirons grumbled.

"How wonderful to ride all day on your own land," India said, looking around, taking in the blue bowl of sky and the red mountains.

"Don't go out too far, Señorita Blackstone," José said. He gave her a grave look and spoke quietly. "There are bandits in the mountains."

"Truly?" This was the first time anyone had mentioned it to her. In fact, the Taos Valley appeared to be a remarkably peaceable spot. She narrowed her eyes at José. "What kind of bandits?"

"Robbers. Men who don't—don't treat women with respect."

India snorted with amusement before she could stop herself. José looked so perfectly the kind of vaquero whose treatment of women consisted of loving them and leaving them that his lecture struck her as ironic. She knew what he meant, though. She saw Johnny watching them, trying, she thought, to overhear the conversation, and found it odd that he had never seemed to think it

dangerous for her. Frank never had either, and he generally had an ear to the ground. He had been more worried
about Pinkertons, and his concern for India had all been
over Johnny Rojas. India flicked an eye toward the other
side of the wagon and saw that Frank was watching her,
too, and had begun a low-voiced conversation with
Johnny.

Impulsively, India kicked her pony into a canter and
rode up beside Eden. "What is the matter with them all?"
she muttered.

"With who?" Eden asked.

"José says there are bandits out in the mountains and
I should be careful. Johnny is giving me the eye. And now
Frank is giving me strange looks and talking to Johnny."

Eden laughed. "Well, they're all interested in you,
dear, although José seems to have come rather late to the
game. I would have said something about Johnny, but
he's a good, intelligent boy, and he knows you're not going to stay here."

India groaned. "Frank warned me about Johnny, but
I didn't listen to him."

"Probably because it was Frank talking."

"Well, yes," India admitted.

"I think he's right, though. Now, José surprises me a
little, but he may just be doing it because of the other
two. José likes to be the only stallion in the herd."

Eden's analogy was so apt that India chortled. She
could just see José, black mane flying, strutting for the
mares.

"I suspect that José's bandits consist of his trying to
cut you out with Johnny," Eden said.

"Men," India said in a disgusted voice and proceeded to ignore the three of them.

*   *   *

Mike Holt set up the Biograph and the rest of his paraphernalia where the Millironses' cowboys were cutting from the herd those cattle destined for the fall trail drive to Kansas. Mike's camp consisted of the camera and its wagon, a rope corral for turning out the mules and ponies, sawhorses and a plank table to feed the crew, and a tent—sporting a flag with the tree and sun emblem of the company, made by Eden—for costume changes and protection from inclement weather. In the case of the latter, it was the Biograph that got the tent. Otherwise, Rachel reclined in it when the sun grew hot.

The tentpole flag added to the gypsylike atmosphere, India thought. No wonder Fayette Millirons liked to hang around the company, she admitted grudgingly. It was as close to a real gypsy adventure as Fayette might get. No Gypsy Davy on the cold, cold ground for Fayette; she'd stay with her wedded lord and her feather bed and soak up adventure the only way she could: vicariously. *I'm not going to do that*, India decided suddenly. She would have a Gypsy if she wanted one, and a feather bed, too, when she felt like it, and she would never be Fayette Millirons, longing for adventure and afraid to go find it.

Rachel disappeared into the tent as soon as it was set up and shed her kimono. She shed something else along with it. When she came back out, she was Mike's prairie flower. India could swear that if Rachel spoke, she would have the accent of the prairies and not of Polotzk. But she didn't speak, of course. That was the magic. The music of her silence, Mike called it.

"She's amazing, isn't she?" Frank came to stand beside India, watching Rachel as Mike set up the shot. "Did I tell you I met her once before, at Mike and Eden's?"

"Rachel told me," India said. She sighed. "I wish I could do that, just stick on another face. It's extraordinary."

Frank laughed. "It would drive me crazy in the long run. You'd never know who you were with. But she was educational. She took me to a socialist rally, to hear Daniel De Leon. That was directly responsible for getting me thrown out of my parents' house."

"Because you went to a socialist rally?"

"Because I came home and started expounding socialist rhetoric to my father." He chuckled. "I was pretty green. I was convinced that all I had to do was repeat De Leon's speech to him, and he would be converted to the cause."

"How old were you?" India asked dubiously. "Even I would know better than that."

"I was seventeen. And I had led a sheltered life."

"You must have. Did you make up with your father while you were home this time?"

"Let's say that we're on speaking terms. He is no longer inclined to take a horsewhip to me. I don't think we've got much beyond that."

"Are you really a socialist?" India asked. Frank seemed to see things from so many sides, it was hard to pin him down, categorize him.

He shrugged. "Rachel would probably say no. I don't have the credentials in a lot of people's eyes. She came here from Russia after Cossacks killed her brother. Her father died on the boat over. Her little sister had trachoma and was sent back with their mother. The kid's blind now; she'll never recover, she'll never get past Immigration. Rachel sends them money every month."

"How awful."

"And what have I had? A comfortable life and expensive prep schools."

"And bumming and digging gold and working the oil fields. Is that why?"

"To get credentials?" Frank grinned at her. "It may

be. Those years go over better in some circles than my family tree does."

"You're as bad as Fayette Millirons. You want to leave all your safe comfort behind and go adventuring."

"I am nothing like Fayette Millirons," Frank said, smiling. "I have gone and done it."

"Is it fun? Or just exciting?"

"For me, the two seem to be synonymous."

India nodded. That was what she had thought. She didn't think it would be for Fayette. She suspected it might be, for herself.

The cattle were passing them in a low cloud of dust, the Millirons cowboys calling behind them. Mike turned the crank on the Biograph as they went by, then set the next scene against the backdrop of lingering dust. Rachel wrestled with the end of a rope that tied a lowing cow while two of the cowboys gesticulated at her to give it up. Stubbornly, she shook her head. They gestured at her again, and she pulled an ancient pistol from the pocket of her dress.

"Perfect!" Mike shouted. "Wonderful. Now you two back off—that's right. You think this woman is crazy. You aren't willing to get shot for a cow."

The cowboys followed his direction, backing away through a clump of snakeweed. Mike stopped turning the camera, and they relaxed and slapped each other on the back, whooping with laughter. "Are we famous yet? Wait till I write my sis!"

"Naw, you ain't famous. It's a wonder you ain't busted the camera."

Gibson Millirons signaled to them. "If Mr. Holt's through with you, get on back to the roundup or you ain't gonna be paid."

"Just one more shot, please, Gibson," Mike said. "Tell you what. I'll trade you Frank and Johnny for these two. Frank and Johnny can both ride. And any Pinkerton thug who's dumb enough to walk into the middle of this setup is too stupid to worry about."

The two cowboys looked pleased and began preening, while Frank and Johnny mounted up. "Don't take it to heart," Frank called to the ranch hands. "We just aren't ugly enough to look authentic." The cowboys laughed good-naturedly.

Mike ground film through the camera until the light failed. At dusk the cowhands returned from the roundup, bringing Frank and Johnny with them. Frank's hair was wet and plastered back. "I hope you got your fill of scenery," he said to Mike. "I personally spent the entire afternoon looking at a cow's back end."

"It's character building," Mike said. "If you want the cushy jobs, you have to make it worth my while." He shot India a wicked grin. "Worm out of yon fair damsel the location of the cliff house she's been painting. I could shoot a heck of a story there," he added wistfully.

"Not on your life," Frank said. "The woman's a viper. I'll stick to defending you against Pinkertons. Rogue cows," he added, smacking the trail dust off his trousers.

India chuckled, and Johnny smiled that interior smile that passed for a grin. All four knew the conversation was pure amusement. Mike wanted to film the cliff house, but he wouldn't be underhanded about it.

José watched them nervously, privy to no such certainty.

Night was coming on fast, and lanterns were lit around the clearing. The cattle lowed in the darkness beyond the lantern light while Fayette, her cook, and Eden set out supper. The Millironses' trail cook had driven his chuck wagon out to the party and then resentfully turned it over to the house cook, a broad-bottomed woman with black hair skinned back in a bun. Though commenting at length on the wagon's deficiencies from the middle of a cloud of chili-scented steam, she produced a dinner that the cowhands tore into ravenously. Normally on the trail they'd get beans and vinegar pie; that night's meal would linger in memory.

India sat between Frank and Johnny on a log at the edge of the clearing, her back to the dark mountains and the cattle. Some bovine murmur of restlessness passed through the herd, and immediately India heard a footfall behind them: José, scanning the darkness, his hand on his pistol.

"What's with him?" Frank jerked a thumb over his shoulder.

Johnny shrugged.

"He says there are bandits in the mountains," India said.

Johnny raised his eyebrows. "If there are, they're probably friends of his."

"He warned me not to go out alone," India said grumpily.

"Maybe you shouldn't," Johnny said.

"Why? No one thought I needed a nursemaid before."

"No one thinks you do now—hellcat," Frank said. "But I'd like to know what kind of bandits José's talking about."

"Eden thinks he's just"—India bit her lip, feeling foolish and resentful of the fact—"well, courting me."

"*La belle dame sans merci.*" Frank hooted at her discomfort.

Johnny looked suspicious. "José likes women from the cantina. Not nice girls."

"India's not a nice girl," Frank said, and she elbowed

him in the ribs. "Calm down. I was speaking of your temperament, not your moral reputation."

Johnny seemed to come to an abrupt decision. "If you want to go to the cliff house, and I can't go—you take Frank."

"Why?" The cliff house was her place. She wasn't at all sure she wanted to share it with Frank. Besides . . . "You said not to tell anyone," she said.

"Not your cousin with his camera," Johnny said. "I give you permission to tell Frank. Don't argue with me." He looked at Frank over his head. "I don't like it if she goes there alone now."

Frank seemed to have grown serious. "I'll swear on anything you like that I won't tell a living soul where it is. I appreciate your trust, pal."

Johnny's eyes twinkled. "Especially don't tell my uncle Luis."

India thought about complaining that she could take care of herself, particularly if she took a pistol, but decided she would look like a complete fool if it proved she couldn't. Two people were probably better than one in an emergency, anyway. And José made her nervous. In fact, he made her more nervous than his supposed bandits.

She sipped her wine, a vermilion glow in one of Fayette's good wineglasses that had been carefully wrapped and packed and brought out from the house. It warmed her as it went down. The night was getting cold. All the women had changed into wool and flannel dresses in the tent, skirts draped over three or four petticoats. They would dance to warm up. A fiddler and an old cowboy with a banjo were tuning up, and India's foot tapped with anticipation.

The musicians began a Virginia reel, and India was about to tug Frank up from his seat when Johnny stood and bowed formally over her. "May I have this dance?"

India blinked in surprise. She wouldn't have thought he knew how. The Pueblo people didn't dance—not like that, not with each other. Their dances were ceremonial, to honor the deer or grow the corn.

"I got Mrs. Holt to teach me," he whispered, reading her confusion. He took her hand and led her into the reel, dancing her down it with some uncertainty but a fair grasp of the steps. "I can waltz, too," he said as they came together arm in arm in the set. "Uncle Luis says I am a disgrace."

India chuckled, but she felt a little guilty. If he was, it was probably her fault. How comfortable would he be, stretched between two worlds? Was it only for her? Would the urge to dance a reel dissipate when she went away again? Or had she enticed him across some cultural border that he could never step back from easily?

The reel ended, and she found herself claimed by a cowboy who couldn't have been as old as she was. Most of the Millironses' trail drivers were young—old bones didn't stand up to the trail. This boy had a shock of reddish hair and a mustache barely substantial enough to give itself encouragement. India took his hand, realizing that she could probably dance herself into exhaustion if she didn't insist on sitting some dances out, since there were far more men than women. Most of the couples in the reel had been two men, half of them with bandannas tied to their belts so they could remember who were the girls. They had argued about it and bumped into each other anyway.

By the time she had danced a polka with her youthful partner, India was warm enough to retreat into the tent and take off one of her petticoats. A pile of them indicated that other women had had the same idea. Beyond the tent the lanterns made a magic circle, and a huge yellow moon rode over Taos Mountain. In the silence before the fiddle struck up again, a family of coyotes yipped and sang to one another across the valley.

Frank met India at the tent flap and held out his hand. "Did your finishing school teach you how to waltz?"

"Certainly. Did yours?" India gave him her hand, and he slipped an arm around her waist. He spun her into the middle of the dance floor, straw whispering under their feet. India found that she was more conscious of the feel of his hand on her ribs than she was of the pattern of their steps. The steps were second nature; her reaction to the proximity of his body, the moist warmth of his breath, was not.

"Mike's talking about staying here through Christmas," she said because she felt the need to say something.

Frank glanced at Rachel. "Is he going to subject poor little Prairie Flower to a blizzard?"

"No, you have to use some kind of false snow. Indoors. Otherwise, you just get a white blur. That's what Mike says. I think he just likes the place."

"I don't blame him," Frank said softly. "It's a place you could stay. Maybe."

India chuckled at the "maybe," feeling back on firm footing. "You couldn't stay anyplace long enough to call it home," she told him. *And you had better remember that, India,* she told herself.

"You never know," Frank said thoughtfully. "If I ended up staying anywhere . . ." The night was crisp and cold now. Their breath puffed out in little clouds as they danced. India fell silent, floating on the music, her skirt rustling above the straw, her eyes bright. Frank tightened his arm just a little about her waist, and his mouth brushed her forehead. Electricity hovered between them. India wouldn't have been surprised to find that they glowed.

The music stopped, and as they ceased to whirl, the

magic slowly disappeared. Mike came over and danced with her, while Frank did the polka with Rachel. Mike was just a nice man, his hand steady against her waist. India let her eyes slide toward Frank, assessing the difference. Did he feel that same glow with Rachel, or was it confined to her? And how did you tell? You couldn't ask.

At midnight, full of wine and dinner, tired with dancing and sleepy with the cold, they packed up the gypsy caravan and rolled home, parting from the Millirons at their gates. India dozed in her saddle, relieved that José didn't seem to want to ride with her. He had danced with her once but otherwise confined his attentions to being near her at all times, which had made her uncomfortable.

On the road home, Frank rode beside her, joking that he would catch her if she fell off.

"Good," India said sleepily.

The camera wagon rumbled alongside them, and Mike and Eden were singing something together in soft voices as they rode at the head of their band. Away in the hills the coyotes had started again, a high warbling conversation that sounded like an argument.

"The missus is blessing him out," Frank said. " 'I *told* you you wouldn't catch anything by the creek bed. I *told* you to go get me a chicken. You *never* listen!' " He finished with a yip for emphasis.

" 'Nag, nag, nag,' " India yapped back at him. " 'All you do is nag me.' "

Frank sidled his horse closer to hers. She was suddenly awake now. Her eyes looked up at him out of her muffling cloak and hood with a fine brightness. Johnny rode a little behind them, his dark face unreadable by moonlight, and José rode behind him, watching everything, including the dark shadows of the brush that whispered in the fall wind.

* * *

As it happened, India didn't go to the cliff house again until after the end of the month, in the first days of October. Mike was trying to make the most of the weather before winter set in and could spare neither Frank nor Johnny. José repeated his cautions about bandits, which kept India from riding out to the ruins alone. In another mood she might have ignored the warning, but for now there seemed always sufficient reasons not to do so—besides being afraid. So she went with Mike's crew or went into Taos and painted the town. Her watercolors of the plaza sold well in Dorothy Brattow's shop.

At the end of September the pueblo held the Festival of San Gerónimo, its patron saint. The night before, they had staged the Sundown Dance, a tribal celebration so lightly linked to Catholicism that India suspected it called for much rearrangement of theology on the part of the padre. Unlike the August ceremonials at Blue Lake, which were, she had been firmly informed, secret, the Spanish and the Anglos were allowed to view the Sundown Dance. Cameras were forbidden, but guests were welcomed and given space around the pueblo plaza. India watched enthralled as the dancers moved between the north and south pueblos and the bridge spanning Pueblo Creek, green aspen branches waving above their heads. She thought she saw Johnny but couldn't be sure in the dying light. They danced in thanksgiving for the harvest and to the sun, to augment its waning strength. Or so Johnny and Luis said. India had no idea whether that was true, or whether they danced some other secret message to their gods. Gods in the plural, she was reasonably sure. Despite the mass to San Gerónimo in the morning, there was more that was Tiwa and ancient about this fiesta than was Christian. She had tried to cajole from Johnny and Luis more information and found she could not.

"Give up," Dorothy had advised her. No Taos Indian

would tell a white person anything whatsoever about their religion. "I asked Luis once, 'What do you believe in?' He answered, 'Life.'"

"Do you have to know?" Frank murmured now. "Just to watch? Maybe the dance gives you what you want to take away from it."

"Well, I want to know anyway," India said, but she watched the swaying dancers appreciatively, Frank's words in her head. You could take grace from it, she thought, and vision. Maybe not the padre's sort.

The day after the fiesta, Paul and Johnny were still involved in pueblo doings, and Mike had given the crew a day off. Frank knocked on India's door early in the morning, waking her with a demand to be shown the cliff house.

"I thought you were supposed to be protecting me," India said, yawning. "What if I don't want to go today?"

"I want to see it. You're just my excuse. Get yourself out of bed."

"Get out of my bedroom, then."

"I'm not in it. I am decorously behind the door." But he closed the door the six inches he had opened it and retreated downstairs to wait for her.

When she came down, the ponies were already saddled, and Frank was packing lunch in his saddlebags. India noted the pistol on his belt and a rifle stowed behind the saddle. "We might bring a deer home," he said. "If I see one."

"Oh." Better than a bandit, India thought. José wasn't around, and she found herself somewhat relieved by that. The stealthily protective air he had adopted had not been abandoned.

The air was crisp and carried the smell of wood-smoke and apples. A porcupine waddled hurriedly across the road in front of them, trying to outpace winter. They turned off into the chaparral, and a roadrunner shot out of it with a resentful hoot and headed down the Pueblo Road the way they had come.

"Everything's in a hurry," India commented.

"Winter's coming," Frank said. "We'd better start being careful of what sort of weather we head out in. We could end up spending a week in the cliff house in a blizzard. An even worse excuse than a broken buggy axle —and I won't marry you."

"Nobody in her right mind would marry you," India said cheerfully. "Besides, I told you, I'm not going to get married."

"Oh, well, then, you might as well go ahead and disgrace yourself."

As they rode, a flurry of yellow leaves tumbled about their horses' hooves, and the ponies snorted and danced. They turned into a canyon, which grew narrower, and then after a sharp bend they came suddenly upon the cliff face. Frank gasped.

"Isn't it a pure amazement?" India said with a proprietary air. She slid off her pony and began unbuckling her saddlebags.

"I want to see the inside," Frank insisted.

"Later, after I paint. The light won't last." India was enjoying her ownership and making him wait. Mostly it seemed she waited for him.

Frank apparently sensed her satisfaction. He sat on a downed log and proceeded to ignore her. He was turned half away from her, in profile, looking at the cliff face she was painting from an angle. The line of his hat was dark against the rosy stone where the light poured down. He seemed a brooding presence, like the hawk of her first visit. He seemed to have something to say about the ghosts of the cliff, so she put him in the picture.

Eventually she decided she had done enough. Light was fading, and she was unsure of her way back in the dark. It would get cold, too. She scrubbed her brushes in linseed oil while Frank ambled over to look at the canvas. He raised his eyebrows.

"If you don't like it, you shouldn't have sat there," India said briskly.

"I *do* like it. I'm flattered."

"I'd like to paint you some more. Johnny won't ever let me."

"Oh, I see. Johnny would be better, but I'll do?"

"Don't be petulant, or I won't take you inside."

"Why do *you* have to take me?"

"I know where the ladder is." She refused to be hurried, studying her canvas with a critical eye. The dark figure in the foreground was not sinister but seemed to possess some power juxtaposed against the cliff house, as if trying to sort out its ancient messages.

"Sometimes you give me the willies," Frank said. "I never knew a girl who could stand the hair up on the back of my neck before."

India flashed him a sunny smile. "Maybe it's just the place. Lots of ghosts on the wind here." She put the canvas away and scrambled up the stone handholds ahead of him.

At the top, Frank slapped his holster and swaggered theatrically. "I ain't afeared of no ghosts, ma'am."

"What's the point in shooting a ghost?" India inquired. "A bullet would just go right through him."

"Not much," Frank admitted. "But it's right handy for folks who turn out to be alive."

"For whoever's been fooling with this ladder," India muttered, looking out over the still canyon. She had dragged the hand-hewn ladder from its crevice to find a rung was split. "This was left here by someone. Johnny quit bringing one when we found it. We thought it had been left a long time ago. But it wasn't broken when we used it."

"Somebody mighty fat to bust that," Frank said. "Or carrying something mighty heavy." He propped it against the cliff wall and tested the other rungs. "Looks like it'll hold us. Who else comes out here?"

"Nobody that I know of," India said. "José's bandits?"

"Maybe." Frank climbed up and stepped onto a ledge at the top of the ladder's reach, then held down a hand to help her. "But there's nobody here now, that's for sure. You can't get into this canyon without being seen, and there's no place to hide a horse unless you haul him up here."

"Oh, come on! Have you ever tried to lift a horse?" India demanded. "It would be worse than trying to lift a live piano. Nobody in his right mind—"

"Sometimes you are the most literal-minded woman," Frank cut in. "I spoke facetiously. Are you really worried there might be somebody here?"

"No, I suppose not. I just don't like the idea."

"Well, we were here first, and we'll hear anybody coming," he assured her. "Come on." Eager to explore, he took her hand and dragged her through a doorway, pulling the ladder after them. They ascended from level to level the way Johnny had showed her. There were rooms with blackened fire circles and odd-sized windows, through which they looked down on the canyon floor. The height was dizzying, and India gripped the rock wall on either side of the windows. The cold air smelled of the dust of unused rooms. In one, a fall of rock spilled from the mountain into the room.

They scrambled higher and came out in a space nearly at the top of the cliff face. A half-broken wall was all that barred them from open air—from a stumble and a swift descent. India edged back from it, through a low doorway into another chamber. Here were the faint marks of a fire and a pile of rounded stones that might once have been the hearth. She sat on one, closing her eyes, trying to envision herself a woman who lived here, who climbed tall ladders to grind her corn and sing her babies to sleep.

"What was after them, do you suppose?" she asked, opening her eyes. "What were they defending themselves against that they needed to live in a fortress?"

"Other Indians, I expect." Frank sat down beside her. "Ancestors of the Navajo, maybe. Raiders. I don't know much about it. These people were farmers, I think, not very warlike."

"Have you ever thought about what if you had been someone else?" she asked abruptly.

"No, I can't say I have."

"I used to all the time. Wishing."

"Who did you want to be?"

"A man."

Frank laughed. "That would be a shame."

India smiled wryly. "Well, I've sort of gotten over that. I wanted to be able to do what I felt like."

Frank put his arm around her, pulling her head toward his shoulder companionably. "I've got news for you. Being a man doesn't help much. Okay, some," he conceded. He studied her carefully. In the light of the setting sun, her skin appeared coppery. She might almost be one of the people who had inhabited this place, the woman of her imagining. He kissed her as he had at the party, this time more gently exploring, and her arms went around his neck.

India felt as she had when she danced with him. She might be dancing now, she thought, on a very bright point of light. There was something about the way Frank held her that was hungry; he seemed to want something more. Let it happen, she thought. With a Gypsy lover on the cold, cold ground. Only it wasn't a Gypsy lover, it was Frank—somehow both comfortingly familiar and terrifyingly unknown. His hand slid up her shirtwaist to clasp her breast, and the sensation was achingly wonderful. She gave an appreciative moan.

Frank sat back, breathing hard. "I have rocks in my head. My mother would kill me."

"Your mother?" India murmured.

"I'm supposed to protect you from people like me."

India opened her eyes and looked at him shrewdly. "Well, that's why I wanted to be a man. Nobody tries to protect them from getting kissed."

"Kissed wasn't all you were about to get," Frank said.

"I thought maybe not. I'm not so stupid I didn't notice. Why did you stop?"

"I'm not going to take advantage of you."

"There you go again." India studied her hands in her lap, embarrassed now. "Everyone thinks women are so ignorant, men can just take advantage of them. What if I *wanted* to?"

"Then I can't take advantage of that," Frank said. He sounded grumpy. "You're making it awfully hard to be a gentleman."

"Maybe you should give up on it. It doesn't appear to be your natural inclination anyway." India took one of his hands and cradled it against her cheek. "You're being sweet. Don't think I don't know that. And maybe it wasn't a good idea." She sighed ruefully. "But it might have been. Let *me* figure it out, okay?"

Frank stood up. He pulled her to her feet before either of them changed their minds.

XVIII

A week earlier, Capitán Alvarez of the Mexican rurales tapped his foot outside the office door of the federal marshal in Santa Fe. His two sergeants consulted their pocket watches alternately every five minutes and clucked their tongues at the results. The clerk at the desk in the outer office watched them impassively. The marshal was in there and didn't have anybody with him, but the clerk knew the marshal wasn't going to let them in until he felt like it. When he'd finished his lunch, the clerk supposed.

Eventually the marshal's door opened, and Capitán Alvarez rose with alacrity and imperiousness. The lawman eyed him suspiciously. "I'm Marshal Baines." He held out his hand after appearing to think it over. "What can I do for you?"

Alvarez nodded at his sergeants to stay where they were. "We have information of illegal activity on your side of the border," he said sternly. "We require that you assist us in the apprehension of the criminals."

"If I don't assist you, you won't be apprehending anyone," Baines said. "This is United States territory." He sighed. "I suppose you'd better come in and tell me about it."

He motioned Alvarez to a chair and closed the office door behind them.

"You understand the Yaqui Indians in Sonora have been conspiring against the government of Presidente Díaz," Alvarez said.

"I understand El Presidente's been trying to get rid of them any way he can," Baines said. He held up a hand. "Not that that's any business of mine. I got a few I'd just as soon part with, if it comes to that. But what's your point here?"

"Ringleaders of the Yaqui have been seen crossing the border into your territory. We have reason to believe they have conspired with Indians here."

"Conspired to do what?"

"Recruit rebels, perhaps. Buy weapons, perhaps."

"Perhaps?"

"They are crossing the border," Alvarez snapped. "That means they are up to no good."

"Well, it may. But it ain't much in the way of legal proof. You say they're making contact with Indians on our side?"

"That is where we require your assistance. To discover who is aiding and abetting them, and apprehend them."

"Uh-huh. For reasons to be decided later," Baines said. "Look, if your Yaquis are crossing the border, I don't blame them, given what I hear is going on in Sonora. Not that I want them up here, but I'm not surprised. You took all their land. You rounded up and shot half of them. I ain't going to help you drag any back unless you got something specific to charge them with."

Alvarez's jaw shot out. He didn't like Baines's tone of voice; he didn't like being lectured to by gringos. "We will determine the charges when we find out what they are doing!"

"Well, if you think I'm gonna roust all my Indians out of their hogans and stir them up just to find out what yours have been up to, you can think again. You got evidence of gunrunning, I'll jump on it. Otherwise, head on back south."

Alvarez leaned forward and smacked his fist on the marshal's desk. "I demand cooperation! These Yaquis are enemies of the government."

"They ain't enemies of *my* government." The marshal leaned back in his chair. He was a big man, with a chin like a bull.

Alvarez glared at him. "Then your government refuses to cooperate with mine?"

"I'm not going to hunt your revolutionaries for you. Give me some evidence that *my* Indians are up to something, or get out of my territory." Baines paused to make his point clear. "If your rurales indulge in any freelance law enforcement up here, they could start an international incident. I don't reckon you want that."

"Certainly not," Alvarez said stiffly. He stood, turned a parade-ground pivot, and jerked the door open. He snapped his fingers at his sergeants, and they rose and followed him out the door of the federal building.

Baines strode angrily out to the front room. "Goddamn rurales," he growled at his clerk. "Too big for their britches. Don't let him in here again. And you hear anything about Indians with guns, you don't tell the Mexicans, you understand? You tell *me*. Any of *my* Indians doing anything stupid, I'm gonna take their heads off." He went back into his office and slammed the door.

The figure was small in the distance, but recognizable. It ought to be. Alvarez had been trailing him for a week. He scratched his head and swore, then focused his binoculars. After his interview with Baines, Alvarez had changed out of his uniform, which made him too conspicuous, into a dusty blue shirt and work pants tucked into

worn boots. He might have been any farmhand or cowboy, most of whom spoke Spanish in this territory.

He squinted as he looked through the binoculars.
There was a connection between this Navajo half-breed
and the Yaqui; therefore, there was a connection to whatever the Yaqui were doing in the north. An aunt who
married into the Yaqui was enough to make him certain.
But he wasn't going to take it to Baines now. He didn't
trust him. If there were guns, Baines would confiscate
them, and he wanted them. If there *were* guns. He swore
again. If there weren't guns, why were the Yaqui coming
north? He doubted the notion that they might be recruit-
ing men. There had to be guns.

"What is he doing, Capitán?" One of Alvarez's sergeants, similarly attired, shaded his eyes and looked
toward the distant figure of José.

"He is riding a horse," Alvarez said between his
teeth.

God save him from dolts. Who knew what José was
doing? They had followed him while he rode shotgun
with a moving picture company, an assignment that baffled Alvarez. Who would rob a moving picture company?
he wondered. They had followed him home to his mother
and supper. They had followed him to the cantina and
waited while he got drunk, having no success in striking
up a conversation with him or with anyone else in the
cantina, the Indians and the locals all being wary of
strangers. Now—maybe—he was going somewhere. After
following him for some time, Alvarez had branched off the
trail and up to the canyon rim for a better view.

Below them in the chaparral José reined in his horse
suddenly. He sat still for a moment and then turned, re-
tracing his path out of the canyon.

"Why does he turn back?" the other sergeant muttered. He sounded aggravated.

"If I know these things, I would have a promotion," Alvarez growled, "and I wouldn't be— Wait!" He swung the binoculars. "He has been following somebody."

"*He* is following somebody?"

"They have gone on, and he has turned back. He's stopping because he knows where they are going. Or because we have frightened him, and he doesn't want *us* to find them." Alvarez's eyes gleamed.

His two men were already swinging their horses around on the ridge.

Alvarez held out a hand. "Wait. Give him time to get clear. Then we will find these people he doesn't want us to find."

"Something about this place is getting on my nerves," Frank said. He looked uneasily about the crumbling cliff house as they made their way back through it, wondering suddenly how stable it was. Might it come down under their feet? He caught a glimpse of India's face, half-turned from him, aglow in the canyon's mysterious aura, and thought it might not be the place after all but his reaction to her, to what had come close to happening. *Better not come here alone with her,* he thought —adding wistfully, *Ah, damn.*

Outside, at the foot of the cliff, the sensation intensified, and he decided that part of it might be India, but part of it was a feeling of being watched. He began to wonder if there *were* ghosts, and he spun around, scanning the canyon. There was no one to be seen.

"Come on," he said abruptly. "It's getting dark."

India followed his eyes around the canyon walls. "Do you see something?"

"No." Frank sounded uncertain.

"Now you've made me feel twitchy." India buckled her saddlebags and mounted, then leaned down for the strap she had devised to carry a wet canvas. As they turned their ponies around, Frank's lifted its head and whinnied.

"Damn it!" Frank said. "Somebody's out there."

"He just knows we're going home," India said without conviction, patting her own pony's neck. "He wants dinner."

"Come on." Frank reined his mount in behind her and hustled her down the trail.

By the time they neared home, he had *almost* lost the feeling of being watched and was inclined once again to put it down to the sensations that India raised in him. Perhaps. India looked equally thoughtful.

Alvarez and his men watched them go. "And who in the name of the Mother of God are *they?*" he demanded.

"Gringos," one of his sergeants said helpfully. "Maybe not the woman," he amended.

"She's not a Yaqui, that is for certain," Alvarez said. "Yaqui aren't coming here to paint pictures. Not even to confuse me. So why is our Navajo watching these people?"

The sergeants were silent, puzzling this out.

"Because he doesn't want *them* to find what he doesn't want *us* to find," Alvarez growled. He turned his pony back to pick up the trail into the canyon. There was no way down the steep sides. You could watch, but you couldn't get there from above. It was twilight by the time they rode around the long way through the canyon to the cliff house.

One of the sergeants crossed himself at the sight of it. "Old," he said. "Very old. Unholy."

"Undoubtedly," Alvarez said briskly, "considering the use to which it has been put. We shall exorcise it."

The men dismounted, hobbled the horses, and then

Alvarez began to climb, grinning at his sergeants' white faces. Reaching the ledge, he sniffed along the base of the cliff house for the ladder he was sure was there. When he found it, he drew the same conclusion that Frank had from the freshly broken rung. "Something heavy went up," he said with satisfaction.

Alvarez and his sergeants went up the ladder in a hurry, fanning out to look. They had no lantern with them, and it was nearly black inside. "We can't see anything, Capitán," a sergeant said plaintively after a few minutes.

"I nearly pitched out a doorway," the other said, shaken.

Alvarez glared at them. He felt like making them search anyway, but they wouldn't find anything and would probably break a leg—or worse—bumbling in the dark. He took a certain satisfaction in telling them they were sleeping there that night.

The ghosts didn't get anyone overnight, but the sergeants looked as if they hadn't slept well. Even Alvarez was glad to see the sun. Something made him twitchy, and he didn't know if it was the place or whoever else might be hiding in it.

The men climbed down to where they had hobbled the horses. After a breakfast consisting of boiled coffee and jerky, Alvarez set them, stomachs rumbling in protest, to ferreting among the rooms and ruins of the cliff house. In two hours they came to the old storeroom with the fallen wall. Alvarez cocked an eye at it.

"Dig," he ordered.

They had brought shovels, and the sergeants set to, rolling away the big rocks by hand, digging out the smaller ones, cursing whoever had laid them there. With the last of the big rocks gone, the boards that kept them from tumbling into the hidden room were finally visible.

"Capitán!"

Alvarez got up off the boulder he had been sitting on —there were, after all, only two shovels—and came to look. He whistled sharply between his teeth. The boards were pried off, and he crawled through the doorway into the space behind. He opened a case at random and then another one. After five cases he was satisfied.

The sergeants watched wistfully. The rifles were better than the ones they carried.

"Put them back," Alvarez ordered.

"Don't we take them?" one sergeant asked.

"Not now. I want the bastards who put them here. And then I want their mothers and their brothers and their wives." Alvarez's face was suddenly vicious, its sharp planes hawklike. "This will be one nest of snakes we won't have to bother with anymore. Another piece of Sonora cleared of vermin." He sat down on his rock again to wait. Like his president and most of his men, Alvarez was part Indian, but that didn't matter. What mattered was who was in power, who wielded the stick. The Yaqui were savages. The forces of civilization would make Mexico a great nation among great nations. El Presidente knew this.

They left, covering their tracks carefully, and counting on the painter woman and her escort to account for any traces that remained. She was useful, Alvarez decided. In two weeks he would be back, with more men and enough supplies to let them wait on the canyon rim for their prey. It would take that long to get what he needed past Baines and the other United States *federales*, but Alvarez thought he had time. There weren't enough guns yet for a revolution, and his informants in the villages had heard no whisper of imminent revolt. There had been no gathering in of men, only these clandestine border crossings. Alvarez felt satisfied. He had stopped it in its tracks.

"Someone was in the canyon tracking the Anglo woman!" José said furiously to Turtle Shell. "I warned you!"

"Maybe he was tracking you," Turtle Shell said contemptuously.

"No one has reason to track me!" José snapped. "You go back to Sonora and don't come north again, or this deal is off. You understand?"

"You kill that woman, *we* will pay for it, not you," Uncle Joe Horseman added.

Turtle Shell sat stiffly, silent.

"You insult him," Scarred Hands said. "He has not been in the canyon. None of us has been in the canyon without you."

"Then who was it?" José waited for Turtle Shell to answer.

"This is serious," Joe Horseman said. He looked at Scarred Hands when Turtle Shell didn't respond.

Turtle Shell folded his arms across his chest. Joe Horseman folded his. Leo Horseman looked at Aunt Mary's Husband. "Best we move the guns," Leo said to him. The Yaqui nodded.

"Who was it, then?" José insisted, prodding Turtle Shell.

Turtle Shell shrugged. "It is your country," he said finally. "I don't know who is in your country."

José reached out and grabbed Turtle Shell by the shirtfront. In an instant, Leo and Aunt Mary's Husband were between them, pulling José off, yanking Turtle Shell backward. Scarred Hands and Joe looked at them thoughtfully for a moment and then stood between the two.

Leo relaxed his grip on José, with Joe handy to collar him if need be. "It does not matter who was in the canyon," Leo said. "It is enough that someone was. The Anglo painter lady was dangerous enough. Someone else is even worse. If someone kills her"—he carefully looked away from Turtle Shell—"then we have big trouble. If she finds the guns, we have big trouble. If someone else was in the canyon and *they* find the guns, we have big trouble. So it is best we move the guns."

"Because this son of a bitch is trigger-happy?" José demanded.

"Because I say so, Nephew," Leo said.

"Because if there is no need to kill the woman, no man can insult any other man over the matter," Aunt Mary's Husband said. He relaxed his grip on Turtle Shell, who stood angrily, stubbornly silent.

"All right," Scarred Hands said. "We move the guns."

"Where to?" José demanded. "Do you know how long it took me to fix up that place? Where do you think you're going to put them? Under a rock? On a rope from the sky?"

"We will have to find a place," Leo said.

"We will send word when we have a place," José said, taking charge. "*Then* you can come north again. To see where we have put them." He gave Scarred Hands a measuring look.

"We will come north to see where the guns are put," Scarred Hands agreed.

"Until then you stay the other side of the border," José said again. "If I see anyone else around that canyon, I'll come after him." He pointed at Turtle Shell. "Is that clear?"

"No, it is ridiculous," Leo argued. "You are like a bad-tempered dog. Stop barking. They will stay here until we move the guns. How long do you want this to take? And how many comings and goings over the border? This last trip was one too many already." He looked at Aunt Mary's Husband. "And all because you were worried about the Anglo woman. Now we are worried about her, too, and you are nearly at blows with my nephew, who is also your nephew. We will move these guns quickly before we begin to fight with each other. And you will stay here and keep out of sight. Has my nephew got any questions about that?"

"No," José said sulkily. "But that one doesn't leave the hogan." He nodded at Turtle Shell.

"Agreed," Scarred Hands said quickly before Turtle Shell could speak. "There are too many comings and goings. None of us will go outside this place until it is time."

"If you don't want to come with me," India said haughtily, "I can certainly go by myself."

"I didn't say I didn't want to come with you," Frank said. "I'm crazy to go back out there—it's the darnedest place I ever saw. I want to see every inch of it. And I *don't* want you going alone. I just said I didn't think it was the world's best idea for you and me to go out there by ourselves."

India looked at him wide-eyed. "Why not?" *And if it embarrasses you to explain, my friend, that's too bad.*

But Frank apparently wasn't embarrassed. "Because we nearly got carried away out there last time. Because I nearly ripped your clothes off and made love to you, damn it. Because I still want to."

"Oh." Now India was embarrassed.

"And you wanted to, too, and I don't think it's the

most intelligent idea in the world, since neither one of us wants to get married."

India thought about it. Frank's bald statement made it easier. "Would we have to get married?" she asked finally. "I'm sure you've—you've done it before. I haven't, but I don't for a minute believe you haven't."

"They were women who knew what they were doing," Frank said uncomfortably. "Has anybody explained to you about babies?"

"Well, of course. There are ways not to. I don't know what they are, though."

Frank started to put his arms around her but hooked his thumbs in his belt instead. "I can't believe I'm having this conversation. You're a nice girl from a good family. You aren't even supposed to talk about things like this. Especially not with a man."

"Maybe I'm a black sheep," India said. "Why do you want to make love to me?" She studied his face. "Do you love me?"

"Probably," Frank said. He looked at her. "I don't know how to tell."

"It's not fair that either you have to get married and give up everything you want to do, or you can't ever love anybody," India said.

"I can love you," Frank said quietly. He put his arms around her now. "I just can't do anything about it. There aren't any neat answers for people like us."

India leaned her face against his shirt. "I'm tired of other people's answers," she said fiercely. "And I'm tired of being a nice girl from a good family. I'm tired of behaving as if everyone in the whole world has to conform to the one set of ideas I was brought up with. As if there's only one way to be and everything else is false. Lots of women who aren't nice girls from good families do what they please."

Frank chuckled. "They get married, though. They all *want* to get married. Believe me. You're the wild card."

"One of them wanted to marry you, didn't she?" India said shrewdly.

"Yeah." Frank sighed. "I just couldn't. Look, it's not fair, but it's different for women. They don't have an easy time if they don't marry."

India raised her head so she could look at him. "I didn't ask for an easy time," she said distinctly. "I want to *do* things in my life, not be complaisant." Then she chuckled. "But maybe I don't want to start today. Mike's not filming today. If we're going to the cliff house, let's take Johnny with us."

It was the start of November and cold. Johnny said they had to watch out for snow. But the sky was cloudless, a cold blue like an icy lake. Vapor rose from their mouths when they talked, and the horses snorted and blew steam from their nostrils. The smell of woodsmoke hung over the plateau, sharply scented with burning pinecones. India was bundled in a sheepskin jacket over a lightweight woolen shirt and a divided skirt of heavy wool. Her saddlebags were packed with paints; this might be the last time she could visit the cliff house until spring. And she didn't think she would be here in the spring. Mike had talked about packing up the household after Christmas. His New Yorkers, Herb and Rachel, were growing restless, complaining about the food, the lack of theaters, and in Herb's case a good cigar.

They reached their destination, and when they dismounted, India took Johnny's hand impulsively. "Thank you for this, Johnny. I will always remember it. It will always be with me."

Johnny smiled. A real smile. It was brief, but it flickered like a fire across his face. "That is why I gave it to you."

India set up her paints while Frank and Johnny sat out of her view, playing poker. "Go explore," she said. "You don't have to watch me every minute." But they shook their heads and dealt out the cards again. India began to paint. If they wanted to behave like bodyguards, that was their business. They were sweet, though, to be worried about her.

Despite the urge to paint until the last scrap of light was gone, she packed up her easel in the early afternoon to give them time to picnic and explore.

She spread their lunch on a blanket and poured hot tea from the pot Frank had heated on a fire, waiting on them to make up for their having been so patient. Frank and Johnny wolfed down tamales and chili verde with the appetite of starving weasels, and India wondered once again how young men did it. A meal that big would make her want to sleep for hours.

Frank and Johnny appeared to have no such problem. They drained the teapot, wiped the stew pot out with pieces of tortilla, then scrubbed their hands dutifully on the napkins Eden's cook had packed. "Let's go up," Frank said impatiently. He doused the fire with a potful of water from the creek.

They scrambled up the steep path to the ledge. When they pulled out the ladder, Johnny nodded somberly over the broken rung. "Plenty of people know the place." He looked around. "Uncle Luis thinks someone's up to no good, but I don't know who."

"What would they be up to?" India asked.

Maybe what we *were up to,* Frank thought but didn't say it.

They went up the ladder clumsily in their bulky clothes. India's hand slipped, and she missed a rung, turning an ankle in her attempt to catch herself. She went cautiously up the rest of the way, and Frank took her hand.

"Are you all right?"

India moved her foot in a circular motion. She grimaced slightly. It hurt, but she wasn't going to admit it. "I think so. I'd better be. You can't carry me down that ladder."

"We'd make a sling," Johnny said earnestly. "Lower you down."

"No, thank you. What do you want to see?" she asked Frank before he could pursue this notion.

"I've been thinking about who busted the ladder since last month," Frank said.

"Whoever he is, he's long gone," India said.

"Perhaps. But something is still here. I can feel it."

"Maybe you'd better not look too close, then," Johnny said. "If you feel it, it may not be human."

"We're here," Frank pointed out. "And India says it wasn't your ladder to start with."

"I don't feel it. I read tracks I can see. Somebody's been here, all right, but they've gone away again."

"Well, then, let's look around. You can tell me what people used this place for."

"Like a pueblo," Johnny said, as they ventured farther in. "To live. Sleep. Store food. Have babies. Be a people."

"Why did they leave?" Frank traced the marks of old tools on the rock wall with his hand.

"Who knows? Maybe there was less danger. Some enemy went away, maybe. Maybe it became unclean somehow. I don't believe that," he said hastily.

"It's all right. I've been in some places I know were unclean, if you count what happened in them."

Johnny shrugged. "What else *would* you count?"

They climbed higher and investigated an interior passage.

"Look!" Frank said suddenly. "What did I tell you?"

"What?" India demanded.

"There." He pointed.

"It's a pile of rocks," India said. "It was there last time."

"It's different. Use your eyes. Someone's moved it."

Johnny narrowed his eyes. "I think it *is* different."

"Why would anyone move a pile of rocks?" India asked, adding, as it dawned on her, "To get at whatever was behind it."

"Come on." Frank began pulling rocks away. Johnny and India joined him. They had no shovels, and they scrabbled with their gloved hands.

"What are we looking for?" Johnny asked.

Frank grinned. "There been any robberies around here lately? As far away as Santa Fe even?"

"José's bandits?" India asked.

"I wouldn't be surprised if the bandit was José. If I had pulled a bank job, I wouldn't want to look rich too soon. I'd find a nice, unlikely place to hide the loot and sit tight. Some place most people would stay away from, particularly my own people. Some place no one would expect *me* to go, if they got ideas."

"Do you think José's that smart?" India wondered. "He strikes me as the type who'd immediately go out and buy a flashy saddle. Or put down big stakes in the cantina."

"Maybe," Johnny said. "But what Frank says is just what *I* would do. I don't know if I'm smarter than José or not." He was eager now, digging rocks away. A bright thread of excitement hung in the air, tying them to one another, linking their digging hands.

Finally they had excavated enough rocks to see the

boards, and Frank kicked them in with a booted foot. He wriggled through the opening, Johnny and India after him. The little room was stacked with wooden crates.

"If that's a bank robbery, he must have hauled it out in a wagon," India said.

"Some of them have been opened," Johnny said. He pulled the lid off one of the crates. He said something in Tiwa.

"Jesus, Mary, and Joseph," Frank breathed, looking over Johnny's shoulder.

The crate was full of rifles.

"Come on!" Frank grabbed India by the wrist.

"That's no bank robbery," India said, stunned.

Frank nearly pushed her through the low doorway. Johnny was on their heels. "We don't want anything to do with whomever those belong to," Frank said, "except at a *very* long distance. Let's get out of here!"

They hurried through the passageway. Then Frank pulled up short in the outer chamber, listening. "Damn!" he swore, his face pale as he looked at India. She and Johnny heard it too: hoofbeats, a lot of horses moving fast. The three of them raced for the ladder, but where would they go to outrun anyone in the canyon?

XIX

Dust rose in the canyon; hoofbeats reverberated from its walls. Slithering down the ladder, India slipped, and her wrenched ankle caused her to freeze in pain for a moment. Reaching the ledge, she gritted her teeth, then went on down the path, scrabbling and sliding to the base of the cliff. The ponies tethered to the scrub there had thrown their heads up, listening.

"We won't get past anybody," Johnny said. The trail and the canyon it cut through were too narrow.

"Well, we can't go back up there," Frank said, gesturing at the cliff house. "They'll know we're there. We'll be sitting ducks."

"We can climb up the canyon side," India said, hobbling around to face the canyon wall. Horses couldn't make it. People might. Or goats. Unfortunately, no one had cut handholds here.

Frank grabbed her arm. "You can't climb that. You can't even walk."

"I can do what I have to." She started for the wall to prove it.

A shot blasted through the canyon behind them, echoing back and forth from wall to wall. Frank spun around but couldn't see anyone yet. The riders were nearly at the bend, though, judging from the sounds they made.

"Turn our ponies loose!" India shouted. "Maybe they won't bother to catch them. We'll need them later."

Their mounts still stood, nostrils quivering, looking down the canyon. Frank untied them from where they had been tethered and hit them hard on their rumps. "Go on! Git!" The ponies flung their heads up and wheeled around. Frank threw some stones at them. They rocketed into the chaparral, trampling the remains of the picnic and India's easel.

Frank turned and clambered through the sage and up the crumbling slope of the canyon wall. Johnny was helping India up a tumbled scree, finding toeholds in the rock, a stunted piñon pine to hang on to. Frank took her waist and boosted her from below.

"I can do it, damn it!" she gasped.

"I know you can do it. Shut up and climb." He pushed her up the slope. Her face was ashen with pain.

They scrambled higher, clinging to rock that crumbled away in their hands, climbing a wall that might suddenly become as insubstantial as the ghosts of the cliff house, tumbling them down upon the real danger below. It hadn't been the chindi or anything else supernatural in the cliff house that had raised the hackles of fear on Frank's neck; it had been men and the dealings of men.

A sheer face of sandstone rose above them. No way up. They edged their way along a narrow ledge, looking for toeholds. Johnny pulled at an overhanging branch, testing it. Another shot cracked in the canyon, and this time the bullet whined like a bee past Frank's ear and buried itself in the sandstone above him. He looked down and saw a rider on a dun pony level a rifle at him.

Frank pulled his revolver and fired back, dropping onto the ledge. "Get her up the rock if you can!" he shouted at Johnny. "I'll try to keep him off."

The rider below wheeled his horse back into the

chaparral as Frank's bullet spat into the dirt. Frank swore. He was too far away. His rifle was still on his pony. *Damn fool,* he thought. Another shot came at him out of the chaparral and went wide. At least the son of a bitch couldn't see very well. More riders thundered into the canyon in a blaze of shots. Frank flattened himself and looked up at India and Johnny in sheer terror, but no bullets hit him or the rock around him.

He lowered his pistol and peered down. A string of packhorses and a dozen or more horsemen were milling in the canyon, and after a moment of confusion he realized that they were firing at each other. He scrambled to his feet, holstering his weapon, wasting no time on puzzling that out. Johnny and India were still climbing, dark silhouettes dangerously visible against the red sandstone cliff. Frank scrabbled after them, expecting to feel a bullet between his shoulder blades at any moment.

He caught up with them as they neared the top. Below they could hear the crack and bang of gunfire, the shouts of the combatants. Who knew who they were? What did it matter? When they had finished killing each other over a cache of guns, they would come after the three of them—of that Frank was sure. India's face was taut, wet with sweat, her hands bloodied through torn gloves. The thought that she might die hit Frank in a wave of terror. Johnny scrambled and slithered, always turning back to help India after him. The top of the canyon loomed above them another thirty feet, but they had come to a slanted ridge that afforded a gentler ascent. Frank briefly wondered if he and Johnny together could carry India, but they couldn't. Even here it took both hands and feet to make their way up.

"Almost there." He steadied India over a boulder that blocked their way. "Look. See the sky?"

"I know." She took a step, and her face went white.

Another on the good ankle. Another on the bad one. The cold blue sky hung above them. Another step up toward it. "Are they shooting at us?" she whispered.

"Not now. They're shooting at each other. They'll shoot at us soon enough."

"Who are they?"

"I don't know." He put his hands around her waist, boosted her up again to Johnny, trying to keep the weight off her ankle. *She can't run.* The thought went clearly through his head. Wherever they got to, they would have to stay and fight.

Suddenly the ground gave way under their feet. The rock shifted and India tumbled backward, taking them both off their feet. Frank braced himself and caught and held her, feeling the yawning canyon pull at them. India got to her knees, knelt there, hands on the rock, eyes shut. He could see a tight white line around her mouth.

Johnny turned back for them. "Go on!" Frank said, pulling his pistol from its holster. He stretched his hand out and gave Johnny the pistol. "Try to keep them pinned if they come after us."

Johnny looked down into the canyon. "Who are we fighting?"

"I wish I knew. Go on. Get up there where you've got some cover."

Johnny began to climb again, moving faster now that he was on his own. Frank watched him disappear over the last ledge in only a minute.

Slowly India got to her feet, teeth gritted.

"Can you make it?" Frank asked her.

"We can't stay here." Doggedly she began to climb, clawing at the rock to steady her steps. An explosion of gunfire from the canyon below made Frank try to put her between the mountain and himself, but she wouldn't stop.

"Move. I can't stop," she said between clenched

teeth. "And it won't do me any good for them to shoot *you*."

"I don't think they're firing at us," Frank muttered, not wanting to discuss why he had tried to cover her. Giving voice to his fears would make them real. If he didn't think about her getting killed, it wouldn't happen.

Up. Up the last step, the last explosion of pain in India's ankle. Johnny reached down and pulled her onto the plateau. She knelt in the cold dirt, head hanging down, and retched, bringing up everything she had eaten.

"It's all right, let it come up; you'll feel better." Frank put a hand to her clammy forehead.

"I couldn't stop it if I wanted to," she said weakly. She retched again, gagging, but nothing came up. Her head was swimming. Frank bent and picked her up, staggering under her weight, his own knees weak, and set her down away from the sharp slope of the canyon's edge. He started cutting her boot off with his belt knife, pushing the heavy folds of her divided skirt out of his way. Johnny lay on his stomach at the edge, watching.

"I'm sorry," India whimpered, wincing as the boot came off. "I nearly got us all killed."

"Stupid clothes," Frank said viciously, furious and sick with relief. "Women wear stupid clothes. No one could climb in these things."

"I didn't know I was going to have to."

Frank rolled the wool stocking down gently over her foot. The ankle was puffy, and India winced again when he touched it. "You've sprained it real bad. You can't walk anymore."

"I'm sorry," she whispered.

His face was tight; there was a little tic at the corner of his mouth. A hank of blond hair hung in his eyes. His hat was long gone. "Be quiet," he said fiercely. "We're going to be fine. All of us. Be quiet and rest." He touched her face, and the longing to keep her safe, to make her world right for her, washed over him in a wave so strong it felt physical. He nearly bent double under it.

"Stay here," he ordered. "Don't stand up." He turned and crawled on knees and elbows to the canyon's edge beside Johnny.

Johnny lay perfectly still, his dark eyes fixed on the men below, the pistol cocked in his hand.

"Can you tell who they are?"

"One is José, I think," Johnny said. "With the silver band on his hat. But I don't— There, those with him. They could be his uncles, the Horseman brothers, but maybe not. It's too far. I don't know the others. They are Indians, though, the ones with José."

Frank watched cautiously, trying to sort them out. A pitched gun battle was raging on the canyon floor. Most of the combatants had dismounted and taken cover, José and his compatriots nearest to the cliff house. They had arrived first, Frank thought, with the others riding after them, but it was hard to be sure. And who *were* the others? They shouted to one another, and to the Indians, in Spanish.

"What kind of Indians are they, with José?" Frank asked Johnny.

"Not Pueblo," Johnny said. "Not Navajo either, except for the Horsemans. Those other three—*some* kind of Indian."

"Surrender!" The shout came from below in Spanish. "Surrender to justice, or we will shoot you down!"

"Bugger your justice!" someone else shouted back. "Rurales don't know justice!"

"Mexican!" Johnny said, eyes wide. "Rurales, they're a kind of police. What are they doing here?"

"The others must be Mexican, too," Frank said. "I'm willing to bet our marshals don't know they're here, either batch of them." He brightened. "Those other three with José, maybe they're Mexican. The rurales are probably after their own folks for something. With luck, they won't have the nerve to shoot American citizens."

"You, maybe. No one is so particular about Indians."

Frank ignored that. There wasn't much he could say since he knew it was true. "I'm betting José and his uncles won't have the nerve to shoot us, either."

"Somebody shot at us," Johnny pointed out.

"Him, on the dun pony." Frank pointed at the rider, now dismounted. "The one with the hunchback. He seems to belong to José. Maybe when José figures out who he's shooting at, he'll use his head."

"What head?" Johnny muttered. "What's José doing with Mexican rurales after him?"

"Running guns to Mexico?" Frank suggested. "Would you put it past him?"

"No," Johnny admitted. His watchful gaze intensified, focusing on the strangers with José. "I heard something."

"What?"

"Just Taos gossip. A woman in José's hogan married out of her people, to a Yaqui down in Sonora."

"So maybe those Indians with him are Yaqui," Frank speculated.

India suddenly slithered into place beside him. "Get back!" he hissed.

"I can't stand it. I have to see. Who are they?" She gasped. "My God, that's José!"

"They're Mexican police, we think," Frank said. "We don't know about the men with José. We think they're *maybe* Yaqui Indians from Mexico."

"Hiding guns here?"

"Sure, if they're brewing up a revolt against the government," Johnny said. He looked angry. "From what we hear up here, the Mexican government is trying to wipe the Yaqui out. They want their land. These rurales just go into the villages and kill. Women. Children."

"All right, I sympathize," Frank growled. "But those guns are a secret that's dangerous as hell. And we know about it."

"Like you said, the rurales won't shoot American citizens if they win." Johnny looked depressed about it.

"Do you want to come in on the rurales' side, so they won't kill us?" Frank demanded.

"No!" India said.

"I didn't ask you. We're trying to protect you."

"Don't!" India snapped. "I've heard about the rurales. They're murderers. I wouldn't give them a drink of water. José has enough sense not to shoot at us."

"That's what I think," Frank said. "But apparently that's not the case with at least one of the fellows with him."

"Well, there's not much you can do with one pistol," India said practically. "Except use it on anyone who tries to climb up here." She laid her head on her arm for a moment. She still looked pallid. "I wish I didn't feel so sick."

"It's your ankle," Frank said. "Pain does that. Quit crawling around. And keep your head down. We don't want them thinking about us."

José knew they were up there. He had seen the trampled easel. And then Turtle Shell had shot at them. It was hard to say who was the bigger fool, but José didn't have time to decide. How the hell had the damned rurales

found them? There was no way out. They were going to
have to kill them all. No one was going to come riding to
the rescue, and their own government would put them in
jail for possessing the guns.

The rurales weren't going to give up, José knew. He
and his partners couldn't let any get away. A bullet zinged
past José's head, and he focused on killing. He had an
advantage. The rurales wanted someone left alive to question. José didn't. He sighted in on one of the five left as
the man came from behind cover to fire at him. The Mexican dropped with a sudden outflung arm that sent his own
bullet wide, ricocheting off the canyon. Four, José thought
grimly. Four left.

It had cost them. Aunt Mary's Husband had crawled
into the slight shelter of the cliff base and was tying a
tourniquet on his thigh. Scarred Hands was dead.

The canyon air was thick with powder smoke and
dust. The horses, quickly tied, were churning up the dirt
with frantic hooves. José scurried along the cliff base,
screened by smoke and dust and the scrub that grew at
the canyon's foot.

India put her knuckles in her mouth. It was like
watching a dreadful play except that what was happening
was real, and she knew some of the players. She knew
José. She knew Leo Horseman, who ran the trading post,
and his brother, Joe. Surely they wouldn't climb the canyon wall to kill her. And surely she wasn't going to watch
them die, shot by strangers.

They watched a figure that might be José moving in
the brush. It was hard to see anything much. Two of the
rurales seemed to be dead, and so did one of José's band.
Another quick burst of gunfire and they saw that José had
killed his man, then taken to his heels, zigzagging among

the stones and scrub of the canyon floor, while the others shot at his fleeing form. One of the rurales was close below where India and Frank and Johnny hid on the canyon rim.

"He's trying to get behind them," Frank said, watching José. He took the pistol from Johnny and lifted it.

India clamped a hand on his wrist. "How do you think the rurales would thank us?" she whispered.

Frank lowered the pistol. Being able to do nothing made him frantic. He gritted his teeth.

Below them the Mexican he had nearly shot suddenly dropped into the barbed arms of a prickly pear. José and his uncles had the advantage of knowing the canyon.

India looked at the sky apprehensively. The light was failing. What would happen when darkness fell? Another burst of gunfire reverberated off the canyon walls, and then the air was unnaturally silent. Below them in the chaparral, bodies were sprawled, one with his hat gone and a dark red patch that seemed to cover his head.

Slowly José straightened up from his cover in the chaparral. Leo Horseman came limping over, a bloody rag around one calf, and then Joe. One of the Yaqui lay dead at the base of the cliff. The other two inched forward cautiously, the man who had shot at India, Frank, and Johnny and another who could barely walk. He had blood streaming down his leg, a makeshift tourniquet wrapped around the thigh.

"Sit!" Joe said abruptly and bent over the man.

India, Frank, and Johnny watched silently from above. There wasn't anything else they could do. They couldn't get down from the rim unnoticed. José shouted for someone and swore when there was no answer. He and Joe set off into the chaparral, each dragging a body and a shovel.

"Are they just going to bury them out here?" India whispered.

"They aren't going to ride home with them," Frank said. "I wonder if they'll bury their own, too."

India thought about it. "I would," she said after a moment. "You're right. They can't take a corpse home. I guess the rurales are lucky to be buried and not left for the coyotes. I wonder why."

"People come out here," Johnny said. "José and his uncles live here. Coyotes make a mess. Someone would find something."

"And connect it to them?"

"Who wants people wondering?" Johnny said.

The thought that the three of them knew the connection remained unspoken. Again José shouted from below for someone who didn't answer. At the second shout, Frank, his pistol in his hand, leapt up suddenly in one movement. A bullet smacked into the rock where he had been, and India and Johnny rolled to one side, terrified. They tried to stand. India stumbled and Johnny picked her up, pulling her to the dubious shelter of a clump of snakeweed.

Frank saw the intruder climbing closer and noted with satisfaction that he wasn't quite over the rim yet. The man's hunchback marked him as the rider on the dun horse. Frank pushed a small boulder loose and sent it rolling down on him. The Yaqui avoided being dislodged and struggled on, over the canyon rim. Before he could aim the rifle again, Frank kicked a booted foot into the man's face. The man grunted, his hands scrabbling for the rocks on the rim, seeking a grip. His rifle slipped, and Frank kicked it into the air.

A hand came up, clawing, and grabbed at Frank's ankle. Frank slipped, his hands flailing. His pistol went flying into the air, and he felt himself falling backward while the clawlike hand pulled at his foot. With his free leg he kicked at the Yaqui's face. He heard voices below, but he couldn't divert his attention from the weight dragging him into space.

Frank strained backward, pushing with his hands on the rocks. He brought the heel of his boot down hard on the clutching fingers. The fingers opened, and the man howled with anger. Frank pulled his foot back and rolled away from the rim; the other man surged over it after him. His eyes took in India and dismissed her, then rested on Johnny with a kind of outraged fury. He launched himself at Frank. He was enormously strong, stronger than Frank had expected. The Yaqui's arms closed around him and bore him backward, but not before Frank saw the knife in his hand.

He twisted in the man's grasp, determined not to fall onto the knife or give the Indian a chance to use it elsewhere, either. An accomplished brawler from his years on the road, Frank had no scruples when someone was trying to kill him. The enemy's ear was within reach, and he sank his teeth into it. Out of the corner of his eye, he could see India crouched in the tangle of snakeweed and Johnny coming at them. Johnny had his own knife in his hand.

Frank and the Yaqui spun, struggling, in a circle, perilously near the canyon rim. Frank felt the Yaqui's knife graze his arm as he pulled from his grasp and retreated from the uncertain footing along the edge. He managed to get his own knife from his belt as Johnny came past him in a crouch, surefooted as a goat in the rubble. Together they edged the Yaqui nearer to the canyon, and his eyes grew angry.

He ran at them, screaming something neither could

understand, his knife out. They separated, coming at him from either side. He spun furiously from one to the other. Spotting India, he ran toward her.

Frank leapt after him and caught him by the humped shoulder, but the man shook him off. With a howl of anger, Johnny rammed his head into the Yaqui's chest, driving him toward the rim. The Yaqui's feet slipped in the loose stone and he fell, flailing, into the air. He landed with a heavy thump, a sickening splatter of broken flesh, on the rocks below, the knife still in his hand.

Frank looked at India. She was sitting with her bad ankle stretched out before her, one hand clutching the belt knife she wore when she went riding and the other braced on the ground beside her.

"You can put that away now," Frank said. India nodded and stuck the blade back in its sheath.

Below them José and his uncles had gathered around the dead Yaqui. Frank stood, hoping they wouldn't take potshots at him. "We don't want anything to do with you folks," he shouted. "We aren't the law. Whatever your business is here, we don't give a damn. You got that? We'd just like not to get shot at by strangers." He noted with a certain amusement that José and his uncles had tied their bandannas over their faces. Big-time gun smugglers. Fine. If they thought they hadn't been recognized, it might forestall their urge to start shooting.

José looked up from the body sprawled on the rocks. "He's dead," he shouted back.

"Come up here after us, and some of you will be dead, too," Frank warned. "Just take care of your business and we'll mind ours until you've gone. We'd appreciate it if you'd leave our horses alone," he added. He exhibited his knife. "We've got a pretty good view from up here, and I'm pretty good at throwing this."

The masked faces peered up at them, then turned

away. The man spoke to the others. "Stay there!" José finally ordered. "Try to come down before we're gone, and you're dead."

Frank nodded and put his knife away so that they could see him do it. He retreated from the canyon rim and sat beside India and Johnny. They were just near enough to the edge to track the men below and be certain of their whereabouts.

India was about to ask, "What do you think they'll do?" but suppressed it, deciding it was an idiotic question. Frank and Johnny had no more idea than she did what the men below would do. Why was women's instinct always to ask men what they thought? Probably because they had been taught to, she concluded. Men were supposed to make the decisions; therefore, you asked what they thought so you had some idea of what the decisions were going to be—and could brace yourself if they were unpalatable. The notion depressed her. One more reason not to marry. Not even Frank—he was already trying to make decisions for her. Assuming either one of them survived to marry anybody. She watched the activity below apprehensively, but no one came toward the canyon wall. The men looked up now and again, but that was all.

Silently the three above watched the four below bury the dead rurales and, separately and with more care, their own dead. José and his uncles buried the rurales' saddles and bridles as well, then turned their horses loose. Horses were too identifiable, as was their government-issue tack. The three above watched ruefully as they scattered. There was no telling where their own ponies had gone.

The men below began to climb to the cliff house, finally returning, to no one's surprise, with the crates of guns. They did this repeatedly, then loaded the crates onto the string of pack ponies they had led into the canyon. It was full dark before they left, riding out single file, with a last shout at the canyon rim: "Stay where you are till morning! If you do not, we will know. We will come after you."

"Oh, certainly," India said with disgust to José's departing back. "In between finding another place to put your guns and hiding a wounded Yaqui in your mother's house."

"We'd better find our ponies," Johnny said. "It's cold." It was an understatement. With the last of the November sun had gone any trace of warmth. Johnny thought a moment. "You stay here. I can catch my horse, I think. Then I'll find yours if they haven't headed home. If they have, I'll go after them. Build a fire." He pulled his coat off and gave it to India.

"You're just as cold as I am," India protested.

"I can walk home if I have to. You can't. Take the coat. You'll need two."

"We could take turns carrying her," Frank said.

"Ha," Johnny scoffed. India was as tall as he was. It was no time for chivalry. "I'm going to catch my horse." He started down the canyon's edge, looking for the least precipitous way down. Before he began the descent he turned to them for a moment. "Will you bring marshals back here?"

India noted that he had said "you," not "we." "No," she said gently, before Frank could make the decision. "There would be white people here forever after that, wouldn't there? You'd never get rid of them." Johnny smiled again. His second. India was counting. "You tell your uncle Luis we know he wouldn't like that," she said.

Johnny's scrabbling on the rocks below became less and less distinct. At last they heard him whistle in the canyon for his mount.

"So you're just planning to let the Horseman family

shoot Mexican law officers and bury them out here in the middle of nowhere without any comment?" Frank inquired, gathering firewood as he spoke.

"I'm not planning on having white people scrambling through this cliff house, ruining it," India retorted. "There'll be archaeologists and heaven knows who else out here in droves, asking all the Pueblo people stupid questions and treating them as if they were specimens."

"What about the matter of a few dead bodies?" The glance Frank threw her over his shoulder was amused.

"I hope they get away with their guns and shoot the rest of the rurales. As far as I'm concerned, Mexico needs a revolution."

"Firebrand." Frank smiled. "I suppose my sympathies incline that way, too. I thought you might be made of more law-abiding stuff."

India was silent, thinking it over. "Apparently not," she said at last.

Frank came back and knelt beside her, piling up deadwood. "We may be here all night," he groused.

India chuckled. "Don't worry. I won't make you marry me." Even with the pain in her ankle, it seemed almost exciting, an adventure—now that no one was shooting at them. She would probably feel differently if it snowed, she imagined. In the light of a full moon, a flicker of movement in the canyon bottom caught her eye. "Frank, look." She put a hand on his arm and pointed with the other. Below them Johnny's horse was dutifully trotting out of the chaparral, following his whistle.

"Nice trick," Frank said. "I hope ours aren't in the next territory." He lit the fire, babying it along. Despite her best efforts, India's teeth were chattering.

The fire bloomed, bright orange tendrils dancing in the cold air. India put Johnny's coat on over her own and sat as close to the flames as she could get without catching on fire. Frank scooted next to her and put his arm around her. "This is strictly for warmth," he informed her. "I am not taking indecent liberties."

"You couldn't, over all these clothes," India muttered. "I'm glad we brought Johnny. You were right."

"Because we needed a chaperon?"

"No, because his horse comes when he whistles." She cuddled as close to him as she could get. "I have a horse that will do that."

"Where is it?"

"In Oklahoma, alas." The wind picked up, biting into her cheeks and ears. Her hands felt numb in her gloves, even held to the fire.

"The very best way for two people to stay warm," Frank said after a while, "is to take all their clothes off and get under the covers together and let their body heat warm each other."

"We don't have any covers," India pointed out. "All we have is clothes. Probably fortunate."

"For the best," Frank agreed solemnly. "We may freeze, but they will find us with our virtue intact."

"That will be a comfort to our mothers," India murmured.

Frank hooted with glee. "You're a joy to me, darlin'," he said. "Is it safe to kiss you, do you think?"

"Probably. It's too cold to get undressed." She turned her head up, and his mouth came down on hers. She was aware of being cold, of the ache in her fingers and toes, but she was also aware of the bright circle of hunger that lay between them. Frank's hand crept up under Johnny's coat and hers, and rested on her breast again. This time he didn't pull it away. *What's going to become of us?* she wondered idly, floating somewhere outside the cold.

It was just beginning to snow when Johnny rode up

later, trailing their ponies behind him. Frank had the decency to pull his hand out from under her coat, even though Johnny was still too far away to see them. *Poor Johnny*, India thought. *Everyone wants what they can't have. Me, too.*

XX

India, sitting in her bedroom in Mike and Eden's house, her foot propped up, looked out the window and watched the snow fall. Her ankle was nearly healed now; she just needed to rest it once in a while. As she stared out the window, she thought about the aftermath of her harrowing excursion. . . .

On the way back, she, Frank, and Johnny met a search party organized by Mike and led by Luis. Their would-be rescuers were told a tall tale of a cougar that had spooked the horses—thus India's sprained ankle. Luis looked at Johnny thoughtfully, or maybe skeptically. Mike was relieved to find them all in one piece—and vastly disappointed the search hadn't led all the way to the cliff house. "You might have stayed lost a little longer," he said plaintively.

José came to work the next morning as usual, his swagger undiminished but cocking a wary eye at India, Frank, and Johnny. Johnny was his usual silent self, and India treated José with the casual aloofness a daughter of the house might employ toward a hired hand who has shown a little too much interest in her. But Frank seemed to enjoy watching him with the puzzled expression of someone who thinks, but is not quite sure, that he has seen a stranger somewhere before. It made José visibly nervous.

Dismayed by Frank's tactics, India sought him out. "Will you quit that?" she hissed. "You're being blatant. Stop it."

"Getting little José uneasy, am I?" Frank laughed.

"He could still decide to lie in wait for us some night."

"He's got more sense. I'm just pushing him a bit, to get those Yaquis and those guns out of Taos. If they get caught, there'll be trouble for *all* the Indians here. Gun-running is serious business."

"Sure," India said. "You're enjoying yourself, and you know it. You have that look."

"I take it where I can find it," Frank said. "I just found out my whole damn family is coming out here for Christmas. Mike's got some grand reunion planned, and he's got a bee in his bonnet that we're all going to make up with each other. God knows how it'll turn out."

"Oh," India said, wondering what his family would think of what had happened between her and Frank—whatever that was.

She was still thinking about that now as she sat looking out at the snow and at the arriving Blakes and Holts, who filled the house to the gills and spilled over into the hotel in town. As Frank had said, Mike had gotten a bee in his bonnet, arranging one of those occasional coming-togethers in which the entire clan congregated en masse for an orgy of *auld lang syne*. The last one India remembered had taken place at her parents' ranch when she was nine. Mike had met Eden there, she recalled. No wonder he was sentimental about family gatherings. They hadn't been but about twelve themselves, India thought. But they'd known, right away, and had been single-mindedly obsessed with each other until they could marry. But what if you knew and couldn't bring yourself to marry? What if you knew he'd make a rotten husband if you *did* marry him?

Shouts of laughter and greetings filled the house. India's parents had declined the invitation, somewhat to her relief, but Mike's parents, Toby and Alexandra, his sister Sally, and his grandmother, Eulalia, had come. They were being put up at the hotel, where Eulalia could get some rest. Mike figured the festivities among the younger members were likely to go on all night. Sally, sixteen, was grown up enough to bristle at having to stay at the hotel with the old folks, so India had done what she considered her yearly good deed and told Mike that Sally could share her room. Mike's older brother, Tim, who ran a newspaper in San Francisco, and his suffragist wife, Elizabeth, were coming—assuming the stage lines could get through the snow. Mike's sister Janessa, the doctor, and her husband, Charley, the doctor, and their twins were coming. India had them all pigeonholed by occupation or avocation or public scandal. Both Janessa and Elizabeth had on occasion achieved the latter.

And Frank's father was coming, with his mother and little sister. Midge's doctors had thought a holiday away from the congestion of Washington, in clear desert air, would do her good. Or at least that was Cindy Blake's stated reason in accepting the invitation. If she wanted instead to throw Frank and his father together again, or force Henry to make his peace with the rest of the family, she was wise enough not to say so.

India watched Frank stalk across the snowy yard, his hat pulled down over his eyes as if he were hiding. He went into the barn and came out with a saddled horse, mounted it, and headed down the Pueblo Road, away from town. His parents were due to arrive in an hour.

There was a tap at the door, and Sally Holt poked her head around it. "Mike says you're going to let me share. You're an *angel*." She came in when India beckoned and flopped down in the Spanish armchair that took up most of one corner. She moved with the instinctive grace of one whose balance is perfect and unencumbered by uncertainty. Her face was heart-shaped and delicate, her hair a soft rose gold, the lashes over her blue-green eyes dark and sweeping. *The ethereal quality of Botticelli,* India thought, *underlaid with a hint of stubbornness.*

"They were going to make me stay in the hotel with Mama and Dad and Gran," Sally said, making a face. "Dad has trouble with his stomach and goes to bed at eight o'clock, and Gran orders health biscuits for breakfast. All the fun is going to be here, while they're in bed."

India laughed. "That may be what your mother had in mind. You'll have to be well behaved. I won't be your nanny."

"I'm always well behaved," Sally said with a smile indicating anything but.

You're a terror, India thought. *I wish I could learn to move like you do.*

"I like to flirt," Sally said. "But I know how to do it. Mama thinks I'm too young. But I know what I want."

India, who had not the faintest idea how to flirt and found it bewildering when she tried, digested this. "And what do you want?"

"A nice life," Sally said cheerfully. "The right man. I have enough sense to know when I've found him. The rest are just for fun. You know, practice."

"Well, the pickings are slim around here," India said. "All cowhands and farmers," she elaborated.

"If they can dance, they'll do fine."

India chuckled. It was hard not to be disarmed by Sally's gaiety.

The muffled rumble of a wagon sounded in the yard below, and Sally ran to the window. "Tim's here!" she shrieked. "And Janessa!" She whirled out the door and down the stairs. India followed, at a slower pace.

Eight passengers, snow-covered and laughing, tumbled out of the wagon, complaining happily to Mike about the indignity of their transportation. India recognized Mike's older brother, Tim, and was introduced to his wife, Elizabeth, who was pregnant, India noted. Peter Blake had come with them from San Francisco and shook India's hand gravely. Janessa and Charley Lawrence corralled the twins, who were whirling in the snow, and handed them off to a black nursemaid. The Lawrences were presented to India as well.

"I saw you once when you were little," Janessa said. "But you won't remember."

"No, I'm afraid I don't," India said. "But I've heard a lot about you from Mike and the Blakes."

"She's probably read about you in the papers," Sally said happily.

India gave her young roommate a squelching look. She took note of Janessa's twins and wondered if Janessa was practicing medicine actively enough to *be* notorious these days. She would ask Sally. Sally knew everything and appeared to have no scruples about telling it.

"When are Uncle Henry and Aunt Cindy coming?" Sally asked Mike.

"In time for dinner, I hope. The stage driver said there was one more coach coming behind him, and it's their last run till the snow clears. Apparently we're in for a real norther."

"They'd better not miss it," Sally said. "It's almost Christmas."

"Two days, brat," Mike said. "Did you bring me a present?"

"Certainly. We brought presents for everybody."

As if to prove it, Peter and Tim were unloading trunk after trunk from the wagon. "Where's Frank?" Peter demanded.

"Hiding," Mike said. "He went off on a horse. I presume he'll have enough sense to come back before he freezes."

Peter didn't ask why, and India surmised that he didn't need to. Mike sent Johnny Rojas into town again with the wagon to look for the stragglers and bring the senior Holts back for dinner. Everyone else bustled into the house and began to shed snow-covered coats. Rachel Poliakov and Herb Lumb looked at them all with curiosity. Rachel seemed relieved to find in Janessa a face she knew among the thundering herd of Mike's family.

"How are you?" Janessa asked her.

"I am good. Already I have sent my mother enough money to pay the blind school for my sister," Rachel said. She sighed. "I don't tell her I am standing up for a camera and eating food that is not kosher. I don't tell her I am in a house where they are celebrating Christmas."

"Oh." Janessa thought about it. "That's bad, isn't it? Rachel, I'm sorry it turned out this way."

Rachel shrugged. "I have money to send. They need money. To be safe, to pay for Sophie."

Janessa nodded and followed Belle and the children upstairs. India watched all the interplay with fascination. She felt half an outsider like Rachel, half a part of it all. She saw Tim's wife, Elizabeth, watching them with what India thought might be her own expression and wondered if she felt the same way. The Holts in a group were daunting. And the Blakes weren't even here yet.

They arrived at dinnertime, as Frank slunk in the back door, snow-covered and dirty. He went to change and came down in good clothes, kissed his mother and Midge, smiled at Peter, shook hands with his father as if with a new acquaintance, and sat down at the table where Eden told him to.

Midge looked better, India thought, judging by Frank's last description of her, but you could still tell she had been ill. Sally seemed to be making it a point to pay attention to her, something India suspected was not always the case.

"I'm trying to grow up," Sally confided to India after dinner. "I feel for Midge so. Uncle Henry looked just like he'd been eating a lemon or someone had stuck a broom handle down his back. At least my father's human. And Aunt Cindy looked like a hen, fluttering every time anyone said anything, for fear they'd all be in a brawl again."

"I think everyone behaved admirably, under the circumstances," India remarked.

"Frank did. But he was watching you more than he was watching Uncle Henry."

"Oh, I imagine you're mistaken about that."

"I'm never mistaken. But I don't think anyone else noticed. What are you going to do about it?"

"I'm not going to do anything about it," India murmured. She gave the merest flicker of a glance at Frank, who was sitting in front of the adobe fireplace talking to Midge. Midge would notice, India thought, that's who would notice. And what *was* she going to do about it?

Everyone drifted off to bed in the accommodations set up in every available nook and cranny—even the young were too tired from the journey to carry on for long. Janessa was sitting on a dark-oak bench under the window in the upstairs hall, just watching the snow, when India approached.

She smiled as India stood hesitantly over her. "I'm

just catching my breath," she explained. "Charley's in bed, the twins are in bed, Belle's in bed. I take my solitude where I can find it."

"Oh. Actually, I was wondering if I could talk to you, but it can wait."

Janessa took stock of India's expression. "I'd be happy to talk. In, er, what capacity?"

"In a medical capacity."

"I see."

Privacy was called for. Since Sally was in India's room and it was as cold as Lapland outside, they tiptoed back downstairs and sat in the dark beside the dying fire. India ran her hand over the smooth warm adobe and said abruptly, "They tell me you got in trouble for teaching women how not to get pregnant."

Janessa looked at her suspiciously. "It's called contraception in medical circles. 'Contra' meaning against conception."

"I see. I want to know how to do it."

Janessa blinked, studying India's troubled face in the firelight. "It doesn't work after the fact," she said tentatively.

"I know that."

"Well, that's a relief. Are you planning to marry? I should tell you that most doctors and most men and a great many women don't approve of it."

"Elizabeth Holt's in the family way. It's her first, isn't it? Yet how long have they been married?"

Janessa hesitated. "Yes, I believe Elizabeth does practice contraception. I do myself. Not that I've spent enough time around my husband the last few years to need it." She smiled. "But we're changing that. And when are you getting married?"

"I'm not getting married," India said flatly.

Janessa paused to consider the ramifications of that

statement. She was shocked. "You aren't getting married, but you are planning to have carnal relations with a man?"

"I'm thinking about it."

"Then my advice to you," Janessa said briskly, "has to be that that is a most unwise course. You will damage yourself enormously. Do not let any man persuade you to go against your own moral convictions."

India shrugged. "I'm not sure I have any moral convictions. Not against that, I mean. I don't want to marry. I'll never have the time or the freedom to be an artist if I marry, certainly not if I marry young. Am I supposed to do without love all my life because I don't marry?"

"That is the accepted theory," Janessa said, but India's bluntness caused Janessa to smile in spite of herself.

"Well, I don't want to. I refuse."

"Do you, um, have anyone in particular in mind?" Janessa asked, feeling her way.

"Well, of course." India did not elaborate.

"Oh, Lord. I hope no one in the family has been trying to take advantage of you in that fashion."

"You have to understand that I do not consider myself taken advantage of when I make my own decisions."

"If I don't tell you anything *or* tell your parents, will you have sense enough to abandon this idea?" Janessa demanded.

"I doubt it," India said.

It snowed again on Christmas Eve but stopped by Christmas morning. Roads off the plateau were impassable, but the Pueblo Road was well traveled on horseback and snowshoes. The elder Holts and Blakes rode out from the hotel in the village for a Christmas breakfast of chorizo, flapjacks, and thick Mexican cocoa. Eden decreed that presents were to be opened later, wrapped her mystified guests to the eyebrows in mufflers and coats, and bundled them onto waiting horses. Frank and Mike had been out since dawn, grooming and saddling borrowed mounts.

"Where are we going?" Sally asked. Her eyes were bright over the muffler that covered her nose.

"Something special," India said mysteriously. "The Deer Dance at the pueblo." She wouldn't elaborate.

The few Anglo residents of Taos and the Spanish and the Navajos were already streaming along the Pueblo Road. There was a sense of adventure about the cavalcade, of exotic sights to be seen. Even Henry Blake had lost some of his stiffness and looked interested.

The plaza of Taos Pueblo was a smooth expanse of unbroken snow. Across it figures emerged from the kivas. Antlered, deer headed, they picked their way along the footbridge spanning Pueblo Creek, deer heads staring knowingly.

"One of them is Johnny," India whispered to Frank. "I can't tell which one." Deerskins hung down their backs below the antlered heads. They carried pointed sticks in their hands, uncannily resembling the brittle forelegs of deer. With them were a few buffalo, plus Coyote and Mountain Lion. Deer Chiefs in white buckskin brought Deer Mothers, white and mysterious as the snow in buckskin gowns and high white boots. They wore head ornaments of parrot feathers; in their hands they carried gourd rattles and sprigs of spruce.

Cindy Blake held her breath and stared, and India smiled. There was something about the ceremony that tugged at one's oldest memories, at glimmerings of a time when man was one with the beasts he hunted because he had to be or starve. He must call to them or wither.

"Do you believe in racial memory?" Frank whispered to India, echoing her thoughts.

"Maybe I do now. They make me want to . . . go into the dance."

Behind the Deer Mothers pranced the Chiffoneta, the Sacred Clowns. Their legs and torsos were bare in the icy air and striped with black. In their hands they clasped bows of twigs and arrows of straw. They pranced to the front of the church, and the drums began, dividing them with sound into dual lines. The Deer Mothers moved in spirals, the others dancing behind, the lesser animals crouching from their fearful presence.

And then Mountain Lion touched a deer, and a Chiffoneta shot it with his straw arrow. The Chiffoneta slung the deer across his shoulder and ran, pursued by vengeful deer. A Deer Chief brought back his creature, and the dance began again.

The other deer yelled and hooted, shouting advice to the participants scuffling in the snow, but it was clear that this was serious business. The Indians watching in the plaza were intent and silent. Three times the Deer Dance wove through the plaza; three times the deer was shot and recaptured; and then the Deer Mothers led the deer away again, winding down into the kivas, into the sacred places.

"They make me want to follow them," India said longingly.

Later, when presents had been opened and Christmas dinner eaten, India and Frank went outside, the moonlight washing over the snow like silver water. Behind them, everyone was singing Christmas carols inside a house warm and scented with burning pinecones and the goose and turkey that had been served for dinner. The table had been stretched with sawhorses and planks and benches made by Mike and Frank, until it ran from the dining room all the way across the parlor. Mike had stood, beaming, and toasted everyone, all twenty of them, with champagne. "To the family," he had said. "To the last Christmas of the nineteenth century."

"What do you suppose it will be like in 1900?" India now asked Frank, looking at the moon as if it might abruptly alter. "Will we all see the light and build Utopia?" She grinned at him. She was still basking in his delight at her Christmas present to him: a small oil on wood of the pueblo in October light, the Sundown Dancers, recalled from memory, moving diagonally across the space, the green aspen leaves whispering above their heads. One of them had Frank's face and yet was still an Indian, an uncanny flash of likeness, half seen beneath bronze skin, that had made him catch his breath and stare.

"Now I have two," he had said, touching it with a fingertip. She wasn't sure whether he had meant two souls or two paintings by her. "No one ever gave me anything this wonderful before."

"It's small enough to take with you. Wherever you're going."

He had given her a polished piece of turquoise that he had bought from among the pawn at the Horsemans' trading post. He had had it set inside a silver circle, to wear on a chain around her neck. Typically, he had not had it made into a ring. "Or a collar either, to lead you around with," he had said.

She wore it now, under her coat, against the breast of her jade-green Christmas dress.

He had given his father a bottle of whiskey, and Henry had given him a box of cigars. "I smoke one cigar a year," Frank told her now. "Maybe. I have to be in the mood. Still, he couldn't know that."

"What mood do you have to be in?"

"Drunk. Showing off my masculinity. I don't like cigars."

They walked slowly across the snowy yard into the stable. It was filled with the rustling of the horses and warm with their breath and their great bodies. India took her coat off and hung it across the side of an empty stall. The jade taffeta gleamed in the shaft of moonlight that spilled through the far window.

"I was thinking inside that I like you in that color," Frank said. "Like river water." He touched the cap sleeve gently, feeling the taffeta whisper against his fingers. "You'll be cold."

"No."

They had come by some unspoken mutual consent, away from the party, from the laughter and the dancing, to dance out their own steps, whatever they might be.

Without a word, Frank unbuttoned the endless row of tiny buttons down the back of her dress, and she stepped out of it and hung it across the stall with her coat. He watched her longingly, yet still whispered, "I'm afraid to do this."

India forced herself to look directly at him. "I talked to Janessa," she said. "I bought what she told me to."

"You what?" He gaped at her.

India gave him a rueful smile. "She didn't want to tell me. She was horrified. She thinks I'm depraved. Or in the thrall of some fiend. But I told her I was going to anyway. So she finally gave in. She kept talking about my poor mother as she was writing it down."

"My God," Frank breathed. He put his arms around her and drew her to him. "You've got nerve."

"I don't think she's actually going to tell my mother. And I didn't tell her who it was. She said she hoped it's no one in the family who's taking advantage of me in this fashion."

Frank groaned. "That's not right. You shouldn't

shoulder all the blame." He no longer talked as if they weren't going to do anything.

"I'm not," India said. "No one knows but Janessa. And if she doesn't know anything else, she won't feel it's her duty to tell everyone, and then they won't feel it's their duty to try to make me marry you or shut me up in a nunnery."

"Horsewhips might come into it," Frank said. He would worry about fathers with horsewhips later. Right now he let his hands rove over her, undoing and un-hooking and untying the endless layers of clothing that well-brought-up ladies wore.

India felt as if she were an onion, slowly shedding layers down to the real person underneath, the person who wanted to join the dance, step out antler-crowned over the snow. Frank pulled at the studs of his dress shirt, his face flushed and his breath ragged now. She thought he was trying not to go too fast. She took the studs from him when he looked for a place to put them so that they wouldn't get lost in the straw. She set them in a row along the top edge of the stall—little white stones to follow home again.

They lay down in the loose straw, and the cold bit wonderfully at her bare feet and cheeks; the rest of her was warm with Frank's warmth. It wasn't what she had imagined, but she hadn't known what to imagine. The feeling of being caught in the dance persisted, and cutting through that were sharp physical surprises. Frank seemed taken by something that went past her. There were times when she could have spoken and he wouldn't have heard. And times when she floated in the arms of a hungry joy, arching with how much she wanted what he was doing. When it was over, she thought perhaps there was maybe more beyond that, more to find, more to the dance, but this was enough for now.

Frank leaned above her, getting his breath back. She could feel dampness trickling into the straw, cold and wet on her legs. Frank bent his head and kissed her gently. He whispered something that sounded like "sweet darlin'" and stood up. India watched him with curiosity. She had never had the chance to study a man's naked body before, except her little brother's when Winslow was a baby. A grown man was different, fascinating, truly amazing. Frank caught her staring and grinned. He got a bucket and some water from the trough, and they washed with it, yipping at the cold.

There was an odd camaraderie between them. India had expected embarrassment, maybe even a fierce desire not to have done it, but it hadn't turned out that way. She had no idea where they would go from here, but it didn't matter. Their dance was complete for the moment.

The house was dark, and they slipped in quietly. Apparently no one had been looking for them. They tiptoed up the stairs, then stopped at Frank's door. Peter's snoring could be plainly heard from within. Frank took India's hand and kissed the palm of it. Then he turned the knob and crept inside.

India slipped into her own room. The moonlight reflecting from the magic snow fell across her pillow and Sally's bundled form beside it. India shed her gown and corset, camisole and petticoats again. As she slid into bed, Sally opened a knowing eye and then let the lid fall shut. She breathed deeply, loudly—elaborately asleep.

New Year's Eve. New century's eve. Frank and India sat companionably across the parlor from each other; they had not repeated their experiment. In the week between then and now Janessa had said once to India, "My dear, I hope you will reconsider," and India had said gravely, "I'll give it some thought."

The clan had enjoyed a late dinner, Belle had long ago put the twins to bed, and now they were waiting for the century to change. The old century was being lit by the jewel flames of a pinecone fire. What would the new century be lit by? Electricity most certainly, Frank thought. Electricity and perhaps sources yet undreamed of. He looked at his father. He had sat down deliberately next to Henry but now could not find talk to ease the gulf between them. Henry looked as baffled as his son.

Anyone watching them would have thought how much they looked alike, how gesture mirrored gesture.

It was Henry who bent first, suddenly, like someone taking the stopper out of a bottle. He turned to face Frank. "Tell me what you've been doing, all these years."

"Do you mean really?"

"Yes. I want to know. I missed a piece of your life."

"And you want it back?" Frank asked. Maybe he could give it to him. Maybe that was what it would take to heal them.

"I want to know," Henry said again. He looked at Frank pleadingly. "I'm *trying* to know."

Damned if you aren't, Frank thought. "I bummed at first," he said. "Most of what I had got stolen till I learned the ropes. Took up with another 'bo and nearly got lynched for killing him."

"Did you?"

"No. But that didn't matter at the time. Then I worked the oil fields. You know that. Peter flushed me out and wired home." He laughed ruefully. "He caught me in bed with his girl. My girl, too. Neither one of us knew about that. I'm afraid he'd been a gentleman and I hadn't."

"That happens," Henry murmured.

"I worked the reptile show in a circus, trying to get north. We'd heard there was gold."

"There never is."

Frank snorted self-deprecatingly, surprised at himself. "There was, but the good claims were gone. I came home when the war started."

"By the long route?"

"That, and there was a woman. Same woman. She up and married a Mountie."

"Did you want to marry her?"

"No," Frank said somewhat ruefully. "I felt I ought to."

" 'Ought to' is a bitter phrase," Henry said. "I've given too much to 'ought to.' "

"I suspect I haven't given enough," Frank said.

"You're young. You have time. Maybe I have time, too." Henry looked across the firelight at Cindy, sitting next to India. Frank saw that the bitter lines in his mother's face had softened. Her eyes had a deep glow like the heart of the pinecone fire, and she was knitting something: the russet-and-navy sweater she had kept buried in her workbasket.

"I nearly left her for a woman in Manila," Henry said in a low voice, feeling he owed his son a story of his own, some piece of his own flesh. "She was young." He sighed. "She made me feel . . . that she would let me own her."

Frank didn't ask why he would want that. He knew the tug of that urge of ownership all too well.

"I don't know what would have happened if Midge hadn't gotten sick," Henry said.

"Tell her so," Frank suggested. "She'll know she's done something good." He glanced at his father. "I was afraid you were dead when I started home. Couldn't shake the notion."

"Nearly was."

Frank studied his hands. The big gold academy ring glinted at him, and he thought of how it had come full circle. He felt as if he had bumped unexpectedly into a mirror and seen himself from an odd and altered angle, an unknown face only dimly recognized. He thought it had turned out to be his father.

"Where will you go from here?" Henry asked.

"I don't know," Frank said honestly. He glanced at India. "Life surprises me."

"You can come home whenever you want to. I want to be sure you know that."

"I know that," Frank said. He wouldn't, though. Peace was made between him and his father, but that didn't mean he could go home. He knew that much.

Across the room, India watched Cindy watch her husband and her son. She seemed fixed on them, on their reconciliation, and there was a small smile on her face. *Thank goodness*, thought India.

Cindy turned to India. "I have something for you," she said, her smile widening. "An offer. I've been saving it until after the celebration and while I wrestled with my conscience. But I think I'm going to give it to you anyway."

India's expression was a mixture of anticipation and curiosity.

"A friend of mine in New York," Cindy continued, "has told me he likes your work very much. He has offered to give you a contract for twelve works a year, to be published in *The Gentlewoman's Handbook*."

"Magazine art?"

"Illustrations," Cindy amended, sensing India was balking. "The subject matter would be assigned, I'm afraid. But it would give you a chance to earn your living while you pursue your serious art. I fear your father will want my head on a plate for passing this along to you, but I'll take responsibility for that."

Are you getting me away from your son? India wondered. But she thought not; Cindy must know by now that she couldn't marry him off to some dutiful daughter in Washington. "What do you think I should do?" she asked abruptly, willing to rely on Cindy as a fellow artist.

"It's possible to become very successful as an illustrator. If you think you can reconcile your parents to the idea, and are willing to put your own work aside for a while, or are willing to take the risk that you can't— Oh!" Cindy threw up her hands. "I don't know what to tell you. Years ago I would have leapt at it. Then other things began to seem more important. Now I don't know. There are never perfect answers. This may be half a one. We take a zigzag path, I think."

Mike stood up and popped a champagne cork. "It's almost time," he announced. "We're nearly there." Everyone looked at the mantel clock as it ticked its way through the last few seconds of the nineteenth century.

Mike handed India a glass of champagne, and she balanced it in her hand. There were times when you just had to close your eyes and jump, she imagined. Surely the start of the twentieth century was one of them. She lifted her glass to the mantel clock. She caught Frank's eye and lifted her glass to him, too, with a small, secret smile.

THE AWAKENING OF
INDIA BLACKSTONE
by
Dana Fuller Ross

The twentieth century heralds a dawn for America, a new way of life to a people ready for change. For a young woman named India Blackstone, it means launching into adulthood and taking the New York art world by storm. Befriended by Sally Holt, spirited daughter of Toby Holt, India sets out on a new life in a new century, and throughout the turbulent decades that follow, the two young women form a bond of friendship that survives distance and tragedy.

From the fashionable bohemian salons of Greenwich Village to the smoky meeting rooms of Big Bill Haywood's IWW, *The Awakening of India Blackstone* features the diverse worlds of art, high society, and the developing labor movement. Sally Holt struggles with her love for a German man whose destiny seems fated to be separate from hers, while India is drawn again and again to Frank Blake, Henry and Cindy Blake's nonconformist son, though she knows he will never stay in one place for long. Frank becomes involved in the cause of justice for all workers, as India fights the influence of a male-dominated art world and Sally works for the rights of the migrants, even risking her own well-being.

From the sinking of the *Lusitania* to the New Mexican art colonies of Georgia O'Keeffe and D. H. Lawrence, *The Awakening of India Blackstone* spans the decades that lead up to World War II—and the lives of three Americans, independent and free-thinking, steeped in the tradition of the Holts.

Read *The Awakening of India Blackstone*, on sale October 1995 wherever Bantam paperbacks are sold.